The Governor's Lady

The Governor's Lady
Thomas H. Raddall

NIMBUS
PUBLISHING

Nimbus Publishing Limited
P.O. Box 9301, Station A
Halifax, N. S. B3K 5N5
(902) 455-4286

Cover design: Arthur B. Carter, Halifax
Portrait of Lady Frances Wentworth
by John Singleton Copley,
New York Public Library.
Published by arrangement with
McClelland and Stewart Inc.
Printed and bound in Canada by
Best Gagné Book Manufacturers Inc.

Canadian Cataloguing in Publication Data

Raddall, Thomas H., 1903-
The governor's lady
ISBN 1-55109-016-3

I.Title.
PS8535.A27G68 1992   C813'.54   C92-098652-8
PR9199.3.R33G68 1992

The Governor's Lady

ONE

*A*LREADY, an hour short of noon, the town was oven hot. There was a faint stir of air from the west, with a breath of warm pine woods; not enough for a breeze, but enough to keep off the cool fog that hung seaward over the Isles of Shoals. Mr. and Mrs. Theodore Atkinson, Jr., dressing for an occasion, moved about the bedchamber languidly and with the easy familiarity of people five years married. Theo had drawn his best broadcloth breeches over his long shanks and now stood in his best ruffled shirt, tying a new stock about his neck. He was a thin man of thirty or so, nine years older than his wife, with somber dark eyes in a face as pale as parchment.

He glanced at his wife. Fannie was taking a lot of time with her toilet as usual. At the moment, fresh from the hip bath behind the Chinese screen, she was putting on the silk stockings she had bought in Boston for today's affair. At twenty-two she had hips as slim as Theo's own, though she was not nearly so long in the leg, and her bosom had just the right plumpness to be fashionable. Perhaps a little more, thought Fannie herself, critically. She paused to inspect her person. She had been all bones as a child and was obliged to pad her bodice when she married Theo at seventeen. There was certainly no need of padding there now, and her legs and arms were sticks no more. Marriage was good for the figure. She had remarked that a year or two ago, and Theo wondered sometimes if that was its chief importance in her eyes.

The looking glass reflected an oval face with a rather tall brow, so that her features seemed to gather in the lower half; a short mouth with a natural pout, a slim nose turned up at the tip, a pair of hazel eyes wide-set and slanting a little above

7

the cheekbones, like those of a watchful kitten. She had a milky satin complexion and took care never to expose it to the sun. Among the ladies of the little aristocracy of New Hampshire that was just as important as in England. In the warm light of the morning Theo admired her, while Fannie admired the image in the glass. She picked up a short set of stays and drew it about her waist.

"Lace me, please."

He obeyed. It was always pleasant to touch her.

"Tighter!"

"Umph. You don't need to lace so, Fan—not with your shape. Besides, you'll be deuced uncomfortable, and the reception's not due for two hours yet."

"Do as I say!"

She expelled the last of her breath and watched the result of his efforts in the mirror.

"There! Now tie the tapes and be sure the knot won't slip." With this done Theo paused, looking over her shoulder at the image in the cheval glass beyond. He pressed his lips to the bare shoulder and slipped his hands forward under her arms.

"Don't be silly," she said, turning away to pick up her panniers. Her gown lay over a chair, a light thing of sprigged muslin.

"Is that what you're wearing?" Theo said in a disapproving tone.

"Yes, with a bodice and petticoat underneath of course."

"Nothing else?"

"In this weather? Don't be old-fashioned—you sound so like your father. Only old ladies wear shirts and drawers in summer nowadays. Besides, who's to know the difference? A woman can be cool on a hot day and nobody the wiser. Not like you poor stupid creatures. Look at yourself!"

"I feel quite comfortable."

"That's because your blood's so thin."

She fastened the pannier belt over her stays and adjusted the three little half hoops carefully at each hip. On went the petticoat and bodice. Then the gown, an airy confection, straight from London in the first mast-ship of the season. The panniers held it outward from her hips in the exaggerated London mode. She put on new shoes with tall painted heels and gold buckles. Then a ribbon and locket about her neck. She made a few light touches with a brush at her hair, the dark brown, almost black hair that swept back from the brow and temples and rose in a mound toward the back of the shapely head. Finally the hat, a wide-brimmed-straw shepherdess thing with a blue silk band that went over the crown and fastened under the chin.

"There! I'm ready."

"You might as well sit down," Theo said. "We can't take our places at the Town House for at least another hour."

Fannie sank carefully on a chair, an armless thing in which the panniers could hang freely without wrinkling the gown.

"Tell me about the arrangements."

"Well, a party of mounted gentlemen rode out to meet Johnnie at the Merrimac ferry. They'll be joined by others along the road back to Portsmouth. Everyone's been notified, from Rye to Salmon Falls—Johnnie wrote from Boston and gave us the date and time. The whole troop will stop outside the town somewhere, at Bellows' tavern, I suppose, to beat the dust out of their hats and coats, while Johnnie's servants wash down the horses and the carriage at the pump. Johnnie's coming in style, I tell you. Four handsome bays and a spanking new Philadelphia carriage. Seven English servants, not counting the coachman. You'll see them first of all. They'll come along King Street as outriders, a few minutes before the carriage, all mounted on hunters that Johnnie bought in England or down South. Nobody's seen a show like that in these parts since the days of Lord Bellomont."

"Why did Johnnie come home by way of Carolina?" Fannie said.

"He left England in January. That's a cold time in our latitude."

9

"He could have waited till summer and come out in a mast-ship."

"Not Johnnie. He's a chip off old Mark's block. Mark don't believe in wasting time. Or anything else."

"Pooh! Mark sent Johnnie to England four years ago—for what? To learn to be a gentleman, it seems, English style. As if anyone could make an English gentleman of Johnnie! After he got through college he was mad about the woods, wasting all his time up there toward the mountains like one of those wild rangers of Colonel Rogers."

"You mean like one of his father's timber cruisers," Theo said. "Mark shoved Johnnie into the business as soon as he came home from college in '55. That was the time of the French and Indian War, remember, and Mark had a mast contract with the Royal Navy. There were guineas growing on those tall pines up the river, and Mark knew how to shake 'em down. And that was where Johnnie came in. Winters here in the countinghouse, and the rest of the year risking his scalp in the woods, hunting for pines that stood clear eighty or a hundred feet below the branches. That, and surveying mast roads to the river, and taking charge of the axmen and the ox teams. Oh, Johnnie wasn't fooling any time away up there in the backwoods, I assure you. Mark saw to that."

"Humph! Whatever he was doing, it didn't improve him. I only saw him once or twice after we married. A shock of hair, a face as dark as an Indian's, awkward in his town clothes—like a Squamscot farmer down for the sessions. Nothing like the jolly student who used to come over from Cambridge with you, calling on Papa in Boston."

"You were only a child then," Theo said. "How could you remember?"

"I remember the pair of you looming over me at my dolls—my country cousins from New Hampshire, that wild place up the coast." She laughed. "You seemed as old as the hills, both of you, and nearly as big. I never guessed I'd marry one and come to live away up here amongst the stockfish and sawdust."

"Has it been so bad, Fan?"

"We're talking about Johnnie. If he was so useful in the business, why was he sent off to England? That doesn't sound like Uncle Mark."

"It sounds exactly like Mark. The war was over, and the French had given up Canada forever. That put an end to Mark's fat Navy contract. He'd made more than a penny out of it, of course, but now something had to be found for Johnnie— something good. And there was old Uncle Benning Wentworth, all fat and wind and dropsy and gout, Governor of New Hampshire, and Surveyor General of the King's Woods longer than anyone cared to remember."

"Well?"

"You remember the talk, surely? Uncle Benning had used his post to make a fortune, granting himself good timberland in every new township of the province. Not that he ever went in the woods himself. He even built a council chamber in that queer sprawling house of his at Little Harbor and made the councilors come out there, by saddle or boat, according to the weather, just to hear his orders and approve 'em. And then, after outliving his wife and all his children, damned if he didn't marry a serving girl at Stavers's tavern—Martha Hilton—a chit young enough to be his grandchild. There she was, all of a sudden, the first lady of New Hampshire. Ha!"

"She's made him a good wife, hasn't she?" Fannie said. "Though how she puts up with that great gouty barrel in bed with her I can't imagine."

"That's not the point, Fan. The point is, old Benning offended everyone in the province, high and low, in one way or another. And the grumbling was getting loud enough to hear in London. So Mark sent Johnnie over there, with letters to Paul Wentworth and others who knew the right people."

"Do you mean Johnnie went, deliberately, to get . . ."

"Not at all. Johnnie went to assist the New Hampshire agent in London. And of course to look about the English shipyards for some new mast business for his father. That was what

Mark said, anyhow. And—as Mark didn't say—if Uncle Benning died of the dropsy, which was likely, or if the Lords of Trade and Plantations decided to swap the old Governor for a new one, which was possible, why, there'd be our Johnnie right under their noses. Johnnie the kinsman of Paul Wentworth, the smartest American in London. Johnnie the protégé of Lord Rockingham, the biggest Whig in England. Johnnie the graduate 'of Harvard College. Johnnie the surveyor who knows New Hampshire like a book. Johnnie whose family goes back well over a hundred years in these parts, a native American, loyal to His Majesty. Eh? Who else could they pick?"

Fannie took a silk-and-ivory fan from the nearby table and waved it irritably before her face.

"How sultry it is. Let's go down to the garden and sit in the shade of the trees."

Behind the big clapboard house of the Atkinsons the garden went down to a shallow creek, a finger of the tide that ran up to a small marsh at the rear of the town. Some wag had called it Puddle Dock in the early days, when a few fishermen sheltered their boats in it, and the name clung. There were still some cottages of fishermen clustered at the mouth where it entered Portsmouth harbor. The rest of its banks were lined with roomy houses and gardens belonging to merchants or officials like Chief Justice Atkinson. It was a pleasant place, not far from the business quarter of the town. On hot June days like this, even with no wind, an incoming tide brought a touch of coolness to the gardens by the water.

Theo sat with Fannie on a rustic bench under the apple trees.

"D'you remember how we used to sit here, Fan, that first summer we were married? Like a pair of children, hand in hand, watching the boys fish for cunners in the Dock?"

Fish! she thought. *That's Portsmouth. Fish and lumber, fish and lumber. Pooh!*

"I still don't understand," she persisted, "why Johnnie chose to come home by way of Carolina."

"Because, apart from being Governor of New Hampshire, our

Johnnie's now Surveyor General of all the King's Woods in North America."

"What's that got to do with it?"

"Those Lords of Trade and Plantations have some quaint notions, my dear. The Royal Navy's got to have a reserve supply of masts for its first-rate ships in case of war. Growing on the stump, you understand, ready to be cut when the time comes. And big ones, not the kind they can get up the Baltic. And there's America, a bristle of mast trees all the way from Maine to Florida—or so they think."

"Well, isn't it?"

He chuckled. "You couldn't find a mast for a first-rate man-o'-war anywhere on the coast south of New York, and not many north of New York till you get up here. White pine's the proper stuff, and it's got to be mighty thick and tall and clear of knots—and handy to tidewater. The only supply like that is here on our New Hampshire rivers and some of the streams in Maine. That's how Mark Wentworth made his guineas in the French war. Brother Benning was Surveyor General then. He put the King's mark on the best trees—his deputies could go on anybody's land and do that—and he made sure Brother Mark got the contract to deliver 'em."

"But Johnnie!" she said impatiently.

"So Johnnie sailed home by the southern route, a sensible way to come. He stopped at Lisbon and Madeira to pick up some wines, and the trade wind carried him over to Carolina in March. From there he's traveled northward with the sun, staying with the leading gentry, showing his commission, and asking questions about the woods. And on the way he picked up a few more blood horses for his stable, and in Philadelphia he got the new carriage you'll see today and ordered a sulky chaise to be sent on later. Apart from all that he's got a lot of furniture, chinaware, silverware, horses, and what not, coming out from England in the next mast-ship."

"How do you know all this?"

"Johnnie's letters. He's kept Father well posted. As Chief Justice, Father had to make the arrangements for his reception—old Benning claims his gout prevents him doing anything. Well, all this. Johnnie's getting home in June, the finest time of our New England year, just right for the show today. Meanwhile he's picked up all the information he needs for a long report on His Majesty's Woods, from one end of the colonies to the other. That'll satisfy the Lords of Trade. Now Johnnie can settle down at home, draw his extra salary from England as Surveyor General, and send his deputy surveyors to look after the King's mark on all the best pines hereabouts. Oh, he's got a clear head on him, Johnnie. And a conscience too. You should see his letters. You'd think he'd taken the whole empire on his shoulders."

"How much pay does he get for all this?"

"Let's see. He'll have to pay his deputy forest surveyors out of his own salary. That leaves him four hundred neat. On top of that he gets seven hundred pounds a year as Governor. That comes from our own Assembly—provincial currency of course. Eleven hundred altogether. A pretty enough income."

"I wonder. He seems to have picked up some expensive tastes in England."

"He'll soon get over that, back home here in New Hampshire. You'll see him settle down like Benning, stowing his money away in kegs."

"Not quite like Benning, I hope."

There was a step on the walk. They looked up and saw the Chief Justice, impressive in his long red robe and dangling wig-laps, coming down the garden. A tall old man, gaunt and shrewd, one of the wealthiest men in Portsmouth. Theo was like him in build and every feature.

"I think perhaps we should get along," Mr. Atkinson said in his thin dry voice. "We'll go in the coach, of course, for the look of it. And for Fannie's shoes."

And so, for the dignity of the Chief Justice and for Fannie's shoes, they rode the short way to the Parade in the huge old-fashioned Atkinson coach. Most of the Council were on the

Town House steps already, with their ladies arranged at each side, a pretty show of silks, satins, lutestrings, hats, and bonnets, in all the tints of the rainbow. The ladies turned as the big coach lumbered into the square, and all the gowns swayed like a tulip bed in a breeze. There was a distinct buzz when Fannie took Theo's hand and stepped down. The artfully simple London gown, the shepherdess hat, the demure manner. She might have been an actress stepping out upon a stage. As Theo and his father took their places on the steps she moved with her light free step to join the tulip bed.

A mass of people stood about the Parade. Fishermen from the Isles of Shoals and every creek between Rye and Ogunquit. Farmers from Dover and the other up-tide settlements along the Piscataqua River. Sawyers and loggers from Salmon Falls. Sailors, wharf hands, clerks, teamsters, shipwrights, blacksmiths, mechanics, laborers, petty merchants, and shopkeepers of the town itself. And their women and little girls, figged out for a holiday, and a rabble of noisy small boys, with all the dogs of Portsmouth scampering in and out.

The fire-engine company and the militia were drawn up in King Street just where it entered the square. Theo regarded them quizzically. Nothing uniform about them except the hard leather caps of the fire company and the blue coats of the militia officers. The men wore the daily dress of a dozen occupations; breeches of homespun and broadcloth and buckskin; linsey shirts, checkered shirts, fringed green hunting shirts; a wide choice of hats cocked and uncocked, most of them faded by weekday suns and rains.

Their guns were an odd assortment too; everything from rusty fowling pieces to long French muskets captured in the late war; and, slung about them, they had a great variety of cartridge boxes and carved powder horns. Some had bayonets. Most had not. The men in the hunting shirts, a company of rangers from up the river, had tomahawks at their belts. A British sergeant major, Theo thought, would turn purple at the notion of drilling such a lot, but they'd fought the French and Indians well enough a few years back. Of course there was no need of militia now at all, what with the French gone and the Indians quiet. No more war. How strange that seemed. He was past thirty, just about the age of Governor Johnnie, and almost as far back as he could remember there had been fighting with the Indians or with the French in Canada—usually both.

A long wait. The square grew hotter by the minute. The midday sun cast little or no shade even from the Town House or the North Church or the Bell tavern, the tallest buildings about the Parade. The wiser ladies had brought fans, and there was a continual small flutter before the faces under the hats and bonnets.

The Town House clock struck one, a sound almost lost in the chatter and the yapping of dogs. Suddenly a youth on the ridgepole of the Bell tavern cried in a cracked voice, "Here they come!" Fannie, peering past the bonnet next to her, saw the fire company and the militia parting their ranks to make way. Then Johnnie's outriders, just as Theo had said, all in new green livery. And now the four bays and the smart Philadelphia carriage, with a green coachman on the box, and a lone figure in a scarlet coat and a gold-laced hat sitting erect on the carriage seat. Governor Johnnie! He was sweeping off the hat now, revealing something new in wigs, a tight white London peruke that fitted his head like another scalp.

He bowed to right and left as the militia presented arms, and then the carriage was bowling into the Parade. Behind came the mounted gentlemen, in two troops, each of a hundred horsemen bobbing up and down in the stirrups, a gallant show of hats and wigs and coats and cuffs, of riding boots and swords.

Young Mrs. Livius, at Fannie's elbow, murmured proudly and a little wickedly, "Could Boston put on a better show?"—and for once Fannie had no answer. She was staring at the stranger in the carriage, abreast of her now, and doffing his hat to the ladies with the ease and grace of a prince.

TWO

*E*NGLISHMEN, in the past year or two, seeing John Wentworth in a London street, and noting his hands and shoulders and the muscular silk-stockinged legs, usually marked him as a fox-hunting squire up to town for a new saddle or a bid or two at Tattersall's new sale. A passion for horseflesh was all over him. And from his lips and air they might have guessed a gentleman's taste for fine wines and food and possibly fine woman-flesh, although on the last point there was room for doubt. A passion for horses can leave a man with little thought for women.

Any American seeing him afoot, watching his stride and the quick wide gaze that missed nothing in street or landscape, would have known him for what he was, a man born and bred close to the American forest, with an acquired English polish but a dignity quite natural to him, the gift of his birth in some proud little colonial aristocracy across the sea.

He was neither tall nor short, a man well thewed and shaped, with large sensible gray eyes and a nose with a somewhat imperious flare at the nostrils. His mouth was small, with sensitive lips, the mouth of an artist or a musician set in a jaw as stubborn as his own New Hampshire granite.

He had gone to Harvard College at fourteen, graduated four years later, and passed at once into the harder school of his father's business. There he learned everything from ledger-keeping to the art of felling a mast tree so that it would not split in the crash. He had liked the woods best. The forest enchanted him, and sometimes, when he was supposed to be ranging for masts, he had traveled far into the wilderness, where the Indian war parties roved like wolves. Then, at twenty-six, Mark

17

Wentworth had plucked him away from these adventures and sent him to England for another kind of education altogether. For more than three years he had studied the life of an English gentleman under the tutorship of his kinsman Paul, living in Paul Wentworth's house in Poland Street, London, and meeting every sort of gentry from the titled spendthrifts who hung about White's and The Cocoa Tree to the great Lord Rockingham himself.

And now, at a little past thirty, he had come to what seemed to him the climax and the purpose of his life. A man with a star, born to make New Hampshire the finest province of New England. All the way across the sea, all the way home through the southern colonies, his mind had fizzed with ideas and plans.

He stepped down from the carriage and walked up the Town House steps, hearing the excited murmur of the ladies and beyond these the murmur of the crowd. He greeted the gentlemen of the Council, each by name, with his quick healthy smile. He knew them all. Many were related to him in one way or another. In the close-knit aristocracy of New Hampshire the Wentworths had ties in all directions. There was Theo, for example, his cousin, and married to another—Fannie must be there among the ladies by the steps. And Theo's father, of course, the Chief Justice, waiting for him solemnly on the platform before the Town House door.

A polite little patter of hands from the ladies and the gentlemen as he moved up the steps. So far the crowd only buzzed with comment. At this point, however, a gang of rough mastmen from the Piscataqua woods burst out of the Bell taproom and thrust their way through the crowd. One yelled, "There's Johnnie! That's him!" At once they all shouted "Spar ho!", the cry of their timber cruisers at first sight of a fine tall pine in the forest.

His Excellency paused and turned. A glance told him that these men had left the mast-landings up the river as soon as they got word of his coming, sailing down from Salmon Falls in a crowded gundalow probably, with their grimy leather breeches, their ragged linsey shirts and greasy pigtails, hooting like Indians and thirsting for Portsmouth rum. The Sheriff, in his place beside the Chief Justice, glared at these noisy intruders and glanced toward the militia. The ladies passed deploring whispers. Fannie herself was indignant. She forgot the raucous holiday mobs of her own Boston and thought, *It's just like Portsmouth, a handful of gentility and the rest a lot of savages.*

But His Excellency did not seem to share these sentiments. He lifted his hat, smiling, nodding to this wild man and that, recognizing them from old days in their company up the river. They shouted again. And now that the ice was broken a townsman cried, "Who killed the Stamps? Huzza for Johnnie Wentworth!" Suddenly everyone was cheering, all around the Parade. Again His Excellency bowed that neat white head. And then, with an easy dignity, he replaced his hat, walked to the top of the steps, presented the Chief Justice with a scroll, and stood aside, facing the people.

Old Mr. Atkinson unrolled the document and scanned it in a portentous silence. He passed it to the Sheriff at last, and that worthy, a stocky man with a tremendous voice, made the most of his great moment. His "Oyez! Oyez! Oyez!" rang like a war whoop in the hush. He spread the scroll with a flourish, taking care to display the great red biscuit of the seal, and began to read aloud. At certain phrases his voice lifted and trumpeted across the square.

His Majesty's royal commission under the Great Seal . . . trusty and well-beloved servant John Wentworth, Esquire . . . Governor over His Majesty's Province of New Hampshire . . . Captain General of New Hampshire . . . Vice-Admiral of New Hampshire . . . Surveyor General of His Majesty's Woods in America . . . Year of Our Lord One Thousand Seven hundred and Sixty-seven. And in one final bellow, *Gawd Save the King!*

As *King* died away in the silence Mr. Atkinson advanced with a Bible to administer the oath, first to His Excellency and then to the members of the Council. Now John Wentworth sat in a carved high-backed chair, placed for him in front of the doorway. His secretary passed the Sheriff another scroll, this one prepared during the careful tarry in Boston. The Sheriff bawled it forth, a proclamation to all officers of His Majesty's Province of New Hampshire, commanding them to continue in their duties and to subject themselves to His Excellency's further orders.

At the Sheriff's last word a mysterious arm flourished a handkerchief from the shadows of the Town House doorway. A group of sailors, lounging about three small cannon at the far end of the Parade, came to life and swept their fuming linstocks down to the touchholes. The guns leaped and spat flame. There was a sound of great planks clapped together by a giant, followed at once by a squealing of silly females and a scuttle of startled dogs. A cloud of white smoke rolled up in the sunshine.

Now the militia swung up their muskets and fired a *feu de joie*. It had the sound of a running boy with a stick at a picket fence as the muskets cracked one after another along the ranks. Here and there a flint missed fire, or a trigger was pulled too soon or too late for an even roll, but on the whole the trick was done with the finesse of His Majesty's own Guards. Whatever their dress or their gait, these men understood firearms as few troops in the world knew their weapons, and Johnnie marked the fact with pride. And now the militiamen followed with three huzzas, waving their hats in a fog of powder smoke and a rain of falling wads. And then like an echo of all this, the guns of the decrepit little fort on Newcastle Island began a slow thudding that rang along the slopes of Kittery.

The Chief Justice touched Johnnie's arm. "Now, Your Excellency, you must be famished after your morning's journey and dry as Gideon's fleece with all this business. The gentlemen are giving a dinner in your honor at the Earl of Halifax—Stavers's place—and your father's waiting there to embrace his new

Governor and to join us in the toasts. Stavers has ransacked land and sea for the food, and there'll be some first-rate wines and brandy. We've got a list of toasts as long as your sword."

"Good! I suppose we'd better ride there for the dignity of the occasion. Will you join me in my carriage—since Uncle Benning can't be here and you represent the retiring Governor? I think that would look well."

The Philadelphia carriage took them along the Parade, followed by the Council and many of the gentry, some on horseback, some in smart carriage turnouts of their own. Mr. Atkinson murmured in his dry tones, "Seems only the other day you were off to Harvard College, Johnnie, with tears in your eyes at parting from your mother—remember that? Your new clothes in a portmanteau strapped to the saddle. A purse of silver dollars from your father to pay your first term's fee and lodging, and a doubloon from me to buy some luxuries. One of Mark's servants riding along to see you safely there. How the time goes!"

Fifty gentlemen of New Hampshire, most of them from Portsmouth town, sat down to a vast meal that filled two hours with the music of knife and fork and spoon. Then came decanters of Madeira and prime Oporto and bottles of Bordeaux brandy; and the list of toasts, beginning with "Gentlemen, the King!" and going on through "His Excellency, Our Own John Wentworth!" to various other provincial notables and subjects, all of which deserved a glass and a well-turned compliment.

The afternoon heat was choking in the crowded room, the toasts went on and on, and halfway through the list most of the fifty faces had the tint of His Excellency's scarlet coat. The toast to "Our Ladies, Absent but Ever Present in Our Hearts" demanded a truly noble sentiment, and a portly gentleman arose and dealt with it at great length. "Our Forefathers, May Their Memory Never Perish" aroused another burst of oratory; so did "The Heroes of the Late War," and "New Hampshire, Youngest and Fairest of the Colonies." When the toastmaster came to "Speed the Plough," and "Fair Wind and Good Fortune to the Fishery," and "The West India Trade," and "The Boundless

Resources of Our Forest," everyone seemed to have important things to say.

His Excellency sat with an air of smiling interest, but from time to time he stole a glance through an open window, letting his mind drift into the fresh air of the afternoon where his body longed to be. Not far away he could see the home of the Atkinsons; a big house of yellow clapboards and white trim, with fine wood carving on every cornice and lintel. It was typical of the mansions of the Portsmouth gentry, with a roomy stable and coach house, a long kitchen garden, a small orchard, and some flower beds. Most of the gentry were merchants like his father, with counting rooms and big warehouses down by the wharves. Ordinary folk lived mostly in the lower streets, in clapboard or shingled houses cheek by jowl, some with paint and some without, and along the water front lived the fishermen, the ship carpenters and warehousemen, in small wooden cottages that never saw paint at all, weathered to the color of a winter sky.

Amid the drone of voices, in the stuffy room burdened with smells of food and wine, His Excellency regarded the Atkinson house and thought of the garden behind, the grass, the flowers, the shade of the apple trees, flickering in a small air from the tide. Five summers ago he had sat in those patches of light and shade, chatting with young Theo and his bride.

In his Harvard days, calling at the Boston home of his uncle Sam Wentworth, he had found a dark thin child named Fannie, always clutching a toy and greedy for sweets. Cousin Theo, a student like himself, had joined sometimes in these dutiful family calls across the Charles River. Long afterward, when Johnnie was happily ranging the Piscataqua forests, Theo had gone to Boston again and found "little Fannie" grown into another person named Frances. And so the romance had begun, a quick one that brought Frances a girl bride to the roomy old mansion above Puddle Dock.

Johnnie, just back from a long journey in the wilds, had come to offer his congratulations and a wedding gift, and found them in the garden. Frances was four months short of seventeen, still thin and *gauche* for all the grown-up dress, and delightfully shy. Theo himself was tall but of the same slight build as his bride, and he had the same features carved in the same pallid ivory. Although he was nine years older than Fannie they looked like brother and sister together. It was touching to see them, hand in hand, talking dreamily on the bench beneath the trees.

Each time His Excellency gazed out of the tavern window his mind brought back that moment and the refreshing picture of the garden and the water. Glancing down the table where the members of the Council sat with him, he wondered if the Secretary had the same thought. But Theo apparently had no longing for fresh air nor old remembrances. He took his post in the Council very seriously. Between the toasts, when the talk gushed up about the tables, he leaned forward and darted his high thin voice into the hubbub. If he thought for a moment of the shady garden by the creek the vision was not a cooling one. In the long white face his dark eyes burned as if with fever. Perhaps it was just the heat and the wine. But he had been high-strung even as a boy. Someone at college had said you could play a tune on Theo with a fiddle bow.

The afternoon sun was well down the sky when at last the gentlemen emerged from the tavern. Johnnie caught his father's arm.

"Let's walk," he said, under the faded Earl of Halifax on the sign. He dismissed his waiting coachman with a wave of hand. The gentlemen, as a final courtesy, fell in behind, escorting them afoot to Johnnie's home. The crowd of people had scattered away to their dinners and occupations long since. The buildings were casting long shadows now, and there was a cool air from the harbor and a smell of salt and kelp. It was an easy stroll past the houses and shops to Chapel Street.

Mark, frugal man, disapproved long drinking, and the length of the toast list appalled him. He gave his son's face a careful stare as they walked along. Johnnie had been obliged to drink bumper for bumper with the gentlemen. The wine had deepened his naturally healthy color to a flush, but his step was firm and his

23

eyes clear. Mark noted this with a touch of pride. No doubt Johnnie had got used to it in England—those English were a hard-drinking lot by all accounts—but still there was nothing like a steady Wentworth head on good sound New Hampshire legs.

"What's next?" Johnnie said. "Just the family, I hope."

"Just the family," Mark said drily. "Including all your aunts and female cousins and second cousins of course. The gentlemen have had their time with you. The ladies must have theirs."

Johnnie sighed. A headache like the strokes of a logger's ax was splitting his skull between the eyes.

"A dish of tea with the ladies," Mark observed, "is just what you need now. All that wine swigging at Stavers'. We didn't drink like that in my day."

"Oh?" Johnnie gave him a wry sidelong grin. "I seem to recall from my schoolboy days that Portsmouth gentlemen—on a good occasion of course—drank just as much, and poorer stuff. Rum and hard cider, eh? And that strong Western Islands wine they favored in those days. What was it called? What *was* it called? Vid-something. Vidonia! No self-respecting horse doctor would wash a nag's foot with it nowadays. I used to carry off some of your precious vidonia, whenever I went back to Cambridge after the holidays, and shared it with my friend Ammi Cutter. It made us very loud and important, I remember, and there was an unfortunate matter of throwing one of the tutors down the stairs. What stuff! Pale and cloudy, like a foggy sunrise on the shoals out there off Smutty Nose, and harsh as sugared vinegar."

"Umph! So that's where my vidonia went. I blamed it on that black boy Nero and whipped him soundly, poor devil. Well, here we are."

And there they were, approaching the bulky mansion at the corner of Chapel Street, freshly painted for his home-coming. Like a man seeking old and cherished friends Johnnie looked at the house across the street, the familiar mansion of the Warners, built of brick from Holland, and the great chimney with one of Mr. Franklin's lightning rods, the first in Portsmouth. And beyond, where the road curved up the hill toward Strawberry Bank and the river, Queen's Chapel pointing a slim white finger to the sky.

He turned to the little procession, doffing his hat, and thanked the gentlemen for all their courtesies to him this day. Off came their hats in return. The afternoon sun, now setting the slender windows of Queen's Chapel afire, glinted on the white-wigged heads in the street as he and Mark vanished into the house.

His mother and sisters greeted Johnnie affectionately within the hall. A servant took his hat. Then he was swept away in a sea of eager ladies in piled hair and swishing silks that seemed to fill all the rooms and even the lower staircase. They were all Wentworth relations, and here together they seemed half the female population of Portsmouth. Johnnie murmured their names, one after another, and lifted to his lips the hands they put out to him.

These gestures, which would have been ridiculous four years ago, were instinctive with him now and done with a grace that delighted every woman in the house. This was not the sunburned young backwoodsman they had seen last, and in their lively voices they told him so. There was not much time for conversation with any of them, but he had a compliment and a laughing remark for each as he passed from one to another. When he came to Fannie it was, "Marriage becomes you, coz. How many little Atkinsons have you now?"

"None."

"In four years? Tut! I'll speak to Theo." And he was away, taking another hand in his fingers, bowing over it and smiling, as if every move of his head were not bringing down another hack of the ax.

It was after dark when the last of the ladies went away in a flicker of carriage lamps, leaving the empty rooms swimming in an invisible mist of bohea tea and warm and scented femininity. Not until then could His Excellency climb the stairs to his old room, fling off coat and waistcoat, wig and shoes, and drop full length on the familiar bed. All day long his easy dignity had masked the Johnnie underneath, a Johnnie as excited as any dog in the crowd.

Your Excellency. He murmured the magic words aloud.

There was a small knock at the chamber door and then his mother's soft voice.

"John?"

"Yes?"

"Would you like some supper now?"

"Oh, ma'am, I don't want a thing," he said, lying exhausted on the bed and staring up into the darkness. Sleep was all he wanted now. But sleep would not come. His head buzzed with duties and plans like a nest of wild bees in a stump. After a time there was another knock at the door. It opened, and his father appeared in a nimbus of yellow light, with a candlestick in his hand.

"You feel all right, Johnnie?"

"Yes."

"You've had a hard day."

"Yes. But I'm not too tired to talk, if that's what you want, Father. Put the candle over there and take a chair."

Mark Wentworth straddled the chair as if it were a horse, with his forearms resting on the high back and his gaunt chin on his hands.

"Well, Johnnie, it's all turned out as I said it would, eh? And you thought it was just a wild dream of mine when I sent you over there. I can still hear you saying 'England!'—like that, as if I'd said China. Will you give me some credit now? 'Twas plain as a pikestaff to me. London was the place for you to go. Tell me about London and all that."

"I told you in my letters."

"Letters! You wrote those to your mother as much as to me. That's not the same as plain talk between one man and another. Tell me now, Johnnie."

His Excellency lay silent for a time. Then he said, "Well, where shall I begin? With Paul Wentworth? I'm afraid our Portsmouth ladies would give a very prim sniff at Paul's way of life. He's one of the richest men in London, with a well-furnished house on Poland Street, in the part they call Soho. Gives the best dinners and *soirées* in London, and nobody who's anybody misses a chance to go."

"I suppose he's got another wife? His first was a rich widow in Surinam that died and left him a fortune. After that America was too small for Paul. That's why he went to London."

"Paul has no wife," Johnnie said. "He keeps a pretty lady, though. Not always the same one. I lost track of 'em in the years I lived with him. Don't look so shocked, Father, it's quite in the London mode. Paul's come a long way since you gave him a hand as a young merchant here in Portsmouth. Oh, he likes to talk about his old days in New Hampshire, and of course he keeps a lively interest in all that goes on here, as you know. But you couldn't drag him back to Portsmouth—not with every horse and all the oxen from here to the head of the river."

"I trust you didn't fall into his way of life," Mark said piously. Johnnie swung his head to regard his father for a moment in the candlelight, and turned his gaze back to the dark shadow of the tester over the bed. A whimsical smile played over his lips.

"Paul undertook to introduce me to the fashionable life, where you meet the people who count in London. For that there's no teacher like a fashionable woman, and Paul chose my teachers. I'll say no more, except that I found them charming, and they seemed to enjoy their young American. It was all part of the game, like learning to play cards well, and how to choose a wine, a snuffbox, or a waistcoat, and what to say and how to say it when you met Lady So-and-so slipping out of Lord Somebody-else's rooms."

He glanced at his father again. "If any of this makes Paul seem a wastrel, Father, I'm giving a false notion of him. Paul's too clever a man to let the little pleasures interfere with the main sport of his life."

"What's that?"

"Gambling for big stakes. I don't mean just cards and dice. Paul has magnificent stockjobbing adventures on the London Exchange, and he speculates in all kinds of things at Paris, Amsterdam, Hamburg—even as far away as India. For success in that kind of thing you've got to have wits and courage and the devil's own luck, and Paul has all three. London's always talking about his coups. And his free spending. During my stay in England he let me have several thousand pounds as if it were sixpence."

"Good God, Johnnie! What for? I sent you an allowance."

"You don't understand, Father. Over there I had to eat and drink and ride and dress as well as any of the gentlemen I wished to meet—better, in some cases. Paul insisted on that. And I learned to drop a fair sum in guineas at the gaming tables as I might a pinch of snuff. Not too much or too often, you understand. Just enough to carry the part of a well-to-do young American gentleman, one who enjoyed the company more than the game and chose not to make a fool of himself."

"I could give you another opinion on that," Mark snapped.

"You miss the point, Father. It paid handsomely in other ways. For example, at one of those card-and-dice affairs I met the Colonel Michael Wentworth I mentioned in my letters. We became friends—he's coming out to visit me here when I get settled. He's a Yorkshireman. Wasn't our own ancestor, the first Wentworth in America, from that way somewhere? We may be relations in a distant fashion. Well, no matter. What's important is that the English Wentworths stick together as our American Wentworths do, and Michael's a close relation of Lord Rockingham."

"Ah!"

"You begin to see. Michael introduced me to him at a race meeting near London in the spring of '64."

"What's Rockingham like?" demanded Mark, very interested now.

"Oh, an agreeable gentleman, about my own age, with a sound eye for horseflesh. But at the time he'd something more than horses on his mind. Lord Grenville was proposing a stamp tax on the American colonists, and nobody over there was paying much attention—except Rockingham. When he found I was an American, and a Wentworth at that, he invited me up to his seat in Yorkshire. You should see it. The estate's called Wentworth Woodhouse, and, like the bumpkin I was, I pictured a small wooden house in the wilds of Yorkshire. What I found was a palace fit for a king, a vast thing of brick and stone set in a private park of fifteen hundred acres. Zounds!"

"Go on."

"As one of the biggest Whigs in England—there's a pun for you!—Lord Rockingham wanted to know what the American attitude might be, and I told him what I knew. Our conversations went on over half a dozen visits. Lord and Lady Rockingham took a fancy to me. Their house was always full of interesting people, and it pleased them to introduce me as a Wentworth from America, as if we were one family."

"Get on with the Stamp Act," Mark said sharply.

"Oh, that! Lord Grenville slid it down the throat of Parliament like a greased patch down a worn musket. I was there with Mr. Trecothick, the New Hampshire agent, expecting a hot debate, but there was hardly a word. The whole House seemed lost in a dream that the Americans wouldn't question a tax that Englishmen were paying already. I felt like waking 'em up with a good loud backwoods yell. But once the news crossed the sea there was yelling enough from America, as you know. Grenville lost favor in Parliament, and Lord Rockingham became Prime Minister. Unfortunately his cabinet were a quarrelsome lot. They squabbled about everything under the sun, and in a year they were out too. However, before he lost office Rockingham had convinced Parliament that the Stamp Act was a blunder. It perished soon after."

Johnnie glanced again at the figure in the chair.

"Those people about the Parade today—they seemed to think I slew the Stamp Act by myself. Where did they get that notion?"

"From me. True, wasn't it?"

"Not at all. I only spoke for New Hampshire, and so did Mr. Trecothick; and we did our talking in Lord Rockingham's ear, where we reckoned it would do the most good. But you seem to forget Mr. Franklin was in London, speaking for most of the other colonies. Besides, Colonel Barré and Mr. Wilkes and a lot of other Englishmen saw the folly of trying to tax the Americans in that fashion, and they spoke up as loud as any of us."

"Well, who killed the Act, then?"

"Who killed Cock Robin?"

"Bah! You're too modest, Johnnie. If you don't sound your own horn, someone's got to blow it for you. So I did, last year, soon as I got your letter about the end of the stamps. Now tell me about the governor's post. Benning says he resigned on account of his health. That true?"

"There was more to it than that. You know what petitions and complaints about him had been going to London for years—all stuffed away in some dusty hole of the Trade and Plantations Office. America was in an uproar over the stamps when Lord Rockingham became Prime Minister, so he had all such things dragged out and examined. He guessed that every one of the American colonies had a sore of some kind, quite apart from stamps, and he was right. When it came to New Hampshire Uncle Benning was the villain. One day Rockingham said, 'John, this man must go,' and asked me if I'd like to take his place."

Johnnie paused.

"Go on, go on!"

"Well, I was in a delicate position, after all. You know why. I decided to tell him everything—Englishmen understand these matters of inheritance. I said, 'My lord, Benning Wentworth is my uncle. He has one of the largest fortunes in New England, and no living child. I'm his favorite nephew and his heir. Except for a modest provision for his widow during her lifetime I'm to get every penny. Everyone in New Hampshire has expected him to die any time these past ten years—an old fat man with the dropsy. Yet he lives, and clings to his post as governor. If he's dismissed, and I take his place at once, what will happen to my inheritance?"

"Very well put, son. Oh, nice—nice!"

"So, to spare Uncle Benning's feelings—and mine—the Lords of Trade and Plantations wrote him a careful letter. They praised his long faithful service. They suggested that he now lay down his burden. In view of the new troubles and difficulties in America, you understand. A task for a younger man. You know the rest. Uncle Benning had got a taste of the new troubles in America—the Stamp Act riots here in Portsmouth—and he didn't want any more. He knew how the people felt about him. So he took the opportunity to resign before some other trouble threw him out. Then, after a careful interval, my appointment was announced, and I stayed away another fall and winter before I came home to take it up. No indecent haste, as Lord Rockingham advised."

"Handsome!" his father said. "Handsome, I call it."

"Lord Rockingham did things handsomely in all ways. To give me countenance in London as well as here. I received the courtesy of a degree, *honoris causa*, from King's College at Aberdeen. With that step, a better was forthcoming. I had the compliment of a degree from Oxford. Oxford! I couldn't help pinching myself and asking, 'Can this be plain Johnnie Wentworth?'"

"What's so strange about that?" growled Mark. "Studied your way through Harvard College, hadn't you? Those Englishmen can't think all Americans wear clouts and feathers and write on the ground with a stick."

"You'd be surprised how many do."

Johnnie sat up and swung his feet to the floor. He passed both hands slowly over the brown stubble of his hair, closely cropped by his Yorkshire valet for a neat fit of the new peruke. His headache seemed easier now. Perhaps it was just the tight wig.

"Now, Father, you tell me a few things. To begin with, Uncle Benning obliged the Council to meet at his house at Little Harbor for years. That was one of the grievances. I intend to live here in town, where I can entertain as a governor should, and I'll meet my Council in the proper place, the Town House council room. But first I must have a suitable residency. It's time the province had a mansion for the Governor. What's the Assembly doing about that?"

"The Assembly," Mark said drily, "is pinching pennies harder than ever. I thought about a residency, as you call it, when you were still on the sea somewhere. As it happened, there was the big house I built on the other side of town for your sister Anna, when she married John Fisher. Last year Mr. Fisher got a Customs post at Salem, and they moved away. So I offered the house to the Assembly dirt cheap—seventeen hundred pounds, provincial currency. They hemmed and hawed, you know the way they do, specially the ones from Exeter and Dover and those other settlements up-tide from Portsmouth. They don't like town folk, and specially they don't like us Wentworths, nor any of the families that married into ours. They figure we've had too many favors in the past. Benning's fault, mostly. He was too crude in all ways. All that land he granted himself, and anything else he could lay his hands on. And the way he lived, eating and drinking like a pompous pig. And then marrying that tavern girl."

"Does she know about the will?" Johnnie asked curiously.

"She must guess, if she's as smart as I think she is, behind that modest face of hers. Benning wouldn't leave all that money to a handsome young widow. Waste it on the first man wags a finger at her. She'll be provided for, that's all, and she must know it."

"I see. Go on about Anna's house."

"Well, our friends on the Council were all for buying it, but the money had to come from the Assembly, and the Assembly wasn't buying. They agreed the Governor ought to live in town, though. After wind enough to blow a ship to Europe they decided to rent Anna's house at sixty-odd pounds a year. That's your residency."

Johnnie pushed out his lips and considered Anna's house. "It's not the genteel part of town, is it? Out of the way, I mean, over there in the pastures by South Pond."

"Some pretty nice houses over there now. They call it Pleasant Street."

"Call it what you like, it's just the lane to Titus Salter's mill-dam." He reflected for a time in silence. "Of course," he said slowly, "the house itself isn't bad. Dignified, in a good square fashion. Nice view of the town and harbor. And the garden goes right down to the shore of South Pond, a pretty stretch of water with the woods behind. I always liked that about Anna's house. Well, I daresay I can make it do till the Assembly's more generous. I'll have to make a lot of changes, you understand; enlarge it for servants' quarters, and so forth. I'll need a stable for sixteen horses and a good-sized carriage house. Those will have to go across the lane—I won't spoil that garden view to the pond."

A cluck of his father's tongue. "Johnnie, come down out of those English clouds and put your feet on New Hampshire. What'll you get from both your posts? Eleven hundred a year. You couldn't afford to keep eight servants and sixteen horses and do all these other wonderful things on twice the money. Forget London, Johnnie. This is Portsmouth in America. And why English servants? Aren't Americans good enough?"

"The English make better servants. And these have been trained in genteel households in Yorkshire. Some even came from Lord Rockingham's place—his own suggestion."

"You don't, by any chance, think you can live here like an English lord?"

"I intend to live in a manner becoming His Majesty's Governor of New Hampshire," Johnnie retorted crisply. "That doesn't mean like Uncle Benning, clutching every ha'penny. That's why our people despised him, as much as anything else he did. Nobody loves a miser."

"Humph!"

"Will you lend me enough money to get myself established in Anna's house, Father? And to pay some bills I owe?"

Mark gloomed at him over the chair back. "Times are hard, Johnnie. Have been, ever since the French war ended. Everything's in the doldrums, including my mast business. I can let you have money—in reason, mind, in reason. But you'll have to pull in those English horns of yours. They won't go 'tween the trees here."

"That remains to be seen. I can always borrow money in Boston."

"Moneylenders want security. What have you got?"

"The biggest fortune east of Boston—Uncle Benning's."

"He may take a long time a-dying, Johnnie."

"In that case the moneylenders can gather a long term's interest. They won't quarrel with that."

Mark shut one eye and gave his son a cold stare with the other.

"Has it occurred to Your Excellency that old men sometimes change their minds? S'pose Benning leaves everything to that tavern chit after all?"

"I could marry the widow."

"Don't jest about a thing like that. 'Tisn't decent."

A hoot of laughter from His Excellency. "For an idle argument, Father, why not? Martha's just my age and not a bad-looking woman, as I recall her. What if she worked in a tavern? She was no common slut—everybody knows that. And she's been a good wife to Uncle Benning. I've seen some noble English spendthrifts marry worse, and for less money. Besides, as Governor I'll need a wife sooner or later to do my entertaining properly, and who's had more experience than Mrs. Martha?"

Mark rose abruptly, moving to the door.

"What you need right now is to souse that head of yours in a bucket of cold spring water. All those bumpers at the tavern have got to your brains at last. Better still, just lie back and sleep 'em off. I'll see to the lodging of your horses and flunkies."

"Will you let me have a thousand pounds in the morning?"

"That's a matter for the morning. Just now, good night."

Mark slammed the door behind him as he went, and the wind of it blew the candle out. His Excellency relaxed in the darkness, smiled, and slept.

THREE

TOWARD the end of the month, June's hot sunshine faded into an east wind and some days of rain; and then July dragged its dusty days away, and August came. All these weeks a company of carpenters, joiners, masons, and painters swarmed about the house on Titus Salter's lane. The best wood carvers in the Portsmouth shipyards came to work their skill on mantels, cornices, stair rails, and banisters. A schooner from Nova Scotia brought new plaster for the walls. New York sent choice wallpaper. The new stable and carriage house arose. At the back of the house half a dozen happy-go-lucky Negroes, under the direction of an English gardener, began to change Anna's neglected shrubs and posy beds into a formal garden, leading the eye down the slope to the long mirror of South Pond.

Writing cheerfully to the Bayards, who had entertained him at Weehawken on his way north, Johnnie spoke of his "small hut with comfortable apartments."

In a letter to Lord Rockingham he was making a "Lilliputian Wentworth House." The cost of it was far from Lilliputian, but when Mark's thousand pounds were spent there were moneylenders elsewhere quite willing to let His Excellency have any sum he wished. Toward the summer's end all was ready, even to a row of young lindens planted before the house. On a starry night in late August he gave a housewarming party and invited the elite of Portsmouth—the Wentworths, Atkinsons, Meserves, Pierces, Odiornes, Langdons, Parrys, Boyds, Sherburnes, Moffatts, Liviuses, and many of the minor ones.

Carriages, coaches, and smart little painted chaises rolled up to the door, set down their ladies and gentlemen, and rolled away. Johnnie's footmen, tall as grenadiers in the smart green livery, bowed the guests inside, and his major-domo bawled their names. Johnnie greeted them in a suit of dove gray, with clocked silk stockings and silver-buckled shoes, a great frilled cravat, and a rich flutter of lace at his wrists.

Even old Uncle Benning came, with his gouty legs huge in bandages, jolting over the stony road from Little Harbor in his heavy coach. Four of Johnnie's servants, sweating under their powdered hair, seated him in an armchair and carried him into the house, like a florid image of Bacchus at a pagan festival. His lady walked in behind. She was still slim at thirty, a blonde woman with mild blue eyes, diffident in the presence of all these people who despised her so, but facing the evening with patience as she had faced the past seven years.

"Martha!" Johnnie said. "How good of you to come—and in such a charming gown!"

She flushed. They had met a few times, briefly, after his college days. He had called her Ma'am on those occasions and kept his distance like the others. The sudden "Martha," the compliment, and the touch of his lips on her fingers confused her for a moment. She gave him a quick apprehensive glance. Was he making fun of her? His steady gray eyes denied it, and she had a little glow of reassurance. He was honest, and he was being kind. She said quietly, "Thank you, John—Your Excellency. It seems strange not to hear people calling my husband that any more."

She drifted away to the east drawing room, where ladies were chattering over the maroon flock-paper on the walls, the mantel and its carved dolphins, the rich carpets and window hangings, the crystal chandelier, and the silver sconces with their candles and polished mirrors.

The Atkinsons, father and son, arrived with Frances in their handsome old coach-and-four. The two men gave Johnnie a bow, a murmured "Your Excellency," and passed on. Frances plucked at her skirts and made a demure little bob. Johnnie caught up her fingers.

"Fannie, my dear, I have a task for these tonight."

"If it's currying your precious horses they refuse."

"You can refuse me nothing—I'm your Governor, remember. D'you know, Fan, you've become another creature in my absence. You used to be all eyes and bones."

"Well?" she demanded.

He paused, thinking of that dreamy pair in the garden. She had looked small then against Theo's gaunt six feet. Now she seemed tall for a woman—as tall as himself anyhow. The flat little chest had gained something that thrust out her bodice. Padding, no doubt, a good many flat ladies padded, and if so the gown was a high-cut thing that kept the secret well. But her carved ivory features were the same, the high cheekbones, the taut look of the skin, the slanted hazel eyes.

"Well, you make a mighty handsome wife at—what is it—two-and-twenty? Theo must tell you so two-and-twenty times a day. If he doesn't he's a dog."

"Hmmm! When a man spoons up compliments like this he wants something—the dog. What do you want of me tonight, Your Excellency?"

He laughed. "Don't be so suspicious, coz. Any man here will tell you the same. But I confess I want something. Nothing difficult. You play a harpsichord very well, I remember that. There's something to be said for Boston music teachers. Now, I have here one of the latest instruments, made by a Swiss named Shudi, the best in Europe. And no one to play it."

"Pooh! If there's one there's a dozen women here who can thump either spinet or harpsichord. As you know very well."

"Possibly, coz. But I'll have no one thumping my beautiful Shudi. I have a tender ear for music. Don't smile. I picked it up in England, the best of my accomplishments. Indeed I even learned to play the flute after a fashion. My friend Colonel Wentworth had a fine skill with the violin—surprising in a soldier—and we formed a little group and played chamber music on rainy London nights for our own amusement."

"You astonish me, Your Excellency. I thought your only interests were trees and horses."

"You wrong me. Look here, Fan, it's time we had a musical society here in Portsmouth, and I intend to make a start. D'you see that footman over there? He can play the cello very well. That's why I brought him out with me. I'm sending to England for another who can play the French horn. And Colonel Wentworth is coming from England to visit me this fall."

"Fiddle and all?"

"Fiddle and all. So we'll have a little group to begin with. If you behave yourself nicely you shall have a part in it. But all that aside, coz, I want some music here tonight. Please try the Shudi for a few minutes. Then I'll join you with my flute, and my footman will play the cello."

"So that's what you invited me for!"

"My dear Fan, I invited you because you're my very pretty cousin, because your husband's the Secretary of my Council, and because you're the daughter-in-law of my Chief Justice. In that order of importance. And you happen to play the harpsichord."

"Very nicely put, my clever sir. Where is your precious toy—in there? I'll see what I can do. But be warned. I've played nothing for five years but that old whispering spinet of the Atkinsons."

The major-domo was bawling again. "Mister and Missus Woodbury Langdon!" Fannie moved away to the west drawing room, where she could hear some idle finger picking at the precious Shudi.

The house filled. All Portsmouth was curious about Governor Johnnie's mansion, and now the privileged ones came to inspect it thoroughly. A female voice asked leave to explore, and Johnnie waved a careless hand. From that moment there was a continual trooping up and down the staircase and passing from chamber to chamber, above and below. They even peered into the busy kitchen, with its new English ovens and a coppersmith's stock of pots and pans, polished like gold, and delicious whiffs and glimpses of the supper that was to be served late in the evening. Great kettles of turtle soup; salmon fresh from the

Piscataqua; richly browned chickens and turkeys; Virginia hams; partridge pasties; wild-pigeon pies; a confectioner's array of sugar cakes and tarts and of iced *orgeat* and *capillaire*, prepared by Johnnie's own cook, a man fetched all the way from fashionable London.

In the dining room a sideboard held a row of glass decanters, each slender neck hung with silver chain and ivory ticket to declare the wine inside. A table of San Domingo mahogany, polished like a dark forest pool, gave back the gleams of candelabra at each end, and in its middle, surrounded by delicate glasses that blazed in the light, sat an immense silver bowl of punch.

Happy and house-proud, Johnnie moved about enjoying the chatter. Once, finding some ladies peering into his own bedchamber, he invited them inside to see his view. The new stable and carriage house across the lane had been designed long and low not to spoil it. The house stood on the first knuckle of the broad green thumb between the Puddle Creek and South Pond. He swept back velvet curtains and pointed past the Puddle to the yellow-lit windows of the town and beyond them to the masthead lights of shipping at anchor in the river.

"On a fine day," he declared, "I can see Mount Agamonticus over there past Kittery. Forty miles away—think of that!"

But the ladies had no interest in Agamonticus. Their eyes with bright feminine curiosity roved over the dressing table and his silver-mounted brushes, combs, and powder box; a wardrobe whose open door gave a glimpse of elegant London clothes; the rich carpet in which their painted wooden heels sank as if in snow; the huge mahogany bed with its tester and valances and looped curtains.

Mrs. Langdon and Mrs. Sherburne looked at each other across the wide counterpane and giggled. They were lively young wives. Mrs. Langdon said in a bubbling voice, "If it please Your Excellency, aren't you afraid of getting lost in this great bed all by yourself?" A tinkle of laughter in half a dozen feminine keys.

39

"I?" Johnnie said gaily. "A qualified surveyor of His Majesty's Woods?"

"Oh come, Mr. Wentworth," coaxed Mrs. Langdon. "We're all dying to know who's to be mistress of all this. Some milk-and-roses English creature, I suppose. When does she arrive?"

"Upon my honor, dear lady, I have nothing of your sex on the way but a pair of very pretty English mares—and they're to sleep across the lane."

"You and your nags!" cried Mrs. Livius. "You can't wed anything on four legs, Johnnie. Confess now! You haven't set up this handsome home just to play the bachelor. There's got to be a lady of the house, and heaven knows it's time you married. But who? If she's not English, then it must be some girl you found on the way from Carolina. Is that it? One of those horsy Virginians, I suppose."

Johnnie smiled and shook his twenty-guinea wig. "Not even one of those, and they grow mighty handsome girls and horses in Virginia, I can tell you. Believe me, ladies, you see a bachelor safely past the perilous twenties, and satisfied to worship you heavenly creatures from afar, like an astronomer."

"A shocking bad example to the young men of New Hampshire," Mrs. Langdon chaffed.

"I'm afraid I can't help that. I must make up for it in other ways. Just now, if you'll forgive me, I hear music and I must go below. I can't play the doting benedick for you, but in a few minutes you shall hear me play the flute, which is not so difficult. With a flute you call your own tune. One can't do that with a wife."

He left them laughing and made his way down the busy staircase. Fannie was running her fingers over the harpsichord keys, and his musical footman stood there in patience with his cello tuned and ready.

"D'you like it, coz?"

"It's beautiful, Johnnie. Too good for a dolt like me, but never mind. What shall we play? We'd better try simple tunes that everybody knows, else they mayn't guess what we're doing at all. We should have practiced together."

"After this we shall, I promise you."

"Get your flute then. I suggest we begin with "Early One Morning" or "Drink to Me Only." Everybody knows those. They may even sing and drown our mistakes."

So they began, falling into discords now and then at which Mrs. Theo shuddered, but the guests came crowding about them, and first one voice was raised, then three or four, and soon the whole company was singing. The gentlemen had been passing a good judgment on the punch, and the deft English servants made sure that no lady was without a glass and no glass without wine. With these useful accompaniments the musical part of the evening was a success that even Johnnie's flat notes could not spoil.

Then it was time for that tremendous supper, and after that for the toasts to His Majesty, to the Ladies, and to our Excellent Host. At last the carriages rolled away under the weak morning stars, and Johnnie could retire to that vast and lonely bed. He was lost in sleep the moment his head touched the pillow, as if there were no women in the world.

Back in the older part of the town, in the privacy of their own bed curtains, young Mrs. Langdon recounted the high points of the party to a husband reflecting drowsily on the evening's fare.

"You know—do stop yawning, Woody, and listen to me—I think he meant it. About not marrying, I mean. And then that little speech after the last toast, saying he wished to devote his life to New Hampshire, and all that. When he said he'd live to see this colony the greatest in New England his voice was, well, passionate."

"Oh, Johnnie likes to be a little pompous, duck. He wouldn't be old Benning's nephew if he wasn't."

"He's nothing like Benning. I tell you, when Johnnie said that, he had a look in his eyes like a monk who's taken the vows. Really! As if women didn't mean a thing to him and never had. Do you suppose there's something lacking in the man?"

A male snort from the adjoining pillow. "Stuff! Johnnie's all man in spite of those dancing-master ways he picked up in England. He's kissed more than ladies' hands, depend on it, if half we hear of London society is true. Johnnie probably had too much of 'em in those four years he was gone. Even good cider loses taste if you go too often to the keg. He'll get over that. He'll marry, you may be sure, if only to carry on his branch of the Wentworth dynasty. And when Johnnie takes a wife, it won't be some little goody pushed at him by you matchmaking wives of Portsmouth."

"Who, then, if you know so much?"

"Ah, that's the question. Some girl of a fashionable society, that's sure, one who can play the Governor's lady to his own standard. She must have looks, of course, and money. A lot of money. That's as plain as Johnnie's debts—as plain as the nose on old Mark's face."

"Then why didn't he marry some English heiress?"

"Because he wants an American, I suppose. Under that fancy English wig our Johnnie's still clear white pine, from heart to bark. Oh, Johnnie didn't come home by way of the southern colonies just to look at trees and horses, my dear duck. Those southern planters all have daughters and dollars, and they're not afraid to part with 'em when the right kind of gentleman comes along. Ha! They don't pinch their money down there. They're not like our aristocrats. Look at old Benning, that greedy moneybags. Look at his brother Mark, for that matter, or brother Hunk. Look at old Atkinson, the way he clings to his post as Chief Justice, the way he got son Theo the post of Secretary to the Council, and the way both of 'em collect their salaries to the penny, as if the old man hadn't one of the biggest fortunes in these parts. Maybe it's the climate. Maybe a rich man up here gets cold and tight with the winters."

"You sound like one of those noisy Boston levelers."

"God forbid. To get back to what I was saying, one of these days you'll see Johnnie Wentworth bring home a Virginia fortune all wrapped up in a pretty bundle of petticoats, and that'll be the end of all this prattle."

"That remains to be seen," said Mrs. Langdon darkly.

"Ah, you women—you'll never believe a man can get along without you. If he does, there's something wrong with him. I tell you Johnnie's just a man with one idea fixed in his mind. After the bad record of old Benning Wentworth he wants to be the best governor we ever had, the Wentworth who made New Hampshire big and famous. His noddle's too full of that to leave room for a woman or anything else just now. This is what he says, and call it a fantastic dream if you like, but at least it's better than Governor Benning's lackadaisy ways. Johnnie swears we must open the back country and settle it quickly. The New Yorkers are claiming the whole backwoods clear to Canada, did you know that? Massachusetts wants a big chunk too. Where do we come in? Johnnie says we've got to busy ourselves, or New Hampshire will be left with a cleared patch on the coast—we'll be left sitting with our tails in salt water, like a hungry cat when the meat's gone into the pickle barrel."

"What's he propose to do about it?"

"To begin with, he'll cut a road right through the forest to the mountains. Oh yes! He knows that back country well. He and Ammi Cutter and some other bold fellows even ranged out lands for 'emselves at Winnipesaukee years ago, when the French and Indian War was still going on. Johnnie says he'll clear an estate and build a mansion up there for his 'country seat,' and he thinks everyone will scramble to follow his example. He talks of farms and sawmills and gristmills in the wilderness as if he could actually see 'em. Even dreams of a college up that way somewhere—a college!—a place where our New Hampshire boys can go for an education, instead of trapesing off to Harvard College and wasting their fathers' money in Boston. Oh, you should hear him! He talks of 'opening new townships' all over the backwoods as if they were clams at a penny a bucket. Says new people will flock into the woods once we get roads cut. People from every colony north of New York—even from England. Says there's no reason why New Hampshire can't have a hundred thousand people—double what we've got now—in a matter of ten years."

It was Mrs. Langdon's turn to say Stuff, and she said it.

"Stuff if you like," her husband said, "but trust our Johnnie to give it a good try. Of course it's hopeless. The only land fit to plow is right down here in the lower river valleys. I give him five years—less—to butt his handsome head against the granite boulders and pine stumps up there in the hills. Then you'll see him calm down, take a wife, and play the little king of Portsmouth like his uncle and grandfather before him. Now go to sleep."

While this conversation was going on, another crackled in a big white house looking out upon the salty gleam of Islington Creek at the north end of the town. Mr. Peter Livius and his wife also were engaged with the evening's affair. A well-to-do Englishman with a law degree, he had met and married a breezy New Hampshire girl when she was visiting in London, and the bride had induced him to cross the sea and settle in Portsmouth. Here they lived in much style, although Mr. Livius was inclined to look down his nose at the little colonial pomps and customs of the place.

"You can say what you like about the Wentworths," said his spouse amiably, twisting her hair for the night. "What if they do run this province as if they owned it? Wouldn't you in their place? Johnnie's going to make a good governor, you'll see. And if he brings a bit of London tone to our little society here it'll do the place some good. You said as much for yourself when we came and built this house, remember?"

"That was five years ago. I've got used to your smug little Portsmouth, my dear, and so will your precious Johnnie. It won't take him so long. Behind all his fine manners he's still got the mind of a backwoodsman. He took some of us over the lane to see his new stables tonight, and we had to listen to a long harangue about the value of the wilderness up there to the north. There may be something in what he says, mind you. I've a notion to buy some land in—what the deuce is the name of it? That fanciful township he and some others laid out years ago. Wolfe something—General Wolfe was killed at Quebec about that time."

"Wolfeborough."

"Ah! Well, it seems to me Governor Johnnie's got an eye to the main chance, like all the Wentworths. If half his plans come true, he and his friends can make a pretty penny from the lands they hold up there."

"What's wrong with that?" cried Mrs. Livius. "Isn't that honest speculation? They bought the grant with good money, and they risked their scalps to run the lines. The Indians didn't make peace till long after General Wolfe died fighting up in Canada. My ancestors took chances like that too. So did Johnnie's. It's not like that fat old Benning, never risking a hair and taking lands all over the country for nothing."

"I still say they're birds of a feather—the Wentworth feather."

"If you're smart, Mr. Livius, you'll pay more respect to His Excellency."

"His Excellency! Bah! His Excellency's great-grandfather kept a tavern, you told me that yourself."

"Oh, Peter, you dyed-in-the-wool snob, you! For heaven's sake, bend that stiff English neck of yours and try to see this country as it is. It's no good sneering behind your hand at the Wentworths and their circle. The thing is to be part of it. Wouldn't you like to be Chief Justice? Old Atkinson can't live forever."

"He plans to do just that, my dear. Old men in fat offices have the knack."

"Benning Wentworth lost his, though."

"It took another Wentworth to ease him out."

"You play your cards properly, and Johnnie may ease old Theodore out for you. He must want younger men about him, with all these fine new plans of his."

"In that case he'd give the post to his cousin Theo."

"I doubt it—I doubt it very much. Theo's no lawyer. Anyhow, didn't you notice him tonight? A living ghost. He's had a cough these past two years. The Atkinsons keep mum about it, but anyone can see it's consumption—the galloping kind. There he was tonight, coughing blood into a handkerchief in a corner, while that bold snip Fannie was giving herself airs at the harpsichord."

"Mrs. Theo? She seemed very nice and modest to me."

"Because she wore that high-cut gown, I suppose, while some other ladies were showing well nigh all they'd got above the stays. Well, if you want to know, old Mr. Atkinson rules that house, and he don't approve women showing. Fannie modest? Ha! A couple of years ago Fannie went a-visiting to Boston. She does that every chance she gets, if you've noticed. She's Boston born and bred, and she finds life dull in Portsmouth. Well, while she was there she took a notion to have that Copley man, the painter, to do a portrait of her. And she posed in a silk gown that would have thrown old Justice Atkinson into a fit. Bodice down to here, and the stays laced tight below. She daresn't take a good breath the whole time she was sitting, lest she pop her pretty dumplings. She told me that herself. The picture was for young Theo, of course. Pearls in her hair and beads at her throat, and holding a tame squirrel on a silver chain. Copley likes to paint ladies with a fine bare show. He likes to paint that squirrel on a little table at their hand too. With his own tongue stuck halfway through his cheek, the rogue."

"Why?"

"The squirrel's the tame husband on the lady's chain."

"Meow!"

"Meow for Fannie too. Only she's a sly Boston house-puss, and I'm your honest down-East wildcat, Peter dear. Which do you prefer?"

"As one of the tame squirrels?" Mr. Livius snorted. "What chance has he got?"

FOUR

COLONEL MICHAEL WENTWORTH, sailing up the estuary in a mast-ship at the summer's end, found himself in a very new world indeed. His friend Johnnie had talked mostly of the sport to be had in America with rod and gun, and of long wonderful rides and marches in a forest where only yesterday the savages lurked with tomahawk and scalping knife.

None of this had prepared the half-pay soldier for a prosperous town of four or five thousand people between the forest and the sea. He had thought of wooden houses vaguely as something made of logs and of the colonists as a half-wild folk with a sprinkling of educated Johnnies. But there was not a log hut in sight. Even the cottages of the fishermen were neat affairs of frame and shingles or clapboards, and it astonished him to see so many tall painted mansions, as handsome as anything in brick or stone across the sea. Later on, when he saw the inside of them, he marveled more, noting the stairways, the spacious chambers with their wainscots and panels, their carved mantels, their elegant furnishings.

The mast trade had given these Portsmouth gentry a direct and regular connection with England for generations. They wore the latest London modes, sat in English furniture, rode English horses on English saddles or bowled behind them in English carriages. They ate on English chinaware, with English silver, and drank from English glasses. Although they sent their sons to Harvard College, they lived independent of bustling Boston, a scant hundred miles down the coast, as if Boston did not exist.

At the age of forty Colonel Wentworth carried the neat figure of a riding man with a military air that made him look younger by ten years. He was handsome in a florid way that came partly from the wars and hunting fields and partly from a taste for good sound port. Johnnie's town surprised him, and he was even more surprised to find that this colonial society, which enjoyed so many things beyond his own slim purse, regarded him with a great respect. Why? Because he was not only a Wentworth but a Wentworth actually related to an English lord!

In England that had got him nowhere. There were so many lords and so many connections better than his own. Yet even his friend Johnnie, who was always proud to call himself an American, seemed to have a devout regard for English nobility. He heard Johnnie dropping great names like Rockingham into parlor conversations as a boy might drop stones in a pool, enjoying the ripple they caused—and never mentioning the titled sharpers, rakes, and scoundrels he had met in the house in Poland Street. To Colonel Michael this was nonsense. He was a penniless younger son, sent into the army as a matter of necessity. The years of war abroad had given him a humorous contempt for the idle castes at home. And now in America he found a liking for these colonial aristocrats who had got where they were by their own efforts, who actually boasted that their own ancestors, two or three generations back, had been poor fishermen or farmers, grubbing for a living with one hand and fighting off savages with the other.

However he soon found other sides to Governor Johnnie. Johnnie could hold court in this little kingdom of his with the ease of a monarch born. But the same Johnnie, with the same ease, could set off through the woods in buckskins and moccasins and live for weeks in the rude fashion of the forest rangers. Indeed Johnnie was amazing. He could ride a hundred miles in a summer day when the roads were fit. In the forest, where there were no roads at all, he could stride forty between dawn and dark, pausing only to glance at his compass now and then. When night came he would sit in the firelight with pencil and notebook, jotting details of the landscape, the timber, the soil, and sketching a map of the country he had passed—

all this before he permitted himself to sleep. He never hesitated on these forest journeys to throw himself on a few poles or a hollow log to cross the rivers, although he could not swim. And in hunting game he could shoot as straight as any of the mountain rangers, of whom people told such fabulous tales.

It was this Johnnie Wentworth, not the polished Governor of the Portsmouth drawing rooms, who held the friendship of the hunters, the small farmers, the tough unruly mast loggers of the Piscataqua. And the mastmen were one of his chief problems. He was determined to carry out his duties as Surveyor General of the King's Woods. Uncle Benning, well aware that his own forest dealings could not stand the light of day, had been lax about the mast law. Many a pine bearing the King's broad arrow and his own big W, clearly marked by his deputy surveyors, had been stolen and floated boldly down to the Portsmouth shipyards or sold to sawmills at the falls.

To Johnnie this was a serious matter. Nobody knew better than he that the demands of a century, and especially the last French war, had played havoc with the biggest and best pines. Those that still stood within short haul of a tidal river or the coast itself were getting scarce. He kept his deputies ranging the woods for them and carving his official JW under the broad arrow. He visited logging camps large and small, stopping a night or a day with the men, sipping their raw Medford rum, capping their rude jokes with witty ones of his own, and then in a quiet moment announcing that the new JW on the King's trees meant a quick prosecution for anyone who cut one without his leave.

"Who'll persecute?" drawled one of them, an old companion of his own mast-cutting days. "Hey? Who'll persecute us, Johnnie?"

"I," said Johnnie frankly. "Myself—no matter who's guilty, no matter how far I have to go to find him."

He meant it, and as the months went by he proved it again and again. Once, traveling through the snow and biting cold of January weather, he arrested some mast thieves on a distant river and brought them to Portsmouth gaol, a round journey of three hundred miles in sixteen days. On these expeditions he seldom had more company than a servant or one of his deputy rangers. He was afraid of nothing, in the forest or out of it.

Colonel Wentworth admired all this. He could see the point of it. But then there was Johnnie's studious side, which the soldier could only deplore as a sad waste of time. This was the Johnnie who pored over books of natural history and science, who read the classics of ancient Greece and Rome, who carried on a busy correspondence with odd fish of every sort from arch-bishops to architects, who was always gathering specimens of New Hampshire minerals, plants, birds, and animals and sending them off to his friends abroad. Night after night when the Colonel, drowsy with negus, had tumbled into bed, the candles burned on in Johnnie's library.

This, decided the Colonel, was a freak of nature, like his own unsoldierly flair for the violin. He indulged his flair a good deal now, in company with Johnnie's flute, with the footmen who played the cello and French horn, and with Mrs. Frances Atkin-son at the harpsichord. There was a musical evening at least once every summer week in the Governor's house when he was at home, and as often as three times a week when winter set in and put a curb on His Excellency's restless travels.

Sometimes young Theo accompanied his wife up the rough lane past Puddle Dock and sat the evening through, regarding the musicians with his white face and haunted eyes like a specter at a wedding feast. Usually she came alone. On wet evenings Johnnie sent his coachman in the little chaise for her. In fine weather she chose to walk, and Johnnie or Colonel Michael went down to the Puddle footbridge to meet her, in case some drunken fisherman wandered across her path.

Privately, Mrs. Fannie marveled at their pleasure in the sounds they made about the harpsichord. Often they kept her late, scraping and squealing and tootling hour after hour, but she never gave a sign that she was tired or bored. Usually it was Colonel Michael who noticed a late strike of the clock, and then after a nibbled biscuit and a glass of His Excellency's best Oporto she made her way home, escorted to her door by one or both of them.

One night, sauntering back from this little duty together, the soldier said lightly, "You know, Johnnie, sometimes these people of yours, specially the women, seem prudish as a set of parsons' wives. Yet nobody cocks an eyebrow at a young married woman visitin' the Governor's house without her husband, and at night."

"Fannie?" Johnnie said, surprised. "Everybody knows about our little musical club. Besides, she's my cousin."

"And a very charmin' one."

"What d'you mean by that?"

"Oh nothin'—nothin'. Mrs. Theo's the image of modesty and all that, my dear feller. Still, I can't help thinkin' sometimes what a dash a gel like that could cut in London, say, with those eyes tipped in that tight little face of hers, and that figger, and the way she walks."

"What way does she walk?"

"Um, well, as if she had legs. Most of our English ladies move as if they just had wheels."

"You're very observant," Johnnie said stiffly.

"Oh, I'm just not blind, my boy. And that husband of hers don't seem up to snuff, if you know what I mean. Oh, a nice polite feller, y'know, but a fish. A nice polite fish, with very little blood, and that cold."

"Theo has a touch of the consumption. His family never mention it, but he's obliged to mind his health."

Colonel Michael noticed a chill in His Excellency's voice and dropped an unimportant subject. The Johnnie he liked best was the one who took him shooting in the woods and marshes up the Piscataqua. He had mastered its crackjaw name ("Pis-KAT-a-kwa, Pis-KAT-a-kwa—phew!"), and he had discovered that the "river" was largely an arm of the sea, curving around the town and opening a broad wet hand whose tidal fingers wandered into the country for miles. A few short streams fell into it, and at their mouths lay salt meadows and reedy channels where in autumn the flocks of wild duck had to be seen to be believed. And there were shoals in the basin behind the town where, under a boat's keel, the long eel grass could be seen swaying with the tidal currents like the hair of a drowned giant. On these shoals in autumn the south-flying wild geese gathered in thousands, diving to feed on the roots of the green sea grass, honking in a chorus that could be heard in the town itself, and resting together like dark rafts on the shallow water.

At home the soldier had often ridden down from Yorkshire for a few days' fowling in the Lincoln fens, but he had never dreamed of anything like this. Lying with Johnnie by the shore in crude brushwood blinds, on the wet and windy mornings that were best for gunning, or in a flatboat hidden in the reeds, he blazed away to his heart's content. For this sport they sailed on a flooding tide from Portsmouth aboard one of the gundalows that carried freight to the up-tide settlements. The Englishman enjoyed a spell at the tiller on the way, especially in the tricky tiderace between Dover and Bloody Point.

He pronounced the word "gondola," although the name seemed to him absurd for such stubby and beamy craft. They were open for the most part, with a short deck forward and another aft where the cabin was. In the forward deck stood a single mast, spreading a big lateen sail. They reminded him somewhat of Thames barges. Indeed the whole aspect here reminded him of the Thames mouth; the broad water, more sea than river, the low green slopes of the fields, the patches of woodland, the small farmhouses, the pleasant smell of hay at harvest time, an occasional windmill spinning its arms in the wind, the coming and going of gundalows and shallops, the tall-masted ships from the ocean sailing in to the heart of the land.

He remarked this to Johnnie one day, and His Excellency looked about him.

"Mmm, yes. Though to me it's more like that bay around the corner from the Thames, where you go in to Chatham. All it lacks is the men-o'-war anchored in Chatham roads. Someday we'll have those too."

"What the dooce for?"

"Someday the Lords of Admiralty will see the folly of fetching masts and ship timber across the Atlantic, when they could build the ships here and save all that expense. Our shipwrights are as good as any in England. In fact our people built one or two fifty-gun ships for the Royal Navy in the old French wars. I keep that in mind. You'll see a time when our Portsmouth here will be a naval town as busy as your English one, or Chatham."

"Nonsense, Johnnie. Dockyards must be close to the enemy, not the woods. Who's there to fight, this side of the ocean? The French left Canada four years ago, bag and baggage."

"And you don't think they'll come back? I say they will, one of these days when they see their chance. The Canadians are still French to the heels, they'll never be anything else, and as soon as a French fleet comes in sight they'll be rousing the Indians again. When that day comes we'll want good American troops—we can't expect your redcoats to defend us forever. That's why I'll insist on keeping our New Hampshire militia trained and armed. We're too close to Canada for chances."

Colonel Michael grinned. "You'll have a job to convince your Assembly. That costs money."

"Oh, I have another argument there, and a good one," Johnnie said. "Just now there's a scramble to claim the backwoods up Canada way. New York and Massachusetts want 'em all. And what about New Hampshire? My uncle Benning issued a good many land grants up there in the mountains, but he never prepared to defend the claims. Well, I shall. I intend to see this province as big as New York, and I hope I live long enough to see it as rich. Just now, of course, the other colonies look down their noses at us. We're too small to count, by their reckoning. So we've got to show 'em that we do count. See here, all the lands east of Lake Champlain belong by right to New Hampshire. Our woodsmen were the first to explore 'em, and our rangers under Colonel Rogers drove the French and Indians out of 'em. We claim everything from here to Canada on the north, and as we're the only government this side of Boston we should have everything to Nova Scotia on the east. Someday we will."

"How?"

"Possession—nine points of the law. We'll cut roads into the back country and build towns and villages. We'll back up our possession with a swarm of well-armed yeomanry. Don't throw me that quizzical soldier's look of yours, Michael. New Hampshire could muster ten thousand armed men even now. They lack discipline, I grant you, and their muskets are an odd collection, as you've seen. But I'll mend all that. I won't be satisfied till I can turn out eight full regiments of foot, all well equipped, and I'll raise a regiment of horse amongst the gentlemen. Then, when I go down to Boston and New York to talk about the New Hampshire grants, they'll listen to me with respect. Nobody's going to tramp roughshod over New Hampshire men if they're armed and ready for trouble."

"Gad, Johnnie, I didn't know you could look so fierce. Forgive me if I smile. I can't help wondering what would happen at home if Yorkshire, say, took a sudden fancy to the Lincoln fens. Imagine ten thousand fen-men turning out with their trusty fowling pieces to defend their bogs and ditches. Ha! What a picture!"

"That's England," Johnnie snapped. "These colonies aren't a tight marriage of small counties, with one government, like yours. For the most part they're big and separate and ambitious, each one jealous of the other and out for all the lands it can grab. When you're playing whist you want trumps, and in this game of land-grabbing there's no trump like armed people on the ground in question. You can talk turkey then. Have you ever seen Americans at a turkey shoot?"

Colonel Michael shrugged and said no more. He thought, Poor Johnnie's new appointments have gone to his head. He can't bear to think he's ruling something small. It's got to be big and important. And he wants to do it all in twenty minutes. He'll break his heart of course.

The seasons passed. Colonel Wentworth, delighted with the new country, needed no persuasion to stay on indefinitely as

Johnnie's guest. In the late autumn of '68, when snow clouds began to climb the sky and fill the air at times with the white shake of a torn pillow, Johnnie took the soldier in a small sailboat to the harbor mouth. Black duck were feeding in Witch Creek and Sagamore Creek and whistlers in the shelter of the islands by Little Harbor. At the end of a successful afternoon, when their bellies were empty and their gun shoulders sore, Johnnie steered the boat into Little Harbor and cast himself and his friend on the hospitality of Uncle Benning.

As they stepped forth on the old Governor's stone landing place and moved up the slope to the front door, Johnnie pointed to the original portion of the mansion, a plain two-story wooden house of the salt-box kind, common in an earlier day, and now merely part of a jumble of walls and gables and roofs that extended down the slope to the waterside. Roughly the mansion formed three sides of a square, open to the water, hidden and sheltered from the land side by a low hill and the woods.

He chuckled. "Uncle Benning had a craze for adding ells and chambers to the old house, year after year. Nothing stopped him but the tide, as you see. This thing must have all of fifty rooms. Imagine trying to warm even half of 'em in a New Hampshire winter!"

"Still, it's interestin' in its way and a dooced pretty situation," Michael observed, looking about him.

"You should see the house when the lilacs are in bloom. See what a mass they make about it. Uncle Benning claims they're the oldest lilacs in New Hampshire, and he's probably right."

The old man, seated in a great padded armchair before a blaze of birch logs, greeted them heartily and commanded them to stay the night. Servants appeared at his shout, and up from the cellar came a decanter of Madeira.

"Tinto," he wheezed, "and from south-side vineyards, gentlemen, I can vouch. I had six pipes of it shipped from Funchal to Jamaica last winter, and brought 'em up here in a trading schooner in the spring. Nothing improves Madeira tinto like a good sea-rocking in warm latitudes—you know that, Johnnie, of course."

Supper followed—a feast of roast beef, potatoes, onions, and squash, of plum pudding and pumpkin pie, of coffee, port, and brandy. The younger men, hungry after their day in the cold air, neglected nothing, but Benning outdid both. The old man's appetite for food and drink was prodigious.

Martha Wentworth gave no protest, no reminder of his gout. If she had ever tried to curb the uproarious Falstaff of Little Harbor she had given it up long ago. She sat in her place at the table's foot, giving quiet directions to the servants but taking no main part in the conversation. While Johnnie and Benning talked lands and timber, Colonel Michael addressed himself politely to her, noting the piled fair hair, the soft blue eyes, the placid face. *Amiable and a little stoopid,* he thought, *like me. Still, she was clever enough to catch Old Moneybags. Plays the lady well enough in a quiet country fashion—much better than he plays the gentleman. What a great barrel of wind and fat the man is.*

After supper Johnnie remarked that his friend would like to see over the mansion, and at Benning's command Martha led them forth with a candle. She began in the great cellar with its vegetable bins, its row of puncheons and smaller casks, and the stalls where a dozen horses had been sheltered in the old days of Indian raids. When they came to the Council Chamber the colonel found himself in a stately room with paneled walls, a great fireplace, and a beautiful mantelpiece. Here for years the councilors had come to the old Governor's summons, in fine weather by boat, in bad weather on horseback by the rough track around the creeks. The hearth was empty and the chamber cold —a chilly circumstance, thought Michael, for the ladies carved in wood on both sides of the fireplace. Each showed a lot of bare bosom with the well-turned proportions of Martha herself. A quip hovered on his lips. Who was the model? But he let it perish there. Martha was moving on, shivering a little, to show them the billiard room, with its spinet and long buffet and punch bowls.

The rest of the mansion was a maze of chambers and closets and presses, with staircases narrow and steep, with erratic little landings, windows of all sorts and sizes, and doors leading off in odd directions. From the small-paned windows they had passing glimpses of Newcastle Island, a dark mass guarding the entrance to Portsmouth, and the dance of cold starlight on the water of Little Harbor and the main channel beyond.

When they returned below their host was still in his chair by the fire, with his swollen and bandaged feet on a hassock. A brandy bottle stood at his elbow and there was a half-empty glass in his hand. His purple face glistened in the firelight. He had doffed his wig and covered his baldness with a common red flannel nightcap.

"What d'ye think of my house?" he demanded of the Englishman.

"It's—it's remarkable, sir!"

"It's the biggest in New Hampshire, Colonel. The biggest! Some people up to Portsmouth call it Benning's Folly. Bah! They're mighty proud of their mansions, up in town, but they can't get over me having the biggest house in New Hampshire, away out here at the harbor mouth. Folly!

"You see those muskets in my Council Chamber? French, all of 'em. Came from Louisburg after our New England forces took the place in '45."

He turned a bloodshot eye on Johnnie. "You take my advice, Johnnie, and keep a good rack of muskets in your house."

"But the Indians are quiet now."

"Injuns! Who's talking about Injuns? You weren't here, you were over in England when we had those stamp riots back in '65. Ods my life, what a mob! All the raggle-taggle of the town and countryside. Sailors, fishermen, servants—black and white— and a flock o' those wild mastmen from up the river. God knows who there wasn't, even some that went by the name o' gentlemen. Ranting through the streets and shouting insults at the King and

Parliament, and at me, Johnnie, me! Their own Governor! There was even some wild talk of coming away out here and pulling old Benning's Folly down about his ears. So I kept all those guns oiled and loaded, and my servants ready, and saw to my doors. Even made ready at a pinch to shift my horses from the stable to those old stalls under the house. And I took care to let all that be known in town. Oh, 'twas touch and go in these parts for a time."

"Well," Johnnie said, "that's all blown over now."

Uncle Benning poured himself another glass of brandy, drank a great swig, and gave Johnnie a leer.

"You think so, Johnnie? The ladies say you can see Mount Agamonticus from your bedchamber. You'd better lower your gaze a bit. Look down to the mouth of Puddle Dock, where the mob planted their 'Liberty Pole' in '65. It's still there. They never took it down. And now those damned fools in London are up to their mischief again, my Johnnie, like puppies in a backwoods pasture that ain't got sense enough to let a porcupine alone. This time it's duties on all tea, glass, and paper coming into America, and the devil knows what else. What's more, they're out to stop the habit of smuggling in America, so they say. So now we have a new swarm of customs officers, and gaugers, and tidewaiters, along o' His Majesty's revenue cutters, a lot o' busy-bodies poking their noses into every hole and corner of the coast. They'll find nothing but trouble, mark my words. And that means trouble for you, Johnnie, you!"

Colonel Michael wondered humorously how many of those casks in the cellar had ever seen a gauger's rod. But the old man was drunk of course. And it was time for bed. He arose, tapping polite fingers over a yawn, and Johnnie arose with him. A pair of servants appeared with candles and led them to chambers in an upper part of the house toward the sea.

In the morning they sailed their boat home, past Pull-and-be-damned, on a coming tide and a stiff east wind. Michael blew on his cold hands and laughed.

"That's a rare old pirate, your uncle. I see now why he lives so far out of the way, down there at the harbor mouth. He can smuggle his own wines and spirits ashore, and nobody in town the wiser."

"A low suspicion," Johnnie said with a grin.

"Anything in that tipsy talk of his? Trouble over taxes and all that?"

"Something, something. Oh, I can keep our people quiet if Sam Adams and those other hot men in Boston will let us alone—and if London will use some common sense. Those purblind fellows over there in Parliament! They learnt nothing from the stamp affair. Now they've sent two regiments of redcoats to Boston to back up their customs collectors, and all Massachusetts is in a boil. Sam Adams and his friends have been scratching off letters and sending 'em to every Assembly in the colonies, including mine. A pretty kettle of fish."

"And what's your recipe for the fish, Johnnie?"

"Time! Parliament's got to give us that. Taxing the colonies without their consent is damned bad policy. Taxes have to be raised. The French war's got to be paid for, and we should pay something toward the cost of the King's fleet and army, I suppose, if we want their help in the future. But it should be our own choice, damme. That will take time and patience. Our Assemblymen hate a tax of any kind, even for our own necessities. And the choice has got to come from them."

"What are you doing about it?"

"Using every influence I have with our Council and Assembly, persuading 'em to set up a proper system of taxation to raise money for our own needs first of all. You can't have good government without that. The rest will come with patience and a bit of schooling on both sides of the water. You'll observe I'm not dealing merely with my Council and Assembly, I move amongst the people, talking with 'em in their homes and camps and the cabins of their sloops. They tell me their troubles, and I give 'em mine, a fair enough exchange. And we don't mince words. For every man who calls me Governor or gives me Sir there are ten who know me as plain Johnnie Wentworth, one of themselves, a surveyor who used to cruise the woods with the mastmen and knows the country like a book. Oh, they think I'm a little touched with my dream of a New Hampshire bigger than all the rest of New England put together, but they can see the sense of making roads and suchlike toward that. If all His Majesty's Governors are doing what I am, there'll be no serious trouble in America. Because I'm not just talking to my own people. I'm writing Paul Wentworth and Lord Rockingham and everyone else with influence in London that I can reach. And I'm saying that these officious new customs men are rattling at a hornet's nest—look at Boston. And the soldiers can only make it worse."

"You begin to sound like your uncle Benning," Michael said.

"The old man was right. I daresay he thanks God every night that I'm in the Governor's seat, not he."

"Did you foresee any of this, Johnnie, when you came home?"

"No. When the news came of Townsend's death last year I thought that was the end of his harebrained scheme for taxing the Americans. I still can't believe Parliament will go on with it, any more than they did with the Stamp Act. If there's one spoonful of brains in the lot of 'em they'll drop these new taxes, call their soldiers home, and give us a chance to work out some kind of imperial revenue through our own assemblies."

The boat was abreast of Four Tree Island now, and Johnnie put the tiller over and swung in to the mouth of the Puddle Creek. On one side lay Point-of-Graves, where the town's first settlers slept under their cold stones. On the other stood a tall spar of pine, firmly stuck in the earth and pointing to the dark sky overhead. Colonel Michael had never noticed it before. But now, following Johnnie's somber gaze, he examined the thing curiously. So this was a Liberty Pole. It did not look like much.

FIVE

THE WINTER passed with a depth of snow amazing to Colonel Michael and a cold that seemed to blow straight from the North Pole. Indoors the climate was much more genial, however, with an unfailing blaze of hardwood fires, very cozy with the harsh wind scraping at the panes outside, and from house to house an endless round of dining and wining and cards. He even enjoyed the American outdoors, well wrapped in furs, dashing about the frosty town in Johnnie's sleigh, to the cheerful tune of harness bells and the cold squeak of runners on the snow. The white road to the Governor's mansion was always beaten smooth, for Johnnie's hospitality was famous even in this hospitable town, and an endless stream of callers came on provincial business as well.

From time to time Johnnie vanished into the forest upriver, tramping on snowshoes with one of his lean rangers, and was gone for days. The little musical circle flourished, however, and the best *soirées* of the winter were those in which the Governor himself played the flute, bending over Fannie's shoulder to peer at the music, or pausing like a music master to beat time while the company sang. Colonel Michael found himself saying aloud at one of these affairs, "So this is savage America!" He was solemn with wine at the time, but in the lively company this passed for wit, and everyone in Portsmouth quoted it as the *mot* of the season.

The New Hampshire spring was a trial, a long and weary dallying between winter and summer, and from Johnnie the soldier learned a bit of doggerel, imitating the nasal New England country tones as best he could:

> Fust it blew and then it snew,
> Then it friz and then it thew,
> Then come rain—
> An' friz again.
> Sure as one and one make tew.

At last the frost and snow and rain were gone. Each day the sun stood taller in the sky, the streams ran full, and the silent woods and pastures came alive with birds alighting from the south. Johnnie had been itching for this time, and off he went with Michael to his "estate" in the backwoods. They left town by the river road, crossed over by ferry to Dover Point, and rode on through Dover village and into the woods. Johnnie had cajoled the various land grantees along the route to cut their part of the road—in some cases he had canceled the grants, sold the lands, and used the money to pay axmen and teamsters working on what he declared a King's highway. Now it was passable on horseback fifty miles into the wilderness. Already people were calling it the Governor's Road. Colonel Michael had his own opinion of a "road" that was nothing so far but an ax-cut slit in the forest, cluttered with stumps and boulders, with dangerous pole bridges over the streams and quivering causeways of loose logs and brushwood thrown down in the boggy places. In the last stretch, where the land began to lift in hills and ridges, the ground swell of the mountains, the "road" became a mere trail, cut no wider than the span of a man's outstretched arms, the accepted measure of the pathfinders.

After two days of rough travel they reined up their horses on the crown of a hill, and at last had a view of something more than trees. Before them the shaggy mass of pine woods dropped away to a blue spread of water.

"Behold!" Johnnie cried, pointing with his riding crop. "My country seat! The water's called Smith's Pond, after the hunter who found it years ago. Most of the land you see along this end of it is mine."

"Pond? Zounds, we'd call that a lake in England! Must be all of two miles long."

"It's nearly four, my friend, and two or three miles wide. It spills down a short stream into another lake twenty miles long—like a big horse trough in the hills—and full of islands. We call that by the Indian name, Winnipesaukee. See that green hill, the one shaped like a sleeping woman? That's Copplecrown, and Winnipesaukee lies beyond."

The soldier chuckled. "Winny-pe-SAW-kee. Gad, that's nearly as bad as Pis-KAT-a-kwa. What names! Thank God for Smith, whoever he was. And where does this Winny-pe-SAW-kee flow?"

"Into the Merrimac River, and that way to the sea."

They rode on down the slope, following the ax-cut path. The horses picked their way around fresh stumps that still bled beads of gum like beeswax. The woods were chiefly pine, tall of trunk, with a somber green gloom under their crowns where nothing grew but moss. Johnnie pointed out some giants among them. Each bore a new ax-blaze, white in the rugged brown bark, with the broad arrow of His Majesty and Johnnie's own JW carved in the wood by a sharp knife.

"How the dooce could His Majesty ever get these things to the sea, Johnnie?"

"Oh, the mastmen could haul 'em with oxen to my pond, float 'em down to Winnipesaukee, and thence by the Merrimac River to the coast."

Gammon! thought the soldier. Still, it's a preposterous country, and they do preposterous things. He thought of the mast roads on the upper reaches of the Piscataqua, each hacked through the woods as straight as a sword cut to the river; the giant logs, up to a hundred feet long and weighing God-knew-what, slung by chains to the axles of great wheels that stood sixteen feet high; the long procession of oxen, sometimes fifty or sixty pairs yoked to the load; and the whole thing groaning slowly but surely down the "road" to the river. Gad!

After a time they caught a whiff of burning brushwood and

rode into a flat open space that gave a full view of the "pond." The whole clearing was dotted with black stumps, some still smoldering. In its edges they could see the flash of axes, and heaps of green brushwood flaming and pouring black smoke into a breeze that blew it away across the water. A cluster of small log huts stood in this charred desert, about a quarter mile from the shore, and in the midst of them gaped a large rectangular hole, with a rim of earth and stones thrown out of it.

"What's that?" Michael said, stabbing a finger.

"The cellar of my house."

They rode to the spot, and the Englishman whistled, measuring the hole with a careful eye. It was more than a hundred feet long and forty wide.

Johnnie pointed eagerly. "My grain barn's to stand yonder, a big one, the size of the house itself. And over here I'll have a stable and coach house—one building—sixty by forty. Back there, by that granite boulder, I'll have another barn, sixty by forty, for my cattle and hay. And of course there'll be other buildings for the care of the estate—a dairy, a forge, a carpenter's shop, and so forth."

"And is that all?" The soldier cocked an ironical brow.

"For present plans, yes. I'll think of more later, no doubt. As for the land itself, in two or three years' time I'll have the whole east side of the pond cleared, just leaving the biggest of the hardwood trees for shade—oaks and maples and suchlike. I intend a six-hundred-acre park, with a herd of deer—and a fence they can't jump. Between the house and the water there'll be forty acres of garden, with a stone wall on three sides. And that way—you can't see it, but it's less than a mile from the house—I've got a beautiful savanna."

"What's that?"

"A big meadow, with a brook flowing through it from the woods to the pond. I intend to drain and plow the savanna and plant it to rye—rye grows well in such places."

"All these buildin's you talk about—how d'you propose to get buildin' material up here, twenty leagues from anywhere?"

A sweep of Johnnie's riding crop. "It's growing all about you. I'll have my foundation beams ax-hewn out of clear pine logs. I'll have my shingles split from cedar, which will stand the weather as long as I live. Clapboards the same. For the boards and beams I'm putting up a sawmill in the edge of the woods, where the brook drops down to the savanna. By-and-by I'll bring in stones and have a gristmill there, too, in time for my first crop of rye."

"But bricks, nails, iron, mortar—you can't conjure stuff like that out of your blessed woods, Johnnie. And what about furniture and all that? You can't bring such things over that goat path you call a road. And it 'ud take a thousand men workin' for years to make it fit for a wagon, considerin' all the bridges, and so forth."

"You don't know America," Johnnie said. "You'll see it fit for a glass coach in three years, maybe less—and with no more than a hundred men. In the meantime I'll bring in my materials that way." He waved a hand toward the green breast of the sleeping woman.

"How?" It sounded madder and madder.

"Winnipesaukee. That lake, twenty miles long, which you can't see. There's a track from the old settlements to Merry Meeting Bay at the foot of it. Our rangers cut it through the woods in the French war, and it's passable now for ox wagons. I'll build a gundalow on Winnipesaukee to float my stuff up as far as Wolfeborough. From there I can haul it by sled in winter to my own pond, or in summer I can drag it up the stream in boats with track-ropes. And on this pond I'll have another gundalow to sail everything across to my landing, down there where I'm pointing now. I've found a good clay on the shore of Winnipesaukee, and I can bake all the bricks I want right there. It's a simple matter to build a kiln, with all the woods for fuel."

Colonel Michael ran his gaze over the burnt stumps, the boulders, the raw hole in the ground, the green riot of forest and mountain running on to some invisible mystery called Canada.

"Ods my life, Johnnie, if I didn't know you so well I'd say you'd got moonstruck sleeping in the open on your travels. What the dooce put all this into your head?"

"Lord Rockingham's estate in Yorkshire. Oh, I don't aspire to anything so grand of course. After all, it took a generation and a fortune in his case, though mind you it wouldn't take so much time and money here. This is America, my friend, where we can do things quickly. Someday, not far off either, this country will be as rich as fifty Englands, and when that day comes our American gentlemen will have estates to compare with any in the old country. You can see some even now in Virginia and Carolina. I'm setting a small example to our own gentlemen at Portsmouth. A mansion in town and another well back in the country. But that's not my chief object. For a hundred years the French and Indians harried our settlements so badly that all our folk kept close to the sea. It became a habit, and a habit's hard to shake. So I'm out to prove that the backwood country's not only safe but good to farm. I'm going to open up this wilderness and let the daylight in—clear to Canada before I'm through."

Here he goes again, thought the Englishman. The phrase had been on Johnnie's lips all through the winter. He broke in hastily.

"Yes, yes, I know all that but . . ."

Johnnie was firmly straddled on his hobbyhorse. "You see those woods beyond my pond? Not there—there!—toward the north, where you see the mountains. That's where the Pequawket Indians used to live. Nearly all gone now. Colonel Rogers and his rangers drove 'em off to Canada during the late war. And even Canada's a British garrison now. As soon as I've got my seat built here and the land under cultivation I'll cut a road through the Pequawket country all the way to Canada. The New Yorkers can get there by way of Lake Champlain, swapping trade goods for furs, a mighty profitable business. So we must have a way from Portsmouth. My Pequawket road will do it. And that's not all."

"Gad's blood, you fascinate me, Johnnie. What else?"

"Yonder"—another flourish of the riding crop. "Less than fifty miles from Winnipesaukee on a compass line there's the valley of a big river, the Connecticut. It rises in Canada and flows through our mountain country, then through Massachusetts, then through the province of Connecticut. Comes out in Long Island Sound. The Merrimac's not a patch on it, and our Piscataqua's just a creek. Settlers from Connecticut and Massachusetts have been pushing up that valley for years, and now they're well into New Hampshire where they come under my government. Yet there's no way to reach 'em from Portsmouth. All their movement and trade goes the other way, by the river to Massachusetts."

Michael grinned. "So you're goin' to change the course of the river?"

"Laugh away. When I was a youngster no one in Portsmouth ever gave a thought to the Connecticut. I didn't give it a thought myself till I was in England. I met a lot of Americans over there. One was Colonel Bob Rogers—you've heard about his rangers in the French and Indian Wars. They fought through all our backwoods country, right up into Canada. Rogers knew all about the Connecticut Valley. So did another man I met over there, a dissenting parson named Wheelock—Eleazar Wheelock. He and an educated Indian called Occom were in England to raise money for a mission school. Wheelock's ideas were modest. He just wanted a school for Indians and maybe the back-country settlers on the Connecticut—up in New Hampshire territory. That caught my interest of course. So I gave him money and introduced him to Paul Wentworth and Lord Rockingham and some more of my well-to-do friends."

"I venture they damned you for that!"

"They blessed Mr. Wheelock beyond all his dreams, or mine, for that matter. Even the King gave him money. Last year

Wheelock and Occom came back to America with pledges for ten thousand pounds."

"What? You're jokin'.."

"Ten thousand pounds. Not even Harvard College had a start like that—and Harvard, mind you, started as a school for Indians and whites alike, the very thing that Wheelock had in mind. So when he talked to me in Portsmouth about a school far up the Connecticut we both began to see something more— a college. His ideas rambled all over the map—the Indians were first in his mind of course—but I kept bringing 'em back to the upper Connecticut, the part that's in New Hampshire. Finally he decided on a place called Hanover. Over there!"

Another flourish of the crop. "So I'll cut a road across to Hanover."

"From this patch in the woods? Why?"

"In the first place to join Hanover with my road to the coast, so our Portsmouth people will have a direct route to the college. In the second place to serve the people in these parts. It won't be many years before there'll be more people living in the back parts of New Hampshire than on the coast. Oh, I know they chuckle in Portsmouth when I talk of that. But you're looking at the start of it, the trickle that begins the flood. We've got some settlers already on the shore of Winnipesaukee, and Mr. Livius and some other Portsmouth gentlemen are buying lands up here. We'll soon have a real town at Wolfeborough."

"Livin' on what, Johnnie?"

"On good growing land by the lake shores, once we've got the rocks and stumps out of it. Plenty of fodder for cattle in the wild meadows. The stream from my pond drops thirty feet to Winnipesaukee, a smart chance for sawmills, as we say. Mast pines all around the slopes. What more could a man want? Apart from all that, my Hanover road will draw the trade of the upper Connecticut settlements through here to Portsmouth. One of these days, when I've got my Pequawket road through the mountains cut and bridged, we'll have a trade with Canada as well."

Colonel Michael felt a sudden need for drink. He drew a leather-covered bottle from his belt and took a long pull at some of Johnnie's choice brandy, warm from the ride. When the smack of it began to subside within he took another. Johnnie was still talking of roads and trade and peopling the wilderness, turning his gray gaze from Copplecrown to the distant peaks that shimmered like illusions in the northward haze. At last he fell silent, lost in that scrutiny.

Michael spoke then. After the day's hard journey the brandy sang very pleasantly in his ears.

"Zooks!" he said. "Johnnie, I almost believe you can do it. Not all of it, mind. Not unless you live twice the age of Methuselah and keep a good seat in the saddle to the last."

Johnnie laughed, with a glance at the bottle. "I might do that too. What's impossible in America?"

SIX

*O*N A WARM EVENING in August 1769 Johnnie rode into Portsmouth by the road from the Newington ferry, a dusty figure astride a tired black horse. He had spent weeks at Wolfeborough, riding in like this at times when his duties in town became urgent, and he had left Colonel Michael there, enjoying the fishing and shooting, and watching the "country seat" slowly taking shape. There was grumbling in Portsmouth about the Governor who spent so much time in the woods; there were people who sneered that the new Governor was worse than the old, who at least lived at the harbor mouth, but he faced this discontent with a sturdy defiance, declaring that when his mansion was ready he would move up to Wolfeborough bag and baggage. Fifty miles—what was fifty miles in America?

There were more people plainly curious. Already one or two rude inns had sprung up in farmhouses along the Governor's Road, and these saw frequent travelers, riding in twos and threes to see what he was about. And their tales grew with the telling. Governor Johnnie was building a "palace" in the backwoods. He had cleared five hundred acres—five thousand when the tavern pots were tossing well. He planned to spend ten thousand, fifteen thousand, twenty thousand guineas. A vision of something fabulous in the blue haze toward the hills arose now in every town and village by the Piscataqua waters. A people whose faces for generations had been turned toward the sea were looking over their shoulders.

Johnnie smiled at the talk. It was not yet time to say, "I told you so." That would come when his estate and his Wolfeborough were visible in frame and roof, with busy sawmills, with green fields and grazing cattle, and when the Governor's Road was fit to pass the finest carriages of the gentry. Five years, say. Seven at the outside. All to be taken day by day. Meanwhile work and patience—work and patience.

A groom ran out of his stable and caught the bridle. He descended stiffly and walked across the road into the house on "Pleasant Street." In the office chamber he paused in his road-stained riding boots to shuffle through a heap of letters, picking out those with official seals from London first and then the ones from Boston. They were filled with troubles, especially the Boston letters—folk there were always troubled nowadays. One of the beauties of Wolfeborough was that you were miles and days from all these nagging pens. He sighed and went upstairs. His valet Grose fetched a tin hip bath, filled it with warm water, and placed towel and wash ball close at hand. He helped His Excellency out of his clothes and scrubbed His Excellency's back with the wash ball vigorously. The back was tanned to the hue of leather, so were the chest and arms and face, and the hands bore the dark stains of balsam. Grose had been trained in Lord Rockingham's household in Yorkshire. He did not know what to make of a gentleman who went off into the woods and spent weeks, apparently naked to the waist and swinging an ax like a common mastman. But Grose had grown used to it now. Nothing in America could surprise him.

"I can do the rest," Johnnie said at last, rising in the tub. "Fetch me a decanter of good port, some of that Lisbon Particular from Captain Langdon's last voyage."

"You'll want something to eat, sir, won't you?"

"Nothing. I supped at the Dover inn."

The summer night was hot and still. After the bath he sat naked in a chair, mending the thirst of his journey. The port was cool from the cellar, and as it passed his lips there was a rich tang of good grapes in the mouth and nostrils and then the genial lift of blood in the body, creeping like warm honey through the veins. One touch of port like that deserved another.

He drank several glasses. Suddenly there was a tinkle of music downstairs. He was indignant, thinking that some servant dared to amuse himself at the precious Shudi. Then he recognized the touch.

Almost at once came a knock and a cough at the door and his valet's voice. "Beg pardon, sir, but Mrs. Atkinson has come in for some practice at the harpsichord, the way she does."

"Ah! Give Mrs. Atkinson my compliments and say I'll be down in twenty minutes or so. Then come back and shave me and help me into fresh clothes."

It took half an hour, and the tall mahogany clock in the lower hall was striking ten when Johnnie came down the stairs in white breeches and silk stockings, a ruffled shirt and a green coat with china buttons. Above the light cravat his face was as dark as an Indian's. The port glowed within him. He was a picture of hard male health and he felt it, a man alive.

Mrs. Fannie sat at the instrument with her back to him. For her short walk in the dark she had put on a long blue cloak with a capuchin hood, and she kept it about her. She heard his step, for her fingers ceased flitting, and she said over her shoulder, "Good evening, Your Excellency." Johnnie came to her side, picked up one of the idle hands, and kissed it.

"Good evening, coz. How did you know I was back?"

"What makes you think I did? Theo's in one of his poorly spells, and I felt dull, so I came up to console myself at your Shudi. I do this quite often when you're gone, did you know? It's so much better than our old spinet."

"Good! A pity we can't summon our own little group for a musical party. But I left Michael at Wolfeborough, my French horn's got the mumps of all things, and my cello's off courting a girl down by the fish wharves somewhere. I'll get my flute, though. Aren't you hot in that cloak? Why don't you take it off?"

She stood up, holding the cloak about her, with a faint smile on her lips.

"You've never seen Mr. Copley's portrait of me, have you, Johnnie? What do you think of the original?"

She tossed off the cloak with a quick movement. Johnnie saw a silk gown hanging in rich folds from her hips but fitting her slim waist as the bark fits a young birch in the forest. Flounces of fine lace dripped from the short sleeves and covered her elbows. A narrow froth of the same lace marked the bodice top. Above that frail border appeared a remarkably well-turned portion of Mrs. Fannie, swelling and sinking as she breathed.

"Beautiful," he said.

"Gown or me?"

"Both. Why haven't I seen this charming thing before? D'you wear it only for painters?"

"Pshaw! Aren't I wearing it for my Governor tonight?"

"You thought I was miles back in the woods!"

"Woods a fiddlestick! My dear Johnnie, there's a view between the houses by the Puddle. I can look up from my chamber window and see the west part of your house, including the room where you sleep in that enormous bed of yours. I chanced to see lights go up in your chamber window tonight, so I knew Governor Wentworth was back from the wilds. And here I am—and there you are, brown as a jug and much more handsome. Now get your flute and we'll play."

She turned back to the harpsichord quickly, thinking, If I give him a moment's pause he'll start talking about his stupid mansion up in the back of nowhere and go on half the night. And she began to play again. When he came with his flute Johnnie joined in the music as he did everything, absorbed and striving for perfection in every note. For half an hour he tweeted away with the energy of a fifer at a parade of His Majesty's Foot Guards, staring over that pretty white shoulder at the music on the rack, as if it were the only thing of importance in the world.

At last she stopped playing, turned her face up to him, and sniffed.

"Port?"

73

"Yes. Oh, I'm sorry—I forget my manners along with everything else when I take the flute in my hands. You'd like a sip of something, wouldn't you, after all this playing in the heat? I'll ring for wine." He moved toward the gilded tassels of the bell-pull and gave it a jerk.

When the butler brought a decanter and glasses they resumed their music, pausing now and then to refresh themselves. At last Mrs. Fannie closed her music sheets with a firm little slap.

"There! That's all for tonight, my Governor. Phoo! It's hot! Take me down the garden and show me your summerhouse."

"The night's as black as pitch, coz."

"There's always some light by the water. Come! Hand me my cloak."

They passed through the rear door and went down the steps to the garden. The gravel of the walk flowed in slow curves down the slope like a dim gray stream. Shrubbery loomed and faded mysteriously as they passed. A humid smell of loam and a faint scent of flowers hung in the still air. The tide was on the flow out of the long salt pond. They could hear the distant rush of water over Titus Salter's dam. Far beyond, seaward toward the Isles of Shoals, there was a grumble of thunder.

At the foot of the garden, as Fannie had guessed, there was a ghost of light reflected from the water.

The summerhouse was a small thing of gilded latticework, with a pagoda roof. Thin strips of glass of various length dangled along the eaves where in any breeze they clashed and made a tinkling music. It was all in the Chinese style made fashionable in Hanover and England by a whimsey of the royal house, and which Johnnie had seen on country estates outside London. Inside was a roomy *chaise longue* of Madeira cane, with a heap of cushions. Here Johnnie liked to sprawl and meditate on hot afternoons. The summerhouse was completely open on the water side, where there was always a cool air. Just now the tide lapped at half ebb, and the air had a salty smell from the wet seaweed exposed along the shore.

"What's this?" Fannie said, finding the chaise with her knees. She explored it curiously, spread the cushions and sat down. "Do you sleep out here on nights like this, Johnnie? I would. I've often wished we had something like this in our garden."

"At my new place up in the hills," he mused, sitting down beside her, "there's a pond much bigger than this—fresh water of course—but I get a cool breeze off the mountains. What's more. . . ."

"Oh, a fig for your ponds and mountains! Johnnie you're here just now, and I like this place well enough. Move down the chaise, please, I want to put my feet up. There!"

It was pleasant there in the night, listening to the tide's chuckle along the shore. A loon cried in the darkness across the pond. Another answered, somewhere on the upper reaches of the pond, at half a mile; first the long sad notes, then the mad laughter.

"Johnnie," Mrs. Fannie murmured.

"Yes?"

"Remember how you used to mimic birds like that for me, long ago when I was small, in Boston?"

"Did I? I'd forgotten."

"I thought you very smart. Much more than Theo, who couldn't imitate a crow."

"But Theo was clever in other ways coz, eh?"

"Because he married me later on? That wasn't clever, not on his part. That was Mama. She was out to match me from the time I turned fifteen. And along came Theo, well on in his twenties, heir to a fortune, and one of the Wentworth blood. He hadn't a chance. No more than I."

Johnnie chuckled. "Put it that way if you like, Fan. But I remember the precious pair of lovebirds I found in your garden that day I came with my wedding gift. What a picture of bliss!"

"You mean Theo was pleased with me, and at seventeen I was pleased with the notion of being a married woman. I wasn't so pleased at twenty."

"Why?"

"Oh, I don't know. Marriage isn't all cakes and ale, Johnnie. Sometimes it turns out to be hasty pudding and small beer. A tedious diet anyhow. We had no children. Theo was never a robust man. And then one day Dr. Jackson discovered the consumption. There's no cure for that, in spite of all the medicines. And it's such a catching thing. It's terrifying. You know the rest."

"No."

"That's strange. Everybody else in Portsmouth does. Our tattling chambermaids made sure of that. I haven't slept with Theo in the past two years."

Johnnie was silent. The subject was uncomfortable, and he wondered how to turn it back to their usual easy banter. The loon's laughter sounded again far up the water, and now there was a reply in the high dark, a swift beat of wings, and then the distant splash of the second bird dropping down to the first.

"I'm young," said Fannie's voice. "Seven years married but still only four-and-twenty. I wonder sometimes. Am I to go on like this till I'm withered and dry, like some pious old maid that never knew the pleasure of a man?"

Still he was silent.

"Answer me!"

"It's too hot for riddles tonight, coz."

"Try!" She prodded him with her outstretched feet.

"I'd rather talk of something else."

"Something like Winnipesaukee, I suppose. Well it's too hot for that as well. Talk about London, then. About Vauxhall Gardens, say, where you and Colonel Wentworth used to amuse yourselves on nights like this."

"Who said so?"

"The colonel, who else? He likes to talk about such things whenever he can get a pretty lady in a corner. Nothing impolite of course. Just a gay little tale and then a pause to see what you'll say. A buck's hint, in other words. So now, my good buck, tell me your little tale."

"I don't know any little tales."

"Oh stuff! You don't have to play the polite Governor with me, Johnnie. And this isn't the Council Chamber. I think it must be somewhat like those bowers in Vauxhall Gardens—you know, where London gentlemen dally with naughty ladies over wine. Can't you pretend? You could kiss me for a start. Come!"

Half amused, half bemused, he arose from the chaise end and bent over her. Except in parlor politeness he had not touched a woman since those lighthearted London days when, not in Vauxhall bowers, but in discreet chambers elsewhere, pretty ladies of fashion had spared themselves nothing to entertain a handsome young man from America.

All that seemed a hundred years ago. The adventures of another man. There were memories of course. Sometimes on lonely nights in the forest they came back to him in dreams, the faces a little vague, the names half-forgotten, and yet all clear enough to stir a longing that surprised him. He had put all that aside when he came back to America. There was no room for it in his plans.

And now, the touch of Fannie's lips and the quick slip of her hands behind his head set a fire running in him, like a stand of his own pines touched off by lightning after a long drought, and with a high wind blowing. Somewhere in the leap of the flame a cold voice insisted that he must not make a fool and a villain of Johnnie Wentworth. But it died away as his lips went from Fannie's mouth to her throat. The next voice was Fannie's, close and urgent.

"Wait! I'll unlace."

The thunder muttered away to seaward, and now and then a flicker of distant lightning changed for a moment the hot dark in the summerhouse. But Johnnie was lost in a sea storm of his own, with waves that swelled and lifted him up to the sky and dropped him into warm deeps, with the sound of a wild surf in his ears, with nothing to save him but a slim pine log, peeled and white, that he clasped urgently in the storm. There were times when he fainted and drowned in a fatal plunge. And then, after a death whose length he could not measure, he was alive and alone with the white log again on the mysterious sea, and with new waves rising.

A dream. All a dream. He was sure of that when he woke and heard a patter of rain on the pagoda roof, and an uneasy little wind tinkling the glasses along the eaves. Then a yawn beside him, and Fannie's voice.

"It's late, and I'm cold. I must go, Johnnie. Move!"

"I'll call a groom to harness the chaise."

"No, don't do that, a fuss at this hour. Just help me dress."

He was awkward, still in a daze, and after some fumbling she threw his hands aside with an impatient little cluck and went on with it herself. It did not take her long. He had an odd feeling that she could see in the dark. In a few moments she was ready to go, with the cloak about her and the hood drawn over her head.

"I'll walk down with you," he said.

"No, you won't. As far as old Mr. Atkinson knows, you're not in town tonight and I've just been dawdling over your harpsichord and forgot the time. It's long after midnight, but he may be up. How far can you trust your servants?"

"Absolutely. Why?"

"Then we can practice again as often as we like."

"Music?"

"Of a kind." She giggled. "You play a lady much more sweetly than you do the flute, coz."

The fire had gone out of him. He felt exhausted, while Fannie seemed refreshed by the past two hours, and the light voice gave him a sick twinge and set him thinking suddenly of Theo.

He heard himself stammering, "Fannie, I . . . I've got to leave for the woods again in the morning. And I . . . I'll be gone the rest of the summer. Yes, and part of the fall."

"Nonsense! The Council sits next week. You'll have to be here for that. All this new bother over tea and Customs men— Theo and his father rant about it every night. Besides, what about me?"

"You don't understand, Fannie. Colonel Michael will be back

here in another day or two. He's staying another winter in Portsmouth, here with me."

"Pish! Get rid of the man any evening you choose."

Johnnie blurted it out then. "What about Theo?" Fannie was suddenly still. Again he had that uneasy feeling that she could see in the dark, could read every expression of his face, even of his mind.

"Theo's my affair, not yours. Bah! I haven't any regret about tonight, Johnnie. But run away and hide in your stupid woods if you want."

She walked away toward the side gate of the garden.

"Fannie!"

"Yes?"

The cloaked figure had melted into the night.

"Fannie, I'm not going back to the woods tomorrow. I don't know why I said that."

Her voice came back mockingly, "I do."

He ran after her and caught the mysterious figure from behind, clutching at its shoulders. He felt them quivering.

"Don't cry, Fannie darling—please don't cry. I love you."

No answer. He appealed to the back of the hood. "Fannie, don't leave me like this. Say you'll come again, sweet, I'll—I'll make arrangements. I'll get rid of any visitors, even Michael, any time you say. I'll do anything."

The figure remained silent and shaking. Desperately he turned it around with his strong hands and tried to see its face. A peal of laughter came from the shadow of the hood.

"How very eager you are, my Governor, of a sudden! Have you really got your courage back?"

"Yes," he said in a gasp. "When can you come again?"

"When would you like?"

"Tomorrow night—can you come then?"

"So soon? You flatter me, Excellency."

"Don't tease me, Fannie."

"Very well. Tomorrow evening, half an hour after dark. And please don't keep me waiting as you did tonight."

SEVEN

*A*ND so Governor Johnnie opened a new door in his busy life, and one that had no part in the plan. There were times when honesty accused him, especially when he made his duty calls at the Atkinson house and inquired with a polite concern into Cousin Theo's health. On these visits Mrs. Theo's manner was cool and distant; there was no meeting of eyes, there was nothing to interest even the most watchful of women servants. Whenever he went out he felt that he had seen another Fannie, the one who belonged to Theo, nothing like the one who came to him on the hill.

When his own Fannie came, there was a careful order of things for privacy. On certain evenings a candle and a half-drawn window curtain in her own bedchamber told him that she would be on her way across the Puddle bridge by ten of the clock. Johnnie had only to drop a hint to Colonel Michael, and that convivial man was glad enough to ride down into the town for a long session with friends at cards and wine. When the time came she went up the lane swiftly, muffled in the capuchin cloak, slipping into the Governor's garden by the side gate. When the September nights became too chill for a rendezvous by the pond she entered the house by the rear door and passed to the library. There, with curtains drawn and a fire blazing, the eager lover awaited her. His English servants, obsequious and wooden-faced, could be trusted to see and hear nothing.

Nothing marred the delicious ease of these arrangements as the weeks went by. If there was gossip about Frances it had nothing to do with Cousin John. All Portsmouth knew that Theo Atkinson was ill, a feeble prisoner of his bed and his ruined lungs, and some tongues were sharp about Fannie's appearance at every party and dancing at every ball. But there were some to defend her, declaring that she was young, and that after waiting on the invalid all day she needed some relief for her spirits. After all the old Chief Justice was at home each night, and there was a night nurse to watch at Theo's bedside. Why shouldn't poor Fannie get out of that big gloomy house for an hour or two of pleasant company?

In the midst of his thronging business affairs Johnnie looked with delight to her more secret ventures. The ghost of conscience vanished the moment she stepped into his firelight. He had ceased to marvel at falling in love like a romantic boy at the age of thirty-two, and with a girl who in many ways still seemed the child he had first seen in Boston in his student days. And each visit was a separate adventure. Her moods and caprices made sure of that.

There were times when she was dull, when she wept in his arms, when she came for comfort and would have nothing more. He consoled her then, with patient understanding, more like an uncle than a lover, and the years between them seemed an immense distance. At other times her spirit leaped like a bird from a cage, and then she sparkled, a slender romp of no more than seventeen. She had a wicked little gift of mimicry. By turns she could imitate fat old Uncle Benning, wheezing about the times and manners; or Chief Justice Atkinson, droning an opinion on the law; or the town crier, ringing an imaginary bell and bawling a list of things lost, strayed, or stolen. She could be breezy Anna Livius, passing a lively comment on Sheriff Packer's self-importance; or Parson Brown, bumbling away at a sermon in Queen's Chapel; or old Mrs. Odiorne complaining of her asthma. When she imitated Colonel Wentworth she was Michael to the life, even to the English accent, rattling on in his cheerful tones about a fox hunt in the Yorkshire fields or the proper way to mix a negus.

Once, springing up from Johnnie's arms, she clapped on the very hat he had worn that afternoon at a public ceremony, with its deep cocks and heavy gold lace, and she played His Excellency the Governor, the way he got down from a horse, the way he walked, the way he carried his shoulders, the way he bowed over a lady's hand and gave forth in his eager tones a long description of "my country seat at Winnipesaukee," while Johnnie lay half amused and half indignant on the couch.

His affairs of state and business did not interest her in the least. When one worry or another obsessed him she was bored, and if he insisted on talking about it she listened with the empty ear of a patient wife or cut him off with the impertinence of a mistress, as she chose.

All these whims Johnnie accepted as he did the sunshine and the rain. Sometimes his mind went back to the house in Poland Street, and he could hear Paul Wentworth saying, "Women, my dear Johnnie. A necessary and delightful part of life. Remember always to keep it private. Hold your public life apart, and you'll have no trouble. All difficulties arise from letting one mix with the other."

And now it seemed that, without any forethought, his life had fallen into these convenient compartments. How long it would continue like this he did not try to think. He had always intended to marry as part of his life's plan, and someday he would. But there was still plenty of time for that. For the present this naive delightful creature absorbed his flesh and spirit and left his mind free for his duties. He could not ask more.

In his public life it was a crowded year, quite apart from his frequent journeys and labors at "Wolfeborough." He was hammering away at the provincial authorities in New York and Massachusetts, demanding recognition of the New Hampshire grants in the mountains, and whenever he traveled to Boston he went in state, with eight mounted servants and his carriage and four, to impress the Bostonians with the importance of his mission, of himself, and of his province.

In the early summer he sailed up the Maine coast in his role as Surveyor General of the King's Woods, watchful for mast thieves in the river ports, and went on to Nova Scotia for a quick look at the mast supply up there. For this nautical journey he traveled in state also, aboard His Majesty's Ship *Beaver*, stationed at Portsmouth to check the smugglers. The merchants of Portsmouth, large and small, had noted her appearance glumly when she came last year, but Johnnie quickly interviewed her captain, and there had been no trouble. Indeed Captain Bellew, R.N. proved a pleasant fellow, a bachelor, an ardent dancer at every Portsmouth ball. At one of these last winter he had met the young widow of Johnnie's brother Tom, whose death had left her with a modest fortune to support herself and her children in a stately house by the harbor. The captain was smitten at once with pretty Mrs. Tom. He courted gallantly and soon persuaded her to be Mrs. Harry Bellew, a whirlwind affair that delighted all Portsmouth. Everyone saw at once that the likable sailor had become one more part of the widespread Wentworth clan, with a stake in the New Hampshire soil, and very much under the influence of diplomatic Johnnie. When the Governor took captain and ship away up the coast for weeks, every smuggler in Portsmouth had his chance, and drank a toast to Johnnie's sense of duty. Or was it his sense of humor? Johnnie smiled and said nothing.

"My great object," he told Harry Bellew, "is to steer clear of a mess like the one in Boston, where you see the Governor being pinched between the people and the soldiers. What's to come of that I can't guess, and it's none of my affair. My business is New Hampshire, and a peaceful government first. Sometimes I wish Boston to the devil. I'm not worried about Portsmouth, but you know the jealousy of Portsmouth on the part of our country towns like Exeter. Those Exeter men have an easy road to Boston, and Sam Adams and his Boston agitators make the most of it. There's a lot of correspondence back and forth. I don't know what's going on, though I hear rumors. All I can do is to make sure our Customs collectors here use tact. Firmness, of course, but tact. And that's my own policy. I want our people to look beyond these squabbles in Boston and see what's good for themselves. We've got too much to do, building New Hampshire, to worry our heads about Massachusetts."

"Umph," grunted the sailor. "But you can't build a fence along the Merrimac, my dear sir. You can't even stop your gentry sending their sons to Harvard College, where they're exposed to all this Boston nonsense."

"We'll have a college of our own soon, don't forget."

"What makes you think this college will teach respect for His Majesty? Parson Wheelock's a Dissenter, isn't he? Most of those noisy Boston people are Dissenters too. They've no loyalty to the established Church, the King, or anything else."

"Most of our New Hampshire people are Dissenters, come to that. The gentry here are the only ones who support the Church of England. I hope to increase the Church's influence of course. A people loyal to the Church are bound to be true to His Majesty—as Defender of the Faith if nothing else. That's one reason why I've tried to get the Bishop of London made one of the college fund trustees. But Mr. Wheelock would have none of it. A difficult man. Even threatened to build the college somewhere else. So I gave in, though I reminded him most of the money came from good Church people in England, including His Majesty himself. And—you'll smile at this—now that he's won his point he's offered to name the institution after me. Wentworth College."

"Well, why not? You've done more for it than anybody else."

"Ah, but consider this. When Mr. Wheelock sought the money in England he had to have some noble sponsor. You can't raise a fund in England, for anything, without that. So one of my friends, the Earl of Dartmouth, agreed to be head of the fund trustees. Dartmouth's a Churchman, but he's deeply interested in the Methodists and attends their meetings—some folk in England call him the Psalm-Singer."

"Just the man for your psalm-singing collegers!"

"They don't know Dartmouth from Adam. Anyhow the actual direction of the college will come from a board of Americans—and if I have anything to say about it they'll be New Hampshire men. What I see further is this. The college will need more money later on, and it'll have to come from England. Americans praise education, but they don't spend money on it. The only schoolmasters we have are drunken wanderers for the most part, drifting about the countryside with a bottle of rum, a Latin tome or two, and a fuddled knowledge of writing, reading, and round figures. And nine out of ten of our settlements haven't even a school. That's why we must keep the noble earl at the head of our college fund."

"And name the college after him?"

"Exactly. Dartmouth College."

Bellew laughed. "Your Excellency, you're a deep 'un, if you don't mind my saying so. Is there anything you wouldn't do to get money or anything else for your precious New Hampshire?"

"Nothing."

On a night in October, changing into a dressing gown for a late session at his letters, Johnnie glanced from the chamber window toward Puddle Dock. It was habit with him now, for he expected no signal this evening. Theo's illness had taken another bad turn, and on her last visit Fannie had warned him not to expect another for some time. The window gave him a view past his stable and between the Puddle buildings. He could see the Atkinson lane and the dark Atkinson garden and trees and house, or rather part of them, framed as if in a loophole. And surprisingly there was the familiar sign, the light in Fannie's chamber, with the curtains half drawn.

He went down and cautioned his servants at once, and had one of them bring wood to mend the fire in his library. She was always punctual, and a few minutes past ten she came, wrapped in the familiar blue cloak. The night was frosty, and she kept the thing about her, shivering and holding her hands to the fire. Johnnie took up the decanter and poured wine in the two glasses on the tray. He came to the fire and put one in her hand.

"To love," he said, smiling. It was a ritual with them. She turned.

"To love." She tipped the glass to her lips, but at the first taste of the wine she shuddered, walked to the table, put the glass down, and went again to the fire. *Theo, of course,* thought Johnnie. He was tempted to ask, but it was part of their ritual that Theo must never be mentioned here. She was in one of her mournful moods, that was clear; the lost bewildered child. Instinctively he began to talk of something else.

"You know, Fan, I like that portrait Copley did of you. He's very good. I'm told he has a first-rate custom in Boston now. I had a portrait painted in England, as a gift to Lord Rockingham. But I've always been doubtful about it. Was it a likeness or not? I couldn't decide. I mean the painter posed me just as I was, in a suit of dark clothes, with a bush of unpowdered hair and a most ingenuous face—the obvious young Yankee countryman—and with a scroll in my hand marked New Hampshire, just to be sure. But I'm not that man now. It's time for a new portrait. So I wrote to Copley, and today I got his answer. He's coming in a week or two—he has some other commissions in Portsmouth—and he'll do me then. Now tell me, coz, what shall I be?"

"I don't know what you mean," Fannie murmured, looking at the fire.

Johnnie poured himself another glass. "Well, as a horseman, say? I'd rather like to have one of me holding Vixen—she was sired by Rockingham, the most famous horse in England, did I ever tell you that? Or should it be one of me as Surveyor General, in woods costume, compass in hand, and one foot on a stump? Or should I be the Governor in wig and gold lace, all deep thought and dignity?"

She was silent, with the cloak still about her and her face to the fire.

"Well?" he said, sprawling comfortably on the couch.

"Oh, as Governor, I suppose."

"That sounds indifferent. What's the matter with you tonight?"

She swung about, and in the light of the candles he saw a face white and drawn. The skin of her face always seemed to stretch like white silk over the cheekbones. Now in a momentary illusion of the light and shadow it was almost like a skull. He was startled.

"Johnnie, I've come to tell you something frightful!"

"What on earth . . ."

"I'm in a family way, Johnnie. Yes! I had the sign weeks and weeks ago. I didn't think much of it at first. I thought that all the excitement had just put me out of sorts."

Johnnie was astounded. He had been so long the blithe bachelor that the inconveniences of women never occurred to him.

"You realize what it means?" Fannie said in a strange thin voice. "All the town knows I don't sleep with Theo. Even if they didn't—everyone knows he's been bedfast for the past several months, racked with the consumption."

Johnnie heard his voice stammering, "But everyone knows that some men with the consumption are quite . . ."

"Don't be stupid! See the awful position I'm in. Portsmouth—under the skin of your lively society here it's a town of old-fashioned Puritans with hearts as hard as flint. What are they going to say about this? You know, Johnnie, as well as I do. Only last year they tried and hanged Ruthie Blay because she had a bastard child—hanged her like a thief out there on the Little Harbor road, with a crowd of people watching. They even tore down a farmer's fences, so they could get a good look, and buried the poor thing in a hole at the end of the field. And who sentenced her to death? My own father-in-law!"

"Oh, but they hanged Ruth Blay because she concealed the birth of her child," Johnnie cried. "And the child died. Her crime was murder."

"Fiddlesticks! They hanged her because she'd committed adultery—you know that perfectly well. And here am I, the daughter-in-law of the Chief Justice, in exactly the same position. Theo will know it's not his child. He's never been jealous of my pleasures, but he won't forgive that. How could he?"

"Fannie, you're overwrought. Do take this glass of wine and

calm yourself, for God's sake. Nobody's going to hang you. That's absurd. Nobody's even going to accuse you, least of all Theo. He's too fond of you."

"Not that much," said Fannie, refusing the wine with an impatient gesture. "There'll be a horrid scene, with him and his father. Apart from that, think of the scandal. You know what everybody's going to say. They've always considered me a flighty thing, too bent on my own pleasure. They'll be going over names—every man I've ever talked or danced with, you amongst them."

"Let them!" Johnnie's jaw was stubborn now.

"Oh, Johnnie, why did this have to happen to us?"

A rush of skirts and she was in his arms, weeping and shivering like a frightened little girl. All her pert assurance had gone. He drew her to the familiar couch, and they sat together, her head on his breast and her arms about his neck.

He kissed her wet cheek gently from time to time. At last she sprang up and pulled the hood of the capuchin over her hair.

"I must go. I told Mr. Atkinson I'd just be gone a few minutes."

"Does he suspect anything?"

"I don't think so, no. He's always busy in the evenings with his law reports, and so on. Whenever I go out after dark he just smiles in his absent-minded way and tells me not to stay too late. He's always been like a father to me."

"What about your maidservant, and Theo's nurse?"

"Servants always make a mouth at my gadding off to parties and routs and suppers while my husband's sick, but so do a lot of other people, and it's no more than that. As for you, I've come up here so often for music parties that no one would suspect if they chanced to see me in the lane. What about your own house? The servants know of course. Does Colonel Michael?"

"I've never told him, naturally. But he must know I receive a woman on the nights I ask him to go out. He's a man of the world."

"Is he a man of honor where a friend's amour is concerned?"

"I'd trust Michael with my life."

She seemed a little reassured, but only a little; and suddenly she was gone, flitting away through the back door like a harried ghost.

A few days later Mr. Copley came, a thin darting man of Johnnie's own age, with the marks of smallpox on his face. A pair of deep-set eyes peered shrewdly from under the bushy eyebrows as he set up his easel and laid out his palette and paints and brushes. He was Boston born, of Irish parents, and spoke with a trace of brogue. There was no doubt in his mind about the subject or the pose.

"I must paint you as Governor of course. And I recommend pastel. I can do a handsome pastel of a gentleman with your looks and manner, sir. Now what about clothes?" He made a careful inspection of Johnnie's wardrobe and chose a red velvet coat with rich gold braid, a waistcoat of scarlet satin, a white silk stock and a frilled shirt. "You'll wear one of these neat little perukes, of course, sir. The newest thing. Fits like your own hair. Those old-fashioned wigs made every man look a spaniel, begob, or a carpenter's brat after a dive in the shavings."

And when it came to the pose, "Sit erect, sir, if you please, facing a little that way. Now turn the eyes to me. Just the eyes. There! Not so stiff, please. You're a handsome man, Your Excellency, I suppose you know that. Now adopt a natural expression, as you would in your Council, say. You're listening to some other's opinion, and you're about to give your own. Common sense, dignity, and so forth. There! Something like that. Though you look just a morsel, what shall I say, somber? Somber and a bit—ah—defiant."

"It's a natural expression, however it looks," Johnnie said.

"I'd prefer it a bit more easy—but you know what's natural. Just now, if you'll take my opinion, you look a bit like a man that sees a storm in the offing and the wind his way."

"That may be right."

"These new taxes on tea, and so forth?" Copley held out his brush, squinted an eye, and measured the Governor's face.

"Why do you ask that?"

"They're making a great touse about the new taxes where I live. Next Guy Fawkes Night they'll be toting a dummy of King George about the streets, instead of the Pope—you know what our Boston mobs are like—and hanging him along with the devil in tar and feathers. Sooner or later they'll be at fists and cudgels with the sogers."

"What makes you think so?"

"I'm a painter, and I mind my own affairs, but I'm Irish enough to scent a fight. Those Boston street gangs are a wild lot, and you'd think the town belonged to 'em, ever since the Stamp trouble. This time it's not just a matter of beating the town watch and breaking the windows of their betters. They'll tangle with the redcoats—lobsterbacks, they call 'em—and the lobsterbacks'll take 'em down a peg, depend on't."

"And will that settle the touse, think you?"

"Governor, one rattle of muskets'll send every blackguard in Boston running for cover. As for the gentlemen like Sam Adams, who talk so much about liberty, they'll take the liberty to be somewhere else when the bullets fly, you may be sure."

"Well, we haven't anything like that here, thank God."

"Then what storm would you be facing—perhaps?" The painter's small eyes peered at him around the canvas edge.

"I told you it's my natural expression."

"Um. Well, you may rest a little now, sir, if you wish. How long a sitting can you give me? I'd like at least five hours a day—two in the morning, three in the afternoon."

But Johnnie could give him no more than two hours a day; There were so many other things to be done; and always he posed with the same half-turned face and steady sidelong gaze, which by chance took his eyes toward the Atkinson house, down there across the creek. When would the storm break? Undoubtedly when poor Fannie's figure gave the awkward secret away. Another four months, say. Five at most. The end of the winter, just when he would be riding out to start the season's work at Wolfeborough. He pictured himself returning to find Portsmouth agog. And what would Fannie say? Would she conceal the guilty lover's name? Or would she cry it out at some family inquisition, with the Chief Justice standing over her and Theo's hot sick eyes burning up at her from the bed? Or could she persuade Theo, by some desperate appeal, to declare himself father of the child to save scandal? Not likely.

Well, you can't see Fannie suffer alone. Speak up like a man, and devil take the consequences. Have to go away, of course, both of us, the farther the better. England? Paul Wentworth would find room in his house for us, and maybe look out for something for me to do. I'll send Paul the first copy of this portrait. Keep up my friendship there, whatever else I do. Couldn't appeal to Lord Rockingham in these circumstances. His lofty moral principles.

And then, in the midst of these resolves, he thought of New Hampshire and his hopes and plans, and a cold night fell on his mind. Whenever this happened Copley said in a discontented tone, "Governor, I'm afraid you had a bad session with the Council today, or maybe you got up the wrong side of the bed. That's all for now, sir. I'll see you tomorrow. And will you, for the love of heaven, come to the chair fresh and in a jolly turn of mind?"

A week later, with the portrait almost finished, there was another interruption of a very different kind. It came after a sharp night and an early snow, a light fall that whitened the streets and roofs of Portsmouth. The Atkinson maidservant, muffled in—of all things—Fannie's blue cloak and hood, lent to her for the errand, came breathing noisily up the slope and into Johnnie's presence. At the first side glimpse of the cloak he was startled. Copley paused, brush in air, annoyed at the intrusion.

"If you please, sir," the woman said, teeth chattering, "Mrs. Atkinson sends you her respects and compliments."

She paused, and Johnnie snapped, "Yes, yes. What is it? Out with it." Whatever it was, it did not matter if Copley heard. If Fannie's secret was out so soon, all Portsmouth would know in half an hour.

"Please sir, it's bad news, terrible." She was blubbering now. "Poor Mister Atkinson—young Mister Theo, sir—a convulsion in the night—blood poured out his mouth something awful." She broke into sobs.

Johnnie held back an impulse to shout at the wretched creature. He sat with a deceptive calm, with the whimsical side gaze of the painter's pose, a habit now. At last the woman blurted, "Please sir, poor young Mister Theo died an hour ago."

"What!"

"Missus Frances felt you ought to know first, being his cousin and fond of him as you are."

For a moment Johnnie remained a graven image in the chair. Then, unconsciously, he relaxed, and the held breath escaped his lips in a long sigh. *There,* Copley thought, *that's a better expression, but it's too late now of course. I've done the head.*

EIGHT

THE PROCESSION was a long one, tramping the frozen ruts and puddles to Chapel Street and then winding up the steep knoll to the church. As was customary at winter funerals no women came. They could only peer from windows as the cortege passed, rubbing little bulls'-eyes in the frosty panes. Frances herself was prostrate, with a watch of solicitous females at her bedside.

A dozen sturdy wharf-porters adorned with black hat ribbons and scarves took turns at carrying the coffin on a bier, and four cloaked gentlemen held the black velvet pall over it, struggling with the thin staffs in the wind. Old Justice Atkinson took Johnnie's arm and insisted on walking at the head of the mourners. All had black bands about their hats and on the sleeves of their greatcoats. It was the first day of November, with a whipping wind, and snowflakes wandering down from a pewter sky.

His Excellency had sent a note to Captain Bellew, and a party of militia to the empty fort on Newcastle Island. As the mourners walked two and two behind the bier they could hear the smart crack of minute guns from the *Beaver* and a more irregular thudding from the island battery. In the bleak air the chapel bell tolled dismally. As they gained the crest of the knoll the men could look down Strawberry Bank to the harbor. The wharves and warehouse roofs were white with snow. The fishing sloops and most of the trading vessels lay tied up for the winter, with canvas unbent and stowed away in the sail lofts. Only His Majesty's sloop *Beaver*, moored off the Bank, showed a sign of life. There was no warmth inside the church. It was like an ice cave in the mountains. Winter worshippers usually had their servants

93

bring little charcoal foot warmers or hot bricks wrapped in cloth, but such comfort was unseemly at a funeral. Cold or not, Parson Brown droned a long funeral sermon to the rows of pinched male faces. Then the prayers. At last the coffin, draped in black cloth, was borne outside. The Atkinson vault gaped for a few moments in the flank of the hill, like the dark entry of a tunnel to the thronged and dreadful world of the dead. The porters trundled the coffin inside and emerged hastily with the bier. The heavy iron door clanged shut, a sound that sent a final shiver through the watching men. Old Mr. Atkinson tottered on the arm of a manservant to his big coach and drove away. Johnnie's groom waited nearby with his carriage—black ribbons on the horses' heads and a fold of black cloth draped over his painted cipher on the doors. He stepped in and went away quickly, head bent against the wind, commanding a roundabout route to avoid the Atkinson lane.

In his own sitting room he flung himself into a deep chair before the fire. Colonel Michael found him there staring into the flames and shivering, and sent a servant for rum and hot water.

"Sad business, eh, Johnnie?"

"Yes."

"Cold too."

"Yes."

"Good duck-huntin' weather, though. Out by Little Harbor, say. We could ride out there, spend the night with old Blubber-gut, and be off the islands in one of his boats by daybreak."

"Sorry, Michael, I'm not up to that now."

"Mind if I go?"

"Not at all. Take one of the servants to handle the oars and load the guns—Skidby's best. And stay as long as you like. Uncle Benning loves company—it's lonely out there."

In a few minutes the colonel and servant were off, with a pair of Johnnie's horses and a brace of his fine London fowling pieces. Apparently the duck hunting was as good as Benning's hospitality, for Michael stayed several days. Meanwhile Johnnie brooded in the house on Pleasant Street. He refused to see anybody, turning visitors away with polite excuses through his major-domo. He thought with longing of Wolfeborough, far in the woods, and of "Wentworth House"—he had decided to call it that. The mansion now stood in frame, sheathed and clapboarded, with the roof shingled, two chimneys built, and the doors and windows in place. There was no floor yet in the ballroom or the guest chambers, no plaster on walls or ceilings, no wainscoting anywhere, but the living quarters were habitable for a man who didn't mind things a little rough. It would be good to ride up there now, before the snow got too deep, and spend some days alone, tending his fire, cooking his own food, reading a book or two, watching from the windows the white peaks of the hills and the wind whirling ghosts of snow across the icy skin of the lake. A chance to sort out his mind's cards before fate opened the next play. Impossible of course.

Each evening he gazed for a sign from the all-important window on the other side of Puddle Dock, but not a chink of light escaped the curtains there. Poor Fannie! A prisoner, with all those doleful women for warders, and tortured with her thoughts! What a fix to be in! Whose fault was it? If she hadn't come to my house that night—but tut!—none of that! A lonely girl, wife-and-no-wife, too full of spirit to know what she was doing—and there I was, a man of the world. Should have boxed her ears and sent her home. And yet how very sweet it was with her, there in the dark by the water; and what a wonderful madness, all of it, ever since. Part of my life now, something I can't do without. I'm only half a man when she can't come to me. What's to be done? Go to her and face it out with Theo's father? That's the honorable thing—and so far you haven't shown much honor in this affair, Your Excellency.

While the moody man was wrestling thus with his demons on the hill, poor Fannie lived with hers amid an endless succession of women who came in the custom to sit with the bereaved wife. For three days after the funeral she did not leave her room, lying silent in the bed while the women whispered and tiptoed in and out. Then she dressed and came like a ghost to the parlor fire, where she busied her fingers with crewelwork. Her mirror showed a stranger with a face like a mask of plaster, with eyes shadowed and sullen. When she spoke at all her voice was hoarse and dull.

To the women she was the picture of a distraught widow, with no interest left in life. When they kept saying, "You mustn't grieve so, Fannie dear, you can't bring poor Theo back," she had a hysterical urge to scream. She wanted to jump up and cry, "I don't want Theo back. You might as well know—I want His Excellency the Governor, whose child I'm carrying. Oh yes! I'm two months gone. And what do you think of that?" Each day was a new ordeal, beginning with the morning spasms of nausea, which she had to hide. It was a boon when at last the ladies grew tired of their glum vigils and departed, feeling their duty done.

On the fifth day after the funeral, as she sat alone in the parlor, there was a stuttering knock of the hinged brass lion at the front door. The hour was well on in the afternoon, and the old judge away at some law business in the Town House. A maidservant went to the door, and at once Fannie heard Johnnie's voice. She sprang up as he entered the room. He began solemnly, "Fannie, I've come . . ." But Fannie put a finger to her lips, watching the slowly closing parlor door. The woman might listen there.

"It's very kind of you to come, Cousin," she said, in the cold dead voice she had used to all her visitors in the past four days. Inside she was furious. Why hadn't he come before? Because he'd lost his courage, of course, as he had that first evening, fearful of consequences. Sulking up there in the big house, wishing he could undo the whole affair, wishing her to the devil for tempting him, thinking of his career. Men were such selfish creatures. They wanted only one thing of a woman, and the moment that was satisfied they were frantic to get out of her hands. Johnnie was murmuring some solemn platitude, mindful of the warning finger.

"Did you walk?" she asked. He wore a heavy cloak with three

capes at the shoulders, still clasped, and stood hat in hand, as if he intended staying only a minute.

"No, I came in the coach. Brand's holding the horses outside."

She said in a diffident tone, "I wonder—would you mind driving me over to see Mrs. Livius? The change and a breath of fresh air might do me good."

"Of course! You'd better wrap up well, my dear. It's cold."

She went upstairs and came down in a warm old-fashioned cloak that had belonged to Theo's mother. She wound a black cashmere shawl about her head and led the way to the door. As soon as they were inside the coach, with Brand on the box, she said quickly, "This was our only chance to talk alone. And there's little time—it isn't far. Why haven't you come to me before?"

"I didn't think you'd want to see me so soon after . . ."

"You know perfectly well that you were the one person I did want to see. Were you afraid I'd say something embarrassing?"

"Not at all."

"Would you mind an embarrassing question now?"

"No."

"Then what are you going to do about me?"

Brand was driving slowly, mindful of the ruts and holes. They were passing people in the narrow street, who touched their hats or bowed politely, recognizing the Governor's coach; and Johnnie was touching his hat and Fannie giving now and then a small nod of her shawled head. To appearance through the door glass she was the sad widow out for air and talking of nothing but her loved one gone.

"Marry you of course," he said. "That's what I came to say."

She was relieved at once, but she gave him no sign of that.

"Because you feel it's your duty?"

"Because it's my duty and I love you."

"Both barrels! What a poor little partridge I am."

"Because I love you, then. Because I want you."

"How much do you want me?"

"More than I could tell you in a short drive through the town, Fannie. I've been in torment up there, all these days and nights,

97

not seeing you, not knowing what you thought, wondering if you hated me for what's happened, wondering if you'd repulse me when we met. . . ."

"Pooh!"

She bowed to old Colonel Boyd, standing with his hat off gallantly in the chill air as they passed.

"When do you propose to make an honest woman of me?"

"As soon as I can—we must wait a decent time, of course."

"I'm afraid your child won't wait a decent time."

"What do you mean?" he asked uneasily.

"The child will be born in less than seven months, so the sooner we're wed, the better. Tongues are bound to wag, whatever we do. Let them wag about me taking a new husband right after Theo's death. I'd rather that than have them clucking about a child too soon after the new husband took me to bed. Marry me now, and when the baby comes we can say it's premature. They may suspect, but they can't prove anything. But if we wait your decent time we'll hear a fine clamor when the truth is out. One look at the child and any old wife in town would know the difference."

Johnnie was silent. Her shrewdness surprised him. This was not the madcap girl who cast her shoe over the moon and forbade him to be serious. The coach rattled on toward Islington Creek and the Livius house.

"Well?" she said at last, staring straight ahead.

"I'll do whatever you say, my dear."

"Ah! Then I suggest this. For the next four afternoons you'll call and be the good kind cousin that's come to comfort me. On the fourth evening you'll take old Mr. Atkinson aside and say how it grieves you to see poor Fannie in such a decline. You'll say you've always had a deep affection for her, that you want to comfort her now in every way you can, that you're a lonely man yourself—you'll know how to put it much better than this, you're so clever, Johnnie. And finally you'll announce that you intend to marry me at once."

"I'm afraid he'll be shocked at that," Johnnie said.

"Let him! It's better for him to be shocked than for me to be ruined, isn't it?" And then, with a glance at his troubled face and in a melting tone, "Oh, Johnnie, Johnnie, if you knew how I've starved to be yours, really yours, all this time. No more of those sly journeys over the creek, like a fish girl stealing away to some sailor in an alley. But to be there with you, in your own house, at your table, on your pillow—and to have the right to be there. And now, you see, now I have, I have! I can't wait to be in your arms. Oh, Johnnie, I'll give you such love as you've never even dreamed. How can you wait, how can you even hesitate when a chance like this has come like a gift to both of us?"

The caressing voice, the dark flash of her eyes, coming suddenly from the frigid image in the cloak and shawl, brought back in a rush the memory of that first rapture in the summerhouse. And as on that night of nights he found himself stammering, "When? When shall it be?"

Fannie thought for a moment, but only a moment. "On the eleventh of this month. That will be ten days after the funeral—all we can afford. As soon as you've told Mr. Atkinson you can pass the word outside. And we'll be married quietly at your house, with just a friend or two for witnesses."

He was silent. She saw that jaw of his setting stubbornly. And then he surprised her.

"No, Fannie. I'll have no more hole-and-corner business. My marriage shall be public, as public as I can make it, with every bit of form and show that goes with being Governor. I'm not ashamed of marrying you, damme! Let 'em say what they like—I'm proud to make you my wife, and they shall know it."

"Oh, Johnnie!" She wanted to throw her arms about his neck, to dab his face with kisses. How wonderful he is! And what a fool I was ever to doubt him! But they were drawing up to the Livius house, and she composed herself.

"Tomorrow afternoon," she reminded him. "At four."

"At four."

"Good-by, Johnnie, my darling. Six more long nights before

I'm in your arms—I can't bear it, but I must. Hand me down, please. There!" And with a glance at the Livius windows, where a vague face peered, "Thank you very much, Cousin John. Mr. Livius will see me home in his carriage."

On the eleventh of November, 1769, just ten days after Theo Atkinson's funeral, a very different procession trampled the thin snow of early winter to Chapel Hill: a long cavalcade of horses and carriages, glass coaches, curricles, and chaises, laden with Portsmouth gentlefolk, well muffled against the cold but wearing their best finery underneath. Once more cannon thundered from H.M.S. *Beaver* and the island fort. Every bell in the town clanged in the frosty air. Seamen went down to the idle shipping at the wharves and hoisted every scrap of bunting to be found. People thronged the route and crowded about the chapel. Everyone was delighted to see Governor Johnnie casting off his bachelorhood at last. Sentimental ladies, married and single, sighed at the notion of him, handsome and impatient and determined as every lover should be, carrying off the pretty widow to his lonely house and heart.

To be sure some declared he was too good for that shallow creature from Boston. But he'd be master, depend on it. He'd soon cure those flibbertigibbet ways of hers. That flighty craft 'ud find herself well-manned at last. And if many female heads were shaken over this leap to a warmer bed so soon after her husband's death, there were Fannie's friends to defend the affair with spirit, declaring how dreadful it had been for her, married— a mere child—to a man slowly dying almost from the wedding day, and how nice it was that goodhearted Johnnie had gone to comfort her on Theo's death, and found himself head over heels in love. How romantic it all was, just like a Boston play, and in their very midst!

Fannie made an appealing figure even to her enemies, wearing a simple black bonnet and a cloak that gave peeps at a severe snuff-colored gown beneath. She was pale, timid, clinging to old Mr. Atkinson's arm as they entered the church. The Chief

Justice had been startled at first by Johnnie's demand, but he was fond of them both, and like a good many others he thought it high time Johnnie married. A charming wife like Fannie would settle the Governor here in town, where he ought to be most of the time, instead of chasing phantoms in the woods and hills. The good old gentleman not only gave his consent but agreed to give the bride away.

Only one thing marred the wedding. Just at its close, as they made their way out of the church, the bride on Johnnie's arm and managing a brave little smile, there was a small flurry behind them. They did not look back, and in another minute they were driving away briskly in the Governor's carriage, with white ribbons fluttering in the breeze and the people cheering and waving as they passed. At the church some of the gentlemen were picking up poor Parson Brown, who had tumbled down the steps. One arm hung at an odd angle. It was broken. An old wife from the docks vowed it a bad omen for the marriage. But some said Pish, the parson had taken a drop too much port to ward off the cold of the morning, and others that all the excitement had been too much for the pious old gentleman, first the big funeral and then the big wedding, both inside a fortnight.

Meanwhile the newlyweds drove on in blissful ignorance to the Governor's residency. Fannie's baggage had gone there by wagon the evening before, and she found it set out for her in the Governor's bedchamber. Johnnie's secretary, Thomas Macdonogh, had met him with important letters in the doorway below, and they had gone to the library to examine them. The servants were bustling about, preparing a reception for the afternoon, when a long list of invited guests would come to dine and to pledge the master and the new mistress of the house.

Alone in the bedroom Fannie unpacked her bandboxes and portmanteaus and drew forth her best gown, the creation of a Boston mantuamaker in the summer past. It was made on the pattern of the one she had worn for Copley, full at the hips, snug at the waist, and frank at the bodice. She had worn it once or twice in Boston but never here, not with Theo ill and people so ready to disapprove. She slipped it on and moved to the long looking glass. The figure there gazed at her mysteriously, smiled, and dipped in a curtsy that spread the skirts in a wide and perfect circle on the floor, the feminine movement known in society as "making a cheese." They nodded to each other and arose.

There was a step and a knock at the door, and she swept a dressing gown about her. Another knock, and Johnnie appeared, closing the door and catching her into his arms.

"I've work to do, my dear. Letters to answer, and then the final arrangements for the reception—I want things to go without a hitch. But I had to have a kiss of my bride first."

"Johnnie," she said.

"Yes, love?"

"The Colonel—where's he?"

"Michael? At Little Harbor. He's gone to stay with Uncle Benning two or three days, to leave us alone for a small honeymoon."

"Better two or three years," Fannie said. "Or forever!" And seeing Johnnie's surprise, "I couldn't bear to be under the same roof with the man—you surely realize that. I mean, he knows about us, and I couldn't abide that smile and look every time I met him in the house. I want to live alone with you. The servants don't matter, but he does. Do get rid of him."

He hesitated. His friendship with Michael rebelled at such a discharge, even for Fannie's sake. He saw she meant exactly what she said. Women were strange. He shrugged and said, "Very well."

She smiled deliciously. "You can put it down to jealousy if you like. I won't share you with anyone, even another man. Johnnie, you've married the most selfish, the most greedy creature in the world."

"And the loveliest."

She made a cheese. "Thank you, Your Excellency. Now run away to whatever you have to do."

As soon as he was gone she threw off the dressing gown and

admired once more the fashionable woman in the glass, twisting this way and that and turning to look over her shoulder. A fetching dress—too fetching for Portsmouth, really. All the flat women, old and young, would drip vinegar at such a show. But just the thing for Boston, especially now, with the British officers and their ladies setting the pace. Johnnie must resume his formal visits there next summer, after the baby was born, and her figure back at its best. She saw herself with him in the dark green carriage with the interlaced JW cipher on the doors, with the green coachman and outriders, and the soldiers and people running out of the Boston shops and taverns to see what great folk came to town.

She saw herself in the gown at one of those fashionable Boston routs, sweeping into the ballroom on Johnnie's arm while a voice behind cried, "Their Excellencies, Governor Wentworth and lady!" There were other delightful pictures. And then, with a sigh, she took off the delectable thing and chose a more sober costume for the reception downstairs. The figure in the glass made a mouth at it.

NINE

ON A WARM AUTUMN DAY of the year 1770 Mr. Woodbury Langdon found himself traveling the "Governor's Road" with his wife. He was not so eager to visit Wentworth House as was Mrs. Langdon, for he had busy concerns in Portsmouth, but he went dutifully and with some curiosity. They crossed over the Newington ferry to Dover Point with their carriage-and-pair and were able to cover much of the way on wheels, although there were places where Mr. Langdon wondered which would founder first, the carriage or the pair. At a place called Plummer's Ridge the road finally became impassable for wheels. The rest of the "Governor's Road" was a mere bridle path winding up the forest slopes. They borrowed riding horses from Plummer, a substantial man, and went on.

"I hope it's worth all this," Mr. Langdon said.

"Of course it is. Thank heaven we brought my sidesaddle. I'm dying to see the place—and Fannie of course. She's been up here with Johnnie ever since their baby died. They were both upset over that. A seven months' child, poor thing; it hadn't a chance in the summer heat and vapors, but such a fine looking boy. Remember how proud Johnnie was, there at the baptism, with the baby in his arms. 'Another John Wentworth,' he said to me. 'My son and heir—and image!'"

"Oh well, there'll be others. We found that out, you and I."

"If there are, I do hope Fannie has an easier time. She's small at the hips, you know; she had a terrible labor. And she was still quite peaked when they came up here. I don't think it was right of Johnnie to drag her off through these woods in her condition."

"Pshaw! Women with a delicate look and a sailor's hips are

the ones who live the longest. You couldn't kill Mrs. Fannie with an ax."

"You don't like her, do you?" Mrs. Langdon said straitly.

"Let's not go into that, my duck. I like Johnnie well enough, or I wouldn't be traveling this damned track to see him."

The damned track took them at last over the shoulder of Moose Mountain. Here in the hills the red maples and sumacs were in full color, there was a deepening tinge of fall on the rock maples, the mountain ash, the birches and beeches, and at the horses' feet the ferns already had gone to rust. The afternoon waned. The sun was getting low and the forest shadows lay in the narrow trail with a hint of frost when at last the horses whickered and there was an answer just ahead. They rode into an open space, and both reined up for a moment.

Wentworth House was no larger than some of the mansions in Portsmouth, but here, standing up on the broad cleared shelf at the foot of the hills, and silhouetted by the red flare of sunset on the lake beyond, it looked immense. A pair of tall chimneys smoked above the gambrel roof. Around it stood the log huts of the Governor's carpenters and laborers, with a log lean-to for the work oxen, another for the Governor's horses. There was no sign yet of barn or stable or coach house. The land gangs were just quitting work. They had been pulling up stumps with chains and oxen, and their days' work, a rough tangle of butts and roots, dragged together at the lower end in the clearing, was burning now with the hot red flame and greasy smoke of pine.

"Gad!" Mr. Langdon said, staring about him. "He's really doing it!" He was astonished, in spite of all he had heard. The place had to be seen to be believed.

The young Negro stable boy, Remus, ran out to take the horses, and Fannie herself appeared in the great doorway, calling out to them. She took Mrs. Langdon in her arms and kissed her ardently.

"Oh, my dear, my dear, how wonderful to see you! If you knew how I ache for company all the time. I scarcely see my

Governor the day long, except at meals. He's off now some-where, riding like the Wild Huntsman in the German tale, down to the falls, I suppose. The more he gets done, the more he wants to do—never satisfied. Come in—come into Wentworth House!"

Fannie was dressed, as if she were in town, in a well-measured blue gown, white silk stockings, and blue silk shoes, with a gold locket at her throat. She looked remarkably well. Her clear complexion even had a hint of brown, as if on some reck-less afternoons she had gone in the sun without hat or parasol. If her childbed illness in early June had done nothing else it had left her as slim as a wand. She took them at once on a tour of the house, Mrs. Langdon exclaiming at every step, and her hus-band measuring right and left with a shrewd eye and a strong temptation to whistle. The mansion faced east toward the road approach, and west toward the lake, with a central hall running through from the front door to the back. These main doors were tall and massive with locks to match. Langdon slipped out one of the keys and hefted it in his hand. It weighed well over a pound. The windows, of many small panes, were each six feet wide and ran up almost to the tall ceilings.

From the main hall a corridor led them to the left, where they inspected the parlor, dining room, billiard room, and library. A door from the dining room opened into a one-story ell on the south end of the house, the kitchen, in charge of Remus's mother, a big cheerful black woman named Hagar. Parlor and library looked toward the lake; and in the library, where already Governor Johnnie had a few choice leather-bound volumes, a fire in a black marble fireplace warmed the tiled hearth and the room.

Returning to the central hall, Fannie threw open a door on the other side of the house, and they peered into the ballroom, which occupied half the lower story. It was empty of all furni-ture, indeed the walls and floor were unfinished, and in this state, as Langdon said, it looked as big as a barn.

They passed up the maple staircase, a straight flight with the balusters unfinished, and found themselves in another hall. Fannie waved a hand. "All that space on the north side, over the dancing room, will remain as it is for a time—even my ambitious Governor can't do everything at once—but I want you to look at our chambers on this side. See!"—throwing open a door and revealing a large room, unfurnished, with tall paneling only partly done and a coved niche left on each side of a gray marble fireplace.

"This will be for official guests—visiting governors from other provinces, and the like. One of those niches will hold a bust of His Majesty, the other a bust of the Queen—the Governor's ordered them from England—and of course we'll call it our King and Queen Room."

Passing through another door into another unfinished chamber, "This is for our special friends—we've put a bed and carpet in it for you, my dears. Of course everything's rough as you see— the house is still swarming with joiners and masons every livelong day, but I hope you won't mind."

Mrs. Langdon noted with satisfaction a brisk fire in the white marble fireplace. The nights now were distinctly cold.

"The Governor's sent to France for a landscape paper for this room, East Indian scenes—elephants and temples and palm trees and rajahs walking with their ladies in gardens—most extravagant, but he would have it. So of course we call this the East India Room."

"Now over here," crossing the corridor, "is the Governor's own bedchamber—rough just like yours at the present, as you see. This will be the Green Room: walls, carpets, window hangings—everything. He's mad about woods and fields, and so forth, so green's his color—that's why he chose it for his carriage and his servants' livery. People will call him The Green Man if he doesn't look out—like a tavern sign. And this," opening another door, "leads to my chamber, which will be done in shades of blue. My Governor can have his wood greens. I like the sea, where the towns are, and the blue sky over them."

"But you enjoy the summers up here?" Mrs. Langdon said. Her husband had wandered away.

Fannie laughed and wrinkled her nose. "Do you want the truth? I put up with Johnnie's notions as a good wife must—but between you and me and the bedpost, my dear, I wouldn't give a bent sixpence for all the groves and lakes and bogs from Dover Point to Canada. Give me the town—the town and lively people about me, and some music and dancing or a good hand of whist in the evenings."

Mr. Langdon gazed from a window to the east, where the Governor's Road emerged from the woods. Already the shadows under the pines were as black as night. The clearing on this side opened to the house in a deep inverted V, pitted like a small-pocked face, where stumps and boulders had been dragged out of the earth. A long carriageway from the edge of the woods to the house had been marked out apparently with saplings or switches, ready for leveling. The ladies found him staring at these objects, and he pointed them out.

"What are those?"

Fannie smiled. "Those saplings along the carriageway? Elms—fetched all the way from Portsmouth, with the roots wrapped in wet moss, if you please. My Governor calls it The Mall. The Mall! I tell you, Mr. Langdon, he talks as if he planned to live a hundred years—as if he might drive along there some day in his coach-and-four with trees and branches arching overhead. What a dreamer the man is."

The sunset glow had faded from the western windows, and the brief autumn twilight had begun. Already servants were moving about with tapers, lighting candles in the lower rooms. Langdon noted that they wore their livery, with freshly powdered hair, as if they were in town; and that the candles were not tallow but of the finest spermaceti.

And now the dreamer arrived, in muddy and scratched riding boots, in stained leather breeches and hunting shirt, swinging down from a tired horse and tossing the reins to the boy Remus. He came into the house with his quick stride and greeted the visitors heartily, at the same time beckoning a servant. "Madeira," he called to the man, throwing out the word without turning his head.

When the wine came Woodbury Langdon offered a toast. "To the lord of Wolfeborough."

"And his lady of course," added his wife promptly, detecting the sardonic note in Woody's voice and covering it with wifely skill.

"I'll give you a better," Johnnie smiled. "Our own New Hampshire, the one that is to be, from the Isles of Shoals to Lake Champlain and all the way east to Nova Scotia. A bumper, if you please."

He tossed off the wine and disappeared upstairs, calling for his valet. When he came down he was in full town fig, from tiewig to silk stockings and pumps. When they went into the dining room they found a white cloth laid, with some of the Governor's best silver and chinaware gleaming under an elaborate candelabra. A servant in livery stood behind each of their four chairs. The meal itself was "plain country fare," as Johnnie said; soup, trout, roast venison, and plum pudding, with a very good claret and brandy.

Thus comfortably fed the ladies withdrew to gossip in the parlor, and the Governor and Langdon in the billiard room amused themselves at a game, with a servant to mark the score. They chatted idly between strokes. Mr. Langdon was too polite to ask, but he was curious about the cost of this baronial establishment in the wilds. It must have swallowed at least five thousand guineas already. The house was still half-finished, and Johnnie talked cheerfully of barns and stables, of tons of furnishings still to come, of his proposed deer park and his gristmill and other matters farther afield. His visitor began to suspect that the wildest guess of the Portsmouth gossips was none too large. Johnnie's ordinary living expenses alone must be taking every penny of his salary from the provincial government and from his post as Surveyor General. He had urged the Assembly to increase the salary, and they had refused. Where was Johnnie getting the money? From his father? Mark Wentworth was well to do, but much of what he owned was in timberlands and suchlike property. He was tight with money, especially now that he had to sell his masts to shrewd local shipbuilders instead of the Royal Navy. Governor Johnnie must be borrowing, and he must be over his ears already. A few more years of this lordly expense at Wolfeborough would send him fathoms deep.

Of course, with Johnnie's wide holdings here, he might sell land for good sums and pay off his debts when the tide of settlement came in. And it had begun. Already a hundred and fifty people were living in the Wolfeborough township. Mr. Livius was making a country estate in imitation of the Governor, but on a much more modest scale. David Sewall and that college friend of Johnnie's, Dr. Cutter, had built a sawmill on the stream from Wentworth's lake, and frame houses and barns were going up in the settlement. But all these were being sustained from Portsmouth by the wagon road to the foot of Winnipesaukee, with water transport up the lake to the village. Wentworth House lay miles in woods beyond, with a tedious approach either way. Who would want land there? And would Johnnie sell an inch if he could? Interesting questions!

In the course of their visit the Langdons were blessed with the warm lazy sunshine of a benign autumn. By day the hills swam in a blue haze like wood smoke, and the hardwood leaves about the lake shores fluttered like the gaudy tatters of a Joseph's coat, especially at sundown when the ruddy light brought out the warm color of the maples. Each night the sky was brilliant with stars, with frost sparkling on the torn earth of the clearing, and the lake reflecting all above like a patch of fallen sky.

Each day Mr. Langdon rode with Johnnie over the estate, watching the various gangs of men at work. Once they rode seven miles around the lake to the settlement of Wolfeborough, where the clearings were growing by the hour, and small but snug farmhouses already dotted the slope looking out on the waters of Winnipesaukee. They called on Mr. Livius, and found him overseeing his work gangs from a rude seat perched on a pine snag, twenty feet above the ground. He resembled a dark watchful statue on a monument, with his wife a symbolic figure at the foot. Mrs. Livius enjoyed these wild scenes and frequently went over to Wentworth House by horseback or canoe. She preferred the canoe, paddled by a pair of woodsmen, even when the Governor's lake was lashed by autumn gales that threatened to swamp the bark in a moment.

Mr. Livius did not visit there so often. He was busy with his own estate. As they rode away Langdon said, "D'you trust that man?"

"Of course, why?"

Langdon hesitated. Johnnie's liking for Englishmen was a byword, and he was especially friendly with Livius and Colonel Michael Wentworth at Portsmouth, and another half-pay officer, Colonel Fenton, newly settled with his Boston wife at one of the up-tide settlements.

"He's ambitious, Johnnie."

"Pshaw! Who isn't?"

Woodbury Langdon said no more. His own brother John, an up-and-coming sea captain and merchant, was one of those who despised the whole Wentworth clan and made no bones about it. Lately there were whispers that Livius was secretly another, that indeed he had consulted the rest and was plotting some sort of mischief for Johnnie in particular. But there were all sorts of rumors nowadays.

Fannie and Mrs. Langdon spent most of their time in the house, amusing themselves at crewelwork and billiards, while the din of hammer and saw, of adz and chisel and plane, rang through the building from cellar to garret.

"I'm an indoor creature," Fannie confessed. "I never feel well in summer as I do in winter. I'm at my best when the fires are lit and the doors and windows closed. My Governor thrives on outdoor air—but all men do."

The noise of the workmen drove the ladies out of doors, willy-nilly, from time to time. Once, sheltering her complexion under a broad straw hat, Fannie led the way to see "My Governor's" sawmill on the Rye Field brook, but she went astray near the swampy meadow with its confusing fringe of cedars and hackmatacks, and by the time they found their way back to Wentworth House she had lost her silk shoes in the muck.

A more comfortable venture with the gentlemen took them on horseback to a ridge overlooking the lake. Here the view was wide and beautiful. A painter's panorama of hills and slopes, green and shaggy with pines and hemlocks; of wild meadows which they called savannas, a lusher green in the folds; the blue lake with its little fleet of islands; the hint of bigger Winnipesaukee in the hill folds to the west; the pointed breast of Copplecrown; and there on the broad terrace at their feet the solitary grandeur of Wentworth House, a toy from this height. They dined on the ground, with food and wine brought in panniers by a servant riding behind. Above their heads towered an enormous pine, one of the finest Mr. Langdon had seen in a lifetime on the Piscataqua.

"I don't see the King's mark," he observed, measuring the trunk with his eye.

"This one's mine," Johnnie said crisply. "And it shall stand as long as I live, mark that. We call this place Mount Delight—Fannie's notion—the view of course. By-and-by I'll have a good bridle path up here, and we'll entertain all our visitors in this fashion. And next year I'll have a sloop on the lake. She's a-building now, down by the outlet to Winnipesaukee. Her name's to be *Rockingham*, in compliment to my good friend and patron in England. If you come early enough in the spring, Mrs. Langdon, you shall christen her. We'll even take you for a sail."

At last the time came for the Langdons to return. As they mounted for their journey a blown horse came out of the woods with a rider in livery, one of the grooms at the Governor's stable in Portsmouth. He fished a letter from the saddle pouch. Johnnie frowned. He had told his secretary not to bother him with anything but the most urgent matters here, and the folded and wax-sealed slip had a superscription in Macdonogh's hand. He did not open it, but stood waving good-by to the Langdons with the thing in his hand until the forest swallowed them.

"What's that?" Fannie said.

Johnnie took a small penknife from his waistcoat, sliced away the seal, and unfolded the sheet. She saw a startled look and then one she could not fathom.

"Well," she cried, "what does it say?"

"Uncle Benning died two days ago at Little Harbor."

Up flew Fannie's brows. Suddenly she smiled. She laughed aloud. She seized Johnnie's hands and whirled him about, dancing on her dainty toes in the mud of the carriageway.

"Dance with me, Johnnie, dance! Why so glum? Nobody loved that fat old nincompoop. And think of all that money!"

But her Governor would not dance. He seemed thunderstruck. Fannie ceased her capers and demanded, "What's the matter?"

"His will was opened yesterday. A new one, drawn up by Mr. Atkinson a few weeks ago."

"Oh?"

"Everything, to the last ha'penny, goes to the widow."

"Martha? I don't believe it. Let me see."

She snatched the sheet from his hand and read Macdonogh's fine looped handwriting at a glance. For a moment or two she was rigid, staring at the paper as if it were Martha Wentworth herself. She twisted it into a ball and stamped it into the mud. Then, seeing Johnnie's countenance, she stepped close and slipped her arms about his neck.

"Never mind, darling. There's other money in the world, and you shall find it. I'll bring you fortune yet—I vow I will."

He remained absorbed, staring over her shoulder into the forest, as if all his creditors were there disguised as trees. She withdrew her arms and turned her back, crying petulantly, "I suppose you think I've ruined you. I suppose you think Benning Wentworth cut you off because of me—those whispers about our marriage. And of course I didn't bring you sixpence, when you might have

113

married a fortune. That was what you always planned to do, wasn't it?"

He made no answer but turned abruptly and strode into the house. Fannie paused long enough to shrivel the gaping workmen with a queenly stare and followed him. He had gone into his library, and when she tried the handle she found the door locked. He did not emerge for supper. Late in the evening she sent the servants off to their quarters, went upstairs, undressed, and put on the most charming of bedgowns. In this and a flowered wrapper, and with a candle in her hand, she came down to the library door and scratched lightly on the panel, an intimate little sound, a trick of hers in the early weeks of their marriage when Johnnie was working late and she came to offer herself for love-making. There had been very little of that since the baby's death.

"Johnnie?"

"Yes." His voice was dull, as if he had been drinking.

"Let me in, love."

"I wish to be alone."

"Johnnie, let me in this instant!"

No answer.

Her mind moved nimbly. "Johnnie, if you don't, I'll do something you'll be sorry for. I'll—I'll throw myself down the well."

No answer.

The well was at the south end of the house, just around the corner from the window where Johnnie undoubtedly sat, staring out at the starlight on the lake. She ran along the hall and slammed the great front door behind her. A swift rush in her slippers carried her to the well with its waist-high stone curb. A chunk of poplar lay there, fallen from the woodpile. It was a good three feet long, dry and light from the past summer's heat, but big enough to make a hearty splash. The front door was opening, and she heard Johnnie's shout.

"Fannie? Where are you? Fannie, don't be a fool. D'you hear me?"

She tipped the log into the well and fled like a deer, around the other corner to the west door, and thence along the hall and up the stairs. One of her chamber windows looked upon the well, and in a moment she swung it open. Johnnie, a dark frantic figure under the stars, was at the well's windlass running the bucket down to the full length of the rope. In another moment he was astride the curb and about to descend. In that moment Fannie's voice startled him, floating from above, not below. She was laughing.

"Fannie—you devil!"

"Disappointed, Your Excellency?"

He ran for the door and came up the stairs two at a time. When he dashed into the Blue Room there she was, with a puckish smile, lying on the bed, arms back and hands tucked under the pillow ends. And now she pouted her lips and began to whistle the air of "Why Should We Quarrel for Riches."

Johnnie himself had to laugh then.

"I ought to spank you soundly, ma'am."

She turned her head and blew the candle out.

"If it please, m'lord," the voice floated up in the dark, "the prisoner submits to whatever infliction Your Lordship may desire."

TEN

*A*T THE END of October they were back in Portsmouth, amid
the thronging roofs and chimneys, the clatter of shoes and hoofs
and wheels, the mingled voices, the atmosphere of life in close
company that Fannie loved. Once more His Excellency threw
himself into the routine business of being a governor. Once more
Mrs. Fannie dictated little social notes to Thomas Macdonogh,
as if the Governor's demands were not enough, and watched his
busy quill turning out elegant trifles such as:

> THE GOVERNOR AND LADY INVITE
> TO TEA ON THURSDAY NEXT,
> MR. AND MRS. LANGDON
> TEA AT FIVE O'CLOCK P.M.
> PORTSMOUTH, FRIDAY EVENING, NOVEMBER 23, 1770

Once more they entertained Portsmouth gentlefolk with
dinners and balls and concerts, although Colonel Michael's face
was missing from the musical affairs and an imported footman
played the violin. Since his dismissal from Fannie's domain the
soldier had quartered himself in a room at Stavers's inn. The
stables of his friends were open to him whenever he wished to
ride, and he remained a welcome visitor in and outside the town.
When they met at routs and dinners he and Johnnie chatted
amicably enough, although the old camaraderie was gone, and
the colonel had only a silent bow for Johnnie's lady. On her own
part, with the occult knack of ladies meeting someone they dislike, Fannie always gazed through Michael Wentworth as if he
were not there.

One rainy day in late autumn, riding in Buck Street, Johnnie met his old friend on a fine gelding coming from the tavern. He touched his wet hat in salute and was passing on when the soldier called, "One moment, Johnnie."

"Yes, Michael?"

The colonel rode in knee to knee and regarded him earnestly.

"I—um—there's somethin' I feel you should know, before anybody else. A matter of passin' interest, o' course, but these are dull days, eh? I owe you thanks, Johnnie."

"Not at all."

"This is somethin' particular. I want to thank you for the day you introdooced me to old Uncle Blubbergut. I've had many's the good time out there at Little Harbor since, shootin', fishin', an' so on—and many a jolly bout with the old feller at the bowl. A tippler after my own taste. And I liked the place from the time I saw it first. Suited me to a T, even that Jack Straw's Castle of a house. Nothin' like England, o' course, but maybe that was why. I'd had a bellyful of England. Well, to get on with it, I was sorry when the old man died, if nobody else was, eh?"

Johnnie gave him a shrewd glance. It was early in the day for drinking, even for Michael's drinking, but he could catch no sober drift to this casual discourse in the rain. The horses stamped and sidled impatiently.

"Johnnie, after your uncle's funeral I got to thinkin'. Here I was, with scarcely one guinea to chink against another—cadgin' from friends between one half-pay and the next. After all my years in His Majesty's service, fightin' the French, an' those wild Scotchmen o' Prince Charlie's, an' so on. An' all the time my brother Peregrine sittin' snug on the estate at home with nothin' but a few pheasant guns to bang about his ears. So, as I say, I got to thinkin'—somethin' I've never done much, not havin' the head for it. And 'twas all quite simple when I came to the point. Here I was, damme, a man that deserved a roof of his own an' some ease an' pleasure under it, specially now in his prime years while he could relish a hearty constitution. And out there, d'ye see, was Mrs. Martha, fine figger of a woman, sunny side o' five-an'-thirty, left all alone with a heap o' guineas an' half the timber in New Hampshire."

"What the devil are you driving at?" Johnnie snapped.

"Eh? I mean to say, damme, one an' one makes two, don't it? Why, Johnnie, even I can do a sum like that! It means I rode out yesterday an' popped the question. Popped it like a man. An' got my answer too. She's agreed to surrender—hand, heart, bag an' baggage. See now? The old stallion's come to clover. Ain't you pleased?"

Johnnie's face was nakedly incredulous. The soldier was tipsy, surely. He seemed quite debonair, but Michael always held his wine well, even in the saddle.

"May I ask when the marriage takes place?"

"Oh, as soon as may be—the day must be the lady's choice I mean to say, hey? But the pretty creature assures me it'll be well this side o' the month's end. So Johnnie, congratulate the happiest man in America—barrin' yourself o' course."

"Very well. My congratulations, Michael."

Johnnie put out a gloved hand, and the soldier shook it fervently.

"An' give my compliments to your lady, Johnnie, eh?"

His Excellency's eyes went winter cold, but there was no subtlety in the soldier's. Michael's ruddy features had only the pleased look of a boy who has found a sugarplum in an old coat pocket.

Abruptly Johnnie gripped his reins and spurred away. He felt as if he were dreaming after mulled wine and mince pie. The neatness—the devilish neatness of the thing! All that land and money, the fortune that was his by right, dropping into the fingers of that cheerful wastrel—the guest he'd invited out from England and then turned out of his house! Incredible! What the deuce was Portsmouth coming to?

In a few days the curious little world of Portsmouth was coming in a body to the wedding of Colonel and Martha Wentworth. The interest was scarcely less than that of Johnnie's own marriage, only a year before. And there was much chaff afterward in tavern and drawing room about these widow-couplings so soon after funerals. Was it a fashion now?

The Governor and his lady stayed at home. Fannie had received Johnnie's news in silence. Her comment to her friends was, "Well, a pretty match, my dears. A penniless English rake and a jumped-up tavern wench. Old Benning must be groaning in his tomb to see his fortune in such hands. But he deserved it, after all. And heaven knows that precious pair deserve each other."

His Excellency made his own comment in another way and quite another place. At the next meeting of his Council he laid before them a proposal of his own as Surveyor General. His voice was impersonal and precise.

"Gentlemen, now that our late Governor, Mr. Benning Wentworth, is gone to his last account, and now that his property has—um—passed to other hands, I think we may consider without prejudice the lands involved. As you know, over a period of many years the old Governor kept a portion of the best woodland for himself whenever he made a township grant. He gathered more than a hundred thousand acres in that way. I have long considered the matter, and now I give you a decision. I find the whole of it unlawful."

He paused significantly. A lone voice broke the silence.

"I beg to differ, if your Excellency will forgive me," Peter Livius said. He had the air of a whist player who sees at last an opening for his trump.

"I speak, gentlemen, as a lawyer of some training in England, and I may say of some observation over here. The fact is, under the loose terms of his office our late Governor was quite within the law in granting himself these lands. We can't upset that, whatever our sentiments now."

He sat back with a tight mouth, repressing a smile, although he could not hide the malice in his glance at Johnnie's face. At once a lively clamor broke out around the Council board, protesting that His Excellency was right. It amused Mr. Livius, gazing from face to face. Barring himself, every one was of the Wentworth clan by blood or marriage. A flock of Wentworth eagles hungry to pick at a nice fat Wentworth corpse! What a spectacle!

Finally His Excellency spoke again.

"Whatever the terms of the late Governor's office, gentlemen, there was a term in the grants that applied to everyone, including him. The land must be improved, at a definite expense, within a definite time, or the grant became void. I'm no lawyer"—an ironical bow to Mr. Livius—"but that's beyond dispute. And what do we find when we examine the lands in question? You know as well as I do. Hardly a single tract in the woodlands held by the late Governor's estate has been improved a pennyworth. They should have been escheated long ago. And I say to you now that the province must take steps, first to place them back in the public domain, and second to grant them to such of His Majesty's subjects as will settle and cultivate them."

Johnnie paused. And then, "Will one of you gentlemen make a motion to that effect?"

The motion was made and passed in a minute. Mr. Livius uttered the only Nay.

"I ask that my objection go on the record," he announced in his dry Middle Temple voice. "For the clerk I shall put it in writing later, but I'll give it to you now."

A hubbub of protest. He held up a hand. Governor Johnnie sat watching him, calm, proud, a little contemptuous, sensing venom to come but not afraid of it.

"Patience, gentlemen," said Peter Livius, turning his dark set face from one to another. "It won't take a minute of your time—though it'll take more later on, that I promise you. I object to this motion on the ground that His Excellency John Wentworth, in proposing to escheat these lands, does so with the intent and purpose of securing them, through other parties, to his own use."

A gasp from eight mouths.

"Does that astonish you? I declare further that Mr. John Wentworth has been guilty of gross maladministration in his offices as Governor and as Surveyor General of His Majesty's Woods, as his uncle the late Benning Wentworth was before him. I shall give detail of these malpractices in due time. The matter is painful to me, of course, but I believe in duty, and my duty is quite clear. For the present that is all."

He sat down, with a saturnine smile at the stir and at the looks on all their faces, as if he had blasphemed and was soon to be struck by lightning. But the god of this little Olympus remained calm. He made no protest. It was a matter for the Council to deal with, and they dealt with it. The verbal remarks of Mr. Livius would not be entered in the Council's journal. His written objection would be placed on the clerk's file, and that was all. And with that the meeting dissolved.

Johnnie told the tale to an astonished Fannie over the supper table that night.

"But why?" she cried. "They've always been such friends of ours, Anna and Peter!"

"Anna, yes. There's nothing two-faced about Anna. But this is Peter's other face, which seems to be ambitious. Woodbury Langdon told me so at Wolfeborough, and I said Pooh. Well, here's proof."

"You don't mean he wants to be Governor?"

"Only God and Peter Livius know what he wants to be. He's acquired a sour jealousy of me and all my kin, that's clear, though he chose to conceal it until now."

"What can he do?"

"Oh, the man's rich and clever, but I've nothing to fear from a bilious English lawmonger. He has no standing with our New Hampshire folk, and I doubt if his vaporings would mean a thing in London, if they got so far."

"But of course you do intend to get Uncle Benning's lands? After all they're yours by right. All that property should have come to you if artful Martha hadn't twisted the old sot round her finger at the last."

Johnnie shifted irritably in his chair. "My dear Fannie, all that's water over the milldam. Forget it. I intend to put those grants in the hands of able men with a bit of money at their backs. Men who'll carry out the terms. And why should I hunt about New Hampshire for men who don't happen to be connected with the Wentworths? My family's been here on this soil for generations, marrying right and left. A boy couldn't blow peas at any town meeting in the province without hitting someone linked with me one way or another."

"That's what Livius knew," she said.

"Ods fish, who cares what he knows? I want those backwoods opened fast, and I know the men who'll do it. What else matters?"

"Must you be quite such a Jack-in-a-hurry?"

"My dear Fan, Uncle Benning kept his grants idle for years, in some cases half a lifetime. I can't see one more season wasted. Time won't wait for us, nor will the New Yorkers. D'you realize. . . ."

"Oh dear yes, Johnnie, yes. Don't go into that."

The spring of 1771 came up from the south, with warm rains and a hot political smell from the Boston pot still boiling merrily. Just a year ago a mob of Boston street roughs had clashed with some redcoats and come off second best, as that painter man Copley had foretold. Johnnie's old friend and Harvard classmate John Adams had defended the soldiers in the courts, but Sam Adams and others were still calling it a massacre of peaceable American townsmen.

Johnnie went on vigorously with the training of the New Hampshire militia; he had formed them in twelve battalions, and in making officers he placed ability first, regardless of family or money. His regular force, to be raised in the province, was still no more than a dream. The Assembly had allowed him no more than one officer and five men, hired on an annual basis, and these only because there had to be some trained caretakers for the old fort on Newcastle Island and the store of cannon there.

In other matters he had more success. He got money and built a lighthouse at the river entrance, something the Portsmouth merchants and fishermen had wanted time out of mind. He took the King's quitrent money, taxed on all grantlands, and boldly spent it on new roads. Before long he could point to more than two hundred miles of such roads opened in the back country. And now, after long urging, he had London's permission to mark off the province in five counties, each with its local justices and seat officials. Under Uncle Benning's regime the outlying settlements had growled incessantly because their people had to come to Portsmouth for the simplest of legal matters.

As Surveyor General his sore problem remained in the King's mast trees. The timber owners chafed more and more at the sight of their best pines marked and reserved for some fanciful war in the future. Portsmouth shipbuilders wanted the trees, and the boisterous crews of mastmen were eager for the work. Johnnie held firmly to the law, while he sought a decent way out of it. One had appeared to him, and he was pressing it by letter upon the Lords of Trade and Plantations. Why not reserve whole tracts of timber for the Navy far up the coast in Nova Scotia, where the population lived almost entirely on the fishery? He had seen good stands of pine up there, every stick handy to the sea, when he visited Nova Scotia in the *Beaver*. The change would be no hardship to the Nova Scotians, who had no interest in timber, and it would relieve this pressure in New Hampshire, where God knew he had pressures enough. So far the Lords of Trade were silent.

They were silent, too, on the hotter subject of import taxes and the methods of His Majesty's collectors. Like other Americans Johnnie was protesting both. So far he could still persuade the collectors in Portsmouth to move cautiously, but they were under the orders of His Majesty's commissioners in Boston, and sooner or later they must seize right and left and be damned.

Every fisherman smuggled when he had a chance. So did the lumber and fish traders on their home voyages from the West Indies and other foreign parts. Indeed most of the Portsmouth merchants were involved in smuggling, directly or indirectly. In America free trade was a custom so old that in every mind it had the respectability of law. Of course a good many solid men who smuggled had no sympathy with the common mob, having seen it in action during the Stamp Act riots. They wanted order. But how many of them would support the Governor when His Majesty's shoe began to pinch them too?

So far the belief in order had stood well at Johnnie's back. Everyone remembered an affair in his first winter as Governor, when one midnight the Sheriff roused him out of bed.

"Governor! That man in the jail, the one condemned to hang tomorrow—there's a great crowd gathering in Water Street to rescue him—fishermen and wharf porters, and the like."

Johnnie thought swiftly as he dressed. The water-front mob— the same mob that had set all Portsmouth by the ears in '65. But no Stamp Act now for an excuse. A criminal who chanced to be popular about the wharves.

Away went his grooms at a gallop to summon the Council and a squad of his best-drilled militia. Half an hour later he was standing before the jail with a group of militiamen, hastily dressed and armed. Such of the councilors as had arrived were huddling in the jail doorway. They could hear the mob approaching, a roar like the sea on the Rye shore after a hurricane, something that prickled the scalps of them all. The jail was a small wooden thing, old and shaky. As Johnnie remarked, an old woman could knock it down.

And now the mob came in sight like a Fundy tide bore rushing up the street, many carrying torches, all brave with rum and hot for mischief. At sight of the resolute Johnnie and his group they yelled and doubled their pace, hoping no doubt to frighten this small guard away. But when they came within musket shot they paused and milled about, for in that moment Johnnie called to his men, "See to your flints and priming!" And then the order, "Present firelocks! Ready! Aim!"

He drew his sword, a bright flash in the torchlight. "Mr. Atkinson, read aloud the Riot Act, if you please."

The Chief Justice held a paper to the light of the jail-door lantern, and his voice sounded sharply in the hush. When he finished Johnnie snapped to the crowd, "Disperse! Disperse, or take the consequence!" And without turning his head to the militia, and in the same voice, "When I give the order Fire, you'll

"Well, as Surveyor General I must earn my salary. That means, just now, that I've got to make another sea cruise along the coast of Maine, to keep an eye on the mast thieves up that way."

"And leave me here in the woods!"

"Oh, come now, Fan. This isn't the woods any more. You've got neighbors all about you—within a few miles, anyhow—and a good staff to wait on you hand and foot. Besides, there's all our summer visitors to entertain—you know you like that."

"All very well," said Fannie with petulance and an edge. "But am I to have the pleasure of my lord and master only in the wintertime? There's no need of all this tramping and riding and sailing. You have rangers and deputies to take care of that. And look at you! Rough and sunburnt, like any of those wild mastmen on the river—the Governor of New Hampshire. What would your noble friends in England say if they could see you now?"

"They'd envy me to the ground."

An impatient click of her tongue. "They would a fig's end! They'd never know the fine gentleman that left them for America five years ago. They wouldn't speak to you on the street, my precious Johnnie. Even in Portsmouth the nice people shake their heads sometimes—their Governor, who's always over the hills and far away, like Tom, Tom the Piper's Son."

"They'll be whistling another tune ten years from now. A great many New Hampshire folk appreciate what I'm doing, Fannie. As for the rest, let 'em shake. I can suffer that if you can, love."

"Humph!"

"Someday, when I'm too old to tramp and ride and sail, I'll sit in Portsmouth twelve months in the year, and I'll want nothing but whist and wine and conversation. Will you be proud of me then?"

"I'll be a lot more satisfied," said Fannie.

ELEVEN

*I*N THE EARLY SUMMER of 1773 Johnnie began his seventh year as Governor, with all the jaunty optimism of that first day in the Portsmouth square. He was thirty-seven, with the same spring in his step, the same cheerful gaze, the same easy courtesy, the same ambition. He could look backward with some satisfaction. In what most American governors had found a very difficult time, he had kept his province peaceful and bustling, with a sound currency and a swiftly growing population. And now the troubles elsewhere were on the wane. London had abolished the detested Townsend import taxes, all but a small duty on tea. At Boston the redcoats had withdrawn to an island in the harbor, where there was no further chance of a clash with the street toughs. Indeed Sam Adams and his fellow rousers of the Boston mob were at their wits' end to find trouble. Their only weapon now was tea; and everyone knew tea sold cheaper in Boston, threepenny tax and all, than in London itself. Sam was arguing the tax as a principle, of course, and so were many others, even in New Hampshire, but the people seemed tired of tumult and agitation. To Governor Johnnie the prospect was a long domestic peace.

Portsmouth's only worry in this pleasant summer had nothing to do with politics. It was a sudden fear of smallpox, the scourge that swept every port in America from time to time. Some folk were so afraid that they were willing to suffer "inoculation," which as everyone knew was something disgusting and dangerous, a process found in Turkey years ago and carried to the polite world by an English gentlewoman. And now two Portsmouth doctors decided to practice this pagan art on their own wives and families, and others were going to them for the purpose. Indignant voices declared them dangerous fanatics, bringing a deadly malady into the town by way of their own flesh, and they must be stopped. The fanatics declared their right as free men to do whatever they liked with their flesh. In a short time the town was in an uproar. With his usual decision Governor Johnnie stepped in, summoned his Council, and laid down the rule. Physicians and patients who wanted inoculation must first get a license from the Council and then remove themselves to Pest House Island, down the harbor. After that, under a distant but sharp watch of town selectmen, they must stay on the island till the last trace of the pox had disappeared. It was quite simple after all, and to Johnnie an example of so many of these foolish human storms. One calm voice and a firm hand were enough to stop the winds and leave everyone wondering what the fuss had been about.

Fannie, regarding her own clear skin in the looking glass, shuddered at the notion of smallpox in the town, where so many pretty faces had been pitted in time past. For the first time, when Johnnie moved her out to Wolfeborough for the summer, she went with actual relief. She even began to enjoy the country life. The stream of visitors had much to do with it. Gay parties of ladies and gentlemen rattled and jingled through the woods from Portsmouth to spend a weekend or a fortnight in the hospitality of Wentworth House. The living quarters were finished now, and it was possible to dance in the ballroom, where the carpenters had laid a smooth floor at last.

The Mall was ditched and graveled, with the young elms well rooted and in leaf on either hand. The great barn, the coach house, the stable for thirty horses, the workshop, the smokehouse, and dairy were all up in frame, and some complete. The park was nearly cleared of thickets and undergrowth, so that Johnnie's guests could stroll over acres of brown carpet, in the shade of immense old maples and beeches and oaks, and watch the moose and deer that his hunters trapped in the outer forest and turned loose inside the park fences. The forty-acre garden had been cleared and plowed from the house to the lake shore, and already some flower beds and a patch of vegetables made a little show of what it was to be. So it was with the savanna, twenty minutes' walk northward, where the wild grass had been burned and the roots plowed under. In that moist soil and under the summer sun Johnnie's shoots of rye now made a delicate green, where only a little while back the moose had wandered out of the woods to drink and to roll in the rank marsh grass. For the sportsmen there was fishing and shooting of many kinds, all in easy reach. Not content with the native game, Johnnie had imported pheasants from England and freed them in the lakeside woods, dreaming of a day when he could entertain house parties of gunners like the landed gentry of the old country. Alas, the bewildered creatures were promptly devoured by owls and hawks and wildcats. He was more successful with cusk, which he fetched from the sea in tubs of ice and water and poured into the lake. A mad idea to the Portsmouth fishermen and to his woodsmen alike—and yet the fish were thriving in fresh water.

Guests of both sexes made easy jaunts by saddle along his paths cut through the woods, and enjoyed outdoor feasts under the giant lone pine on the crest of Mount Delight. When the heat was oppressive, or mosquitoes and black flies troublesome, they skimmed about the lake in Johnnie's sloop; and his cook put up hampers of food to be eaten on favorite islands, which they called whimsically Turtle, Stamp Tax, and Tea Rock.

Dr. Ammi Cutter was often there, talking of old Harvard days, acting as physician to the household, and keeping a shrewd eye on his sawmill interests at Wolfeborough. Another frequent guest was clever young Benjamin Thompson, newly married to a widow of property. He was able now to absorb himself in mathematics, astronomy, chemical and mechanical experiments, the art of engraving and a dozen other things that filled his ingenious mind.

Each Sunday the ballroom became a chapel, with service by a Church of England parson invited there for the purpose; and at Johnnie's further invitation the settlers rode in from all the country round to join his household at worship. He still hoped to see New Hampshire a province of the Church as well as the

King, with Dartmouth College a Church institution. His devotion was sincere, although his zeal was something more than religious. Going over in his mind the past American disturbances, especially the fiery talk of the Boston levelers, he saw danger in anything that drew gentry and common folk into separate groups. If, by degrees, the people could be inclined to join the gentry in one Church, at least one of those dangers would be gone. He still worked quietly in that direction, although so far with no success. Early this year he had invited young Ripley, a graduate of Dartmouth College in that lively first commencement, to leave the Presbyterian sect and become a Church of England parson. But Ripley's adviser, the watchful President Wheelock, had defeated that. Johnnie showed no resentment, indeed he had none, accustomed as he was to obstacles. And when, to keep his patron happy, Mr. Wheelock offered an honorary degree from Dartmouth College, Johnnie accepted it with grace.

Now, as usual, leaving Fannie to play chatelaine at Wentworth House, Johnnie went off on his summer concerns. First the routine cruise up the coast, this time as far as Machias, to check the timber cutters there. Then the backwoods journey he had planned last year. It took him and his rangers through the White Mountains by a remarkable notch, where a giant stone face, carved by nature, looked forth from the mountainside. They went on through the rugged hills and woods to what his quadrant showed him to be the forty-fifth parallel of latitude, the assumed border of Canada, and returned through the wilderness by another route down to the coast. He came back to Portsmouth in a coasting schooner, a ratty little thing that stank of fish, and paused at his town house to read the accumulated letters and to change his worn and tattered buckskins for some decent clothes. There was a fat letter from Tom Macdonogh in London, and he opened it in easy expectation. Livius had set forth his accusations for the Council clerk's file, and in the packet that Tom Macdonogh carried to London the Governor had refuted them carefully one by one, backing his defense with affidavits and letters from leading gentlemen of New Hampshire.

And now Tom described the outcome. A small subcommittee of the Lords of Trade had sat upon the matter in May, and they had given Mr. Livius a careful hearing, for he too had letters and affidavits from New Hampshire. In putting the charges he had gone all the way back to old Governor Benning Wentworth's regime—and Benning's greed and favoritism had been proved long ago. From that pot of authentic tar shrewd Peter had swept his brush to Benning's nephew and successor.

When Tom Macdonogh put to them the Governor's defense the committee gave it the same hearing, and examined Johnnie's documents with care. Apart from these they had information from independent sources, and plainly they were puzzled. In their report to the Board they declared—and here Tom quoted them at length:

". . . the reports which we have received, through different channels, of the situation of affairs within your Majesty's government of New Hampshire, do all concur in representing the colony to have been, ever since Mr. Wentworth's appointment, in a state of peace and prosperity; that its commerce has been enlarged and extended, the number of its inhabitants increased. And every attempt made to excite the people to disorder and disobedience has been, by the firm and temperate conduct of Mr. Wentworth, suppressed and restrained."

This naturally made handsome reading; but the report, like many a handsome creation of nature, had its sting in the tail. Despite Mr. Wentworth's good works the committee found him guilty of manipulating public lands for the benefit of his friends, of dismissing Mr. Livius without cause from a post as justice, and of failing to send reports of his Council to the Board in London. And in view of all this they doubted if he was "a fit person to be entrusted with your Majesty's interest in the important station he now holds."

Johnnie sank into a chair, stunned. His valet, coming into the room to announce his bath and fresh clothing ready, saw the blood gone from under the tan of his master's face, and stammered, "Are you—are you all right, sir?" Johnnie waved him away, sitting in the torn and greasy buckskins, wigless, with his own dark hair grown long and tangled from weeks in the backwoods, gripping the chair arms with hands calloused and stained with balsam, a very different picture for Mr. Copley if that deft man could have been there with his paints and brushes.

He sat long without moving, with the letter tossed on the floor at his feet. At last he picked it up and read Tom's postscript.

"'Tis evident, sir, that Mr. Livius has influential friends here, and you have more enemies in New Hampshire than we thought. The gentlemen of the Committee plainly did not know what to think, but in view of the late troubles in America they are anxious to allay all complaints, and therefore chose his side. I have consulted Mr. Paul Wentworth and Lord Rockingham, and they agree 'tis monstrous. So the battle is not over yet, depend on it. We shall go to the Council for Plantation Affairs, and if necessary to the Privy Council itself."

Johnnie went upstairs, letter in hand. The afternoon was far gone, and he had intended staying the night, but now he could not rest in Portsmouth—not in this sudden atmosphere of hidden enemies. He was shaken, and his whole thought turned to Fannie. Suddenly he craved her as a man craves warmth and light in the midst of a polar night. Whatever worries harried him he had always found ease in her arms, the lover slipping out of the Governor's coat. Changing into riding clothes, he swung into the saddle and headed for the Dover ferry. He rode hard and stopped at nightfall in a wayside inn at Rochester, kept by one of his poorer kinsmen, lame Stephen Wentworth.

The next evening he reached Wentworth House, completing the long ellipse of weeks and leagues that began when he set off so blithely for the edge of Canada. A party was in swing. A fiddle scraped merrily in the ballroom and Fannie was in the midst of a lively country dance when he appeared in the doorway, dusty from the road. He put on his best smile and manner, clapping hands at the dancers, refusing to join them, pointing to his boots and spurs. Fannie, in one of her impudent gowns, came over, still prancing to the tune and holding the arm of a young naval officer. He was from the current warship on the Portsmouth station, about Fannie's own age and taller than Johnnie. They looked remarkably well together.

"So ho!" she cried. "Here's the creature who calls himself my husband, though I vow, Lieutenant, I've not seen the man to touch him since the snow went off the ground. Johnnie, this is Lieutenant Halford." The men shook hands.

"What brings you to these parts, Your Excellency?" Fannie said. "Have you paused to light and bait on your way to anywhere, or is this a formal call?"

Her face was alight with the warmth and glee of the dance. Her eyes were impatient, as if Johnnie were a servant intruding on some unimportant errand. She kept her hand tucked in the sailor's arm, but for some reason the young man felt uncomfortable under the Governor's gaze, and in a moment he excused himself and returned to the dance.

Fannie glanced back at him. Then, with a careful look at Johnnie, she led the way across the hall into the library and shut the door.

"You look as if you'd come upon the devil in the woods. What is it? Not my nice Lieutenant Halford, surely?"

Wordless, he put the letter in her hand. She read it through swiftly, and again with care. Her face was still flushed, but the giddy pleasure faded out of it. It was like that other time when Macdonogh sent the word of Uncle Benning's will. That man's news is always bad, she thought. She looked up from the offending sheets and stared past Johnnie at the wall.

"This explains a lot of things," she said in a nipped voice. "You don't care for gossip, and I didn't bother to tell you, but last winter and spring there was a lot of malicious talk in Portsmouth. Mostly about the way you favored your friends and relatives. And not forgetting the handsome horns you favored Theo with on his dying bed—oh, don't stop me Johnnie—you might as well know what's being said."

"I don't care a damn what's being said."

"Well, it isn't the talk, it's the talkers. Not just the enemies we knew, and not those Portsmouth tavern louts who shout abuse at our servants because they're English, but people of family—people that we thought were friends. I daresay they've sneered at us right along behind their hands. Last spring they dropped the pretense. Oh yes, and quite bold about it, Johnnie, some of them. They reckoned it safe, you see. Because Peter Livius sent word that he had your scalp at last, and you'd be out of office by the summer's end. That—that skunk! After all you'd done for him! And the great joke amongst them was that Peter Sly—nobody likes the man really—was doing to Governor Johnnie exactly what you'd done yourself to Uncle Benning. Old Benning's barmaid and her precious colonel must be laughing up their sleeve at that. How I hate that pair! They look down their noses at me of course. They feel so virtuous with that brat of theirs, born a nice respectable two years after the wedding—while I'm little better than a whore."

"Don't say that!"

"Other people do. That and a good many other things you wouldn't care to hear. Well, there's this about it. We begin to see where our true friends are, and where they're not. Can that sneaking Livius really put you out?"

Johnnie shrugged. "Lord Rockingham's out of favor at the moment. In London that can be fatal. And it seems Livius has friends that sit in the right quarter of the wind. Sir Tom Wentworth sits there too, of course, but I think my best hope lies with Paul. His influence goes to Whigs and Tories alike, in all their factions, right up to the palace gate. And after all he's got a good case. What's in these complaints—even if they were true—that isn't done by men in office in every parish of England—or America, for that matter? Besides, I've given myself mighty little favor when you think of my opportunities. I could have been like Uncle Benning, squeezing out a fortune for myself and doing nothing in return. As it is I've slaved body and mind for the province and sunk myself in debt."

"Then what's your crime?"

"It seems I've been loyal to my friends as well as my King. Some men here are jealous of one and some the other. Livius was clever enough to bring 'em together."

"Well, what are you going to do now?"

"Make love to my wife."

A vexed look. "Oh, be serious."

"I was never more serious in my life."

He put a convincing arm about her waist. Fannie gave him a quizzical stare and sniffed, as if she suspected a brandy bottle along the road. Then, with a sharp little laugh, "Well, you've managed to wait all summer, my jockey, and you shall wait a bit longer now. We've guests and there's dancing to be done. When the news gets abroad I want everyone to know the Governor's lady doesn't care a fig. Now go and wash, and change those boots and breeches, do! You stink of horses."

She plucked his arm from her waist, crammed the letter contemptuously into the V of his waistcoat, and stepped away quickly to the music and laughter across the hall.

When they returned to Portsmouth and the sea there was no further word from England of Johnnie's fate. The town was openly divided now between those who hoped for his downfall and those who admired him still. And the feeling had spread through the countryside. The old resentment against the Wentworth clan, gathering fire slowly through two generations of their rule, was now smoking merrily. Johnnie was debited not only with his own family favors but those of his uncle and grandfather. Even the settlers who had flocked into New Hampshire since he came to office felt the heat of these old coals. His friends the woodsmen, much as they liked him in person, saw his mark on the King's trees now as a personal theft of their rights. The fishermen of Portsmouth and the outer islands and creeks, smugglers to a man, observed the intimacy of His Majesty's customs and naval officers with the mansion on Pleasant Street. Merchants outside the magic circle of Johnnie's friends were openly hostile, like John Langdon, and some inside it had become cautiously neutral, like John's brother Woodbury.

Even old Mark was critical. "Truth is, you've let your common sense go a-dozing, Johnnie, here and there. Take that Colonel Fenton, up in Grafton County. There's men up there, settled for years on no more'n a grant of a hundred acres. But this Englishman comes along, and you give him three thousand, first chop, and no questions."

"My dear father, Colonel Fenton's a half-pay officer who fought in America during the late French war. Under our law he was entitled to land according to his rank and he got it. Besides, his wife's an American woman of money, he knows how to farm, and he's built a mansion and cleared a plantation at Plymouth as good as my own at Wolfeborough. I wish I knew more men like John Fenton. I'd find 'em lands, and the deuce with what anybody said."

"And would you make every one of 'em a colonel of the militia, and clerk of the Court of Common Pleas, and judge of probate for his county?"

"That depends on the man's education and experience. John Fenton has those, and I can use 'em."

"Humph! Well, getting back to Livius, 'twas a mistake to make an enemy of that man."

"Oh, come now! I did the best I could for Livius. He hankered to be Chief Justice, but of course that appointment comes from London, and the Lords of Trade and Plantations look to me for advice. He knew I'd support old Mr. Atkinson in the post. So he asked for a seat on the bench, and I made him a justice of Common Pleas. He's the lofty sort of Englishman, and I suppose he considered that barely worth his attention. Anyhow he was careless with his accounts, and I had complaints. Last year I had to give the office to someone else. That's what set him off against me. Still, what does he expect to get with all this hullabaloo? I know he'd like to be Chief Justice. I suspect he'd like to be Governor. But he can guess what our people would say to that.

Even the men who signed their names to his complaints would cry murder at the notion."

Mark Wentworth shifted himself on his bony haunches in the chair, swaying from side to side like a pendulum upside down, a repeated motion that came upon him whenever his mind was busy with a problem.

"Johnnie, I don't know what to say, really. I've got a queer notion that this Livius affair's just a beginning of something. Livius himself doesn't count. He just happened to touch it off, like a boy playing with a tinderbox in a hay mow. Down in my countinghouse and around the mast booms in the river I hear a lot o' things you don't get in your drawing room up there on Pleasant Street. New Hampshire's not what it used to be when you went off to London, Johnnie. There's boxes inside o' boxes, inside o' more boxes, like one o' those little wooden tricks the sailors make."

Mark stuck up a hand and counted off the long fingers, one by one.

"There's the smugglers and their friends, which means pretty nigh everyone within the smell o' salt water. There's the mast-men on the rivers. There's the farmers—specially the new settlers that have flocked in from Massachusetts in the past ten years, chock full o' those Boston levelers' notions—that 'ud like to pull all the gentry down. There's some o' the gentry like Livius, that reckon 'emselves above common folk and 'ud just like to pull down Governor Johnnie and his friends. Finally there's this."

Mark closed his fingers and stuck up the thumb. "There's a lot o' people, common and gentle folk alike, that have no particular quarrel with Johnnie Wentworth but see things wider. I mean this feeling that the Assembly shouldn't be under the Governor and Council—that it ought to be the other way round."

"Pooh!" Johnnie said. "The Assembly's mighty independent as it is. Look at the way they've refused to increase my salary, again and again. Or look at the way they refused a penny for Captain Holland's land survey, and a dozen other things I've asked 'em for, things that were for their own good, not mine."

"Petty funds! Petty funds!" growled Mark. "That's all they control, so they make a point of it, like a pauper with his dog. What they really want is the final say in everything that has to do with New Hampshire. Which includes the King's woods and the tax on tea. A long reach, that, eh? All the way to London. Well, they believe in it, and a lot o' the others are drifting to their way o' thinking. Some that might surprise you, Johnnie. My own brother Hunk, f'rinstance. My brother John. Gentlemen—and Wentworths at that! Well, all this—d'you see what I mean? Five groups o' people, each with their own ax to grind. And they've all got a foot on the treadle. The makings of a damned fine squabble. They could tread you down while they're at it."

Johnnie put up his chin. "I'm not so sure. A grindstone's got four legs and a wheel, besides the treadle, but how far can it travel? Where can it get? Pshaw! People are always at odds with someone or something. It's human nature. In another year or two they'll have other brainstorms, and all this fuss, including Livius, will be forgotten."

"Then you think you've nothing to fear?" Mark said.

"Not here. I'm afraid of those gentlemen in London, though. God knows what they'll do over this Livius affair. I can only trust in my record and my friends."

The news came toward the middle of December, and Tom Macdonogh's letter was triumphant. There had been a further hearing, and this time the Lords of Trade and Plantation had found quite another verdict. He quoted their report to His Majesty in Council: "There is no foundation for any censure upon the said John Wentworth, Esq., Your Majesty's Governor of New Hampshire, for any of the charges contained in Mr. Livius's complaint against him."

A great crowd at the hearings, said Tom, including many American gentlemen from various colonies and even some visitors from the West Indies. The affair had made a sensation. Still, he added, there was a fly in the salve. To satisfy Mr. Livius's friends, and to hold things even in the province, Lord

Dartmouth had decided to make him Chief Justice of New Hampshire.

"Your friends here urge you to make the strongest representations against it, knowing what troubles this will cause. Mr. Livius remains here, thinking to sail for America in the spring with the appointment in his portmanteau."

Johnnie pulled his nose over that. There would be time to cook that goose of Peter's too. Just now there was the pleasure of serving up his first bird. Away went Johnnie's grooms, well mounted, with notes to pass among his friends. The news would burn his enemies' ears mighty soon after that.

And so the word of Johnnie's triumph flew about the province. In Portsmouth his friends arranged a grand dinner and ball at the Earl of Halifax tavern, and nine days before Christmas a crowd of the town's elite gathered to enjoy Stavers's food and wines. When the long room was cleared for dancing the fun went on for half the night. Stavers's fires and the energy of the dancers defeated the chill of a dark rainy night so utterly that windows had to be opened for air, and common fold standing in the mud outside could peer over each other's shoulders and watch as fine a show of happy gentility as could be seen anywhere in the colonies. What music, what laughter, what swishing and prancing of silks and satins and paduasoys, of ruffles and flounces and clocked silk stockings and nimble silver-buckled shoes! What a constant buzz about the great punch bowl, kept filled like the basin of an inexhaustible fountain, and what a continual raising of glasses to the Governor and his lady!

Fannie was in her element; now playing queen of Portsmouth with ease and dignity, now flirting with the best-looking gentlemen, now appeasing their wives with deft and sprightly compliments. Even those who disapproved her had to admit her looks and charm.

There were other goodlooking women in Portsmouth, and many in this room, but none had the exotic note of Mrs. Fannie's slanting eyes, the tilted nose, the pouting red lips with their strange little half-smile when she danced, the clean white flash of teeth whenever she laughed. Who could match that figure, supple as a willow switch and shapely as a nymph's? And where could anyone find such a delicious feminine wit? No wonder the gentlemen clustered to her like wild bees to meadowsweet. Four years as the Governor's lady had developed Mrs. Fannie in all ways, everyone agreed. It was as if she had been made for Johnnie's wife—as if Johnnie had found some sort of Sleeping Beauty beside Theo Atkinson's coffin and wakened her with a kiss.

Rolling home in the glass coach, wrapped in her warmest cloak and snuggling against "my Governor," she had never been so utterly delighted with herself or with life. And dear, good, handsome Johnnie! When they went to bed she was in his arms in a moment.

They slept late, and when Johnnie arose Fannie remained in bed, with a drowsy smile, watching him dress. He was gone about his affairs for the day when she arose at noon. The bedchamber fire had been lit long before and now warmed the room. She went to the glow of it, pulled off her chemise and threw it on the floor. Her maid was bustling to gather clothes and stockings and shoes for the day's wear, chattering about last night's affair, and how "right lovely" my lady had looked.

"What's your gossip?" Fannie yawned, turning her bottom to the fire. "You always have some."

"Oh nothing much, ma'am. I guess there was something a-doing in Boston last night—another of those rows they're always having. Some fellow brought the tale today from Exeter— they get Boston news there mighty prompt, it seems."

Another yawn from Fannie. "What was it this time? Broken heads or broken panes?"

"Oh, nothing like that. A crowd of men got 'emselves up as Indians and threw some merchant's tea in the harbor. Will you sit, ma'am, so I can slip your stockings on?—I've warmed the chair. A sinful waste, and there's the lor besides. They'll smart for that, we may be sure."

"And serve them right," said Fannie, sinking into the chair and putting out a white leg for the stocking.

Johnnie came home with a face of thunder at four o'clock in the afternoon, and she heard him swear at the groom for some fumble with the horse, a very strange thing for him. She greeted him with a wagging finger and a cry of "Temper! Temper!"

Her Governor snorted and threw his hat and cloak at the footman.

"D'you know what was going on in Boston last night—at the very time we were all so merry at the dance? Those rascals of Sam Adams went to the wharves and pitched three whole cargoes of tea in the harbor! Tea that belonged to the East India Company, lately out from England. I'm told there was a tide-rim of it this morning all along the shore from Griffin's Wharf to Dorchester."

"Another of those foolish Boston pranks."

"There'll be a piper to pay for this one, mark my words. In London the East India Company's well-nigh sacred. Gad, it's like setting fire to the Funds. I'm afraid the government's going to take a damned hot view of this prank, as you call it."

"Well, why not?"

"Hot men do rash things. And a rash move from London now is just what Sam Adams and his crew want badly. That's why they threw the tea overboard. Like throwing gunpowder at a candle. We used to play that game when I was a boy—we called it 'making lightning'—and I got my hide tanned for it more than once. There'll be a pretty tanning over this affair. Sam Adams is so sure of it that he's sent off messengers to warn the other colonies—amongst others, I'm told, that mischievous tinker of a Paul Revere is heading for New York and Philadelphia. And of course they sent word here by way of Exeter."

"Fiddle! What mischief can they do here, with you as Governor? You've kept New Hampshire out of trouble the past seven years."

"I wish I could say that of the next seven months." Johnnie's face was cloudy. "You don't understand politics, but I may as well tell you that in some ways we've been living in a fool's paradise. Ever since the Stamp Act there's been something itching the colonies. I don't know how else to describe it. A feeling that Americans are a different set of men from those in England. A separate tribe. Another creation somehow. As if they spoke a different language and had a different God and everything else. Something in the mind so far, you understand. I've even had the same feeling myself at times, and it's troubled me."

Fannie was only half listening. Her own mind was going over delightful memories of the ball.

"Those impudent rascals in Boston don't amount to much," Johnnie mused aloud. "Sam Adams himself failed in every business he ever tried and stole money as a tax collector. But suppose something should happen that set Americans in arms against the King. Even a few. With that feeling in the back of every other mind?"

"You're always dreaming nonsense," Fannie said.

For once he was angry with her. "Listen to me! Those men, those Sons of Liberty in Boston, they've arranged Committees of Correspondence all over the colonies, including every town and village of New Hampshire. Ours hold their meetings on the sly, but I hear about 'em. In Portsmouth they meet at the Bell, at the Freemasons' rooms, and half a dozen other places. The Assembly itself is one big Committee of Correspondence if rumor's even half true. A lot of these people are my friends— even two of my own uncles—so it's nothing against me as a person. The odd thing is, I'm a Whig myself by every instinct—most of my English friends are Whigs, from Lord Rockingham down. They're all against these pigheaded actions of Lord North and his Tory cabinet. And mark you, I was made Governor in the days when the Rockinghams and the other great Whig families had the power in London. Now they're out—but I'm still Governor, sworn to serve the King. You see? I'm a limb of a Tory King and a Tory government. So I must be abused, like a thief in the stocks, with every rotten thing that comes to hand. What do they want me to do? Resign my post? Under fire? They know me better than that. Besides, if I went, London would put Peter Livius in my place as sure as lightning in a thunderstorm—and what would follow then? A worse mess than Boston by a damned sight!"

"Stop shouting!" Fannie snapped. "Raise your voice to the servants as much as you like, Your Excellency, but spare me, if you please. You're making a tempest over nothing. All those silly men whispering and scratching letters, like boys at mischief, what can they do? Good heavens, you're the Governor, and you've got your militia. If the riffraff here start any real trouble you can call out your men and threaten to shoot. You did that once, years ago, remember? And you've had no trouble since."

Johnnie lowered his voice, but it had a sharp edge still. "I'm afraid you don't understand our situation, ma'am, and it's time you did. This is no matter of a drunken mob and a thief. It involves a lot of respectable people, including many of the militia— the militia that I've trained so carefully. A good many of the officers, the really able ones, are in the thick of these secret committees. Men like Colonel Nat Folsom and Major John Sullivan."

"But you've got officers like Colonel Fenton too."

"Their own companies would knock 'em down if it came to the pinch."

"What pinch?"

"An order to shoot at their friends."

"Pooh!"

"God's blood, Fan, try to get this in your pretty head. If it comes to pointing weapons here, they'll be turned our way, make no mistake. New Hampshire men don't flare up at a touch like those Boston townsmen of yours, that's why we've had quiet here so far. But I tell you if they ever decide to move against anyone or anything—the King included—they'll outdo all the rest. I've tramped and hunted and worked with 'em all my life, and I know. They can outmarch, outsuffer, outshoot, yes, and outwit any troops that could be brought against 'em. Mind you that's true of a great many other Americans, specially the backwoods men. Don't look so incredulous. You're thinking of those well-drilled redcoats in Boston. They'd be fine on a battlefield in Europe. Here, too, if the fighting was just about the towns. But the fighting wouldn't be just about the towns. Americans would choose to fight in the country, and the King's troops would have to carry the war there. God knows where or how it would end, but one thing's sure—it'd tear our own people apart. Men like John Sullivan in a civil war against men like me, and blood such as we've never seen before, not in all the French and Indian Wars put together. So, my dear girl, pray the pinch won't ever come. If it does, we're ruined, all of us."

Fannie sniffed. What a lot of gloomy nonsense! And so unlike Johnnie, always so cheerful and calm about everything.

"What you need just now isn't prayer," she said tartly.

"What, then?"

The familiar roguish smile.

"A spoonful of sulphur and molasses."

TWELVE

FOR MRS. FANNIE the winter and spring flew away in the social round. She was truly a creature of the indoors. Her spirit bloomed best in the season of fires and candles, when the easygoing gentry of Portsmouth drew together to pass the winter like a troop of lords and ladies in some old tale, storm-stayed at a wayside inn. Compared with that lively season Fannie found the summers dull and tiresome. The company scattered then and went visiting abroad, or riding or sailing or merely vegetating in their own shady gardens. There would be country parties at Wolfeborough, of course, but there were always gaps between, and then the days and nights were long, without even Johnnie's restless company half the time. Nothing to do but write long aimless letters to her friends, complaining of migraines and fevers and vague summer ills of other kinds, and never failing to mention the heat and mosquitoes and the tedium of the country life.

In May, with all this before her again, she discovered something else in store. When she was sure she counted off the months and uttered a cry of vexation. Pregnant—pregnant and swollen past all public shape by fall, in childbed the middle of January, and with a puling infant on her hands after that! All in the best time of the year! When she told Johnnie she tried to be arch about it—"Well, my jockey, here's news, and I trust you're proud of yourself"—but her face and voice held nothing but complaint. To make injury worse he met the news with a smile and an absent-minded kiss, and went off again, calling for groom and horse. He was always busy nowadays, too busy even to make his cherished spring journey to Wolfeborough. She rarely saw him except at meals, when he ate his food quickly and disappeared. There were long closed-door sessions with his secretary in the library, and others late at night, when she had gone to bed. Mysterious visitors came after dark, and she could recognize only Colonel Fenton's voice, and that of Bartholomew Stavers, the tavern man, who operated the flying-coach service on the King's Highway from Portsmouth to Boston.

She had been indifferent to Johnnie's official concerns for so long that all of this gave her nothing but a vague feeling of annoyance. On a day in June, when even the house dogs were listless, when the harbor and the Kittery shore were quivering in the heat, her Governor flung himself off a horse in the lane. He came running into the house in his riding boots and calling for Tom Macdonogh. In a moment they were in the library. Fannie put aside her book, glanced right and left to make sure that none of the servants were in sight, and stole in her silk shoes to the library door. It was ajar.

"Take this down," Johnnie was saying, "and fair copy it. When I've signed the fair copy you'll take it at once to the Assembly and present it to the Speaker." He began to dictate, and she heard Tom's quill scratching rapidly.

Mr. Speaker and Gentlemen of the Assembly:

As I look upon the measures entered upon by the House of Assembly to be inconsistent with His Majesty's service and the good of this Government, it is my duty, as far as in me lies, to prevent any detriment that might arise from such proceedings. I do, therefore, hereby dissolve the General Assembly of this Province, and it is dissolved accordingly.

Portsmouth, June 8, 1774.

More scratching, while Johnnie's spurs chinked up and down the floor. Then, "Done? The pen if you please." And then, "Clap my seal on the wax and be off with you. My horse is saddled in the lane."

She moved away a few steps as the young Irishman darted out, document in hand. In a wink she was inside the study and shutting the door at her back.

"Johnnie, what are you up to?"

"Hello, my dear. Eh? Oh, business—just business."

"What business? What's the meaning of all this rushing and fussing, and midnight callers, and heaven knows what, the past six weeks?"

Johnnie cocked an ironical brow. "Why this sudden interest?"

"If I were any other wife in my condition I'd say you and your friends were up to no good, and women in it somewhere."

He stared at her for a moment. Then a smile melted the set lines of his face. He broke into a long shout of laughter, leaning back against his desk and grasping the edge with his hands. And then, as suddenly as it came, the humor vanished.

"I'm up to no good for certain people, but they're all men, so far as I can see. D'you really want to know?"

"Of course I do."

"Well, sit down. It's a story that'll tire you, standing up. God knows it's tired me. You'll remember back in May I was about to set off for Wolfeborough. Then something changed my mind. I learnt that the Sons of Liberty, or Sons of Freedom as some call themselves, were up to something new. There's to be a gathering of delegates from all the American colonies, a congress as they call it, at Philadelphia next fall."

"What for?"

"To get the whole country into Sam Adams's stew at Boston. You don't follow these things, but last March the British Government passed a bill to punish those Bostonians of yours for their tea party. They took away from Boston the courts of justice, the customs, in fact all government offices, and removed 'em to Salem. In fact they've closed the port of Boston for good measure. And those gentlemen in London are determined to enforce their Act. They're sending troops and warships, and they've recalled Governor Hutchinson and put a soldier, General Gage, in his place. In short they've done everything that Sam Adams and his Liberty boys could have wished for. The whole damned thing went into effect the first of this month. All Boston's in a roar, of course, and this so-called congress is to make sure the roar is heard clear down to Florida."

"What's that got to do with dismissing our Assembly?"

Again that ironical brow. "Eavesdropping, Fannie? Tut! Well, you might as well know. Our Assembly, including the Speaker—my own namesake, Colonel John Wentworth of Salmon Falls, more's the pity—appear to be Sons of Freedom almost to a man. Today, if you please, they were going to choose delegates for Philadelphia, which is certainly not the business of His Majesty's Assembly. So I dismissed the session."

"Well! What next!"

"My dear, I can tell you exactly. They'll call a meeting in the Town House—as private individuals, you understand—for the same purpose. Tomorrow or the next day perhaps. And I shall go in person, as Governor, to tell 'em, as amiably as I can, that they can't hold such a meeting in a government building."

"And what then?"

Johnnie's strong lips had a whimsical twist. "They'll hold their meeting in a tavern, where I can't say a word. And there they'll pick their delegates."

"Then why bother about them doing it in the Assembly?"

"My duty—just my duty."

"You mean to say you can't really stop them?"

"No more than I could stop the tide with a finger. What's to prevent a peaceful traveler going to Philadelphia?"

Fannie inspected his face. Something's changed, she thought. I can't read his mind any more.

"When shall we be leaving for Wolfeborough?"

"Not for some time yet. I've another little problem in the offing. A mast-ship called the *Grosvenor*. She's due from England any day."

"What problem is that? Anyone can load masts."

"She happens to have aboard some chests of East India Company tea, consigned to Mr. Parry. He's somewhat rash, I think. There'll be a tea party at Spring Market Wharf if I can't find a way to avoid it. Some clerk in Parry's countinghouse has let his tongue wag, and everyone's watching for the ship."

As it chanced, the *Grosvenor* was delayed by weather, and the Portsmouth watch was long, but she turned up toward the end of June and anchored below the town. In a few minutes the word ran through the streets. Men gathered in groups outside the taverns, and a mingled scent of rum and mischief hung in the air. Some went off to watch the movements of the Governor, sure that he would try to muster a guard when the tea was to be landed.

One of his movements they missed. Edward Parry's mansion lay only a short way along Pleasant Street from the Governor's, and both gardens went down the back slope to South Pond. It was an easy matter for Johnnie to stroll along the pond shore in the screen of trees and confer with the merchant in his garden.

He found Parry cold and stubborn. "I'm a merchant engaged in legal importation, and no mob is going to frighten me out of it, Johnnie. You're Governor and you must secure order."

"How? Call out the militia? They'd only help the mob throw your tea in the harbor. The first thing is to get the stuff safely ashore and locked up in the Customs house. And peaceably, my friend."

"How d'you propose to do that?"

"By an innocent little ruse. They're all watching me. So tomorrow I'll ride up the river for a sociable call in Dover. That night you'll bring in your ship and whisk your tea ashore. Colonel Fenton and a few other gentlemen that we can trust will stand guard over the Customs house, and I'll come in from Dover in the morning."

"What happens after that?"

"We'll see."

The ruse worked very well indeed, but when Johnnie rode into the Parade next day he found it buzzing with men. He moved among them in his genial way, calling out greetings and pausing to chat in the saddle. They were mostly workmen and tradesmen of all kinds, but he was quick to notice among them a good many of the merchants, with their clerks and warehousemen. Whenever he asked, smiling, "And what are you doing here on a busy day?" the answer was a chorus. They wouldn't see the tea tax paid in Portsmouth, not they, no more than the Boston folk. The voices were civil, but there was no mistaking the undertone.

To the chief group he said at last, "Gentlemen, let's have no disorder here. The tea's under guard at the Customs house, and I intend to keep it so. I promise you not an ounce shall be removed for sale without my permission. I'm on my way to consult with Mr. Parry now."

And off he went. When he entered Parry's countinghouse he wasted no words.

"Ned, you'll have to give up any notion of selling that tea. You've seen the crowd in the Parade? Well, I've talked to 'em, and you haven't got a chance. One move to put the tea on sale and they'll storm the Customs house and burn your warehouse into the bargain. Any attempt to stop 'em would just mean bloodshed to no purpose—and the end of everything I've worked for, the past seven years."

"Then what am I to do with the tea? Ship it back to the East India Company? If so I'll have to tell 'em why, and you know what'll follow. D'you want a Port Bill here, the same as Boston?"

"Not at all. So you'll ship the tea away up the coast to Nova Scotia—our troubles don't seem to reach that far—ship it on consignment to some merchant in Halifax, say. I must have your promise to do it in the next four-and-twenty hours, so I can tell the people."

Parry was indignant, but Johnnie was not to be moved. Nor was he moved by Colonel Fenton at the Customs house. That lively and peppery Englishman was all for a fight, both for Parry's tea and His Majesty's law. He had ridden in from his country place, scenting trouble and armed with sword and pistols, the moment he got Johnnie's note to "pass a lively day or two with me in town."

When Fenton rode home, still snorting, the tea chests had been loaded into a schooner for Halifax and were on the way out of the harbor. And now the Governor could set off with his lady for Wolfeborough at last. They made a familiar procession on the Governor's Road: Johnnie riding ahead, then Fannie and her maid in a light carriage with strong pig-yoke springs, and then a pair of mounted grooms, each leading a horse with a lady's side-saddle for the final rough stretch over Moose Mountain. Fannie rode a good seat a-horseback. She had mastered that since her marriage, chiefly because it enabled her to show forth the fashionable riding habits in which her slim figure looked so well. But she dreaded the lonely mountain trail with its mudholes and boulders and its shaky poles over the streams, which hard-riding Johnnie took as a matter of course. She was always thankful when the track came down the farther slope and the pine woods opened into the Mall, with the civilized comforts of the big house before her and the servants and dogs running out to welcome them.

Once settled, she faced the summer with resignation. This year at least she had her Governor close at hand. No sailing up the coast, no feckless ventures into the mountains. He busied himself about the estate from morn to night, working fiercely with his hands when he was not in the saddle, as if an excess of energy and sweat could dissolve some nagging shadow in his mind. A succession of riders from Portsmouth carried the post-bag, and whenever it came he sat late by candlelight, poring over letters and newspapers.

He said little to Fannie of their contents. Late in July he remarked that the Sons of Liberty had set up a sort of provincial congress at Exeter, and had chosen Colonel Folsom and Major Sullivan, that country lawyer, to speak for New Hampshire at Philadelphia. He offered no comment. The parties of guests who came out from Portsmouth were not so many now, nor were they so gay and talkative as in the past. A strange new tension of the times was pulling the gentry apart, and the more cautious ones—a surprising number to Fannie—seemed to avoid Wentworth House as if too close an acquaintance there were dangerous. Some old close friends like Woodbury Langdon were actually hostile. And now Peter Livius was back in New

Hampshire, without the post of Chief Justice, hobnobbing with John and Woodbury Langdon and working his mischief as busily as ever.

At the summer's end persistent Mr. Parry tried again with East India Company tea. This time there were thirty chests of it aboard the mast-ship *Fox*. Johnnie rode in from Wolfe-borough to find the town in another uproar and a crowd stoning not only the panes of Parry's countinghouse but those of his mansion, a bare musket shot from Johnnie's own. It was strange and disturbing to find a shouting rabble from the docks up here among the quiet trees and mansions of Pleasant Street. Again Johnnie obtained order, this time by a frank appeal at a town meeting, and again the offensive tea went off to Nova Scotia.

When Johnnie got back to Wolfeborough, Fannie asked, "If things did get really bad, how many men could you count on?"

Johnnie called a roll in his head. It took some time.

"Less than a hundred."

"In all New Hampshire, I mean."

"So do I. Does that surprise you? I'm no Messiah, but I've got my betrayer—Judas Livius—and most of my disciples will deny me when the pinch comes."

"Don't say that! It's not true and it's—it's blasphemous."

"Well, I'll put it a longer way. This coming congress at Philadelphia means a warm feeling in all the colonies for Boston. You can see why. If the King's ministers can close up the port of Boston they could close any port in America. Mean-while they're pouring soldiers into Boston by the thousand—an army, not just a garrison. You know what happened in Boston when the troops were there before. Blood on the cobbles. This time, if there's a clash, the blood'll be on the moon. Because this time the Boston men won't be alone. And that's when the pinch will come, for me and every other governor in America. What's to support me here? My regular force is a Portsmouth joke—Captain Cochrane and four or five uneasy men in the old harbor fort. The militia? You can see the mind of the militia when they send their own officers to the congress. These fellows, these Sons of Liberty, they're a minority in New Hampshire but a strong one. On the other hand, the men that'll stand by the King—we're mighty few. Most of our people are in the middle, rich and poor alike. They don't know what to think. When they see the pinch coming they'll stand aside—a lot are doing it already—till they see what's to come out of all this. My own kin with the rest. Oh yes! And I don't blame 'em, really. Maybe I'd do the same in their place, specially if I was a merchant like Father, say, with a lot to lose."

"Heavens, Johnnie, you talk as if you stood to lose nothing."

"Ah, but there's something more important than property in my case. I gave my oath to serve the King and the people of New Hampshire. If the people do reject me there's still the other half of the bond. My word's involved. My honor, if you like." Johnnie glanced at her and smiled. "Do I sound like a play actor? Maybe I could make a trade of it if the worst came to the worst."

An impatient cluck from his spouse. "Sometimes I don't know what to make of you, Johnnie. Do you really believe all this?"

"I only tell you what I fear. I hope for the best of course. Maybe it'll all blow over—a tempest in Sam Adams's teapot. Who knows?"

Frequently the postbag contained heavily sealed letters from General Gage. For the most part they were routine things that went to all the governors, telling them of affairs in Boston and the measures he was taking, but usually there was a postscript in the general's own hand, inquiring the health of Johnnie and his lady, and hoping to see them again over a good dinner when all this bother was past. Johnnie knew Gage fairly well and had some hope in him. A middle-aged soldier, long stationed in America and married to a Boston woman. He had fought against the French and Indians and was well liked by Americans. A bit old-fashioned in the military art perhaps, but an affable man who didn't like his present job at all and was anxious to have peace.

In September he wrote to Johnnie with a casual request. He'd been obliged to quarter many of his troops on the townspeople, a bad situation. He was anxious to get proper barracks up in time for winter, but there was a lack of carpenters—Boston carpenters seemed unwilling or afraid to work for him. Could Johnnie provide a few? He was asking other governors to do the same.

Johnnie sat long over the letter. It was an order, of course, couched in Gage's polite way. Something he could not refuse. But where to get the men? He thought of the tea crowd in the Portsmouth square. Most of the carpenters had been there. They had swarmed up in their aprons straight from the shipyards. The same would have been true in any of the up-tide towns. Inland, then. Exeter? A hotbed of the Liberty men. Rochester? Maybe Rochester. He sent for Nicholas Austin of that town, a capable man. Austin had recruited good workmen for him in the past, building the house at Wolfeborough.

But when Austin came he was dubious. "We've got a Committee of Correspondence in Rochester now, and among 'em some pretty feverish men. They talk of those sogers in Boston as a preacher talks of the devil."

Johnnie pinched his nose and considered. Rochester was halfway up the road to Wolfeborough. This thing was spreading like a fever too. Still, it hadn't reached through the woods to Wolfeborough. Not yet, anyhow.

"Well, Nicholas, what about our settlers here? They're all handy men with carpenters' tools—they have to be. General Gage is offering good wages, and money's hard to come by, here in the backwoods."

"That's true, sir, God knows. Well, why not? The settlers hereabouts have their crops in now, and their winter's wood. A couple o' months' wages in Boston'd suit 'em handsome. I'll see what I can do. How many d'ye want?"

"Not many. The general's getting men from other directions too. Say fifteen."

"Right, sir. I can get fifteen easy."

And easy it was. The Wolfeborough men departed happily for Boston, and for three weeks Johnnie worked away in peace and solitude. Then one day, as he rode to look at the little mill on the Rye Brook, a lean figure in buckskins stepped out of the cedar thickets. An old man with a long straggle of white hair, one of Johnnie's guides in the mountains, and a veteran of Rogers's Rangers in the old war.

"Hello, Cephas," Johnnie said. "It's odd to see you without the long rifle in your hands and the tomahawk in your belt. You look naked."

"Just come from Portsmouth. Bin to see my marrit daughter."

"She's well, I take it?"

"Never mind her, Governor. Ye've got trouble back there." He jerked a thumb over his shoulder.

"How?"

"Over them carpenters ye sent to Gage. Portsmouth's crawlin' like a nest o' rattlesnakes. Ways an' Means Committee held a meetin'—your own Uncle Hunk was chairman—an' passed some mighty hot resolutions agin ye. Resolved ye were 'an enemy to the community.' Resolved your conduct was 'cruel an' unmanly.' Lot more like that. Every time they resolved somethin' the hull crowd screeched like Abenaki at a war dance. Every man an' boy in town, seemed like. Watch your scalp."

"I think I can keep my hair up here," Johnnie smiled.

"Not so sure. Come through Rochester last night. Crowd there. Had Nick Austin down on his knees in the middle, beggin' fer his life. Made him 'pologize fer gittin' ye the carpenters. Made him promise to tell 'em to come home. They better too."

"Why?"

"Some talk o' comin' out to Wolfeborough an' puttin' fire to their houses. Teach 'em to carpenter closer home. Yours too."

"If they try that game they'll meet another kind of fire,

I promise you. I've got a good eye for a rifle myself." The old man was moving off. "Hold a moment, Cephas. You mountain men—what d'you think of all this business?"

The old man spat on the grass and stirred the spittle with his moccasin.

"Dunno what to make of it. Liberty? Got that naow. Anybody tries to interfere with us—York men, King's men, no matter who 'tis—we'll make 'em sorry."

"Um. Well, give my respects to Ethan Allen when you see him. Brother Ira, too, and Seth Warner. I hope to have another good crack with 'em over a bottle the next time I'm in the mountains."

"I'll do thet, Governor."

And he was gone like a shadow in the woods.

It was October now, and the frosts had made the usual gaudy splatter on the landscape about Johnnie's lake. As always the scarlet was most prominent. One morning, sitting his horse under the monarch pine on Mount Delight, Johnnie had a queer twinge of thought. The clumps of maple and sumac on the slopes, the wide patches of huckleberry by the shore, all shone with a night's dew and the morning sun. And they shone like pools of blood. As he turned slowly in the saddle all the hills were smeared with it, as if the whole countryside were bleeding from mysterious wounds. At that moment the horse shuddered, perhaps from the nip of some belated fly, and the shudder ran through the rider's knees and thighs. On a sudden impulse he spurred away down the path to Wentworth House.

Until this moment he had resolved to stay until mid-November, despite Fannie's protest that the trail over Moose Mountain would be slippery with the first snow and every brook a torrent. He had a deep reluctance to return to Portsmouth. It was not fear for himself but a foreboding that his appearance might be the signal for an explosion of some kind. While he remained in the country there was no way of discharge for this wild hate in so many of the people, which he still could not understand. What had he done in seven years that was not for their good?

He had slaved for them the whole of that time. And now what was his offense? Refusing to allow unlawful business in the Assembly? Everybody knew the law. Everybody knew he was bound to uphold it. Finding some work for a few poor carpenters? What was wrong with that?

It all seemed like a dreary nightmare, from which he still hoped to awake. Meanwhile in the fantastic manner of nightmares the ordinary things of life went along side by side with the grotesque. The courts of justice, the routine of the militia drills, the work on the roads, the grants of land, the thousand and one details of his administration went on just the same. The postbags brought him the usual stream of reports to be read, the documents to be signed or rejected. Regularly he wrote his dispatches to the Lords of Trade and his official letters to General Gage. Regularly he kept up his correspondence with Lord Rockingham, Sir Tom Wentworth, Paul Wentworth, and other friends of America in England. And the other things. He had urged the Reverend Jeremy Belknap to begin a history of New Hampshire, and now the manuscript of Belknap's first volume came to him for reading and suggestions. So it was, too, with Captain Sam Holland, still working on his map of the province, indeed settled in the province and consulting the Governor on this point and that.

Like a shadow of this outward and visible government, functioning in all its detail, lay the new provincial body at Exeter, with a committee in every parish. As with Uncle Hunk's committee at Portsmouth they were turning now from mere "Correspondence" to the more ominous "Ways and Means." In a letter to Lord Rockingham Johnnie excused his uncle as a "superannuated weak old squire, already forgiven," and blamed the carpenter fuss on a combination of Peter Livius and Woodbury Langdon.

But when he rode into Portsmouth at the end of October, with the streets deep in mud and a sea wind blowing the last leaves from the elms and maples and birches, he could see a change in the people beyond any mischief of two men. Only a few workmen touched their hats to him, and these quickly and furtively, with a glance up and down the street. Most gave him a stare and made no answer when he spoke. Some knots of idlers sent catcalls after Fannie in the carriage behind.

In the house on Pleasant Street his major-domo greeted him nervously. The servants were uneasy. Some had gone. For months past they had been afraid to go into the town, where the mere sight of Johnnie's livery brought threats and sometimes blows from the street roughs. Meanwhile Fannie's young brother Benning had come from Boston and was staying in the house. She greeted him with an ecstatic cry—"My darling little brother!"—although the boy was seventeen and tall. He had her own features, indeed he looked like Fannie at that age, as if the naive bride of Theo Atkinson had turned up as a ghost in breeches.

The boy had bad news, startling news. Well-to-do Tory families were fleeing into Boston from the Massachusetts countryside with tales of persecution by roving gangs of Liberty boys. Only the out-and-out Whig gentry were safe. There seemed to be no law or order or even common humanity for a Tory anywhere in Massachusetts outside the ring of Gage's bayonets; and even inside the town there was doubt, with the sullen mass of townsmen out of work and ripe for trouble. Some of the Boston Tories were sailing away to visit England until matters eased— the painter man Copley was one of them. Indeed a tour of England and the continent was suddenly popular, and Johnnie learned now that some of Portsmouth's own Tories, like old Colonel Boyd, who had made a fortune in shipbuilding, were taking passage overseas. Yet things were not bad in Portsmouth. No Tory house had been pillaged, no Tory hurt. Whatever their politics, the gentry and the middle-class folk wanted no such antics here, and their influence was strong. They've got to back me, Johnnie thought. They can't risk a whirlwind that may blow 'em all away.

THIRTEEN

ON A DECEMBER AFTERNOON of 1774 Fannie lay on a couch before her sitting-room fire, hating the sight of herself, bloated and hideous, with still more than a month to go. And now in addition to the lassitude and discomfort she was afraid. She had put that other childbed nightmare out of mind long ago, as she had put aside the memory of Theo and everything else that was dull or unpleasant, but now it crept back with all its terrors and set her shuddering. And it was small comfort that her Governor gave her much more attention now that her time drew near.

The first delicate snowfalls had relieved his other concerns. Most of the shipping was laid up for the winter, the roads would soon be snowbound, and the quarrels of Boston and the intrigues of the Liberty boys in New Hampshire must bow down to the weather like everything else. On this dark chill day, with ice tinkling on the reeds about the edges of South Pond and a clean cloth of snow on the slopes, the world had closed in comfortably about the house on Pleasant Street.

Johnnie came out of his library and bent over her with a kiss.

"How are you, love?"

"Wretched."

"It'll be all over soon."

"That's easy for you to say."

"I know," he said humbly. And infected somehow by her inward panic he fell on his knees and took her cold hands in his.

"Oh, darling Fan, I love you so." His eyes drowned in sudden tears. He was actually trembling. He wanted to cry out, "Don't die, Fan, don't leave me, ever!" But he shut the cry away in his mind, where it went on, echo after echo, like a cry on a still night in the mountains. Fannie gave him a faint smile, tolerant, a little contemptuous, as if he were a guilty boy afraid of punishment for his crime. She felt the child stir in her belly. For something to say she asked without interest, "What do you want, a boy or a girl?"

"I want you."

"You have me. What else do you want?"

"A boy, I suppose. Yes—a boy."

Fannie turned her eyes to the ceiling. He had never said a word of that first child, not since he saw it buried in a small white box on Chapel Hill. But he dreamed of another son of course. A son to carry on his name and some day to be Governor of the greater New Hampshire he was making. As if the Wentworth dynasty must go on forever, along with all his other wonderful dreams.

"And if it's a girl?" she said.

"She'll be clever and beautiful, like you."

She was a little mollified. "She'll probably be a minx like me. But never mind. I'm only twenty-eight. There'll be time for a son too." She did not feel half as brave as that. The notion of going through all this again revolted her. And yet, seeing "my Governor" on his knees, with this frantic emotion in his eyes, she felt pity for him. Poor Johnnie, he does love me, in spite of all that stupid mania for his work. Whatever would he do without me? He'd never find another woman like me. He wouldn't even try. He's so loyal in everything. One king, one province, one woman. If he ever has a coat of arms, that should be on it.

Johnnie's head was bowed over her hands, touching them with his lips, and she was still looking upon him with that almost maternal gaze, when there was a sharp rat-tat-tat from the street door knocker and a rasping of snowy boots on the foot scraper outside. Several men came into the hall, and Johnnie arose hastily and went out to them. Through the sitting-room doorway Fannie could see grim old Mark Wentworth and the Chief Justice, well muffled against the cold, and she could hear the voices of Bart Stavers, the postrider, and others harder to define. They wasted no time about their business. Old Mark burst out, "Johnnie, why the devil did you send to Gage for troops?"

"Troops?" Johnnie snapped. "What are you talking about?"

"All hell's to pay! Paul Revere's at Sam Cutts's house—must have ridden like the wind—sixty miles over these winter roads."

"Well? Well?"

"He's come from the Boston committee. They say you sent to Gage for soldiers, and he's about to ship two regiments."

"Pooh! They lie. Soldiers?—the last thing I'd want on my hands here. That fellow Revere's had his gallop for nothing but a sore backside, I give you my word."

The Chief Justice spoke. "I'm afraid it's not as simple as that."

"Eh?"

"Sam Cutts has called his Committee of Ways and Means. Sullivan's rousing Durham and Exeter. In fact messengers are off to all the up-tide villages, and to the fishermen at Newcastle and Rye. There's mischief brewing."

"What?"

"I hear a crowd's to be drummed up to go to the Castle, and they aim to remove all the powder in the magazine before the King's troops get here."

"Ha! I'll send a warning to Captain Cochrane at once."

"D'you think five men and a boy in that crazy ruin can hold off a mob of fanatics?" This in the voice of practical George Meserve, the shipbuilder.

"Why not?" Johnnie said. "The fort's got walls and a gate, and Cochrane's cannon and muskets are in good condition—I've seen to that."

He stepped away to his desk to scrawl the note to Cochrane. Fannie lay ignored and indignant while the men muttered together in the hall. In another minute they had passed outside, and Johnnie was clapping on hat and cloak to follow them. Through the doorway he gave her a glance, an unspoken message of apology, and was gone.

His mind was back to business now. The "troops" were

another of those Boston canards of course. Anything to stir up trouble in the countryside. And possibly they wanted the Portsmouth powder for their own concerns. Well, Cochrane could take care of that. He crossed over the lane to the stables and sent off a groom with the message.

The next day was bright but sharply cold, even at high noon. And about that time a group of men appeared in the town parade, one beating a militia drum. They marched on through the thin snow of the streets, shouting at doors and windows, and gathering a long tail of men as they went, all armed with guns or cutlasses or clubs.

Mark Wentworth brought word of this, and Johnnie promptly sent across the Puddle bridge for Mr. Atkinson.

"You must go and read the Riot Act," he said crisply. "I'll come with you—— Grimes, bring my sword and saddle cloak. We must stop this nonsense before it gets out of hand."

"You keep your face out o' this, Johnnie," his father growled. "Those people believe the redcoats are coming—and that you're the man who sent for 'em, that you're the man who'll quarter the soldiers on 'em and all the rest of it. They're as mad as hornets, and the sight o' you can only provoke 'em to something we'd all be sorry for. No, Johnnie, let Mr. Atkinson go alone. He's the Chief Justice, and they know he's fair. They won't molest him, whatever else they do. Go on, Thode, go on down there! Read the Act from the Town House steps, and then appeal to their common sense. No redcoats are coming. You can give 'em Johnnie's word for that. But if they persist in this folly and take the powder, we'll have Gage on our necks in no time, just like Boston. Tell 'em that."

Johnnie was doubtful, but Mr. Atkinson said in his thin mild voice, "It's the wisest course, Your Excellency," and away he went. Half an hour later the old man was back in his coach, defeated and pinched with the cold.

"They wouldn't listen to me. Not a word."

So Johnnie set forth himself, sworded and booted and spurred, with a pair of horse pistols in the saddle holsters. He found the streets empty. The crowd had vanished toward the docks. Furiously he rode from home to home of his own provincial officials, and of the customs officers and the other King's men who had drawn their pay so long and comfortably. He would raise at least one resolute platoon among them, armed with their own swords and pistols, to confront the mob before this mischief went further. But they shrank away from him at the mere suggestion, their minds filled with that sight of the angry crowd pouring through the streets. At the end exactly nine, including Tom Macdonogh and the eager boy Benning, were gathered at his house. So small a company was worthless, and he dismissed them. Mark had already gone home, and so had Mr. Atkinson.

From the upper windows he and Macdonogh peered with a spyglass toward the gray harbor and the long bulk of Newcastle Island. There seemed to be much activity on the water with boats and gundalows. About midafternoon they heard three cannon shots from the east, where the old fort stood invisible at the far tip of the island.

It was dark before they knew what had happened. Captain Cochrane himself appeared at the back door, a stout man with eyes still popping from the afternoon's adventure, and very short of breath. He had shed his blue uniform coat and silver-braided hat for the rough dress of a fisherman.

"Cochrane!" snapped Johnnie. "How did you get here? A brandy, there, quickly!"

The captain drank the brandy at a gulp and wiped his mouth. "Slipped across by boat to Little Harbor and borrowed a horse from Mr. Wentworth there. Left the horse in a field beyond your pond—had to cross over the stream by Titus Salter's dam, and he's a hot Liberty man."

"Well, what's happened?"

"Could I have another brandy, sir? 'Twas a long way around the creeks, and mortal cold."

"Another brandy, there! Go on, man, go on!"

"Well, sir, I got your note, and we stood guard at once, all six of us. About three o'clock in the afternoon they came along the island road from the direction of Newcastle village. A mad lot, I tell you, about four hundred as near as we could judge. Yelled at us to open the gate. Said they'd come for the powder, and they'd have it with or without our blood, we could take our choice. We fired off three of the cannon, warning-like. But they just slipped aside amongst all those wild rocks and ledges out there—you know what it's like—and crept forward on all sides, even amongst the boulders on the shore. Well, the Castle's a poor thing—never built against an attack by land, as you know. The embrasures all aim to the harbor channel, and besides the walls are low and old and ready to fall down."

"You had muskets," Johnnie said accusingly.

"Ah! Well, sir, we fired a few musket shots over the gate, but we didn't hit a soul. By that time they were at the other walls, climbing on each others' shoulders, and in a moment the whole crowd was inside and upon us."

"Well?"

The captain looked glum. "What could we do—six men against four hundred? They were all screaming like Indians and armed with all kinds of weapons. So we—well, sir, we just dropped our guns. Someone took away my sword. They put a guard over us, and some fellows hauled down the flag and threw it on the ground—the King's color, sir!—as if it were an old rag that they'd finished with. I'd locked the magazine. They demanded the key, but I swore I didn't know where 'twas. Well, sir, they'd come prepared for that. They had axes and crowbars, and it didn't take 'em long to break through the door. Next minute they were rolling powder casks out through the gate and down to the shore."

"How much did they take?"

"All there was, sir. Pretty nigh a hundred casks. I watched 'em transfer the stuff to a pair of gundalows they brought down the channel. Altogether they were at it about an hour and a half. By that time the tide had turned, and they sailed the gundalows up the harbor on the flow. They'd picked their time very neat."

"You weren't hurt, it seems. Were any of your men?"

"No, sir, they didn't molest us, though some threatened us and gave us some pretty nasty names afore they left. But Mr. John Langdon—he seemed to be one of the leaders, him and Tom Pickering and Pierce Long—Mr. Langdon said they'd no quarrel with us. Said the powder belonged to the province, and they were just making sure those bloody-backed soldiers of Gage didn't get it."

"What have they done with it, d'you suppose?"

"I heard 'em talkin' amongst 'emselves. The powder's going to one of the up-tide towns. They plan to keep it safe and dry under a meetinghouse somewhere, Squamscot, probably. That's handy to Exeter, and there were some Exeter men amongst 'em that seemed to have a lot of say."

"I thought as much," Johnnie said. "Did they take any cannon?"

"No, sir. They didn't even touch the muskets—sixty stand of arms. All they seemed to have in their minds was the powder— that and the tide. They kept watching to seaward for the King's ships. Seemed in a great hurry at the last."

"Where are your men now?"

"Still in the fort."

"Umph. Well, Cochrane, you'd better sup and stay the night here. Tomorrow you must get back to your post."

Supper was a silent affair, with Johnnie brooding at the head of the table, Fannie watching him from the foot, and Macdonogh, Cochrane, and young Benning busy with food. At the end of it Johnnie called Macdonogh into the library.

"Tom, I fear I must ask some kind of force from Boston after all. Without that I've no power here whatever."

The secretary's Irish humor sprang to his lips at once. "One regiment or two, sir? Better make it two, or Paul Revere's a liar."

Johnnie was in no mood for quips. "No, no! I'll have no soldiers in the town—they'd be into the taverns and brawling with our own tosspots in no time, just like Boston. What I want is a warship or two, with say a hundred marines aboard, so everyone can see I've got force at hand if I need it. I'll keep 'em anchored in the harbor—not a man allowed ashore except the officers. These hotheads of ours will cool fast enough when they see I'm not helpless any more, and by the same view I should be able to rouse a better spirit in our gentlemen. The great thing is to keep order with our own hands, while the sailors and marines do nothing more than consume their beef and biscuit in the river. Take your pen and ink. I want a letter to Gage first, and then one to Admiral Graves."

With the letters signed and sealed, Johnnie sent for Bart Stavers, and that alert brown man set off at once, riding through the night to Boston. The next day, in boots, breeches, and scarlet coat, and with a warm green riding coat over all, Governor Johnnie rode slowly and alone through the streets. The loungers at the street corners and outside the taverns hushed their voices, as he passed, and offered not a single insult at his back. There was a look of uneasiness in every face. They were expecting the redcoat regiments any hour now—and so apparently was he.

Near the old North Church he came upon a smart new coach, with Michael Wentworth's coat of arms on the doors, and Mrs. Michael stepping out of it wrapped in a fur-trimmed cloak of London cloth that must have cost a pretty sum. She was turning toward a shop when he rode up and flourished his hat.

"A good day to you, Martha. We haven't met in a long time. You're well, I see."

She flushed. "Very well, thank you, Johnnie."

"And the little daughter?"

Martha smiled with the instant pleasure of a doting mama. "Fat and beautiful."

"And where's my old friend Michael?"

Her eyes went toward the Bell tavern and flicked back again. "I'm not sure, but he's to meet me at the coach in a few minutes." She nodded in her shy way and went on, picking her way through the snow on a pair of small iron pattens, strapped to her shoes.

Johnnie swung his horse toward the Bell and met Colonel Michael coming out of the door. Michael nodded and moved on toward the town pump where the coachman was busy with bucket and trough. Johnnie dismounted and walked along with him, leading the horse by the reins.

"Thanks, Michael, for getting Cochrane to me."

"Nothin', Johnnie, nothin' at all." The soldier, with two or three quick drams of the Bell's rum under his skin, seemed to be in cheerful trim.

"Michael, there's a matter I want to talk to you about. You know what happened at the Castle yesterday. These are warm times. I expect one or two of His Majesty's ships here shortly with a company of marines, but I don't intend to use 'em except as a warning. After all, most of our people want order, whatever their politics, and we should be able to keep it ourselves, eh?"

"What's in your mind, Johnnie?"

"I can't depend on the militia—too many of 'em had a connection with that Castle affair. What I want is a troop of mounted gentlemen who can muster quickly if there's need, each providing his own horse and weapons. I think I can raise fifty or sixty here in Portsmouth. And I must have a commander with military experience and one who knows the country roundabout."

"What about Fenton?"

"Fenton lives too far outside. Besides, I prefer to have him where he is. He's loyal and outspoken, afraid of nothing, and up Plymouth way he's exerting himself to keep the country people on the side of law and order. No, Michael, the man I want is you."

Colonel Michael's ruddy face betrayed a deeper flush. He halted before speaking, and then turned his gaze past Johnnie, as if he saw something of interest far away.

"If it comes to the point you'll fight, eh, you and these gentlemen-riders?"

"If we're pushed to it, yes," Johnnie said.

"You don't really think you could stop all these Whiggish fellers—I mean if they took a warlike turn of mind? I'm not thinkin' of those wild clowns at the Castle yesterday—town idlers an' fishermen an' such. I mean all the able fellers of a Whiggish turn upcountry, the mastmen and the backwoods farmers an' rangers. 'Cause they'd all be in it, at the first snap of a flint, with active an' darin' fellers like Jack Sullivan or Ethan Allen to lead 'em. You must know that yourself."

"This is no time to be guessing odds," Johnnie said stiffly.

"Johnnie, I'll be frank with you. I served His Majesty in my time and got beggarly thanks. And now by chance, by no grace of His Majesty or anyone else, I'm nicely set up in America. I've got my cake, and I can eat it too. Now, dead men have poor appetite. Why should I risk either cake or appetite for some notion that don't concern me? Hey? I don't care a fig's end how this business goes, or who's top dog at the finish, so long as I'm out of it."

Johnnie swallowed a sharp reply. It occurred to him that Michael might be sulky over that business of Old Benning's woodlands—Martha's by inheritance.

"My dear Michael," he said evenly. "This isn't merely a matter of property. It's a matter of principle. What property will be safe—what cake if you like—if these levelers have their way? It's a question of who's to rule, the King and his governor or some noisy rabble that takes its orders from Sam Adams in Boston. You're an English gentleman and a soldier. You can't put that aside."

The gentleman soldier looked him straight in the eye. "Oh yes I can. I'll make it clear. Johnnie, the King can go to the devil for all I care, and the rabble with him. All that matters to me is Michael Wentworth, Esquire, a man of independent means and mind. And he intends to keep 'em both. So a good day to you, my friend. You may govern away and good luck to you. You have my interest, I might even say my sympathy, but no more, Johnnie, no more."

And off he went, reeling slightly, toward the waiting coach and the wife coming out of the shop.

Soon afterward, as Johnnie was about to rein away home, he noticed a column of men coming up the King's Highway with a drum and a horseman at their head. He paused where the highway opened into the Parade. Their leader proved to be lawyer John Sullivan of Durham, in the blue coat and silver-braided hat of a militia officer, and his followers Johnnie soon recognized as militiamen from Exeter and Durham and the country round about. Farmers and woodsmen in every sort of winter dress, including a good many in buckskins and fur caps, and shouldering a queer armory that ranged all the way from well-oiled long rifles to rusty old fowling guns and even a blunderbuss or two. When they recognized the Governor they uttered a yell, broke their ranks, and rushed up and surrounded him. He made no attempt to ride away. They seemed a little puzzled, standing about him, some with guns pointed at his breast. Sullivan rode into this menacing circle and snapped, "Order firelocks!" They obeyed at once, dropping the butts on the snow. Clearly he had them well trained and in hand.

"Well, Captain," Johnnie said, "what's all this?"

Sullivan was not unlike the Governor, an active man in the middle thirties with an air of smiling resolution. His Irish father had settled as a schoolmaster years ago in one of the upcountry towns, and Captain John spoke with a faint brogue.

"Why, sir," he said blandly, "we heard there's some excitement here in town, a foreign invasion or something of the kind."

"I'm sorry you've had your journey for nothing," Johnnie said. "There's no invasion, and no danger of one either."

"No danger," Sullivan said, "because you've got two regiments of the King's troops on the way from Boston, is that it?"

"I've sent for no regiments."

The lawyer gave Johnnie a searching look. "You're a man of your word, Governor," he said. "Would—um—would General Gage send troops here without your asking?"

"In winter? You must know two regiments can't be transferred in winter without arrangements for their food and fuel and quarters. There's this, though. You know about yesterday's powder theft. I believe the powder's been stowed up your way somewhere. What General Gage may do about that I can't answer."

A buzz of comment broke out in the ring of men. They were being joined now by townsmen slipping out of the houses and taverns to see what was afoot, and there was soon a roar of talk, with fingers pointing now toward the invisible Castle and now toward the villages upriver.

"You reckon Gage may come after the powder?" Captain Sullivan said shrewdly.

"It's possible. I'm not a soldier, but if I were I'd certainly do that. And I'd punish the men who stole it, Captain Sullivan."

Sullivan drew aside to confer with his men in the general hubbub. They seemed at odds. Johnnie sat his horse quietly in the cold. A delegation of townsmen emerged from the crowd and came up to him. Most of them were tradesmen of the solid sort. Their spokesman said, "Governor, if—uh—if the powder was put back, or say handed over to you, what then? Would you promise not to prosecute the men that took it?"

"I promise nothing. I'd consider it an alleviation of the offense, though. Especially as none of my men were hurt."

Back went the delegation to the crowd. The hubbub arose again, with obvious disagreement between the cool heads and the hot ones. Captain Sullivan seemed to be listening but taking no part in the debate. At last he spurred his horse over to Johnnie.

"Governor," he said with a straight face, "since there's nothing in this tale of two regiments coming here, why, I'll see if I can persuade the boys to go back home."

"And what about the powder?"

"Powder, Governor? What would I know about that? I was in Durham yesterday from morn to night."

"I'll take your word for it, Captain. Well, tell these people to disperse and go about their proper business."

Off came his hat. Off came Sullivan's. Johnnie rode away, stiff and chilled, but satisfied. That night he retailed the encounter to his supper guests, Meserve, Parry, and the merchant brothers Thomas and Archibald Auchincloss, stout Tories all.

"So you see," he said, "it changes an odd position. As things stood, I'd plenty of cannon but nothing to fire in 'em, while those misguided rascals had powder but no cannon. Now it looks as if I'll have the powder back by morning. I shouldn't wonder if the stuff was on its way here at this moment."

He went to bed with an easy mind and slept well. In the morning he enjoyed a hearty breakfast, and when Edward Parry came in about ten of the clock he called out cheerfully, "Well, Ned, what's ado at the docks? But don't tell me—I know. The powder's back."

"Bah! The powder's still under a meetinghouse up the river, by all accounts." Parry put his fists on his hips. "I've news for you, Johnnie. Sullivan didn't take his men home yesterday. They stayed out of sight, in various houses with friends, till dark. Right here in town. Truth is, Jack Sullivan fooled you nicely. So did they all."

"Pshaw! Because they didn't disperse at once?"

"Because they went off to the island again with Sullivan last night! Oh yes! Busy as beavers they were, too, the whole of the night. My dear Johnnie, they've robbed the Castle of sixteen cannon, five dozen muskets, and every ounce of shot to be found in the place."

Johnnie could not find a word to say. He sat confounded, not so much by Sullivan's guile as his own blind confidence.

"It was a heavy job," Parry went on in his ironic voice. "They barely got the gundalows up to town before the turn of tide this morning." Johnnie sprang up. "Ah! Then they'll have to await another tide to get 'em away up the river!"

"Sit down, my friend. There's nothing you can do. True, the gundalows are lying at a wharf just below mine, with the cannon plain to be seen; and those fellows who worked all night have gone off to sleep, including Sullivan. But the whole thing was neatly planned, I assure you. Right now a fresh force of Exeter men under Colonel Nat Folsom are standing guard over the cannon, and all armed with good muskets from the fort. The town's in their hands and you might as well admit the fact." He paused. "I'll tell you something else, Johnnie. This is no crowd of tavern louts. They're sober countrymen, and well trained. They obey Sullivan and Folsom on the instant. They've molested no one in the town. They've offered no insult to anyone—not even a Tory like me, standing there watching 'em. You couldn't find much better discipline in the King's own troops. If they're any sample of what's drilling up the river you've got a bigger problem than you thought."

"If only those warships would come!"

"What if they did? They couldn't sail in past Pull-and-be-damned till the evening tide. By the time they got up to the town your guns will have gone up the river—by that same tide."

And having delivered this, Parry went out with his savage I-told-you-so air. He had never forgiven what he considered Johnnie's weakness over the tea.

It was not until the following day that His Majesty's ships appeared. Both anchored inside Newcastle Island. Captain Barkley of the *Scarborough* and Lieutenant Mowat of the smaller *Canceaux* came ashore. Barkley had dispatches from Gage and Admiral Graves, which Johnnie read with a gloomy satisfaction. His request had been filled to the letter. The ships had a hundred marines on board, and they would remain in the anchorage as long as Governor Wentworth wished.

Mowat was a polite young man, Barkley a gruff old salt. Johnnie invited them to dinner on Christmas Day; and over the port and brandy, when the dishes and cloth had been removed and Fannie had gone to bed, the captain spoke his mind. He did not like his orders at all. It was all very well for his officers; they could wine and dine ashore whenever they wished. But how long must his seamen and leather-necks remain cooped aboard, like a lot of convicts in a hulk? This thing might go on for months. Why not pass up the river, land the marines, and search the up-tide villages for the stolen guns and powder?

"That would bring on a quarrel of arms," Johnnie objected. "Just what I want to avoid."

"Then what d'ye propose to do, sir?"

"Now that you're here I shall send out a proclamation to all the magistrates, commanding 'em to find the guns and powder, arrest the men involved, and bring 'em to punishment. I want this matter settled by our own law and our own people."

"And you think they will?"

Johnnie gave him stare for stare.

When the officers departed in his coach for the docks he called Tom Macdonogh, and in a dispatch to Lord Dartmouth he described the theft of the guns and powder and admitted, "With regard to bringing any of them to punishment, the very transaction shows that there is not strength in the government to effect it in its present state. No gaol would hold them long, and no jury would find them guilty."

As the days went by he knew the truth of what he wrote. Not a single arrest was made or even attempted. The guns and powder remained hidden up the river. And now even the weather turned Whiggish. The winter proved one of the mildest ever known in New England, especially east of the mountains, where every snowfall was light and vanished in rain. The Piscataqua never froze of course—its tides were too strong for that—but this year the smaller rivers of New England remained open the whole winter. So it was with the roads. Men and their notions could move freely about the countryside instead of being snowbound until spring. Folsom, Sullivan, and the other leaders of the Castle affair were often seen about the town, fearless and at ease. Johnnie had revoked their militia commissions, an empty gesture as he knew. The shadow government at Exeter seemed to be the real power now, and his had become a formal show, going through its accustomed motions like the painted wooden figures of a German clock at each strike of the hour.

FOURTEEN

FANNIE's mother came by a packet schooner from Boston to attend her daughter's lying-in, with a welter of baggage and bundles of baby clothes and a beautiful canopied cradle of mahogany. And on the twentieth day of January poor Fannie's ordeal began. Johnnie sent hastily for the best doctor in Portsmouth and, for that matter, in all New Hampshire. He disliked Hall Jackson's politics; the man was an outspoken Son of Liberty, a confidant of Sullivan and the Langdon brothers and the rest; and Jackson had never concealed his contempt for Johnnie and all his caste. Still, the man was highly skilled in his profession. He had begun as a youth under the teaching of his father, old Dr. Clement Jackson, and followed that with several years' study abroad in the best surgical school and hospitals of London.

And so Jackson came, a hale witty man, with his case of phials and his leather bag of instruments. He went straight up to the bedroom, spent about half an hour, and came down to the anxious Johnnie in the parlor, leaving the nurse and Fannie's mother in charge.

"This is going to be a long labor," he said. "Narrow pelvis. Always difficult. Matter of time—and strength in the woman of course."

"My wife is frail," Johnny said painfully.

Jackson's eyes twinkled. "Frail ladies are deceiving, Governor."

"In what way?"

The doctor regarded him shrewdly. "Well, for one, they complain a lot of their health—it's fashionable to be delicate, eh? And they take no exercise and suffer from migraines and vapors and so on as a consequence. You never see a serving girl so afflicted. The chief mark of a lady, if you don't mind my putting it plainly, is a costive bowel. Ha! Well, enough of that. Your wife has more strength than you think—and she'll need it all, with those hips. Meantime I'll remain below here. There's nothing I can do in the bedroom for hours. Have you a late Boston newspaper?"

Johnnie was amazed at the man's easy air, but he was too afraid for Fannie to be angry. Her groans sounded down the stair well, and he shuddered. Between her spasms there were long silences, and somehow the silences were worse. The doctor read the newspaper and then walked out to the kitchen and struck up a lively conversation there. Most of the English servants had gone, and in their place were young men and women from poor homes down by the fish wharves. The doctor amused them. Their chatter and laughter came to the distraught Johnnie as clearly as the sounds from the chamber upstairs.

All through the day Fannie's torture went on, and Johnnie's with it. From time to time Dr. Jackson emerged, spent a few minutes upstairs, came down with a shrug to Johnnie, and disappeared once more into the servants' quarters.

Bits of his hearty conversation floated through the door at the end of the hall; obstetrical tales and surgical oddities told with a comical twist, military history and theory—he was much interested in the militia—and a good deal about Liberty.

Meanwhile Fannie's shrieks rang down the stairs, together with the hoarse comments of the midwife and the soothing Boston tones of old Mrs. Wentworth. Johnnie paced the floor in anguish, drenched with sweat, and alternately threw himself face down on a couch and covered his ears.

It was after midnight when the end came. The doctor had been upstairs the past half hour, the servants' chatter had ceased, and the wretched Johnnie heard only a succession of harsh deep shouts and snarls, not the voice of Fannie at all. Then a long drawn-out yell, more frightful than any whoop of the savages in his early days in the forest, and a silence, a quick murmur of voices, and the first thin cry of the child. Johnnie arose then and went out into the snowy garden and was sick.

About two o'clock in the morning Jackson came down the

stairs with his case and bag. Johnnie sprang into the hall at his step. The man looked tired.

"You have a son, Governor."

"But my wife—Fannie?"

"Your wife's had a very severe labor—seventeen hours—and she's exhausted. I've given her opium—she'll sleep now. You need have no fear. I never saw so much strength in a slender body. She'll recover quickly, and she'll be able to give suck to the child herself. As fine a pair of breasts as one could wish."

"Thank you—thank you, Jackson."

"You may thank God, Governor. My fee will be ten guineas at your convenience—no, not now." Jackson paused to put on his greatcoat and hat. "I should mention one more thing. Your wife required some quite delicate surgical attention. She'll mend well, and as I've told her, she need never fear another ordeal of this kind."

"Oh?"

"She will never conceive again. A blessing to a woman of that frame. She'll remain a normal healthy female in every other respect naturally. Good night, Governor."

One touch of nature, in Portsmouth as in Johnnie's own well-thumbed Shakespeare, made the whole world kin. For a time the people, Whig and Tory, forgot the nag of politics and trooped to congratulate the Governor and his lady on the birth of an heir. It was like his inaugural, like his wedding, like old days indeed; and he rejoiced, not only as a father, but as the plain Johnnie Wentworth of those days when he had not a single enemy between the mountains and the sea.

Fannie's delighted mother took pen and paper and addressed a letter to Boston:

My dear sister,

Mrs. Wentworth is safe abed with a fine hearty boy. I need not attempt to tell you the pleasure this child has brought to all its connections. The Governor's happiness seems to be complete; and had a young prince been born there could not have been more rejoicing. The ships fired their guns. All the gentlemen of the town and from the King's ships came the next day to pay their compliments. The ladies followed, and for one week there were cake, caudle, wine &c. passing. This house has been full ever since.

Fannie was recovering beautifully, as the doctor had promised, and Johnnie's cup was truly full. He was dashing off letters in all directions: "A hearty boy—he'll do to pull up stumps at Wentworth House."

But as the days went by the other concerns came back with a vengeance. The provincial Whigs, meeting again at Exeter, chose Sullivan and John Langdon to speak for New Hampshire at another "Continental Congress." The stolen guns were distributed among the towns up the river—and men were training for their use. From time to time companies of armed countrymen came down the tide in gundalows and marched behind their drums about the Portsmouth streets, a challenge to Johnnie's authority and to every indignant Tory in the town. Even small boys were thumbing their noses at the silent warships in the stream.

Parry and other angry Tories now were pressing Johnnie hard. The two small warships and their handful of marines were worthless. He must send for troops, and a lot of troops; enough to march and scatter the unlawful assembly at Exeter; enough to search and find the stolen guns and powder; enough to arrest and bring to trial the leaders of the whole affair. They accused Johnnie of weakness, of shutting his eyes and ears to what was going on, like a frightened old woman under a bed. It was time for him to assert himself or resign his post to a man who would.

And so, in the last days of January 1775, Johnnie did what his instinct had fought against all along, and in his letter to Gage he specified two regiments—exactly the strength of that Boston canard.

While he awaited a reply he heard more accounts from Exeter. John Sullivan had recommended a direct challenge to the Governor—a demand that Johnnie recognize the Exeter assembly as the true Assembly of the province, and a body whose proceedings he could neither question nor dissolve. Some of the more moderate men had spoken against forcing Johnnie's hand, but they were shouted down. And it was no coincidence that Paul Revere had come to Exeter on another of his mysterious rides. The New Hampshire Whigs were moving in complete agreement with those of Massachusetts, where every village was now arming and drilling for war.

Johnnie mentioned Revere's visit in a gloomy note to his friend Waldron in the country.

"It portends a storm rather than peace. Peace, my dear friend, has by unwise men been driven out. They shut the door against its return. God forgive them, they know not what they do. Our hemisphere threatens a hurricane. If I can bring out of it, at last, safety to my country and honour to our Sovereign, my labor will be joyful." He paused, twirling the quill just above the paper. And then, bravely, "I yet think I shall. My heart is devoted to it."

A British army captain arrived from Boston to confer with Johnnie, and his name had an ironic sound. It was Gamble. Johnnie rode with him about the town and examined various buildings that might be converted into barracks without much work or material. Gamble, a brisk man, departed at once for Boston. He was noncommittal about the troops. His visit had been well observed by the Portsmouth Whigs, and the street gangs again had an ugly tone. The final irony came to Johnnie with a letter from Gage himself. The general was polite but firm. He could not spare a single soldier from Boston in his present situation. Johnnie must do the best he could with what he had.

Everyone now could see the weatherglass and sense the coming storm. For Johnnie there remained a pleasant interlude toward the end of February, when he and Fannie and their friends drove to Queens Chapel for the christening of the baby. They had chosen the name, Charles-Mary, in compliment to Lord and Lady Rockingham, and as soon as he got home from the chapel Johnnie dashed off a happy letter to tell them of their godchild.

Fannie's mother packed up her trunk and boxes and returned

to Boston by the packet schooner. She wept with her daughter at parting, and Fannie, shivering in the cold wind on the wharf, wished nervously that she and the baby were going too. Portsmouth was no more the little social playroom in which she had danced and flirted and played the queen. Only the Whig gentry now could visit each other without insult in the streets. The small group of outspoken Tories held a dance or dinner at their peril. The sight of a few coaches drawing up outside a Tory house attracted a noisy crowd at once. Even Peter Livius was in the crowd's contempt. Everyone knew that he had tried to unseat Governor Johnnie for his own ends, and to the common mind his boasted influence in London made him another limb of the King, like Johnnie himself. The more cautious gentry held themselves apart from all this, and their policy commended itself even to old Mark. Indeed the Wentworth clan was now either neutral or out-and-out Whig, while Johnnie stood alone for the King.

As the schooner vanished down the harbor Fannie returned with Johnnie to the house on Pleasant Street, which had become a prison with locked and bolted doors, almost as lonely as Wentworth House, far away in the hills. Even Wentworth House was not safe now. The popular fever had spread into the very mountains, and at Wolfeborough there were threats to burn down Johnnie's backwood nest. When he sent off wagonloads of supplies and furniture, preparing for another summer there, his friends thought him mad, but he answered them crisply, "If one goes, all goes. It may as well burn there as here."

He set off for Wolfeborough in April with one of his staff, John Fernald, leaving Tom Macdonogh and the boy Benning to guard Fannie and her baby in the Portsmouth house. He had been there only a few days when a hasty note from Tom informed him of an outright fight between the King's troops and the Massachusetts rebels at Lexington. The paper in his tense fingers seemed to crackle like flames. He packed up the silverware, locked the house, and turned over the great keys to his caretaker. Before leaving he rode with Fernald to the crest of

Mount Delight, and sat his horse under the mighty pine for a long gaze at his beloved lake and the hills.

There lay the house, the outbuildings, the fields, the park, the mill. The islands where the herons nested. The long green breast of Copplecrown. The thin blue smokes of Wolfeborough above the distant woods, where two hundred people lived now. The air was calm in the sunshine, the lake a looking glass. Stamp Tax, Turtle, and the other islands swam on it like water birds absorbed in their reflections. The bushes and hardwood trees were still winter-bare masses of black trunks and brown twigs, but the pines, the cedars, the hemlocks, and firs had their imperishable green. There were patches of snow in their shade, but Mayflowers were blooming on the sunny banks, and down by the Rye Field he knew the alders dangled their yellow catkins. The first song sparrows and robins were back from the south, and so were the loons. As he sat there a loon uttered its crazy laughter, passing overhead, and back to his mind came that mad wonderful night in the Portsmouth summerhouse, when the loons laughed on the pond. Darling Fannie! And now a breath of wind from the mountains sent a cats-paw along the lake and stirred the big pine overhead.

"This sylvan abode," he said. He liked that phrase from one of his books and often repeated it aloud up here. At last he turned the horse down the bridle path toward the Mall. "These contentions will cease, Fernald. Sooner than we think, perhaps. I'll come back." With the chests of silver strapped to a pair of led horses, they rode over Moose Mountain and on through the flat lands to the Dover ferry.

In the parlor he found an agitated Fannie, and soon afterward Edward Parry arrived with a group of Tory gentlemen. They had made their way through an excited crowd in the streets, and they looked grim.

"This," said one, "is what comes of trifling with rebellion—mark that, Johnnie. Gage ought to be kicked. Sending a few troops like that to seize the rebel powder at Lexington—a boy on a man's errand—what did he expect?"

"Well," Parry said fiercely, "I think it a good thing. Gage must act now, with his whole army. Boston and the country round about are the heart of all our troubles in America, and one good trashing in open battle will perish the whole damned treason!"

"I wonder," Johnnie said quietly. "My reports say the whole of New England's up in arms, in fact our own New Hampshire-men have begun to march for Cambridge. I'm told over a thousand are on the road at this moment."

"Then now's your time," cried Parry. "Send those warships up the river on the next tide, Johnnie, and land the marines and search every village from Salmon Falls to Squamscot! Get back those cannon and the powder while you have the chance."

Johnnie put his chin up. "No."

"In God's name, why?"

"I'll have no senseless bloodshed here. What if a thousand of our men have marched for Boston? There are ten thousand more at home. Those poor devils of marines would be slaughtered just like Gage's redcoats on the road from Lexington—worse!"

"Bah! Shooting's a game that two can play."

"I well know that. And if the marines shot a few rebels in the fight—what then? You know what happened at Lexington— the whole countryside swarmed to attack. One clash of arms here and you'd have 'em all on your necks, even those wild men from the mountains."

"Then what d'you propose to do?"

"I propose to carry on government with my appointed Council and with the support of our proper Assembly, so far as I can get it. I'll continue to do so whatever insult I may have to endure— and from whatever quarter."

"A hopeless policy!"

"On the contrary. I have a letter from Lord Rockingham. He stands with Lord Chatham and other powerful men opposing all the present measures in America. He says the government are now inclined to abate their taxes on the colonies, the cause of all our troubles. With that gone we can appeal to all reasonable men to bury the quarrel and go back to their work. Gentlemen, here in America we have in our hands a golden future, something that can only be worked out in peace. I keep my heart and soul on New Hampshire's part in it. Is that a hopeless policy?"

They went away grumbling. Johnnie and his dreams!

May came, with its bright days after the bleak April rains, and Johnnie rode over to the Town House to open the new session of his Assembly. In his address he urged them to approve the conciliations offered by the British government. But it was wasted breath. The members refused to consider anything from London at all, fearing the wrath of the people. Patiently Johnnie adjourned the session until mid-June, hoping for a change in the American weather in a course of weeks.

But toward the end of May there was another cloud, and it arose from the anchorage where the King's ships had lain so long idle at his bidding. Provisions were scarce in Portsmouth, as always in these months between the end of the winter stocks and the harvesting of a new summer's crops. To fill the gap the Portsmouth merchants had ordered supplies outside, and two vessels arrived from Long Island loaded with salt pork, flour, corn, and rye. They were promptly boarded and seized by Captain Barkley's men from H.M.S. *Scarborough*. The merchants came to Johnnie in dismay, and he went off in a boat to settle the matter.

The *Scarborough's* boatswains piped the Governor over the side with all formality. The captain greeted him in full fig, including a square-cut blue coat with enormous cuffs and silver buttons, in the fashion of twenty years before, and a vast three-tailed wig of much the same vintage.

The old salt was in no mood for questioning. A pair of hard blue eyes stared forth in challenge above his pitted purple nose, like those of an old peevish seahawk who has a fish in his talons at last. He had chafed at anchor ever since Christmas with his glum sailors and marines, and no doubt Parry and the other hot Tories in the town had given him their opinion of Johnnie's policy ashore.

He listened with half-shut eyes and a mouth like a crack in granite while Johnnie explained the need of these cargoes to the town. But when Johnnie demanded their release the mouth opened, and there came a shocking broadside.

"God's blood, I was sent here to your assistance, as I thought! I was ready to do my part against those swabs ashore, any time you called upon me. And what have you done? Eh? You've kept me here rotting my cables these five months—five solid months sitting here in your damned river, sir! A joke to every grinning jackanapes in Portsmouth!"

"Do you question my orders?" Johnnie snapped.

"I take my orders from Admiral Graves at Boston, not from you, sir. My orders are to remain here, so here I stay. But now I have orders additional, and damme I'm putting 'em into effect. The army is short of provisions, and I've word from the Admiral to seize all vittles, of whatever sort, that come in here, and send 'em off to Boston. I've made a beginning, as you see."

"Of whatever sort?" repeated Johnnie, thunderstruck. "Why, that could mean anything in the way of food. It could even mean the daily catch of the fishermen."

"So it does. And the salt they use, for that matter."

"D'you realize what you're saying? Half our people here depend on the fishery for a living, not to mention our merchants in the salt-fish trade."

"I can't help that."

"Why, it's infamous! Our people would starve!"

"That's their lookout, not mine. And here's something else you may not like. I have orders to secure my position here, in view of possible reprisals. There's that fort at the harbor mouth you call the Castle—Castle William and Mary, ecod! It commands the channel, yet you don't maintain a proper garrison. In fact you let those rebels of yours run off with the powder and take their pick o' cannon. I'm told there's dozens of other guns lying about the place that only need new carriages. What's to stop the rebels taking possession and mounting those guns? Eh? Nothing! And there we'd be, caught up here like a pair o' flies in a bottle."

"In that case, why not land your marines and man the Castle? I thought of that before, but there's a big fishing population on the island, and I chose not to risk a quarrel. If it's a necessity, put your men in the fort."

Captain Barkley favored Johnnie with a fierce grin. "Who'd vittle 'em there? You?"

"Not while you're seizing every scrap of provisions hereabouts. How could I?"

"Ah! So I'd have to vittle 'em from my ships, up here in the anchorage. Nunno, I've a better plan. Tomorrow I drop down to the island, land my men with handspikes and powder and such, tear down the walls as much as I can, and sling off those other cannon. Then I can sit here safe, and with the town under my guns, according to my orders."

Johnnie swallowed his wrath and turned to the gangway and the boat. "Your orders must be changed. I shall write Boston at once."

The sailor merely twisted his mouth and closed one eye.

The next day, true to Barkley's word, a strong party of seamen and marines from the *Scarborough* landed on Newcastle Island and pulled the last rotten teeth of the fort, while the *Canceaux* sailed with the captured provision ships for Boston. And now, as Johnnie foresaw, the fat was in the fire. At the news of Barkley's actions the townsmen seized whatever weapons came to hand and poured into the streets. Companies of armed men arrived every hour by road or by boat and gundalow from the up-tide towns. The Whigs' Committee of Safety sought hurriedly to take charge, but in the excitement they could do nothing. Bands of men broke into Tory houses and stores in search of weapons and food. From time to time Johnnie himself was besieged behind locked doors on Pleasant Street, with groups of ragged fellows, the scum of Portsmouth, gathering outside and demanding admittance.

It was June and hot weather. The lindens outside the house were in leaf, the grass was lush at the wayside, in the garden the lilacs bloomed, and already the apple blossoms were beginning to shed on every stir of the air. About the shores of South Pond the wild flag made a running blue flame. Strawberry Bank was speckled with white blossoms below the little chapel, violets were blooming among the fish flakes at the mouth of the Puddle Creek, and in the edge of the woods behind the town the blueberry and huckleberry bushes were all in flower. The loveliest month, except October when the leaves changed, but a black one now for Johnnie and worse for Fannie, cringing at every hullabaloo at the big street door, starting whenever a June bug smote the windowpanes after candlelight.

On the thirteenth day of June the official Assembly of New Hampshire met again in the Town House, and Johnnie set forth to open the session, riding with Tom Macdonogh through the streets in a hubbub of hoots and jeers. The Parade was a human swarm, many of the men armed with musket, bullet pouch, and powder horn; and he noted these with a pang—his own militia, his care and pride in the days before the trouble, and now being mustered for war against the King. Inside the old shabby assembly room sat the official representatives from town and country, much aware of the throng outside. There was a new face among them. Colonel John Fenton represented Plymouth—one fearless Tory in the gathering. Governor Johnnie opened the session with all its ancient form, read his address, and departed. The crowd set up a great roar when he emerged with Tom Macdonogh. A trotting swarm of men and boys escorted them all the way to Pleasant Street, whooping like Indians and flapping their hats to make the horses rear. But not a single stone was thrown until they disappeared into the house. It struck the door just as the boy Benning shot the bolts home. An echo boomed through the hall and up the staircase.

From her chamber window Fannie peered at the crowd in mingled fear and contempt and saw them finally drift away toward the town. She glanced at the cradle. The baby had slept through the tumult. She could hear the murmur of Johnnie's and Macdonogh's voices in the library with young Benning. There was a strange stillness in the rest of the house. She ran down the narrow and winding back stairs that Johnnie had installed at her demand—it had affronted her to see the servants using the main stairs at her receptions. It led into the kitchen. No one was there. She ran to the servants' quarters. No one there, either. She saw signs of a hasty gathering of their belongings, and the back door stood open. They had slipped away unnoticed in the noise from the street.

When she came to Johnnie with this discovery he sighed.

"I suppose we should have expected that. I'm not safe to work for, any more. In the Assembly today I couldn't see one friendly face, except John Fenton's, and I daresay by this time they've dismissed Fenton from his seat. They dislike that man even more than me. And then the crowd in the street—like a Boston mob on Guy Fawkes Night—with me the Guy. I never thought to see that in Portsmouth. I was tempted to draw my sword and teach a few of 'em better manners, but of course there'd have been one end to that—they'd have pulled Tom and me off the horses and bludgeoned us to a pudding."

He plucked off his wig, tossed it on a chair, and ran a hand over his cropped head. It came away wet with sweat. "Fan, d'you realize what day this is? Eight years ago, to the hour, I rode into Portsmouth and took my oath as Governor. And the people cheered, remember? Every man, woman, and youngster. I can still hear that gang of mastmen yelling, 'That's him, that's Johnnie!' And the ladies curtsying and gentlemen making a polite leg to me—people that won't admit they know me now, except in a distant way, as if I were Agamonticus or one of the Isles of Shoals. Even my own family. Father and mother afraid to show their faces here. Father's brothers amongst my worst enemies. And Peter Livius—Livius of all people—lumped with me as a King's man! My God, is it real, all this?"

"You're always asking that," Fannie said straitly. "It's time you saw these people as they are." Her mind was murmuring, I never liked any of your precious Portsmouth folk, not really, from the time Theo brought me here. Things like this couldn't happen in Boston.

Johnnie went on in that dazed voice, "I can't believe that people hate me, not really. I still think I could have held them to me somehow if we'd been let alone. All this trouble came from outside. And that oaf of a sailor—that was the final straw."

"He was obeying his orders—you said that yourself."

"Graves then—and Gage. They must have known they were cutting away my last position when they sent such orders here. As if I'd ceased to matter. As if New Hampshire could go to the devil and me with it."

A silence, and then Fannie said, "Well, you might as well admit our situation. We can't go on living here without servants—without even food in a few more days, for the butcher and the market women will be afraid to come to the door. Those rude gangs will be back again, you may be sure, howling for you to throw out your guns and pistols. Sooner or later they'll be breaking in and taking them and swilling your wines and spirits, and God knows what will happen. Think of me and the baby."

"What do you want to do?"

"Leave! Leave now in the *Scarborough* and go to Boston."

Johnnie put his folded arms on the table before him and rested his head on them. After a time he said in a muffled voice, "I can't do that, even for you, love. How could I show my face in Boston? The governor who ran away from his post because some noisy fellows cried Boo! And what would they say here in New Hampshire—my own people?"

"Those! You heard them. They were calling you and me every foul name they could lay tongue to!"

"Bar one." He brought his head up now and sat very straight in the chair, as he had sat his horse that morning. "No one's ever called me a coward."

Fannie uttered a cluck of impatience. "You're worse than a coward. I could forgive a coward—I'm one myself. But you're a fool, Johnnie. A fool! And if you don't take me away tomorrow I won't forgive you—never!" She flounced away upstairs and threw herself on the bed in her chamber.

The afternoon dragged on. From time to time a cluster of men and boys came up the street, yelled outside the house for a time, and then went on to pay their respects to Edward Parry. Toward sundown there was a knock at the back of the house. Johnnie went there and looked from a window. He threw open the door at once.

"Father! How did you get here?"

"By the shore of the pond." Mark's old wise face regarded him intently. "I've come at some risk, as you can guess, and I can't stay but a moment. Johnnie, you must get out. Take Fannie and the child and go off to the *Scarborough* while there's time. Your boat's at the foot of the garden. All you've got to do is to row down the pond, lift the boat past Titus Salter's milldam—the thing's light and a few hands can do it—and make off to the anchorage. There's not a house to pass but Salter's, and you can stand him off with a pistol if need be. At present the mob's hunting Colonel Fenton—he's in the town somewhere."

"Father, I'll not run away."

"Listen, Johnnie! You can do nothing here now—nothing. I'm not asking you to go just for your own sake or Fannie's. I'm asking you to go for the sake of every peaceable man and woman in Portsmouth—Whig or Tory or whatever. The only government in New Hampshire at this moment is the rebel one, with able men at the head of it. Make no mistake about that. With you out of the way the Committee of Safety can take a firm hand and establish order. While you remain the mob's got an excuse to run wild. So go, in God's name—don't waste another minute. Don't argue. Good-by!" He seized Johnnie's hand in his bony fingers and gave them a crushing grip.

"Your mother's love and mine, Johnnie." Mark turned and trotted down the garden, with his old man's bent-kneed gait, and vanished in the shrubbery.

Toward dusk young Benning's sharp ears caught a murmur in the distance. He called, "They're coming back." In another minute the sound was unmistakable. A crowd, and a large one, was coming up Pleasant Street at speed. Macdonogh and the boy armed themselves with guns from the rack in the library, and

Johnnie fetched his horse pistols and loaded them. From the windows, as the uproar drew near, they saw Colonel Fenton coming at a run, with the crowd a few yards behind. He was hatless and wigless, and a flung stone had cut his head. His sword was in his hand. As he came to the door some of the more daring youths pattered up at his back, and he turned and drove them off with a quick sweep of the blade. Johnnie himself threw open the door, and Fenton stumbled inside and leaned against the wall, panting like a hard-run dog.

The crowd made a rush for the doorway but stopped at the sight of Johnnie with a pistol in each hand. In the sudden stillness he said clearly, "I'll shoot the first to touch my doorstep."

"We don't want you, Governor. We want Fenton," one of them said.

"He's my guest," Johnnie said. "Now be gone, you villains, or you'll be the worse for it." Some of them were stooping, and Tom Macdonogh shouldered Johnnie aside and slammed the door just as the first stones flew. He shot the bolts. The mob was roaring again. The flung stones made a drum tattoo on the door. Then came a crash of glass, and another.

"Benning," Johnnie called. "Run upstairs and move Fannie and the baby to the back of the house—the kitchen." He turned to Fenton. The Englishman mopped the blood from his head with a handkerchief. He was dusty and drenched with sweat, and there were bits of straw on his clothes, as if he had hidden in a stable somewhere through the day. Some minutes passed before he could speak, and then he gasped, "Sorry to bring this damned rout upon you, Johnnie. Thought I'd get off to the *Scarborough*. No chance through the town. Waited for sundown and came this way. Got some distance too. Then a yell and the whole pack on my heels. Zounds! There go more of your windows."

They were standing in the hall, where the big door gave its protection. Stones were crashing through all the street panes, upstairs and down.

"Why do they want you?" Johnnie asked.

Fenton shrugged, with his familiar reckless grin. "I talked too much, I suppose. I'm not a diplomat like you, Johnnie. I told those fellows in the Assembly what I've been telling the people up my way—that according to scripture the devil was the first rebel, and hell was the right punishment."

"Umph. Well, you're safe for a time, at any rate. Those fellows know we're armed. When there's no more glass to smash they'll go away."

"I think not," Fenton said.

And he was right. The mob remained and grew. It was dark now, and crude torches appeared, bunches of tow soaked in whale oil and fastened in cleft sticks. When all the front and side panes of the house had gone the patter of stones ceased. So did the yelling, although the crowd's wild talk was a roar in itself. The house itself was dark and silent. Benning watched the garden while Fannie crouched with her baby on the floor nearby. Soon after nightfall three of Johnnie's faithful grooms, the last of his servants, slipped out of the stables across the road and made their way by the roundabout route of the South Pond to the back door of the house. Benning let them in, and Macdonogh put loaded fowling guns in their hands. Johnnie, Macdonogh, and Fenton watched the street. Now and then some bold fellow ventured toward the battered front door, thought better of it, and skipped back, amid shouts of derision from the others.

Toward midnight came a new uproar, a sound of cheers along the street. A dray pulled by two horses drew up outside the stables across the way.

"Zooks!" Fenton muttered, peering. "They've fashioned 'emselves a field gun." Johnnie looked and saw a four-pounder cannon, fastened with blocks and tackles to the heavy dray, and busy hands loading it. The muzzle pointed straight at his door. And now a party of militiamen made their way through the crowd, marked by their muskets and the slung powder horns and bullet pouches. One of these stepped forward, a lean farmer in breeches and hunting shirt and a shabby round hat.

"Governor!"

"Yes," Johnnie called.

"I have a warrant from the Committee of Safety for John Fenton's arrest. Send him out, and we'll warrant him safe conduct to the jail at Exeter. If he stays in there I won't answer for the consequences."

Johnnie was about to answer No. The word was on his lips when Fenton seized his arm. They could hear the baby wailing at the back of the house.

Fenton called out loudly, "Very well, Joel, I'm your man. I'll be out in a minute."

"You can't go out there," Johnnie snapped. "They'd tear you to pieces."

"I know that man," Fenton answered coolly, "he's a decent fellow, a sergeant in the Exeter militia. He and his men will see me safe to the jail up there, never fear."

"But I do fear. What'll they do to you at Exeter?"

"Exhibit me behind the bars—a Tory locked up like a common thief. That's all. Johnnie, listen to me. I'm going out there whether you like it or not. You're the one in danger—you and your wife and child. When the militiamen march me off you'll be at the mercy of that crowd. You've seen 'em. You know what they are. The lowest ruffians in Portsmouth—with a cannon in their hands. You haven't got a chance unless you do what I say."

"Well?"

"There'll be a rumpus when I step outside the door, you may depend. The militiamen will have a lively scuffle to get me away, with all that scum howling for my blood. And that's your chance. Slip out the back door and go to Parry's place—go anywhere—but go! Now, here I go myself. Bolt the door at my back and be off with you."

As Fenton stepped, bareheaded and empty-handed, into the torch glare the crowd uttered a mighty "Ahhhh!"

FIFTEEN

*T*HERE goes a brave man, if I ever saw one, and an Englishman begod," said Tom Macdonogh, slamming the door and bolting it. "Come, sir, quickly, or he's bet his life for nothing."

Johnnie, reluctant, still clutching his pistols and principles, had a last glimpse of the street. The militiamen were leaping to surround Fenton and already warding off a torrent of cudgel blows with their muskets. Macdonogh caught Johnnie's wrist and half dragged him to the back door. The three grooms followed. Fannie was there with a cloak swept about the child and herself and at her feet a portmanteau crammed with clothes. Young Benning opened the back door cautiously and crept forth, gun in hand. The garden was pitch dark, and as they ran down the winding path to the little summerhouse Johnnie had a queer flick of memory of that other night with Fannie, the night that changed his life.

Fannie herself had no room for romantics. She had heard all that Fenton said and was thankful that someone had his wits about him. The long pond gleamed before her now. Macdonogh threw the portmanteau into the boat, and Johnnie gave her his arm as she stepped in with the baby. When they were all in, the gunwales came perilously close to the water; the boat had been built for four people at most. The men rowed cautiously for that reason and to avoid a creaking of oarlocks. It was not far to the seaward end of the pond. The gardens of the scattered mansions on this side of Pleasant Street all came down to the pond, separated by strips of pasture and wild shrubs. On the opposite shore there was nothing but a rim of pasture and the brooding dark shadow of woods. Fannie had always disliked the loneliness of the house that the Assembly had rented for the

Governor, but she blessed it now. The tide was on the ebb, and at Titus Salter's milldam the sound of the sluice was loud. There was still a clamor beyond the dark trees and pastures. Then a shocking blast of the cannon, that seemed to tear the night apart, and a hubbub of muffled yells. The rag, tag, and bobtail of Portsmouth were storming the Governor's "residency" at last. Fannie thought of her elegant furniture, her silver, her chinaware, her presses of linen, and her wardrobes filled with clothes. A rush of hot and angry tears stung her eyes.

The small wooden house of Titus Salter stood on the dark slope just above the dam, where the road led off toward Little Harbor. The lower windows were lit, and as the six men lifted the boat over the dam the baby stirred in Fannie's arms, with a hungry cry. The men froze. Fannie tore open her gown and gave the child her breast. It seemed an age before the men had the boat in the harbor water below the dam, and Fannie walked down, feeling carefully for footing on the wet stones, and stepped into it. The portmanteau was there, she made sure of that. Then they were rowing again. The baby sucked contentedly. Johnnie clutched the tiller, with a watchful gaze on the yellow-lit panes of Salter's house.

It was a warm night, full of stars, and calm—a blessing, for with a sea swell running against the outgoing tide the overburdened boat must have swamped. Even as it was, Johnnie realized at once, there was no hope of reaching the *Scarborough* at her anchorage between Langdon's Island and the town. The tide was ebbing too strongly.

We must go with the tide, he thought. But where? Down to Little Harbor and put ourselves in the hands of Michael and Martha? The memory of that talk with Michael in the Parade still burned him wrathfully. Anything but that! Where, then? Newcastle? The island was thronged with fishermen, rabid Whigs all. But the fort—the fort at the tip? Cochrane was still there with his faithful few. A long way to go, two miles or so, but the tide stream went that way.

"Where are you going?" Fannie demanded. She could see the

lights of the town, very peaceful, as if nothing had marred the night, and over Johnnie's shoulder the masthead lantern of the *Scarborough*, half a mile upstream.

"To the fort."

"Why?"

"Because we can't row against the tide, and I must have safe shelter for you and the baby tonight. We can go up to the ship in Cochrane's big shallop on the flood tomorrow."

It was a long cramped journey, and frightening in the tide lops as the boat rode down past Pull-and-be-damned. Toward the black loom of Newcastle Island they met a dank air drifting low over the sea's face from the east, and they were all shivering before they made the shore near the Castle. The lighthouse, that useful creation of Johnnie's, marked the point with a solitary yellow gleam. A lone sentry challenged them as they stumbled to the gate. Then they were inside, with a tousled Cochrane, aroused from sleep, coming out of his quarters to greet them.

Castle William and Mary, never more than a small work of earth and rock and timber, built in the olden time, was now a sorry place indeed. The Assembly had refused to spend a penny on it since the end of the French wars, and Barkley's sailors had removed the last of the ancient cannon and torn down much of the walls. Inside remained a small wooden guardhouse and a smaller cottage for the commandant. The poorest fisherman on the island had better shelter. Both buildings were rotten, the roofs leaked in every rain, and every sea wind whistled through the walls. Cochrane turned over his hovel to the Governor and went to share the drafty guardhouse with the men. Fannie crept shivering into Cochrane's bed with the baby, but Johnnie sat long by the driftwood fire. He could not sleep. The day's affairs returned to mind in a dismal cycle with no end.

He was still there in the morning, nodding over the ashes in a crude half-barrel chair, when one of Cochrane's men came with breakfast, a pot of pale tea flavored with molasses, a half loaf of stale bread, and a dish of fried herrings. Fannie arose, looked at the baby, sleeping peacefully, dressed herself, and came into the outer room. She was hungry. She had always despised herrings, the bread of the poor, but this morning she took her place at the rough pine table and ate with appetite.

Cochrane joined them, and as they finished Johnnie said, "Captain, step the mast in your shallop as soon as the tide makes. I'll give you a note for Captain Barkley."

"But aren't we going to the *Scarborough* ourselves?" Fannie cried.

"Fan, I've changed my mind."

"What!"

"We stay here, at the fort. I must ask you to put up with these inconveniences for a time. After all, it's summer weather, more pleasant here than in the heat of the town."

"What's in your mind now?" she said in a withering tone.

"Fan, I remain the legal head of the government so long as I stay somewhere on New Hampshire soil, and no grant of land or money, no opening or closing of courts or assembly—nothing is valid without my signature. That's the constituted law of the province. Those noisy villains in the town streets can't change that, let 'em rant as much as they like. I'll have the *Scarborough* come down to anchor near the fort and cover us with her guns, so we'll be safe enough. Tomorrow Tom Macdonogh goes up to town disguised as a fisherman. He'll carry my instructions to the Chief Justice and others. By now the gentlemen of the town will have restored order, in their own interest if not mine. And keeping order means the regular operation of courts and so on, using my law officials, because any law's better than none at all. They're in a pickle, and they know it."

"Indeed! And how long must I stay with my poor mite in this pigsty?"

"Not long, I hope. The rebels have gathered some sort of army outside Boston, with very little powder and no discipline at all. Gage has thousands of British regulars, with everything an army needs. Any day now he'll march out. If the rebels stand they'll be slaughtered, and they'll be laughed out of all countenance if they run. Whichever it is, the whole seditious movement will collapse, there and everywhere in the colonies. Then we can move back to the town and pick up our old peaceful life again. A matter of a week, or at most a month."

"You're sure?"

He hesitated, thinking of his words to Parry. And then, "I'd wager my life on it."

"And mine, it seems, and my poor baby's," she said bitterly. "Very well. But if these wonderful things don't come to pass in a month I won't stay here, I vow. I'll go to Boston if I have to beg passage in a fishing sloop, and on my knees."

Captain Barkley received Johnnie's note with a snort. He had heard of the riots ashore and that the Governor had fled. The whole town seemed to have gone over to rebellion. He did not like Yankees, Governor Wentworth included, and the tall wooden warehouses along the foot of Strawberry Bank were a tempting target for his guns. However, his sense of duty compelled him to hoist anchor and drop down to cover the Castle, as Johnnie requested. It was not a good anchorage, he would have to run up the harbor again at every easterly blow, but it had a certain advantage. There he could stop and search not only the craft bound up tide for Portsmouth, but those that slipped in and out of Kittery as well.

Five days after Johnnie's flight from Portsmouth a furtive man appeared at the fort gate, delivered a note for Mr. Wentworth, and vanished. Johnnie opened it curiously. The handwriting was Colonel Michael's, but it was not signed.

"A great battle outside Boston yesterday. The British army drove the rebels off and killed many, including Dr. Warren, one of their leaders."

He showed it to Fannie and Captain Cochrane. "So it's happened," he said somberly. "I venture Sam Adams was safe somewhere else, but this ends the machinations of Adams and those other wicked men." The rolling slopes and woods of the island shut the town from his sight, but he turned his face that way. "Now we shall see."

Next day Tom Macdonogh sailed down from the town in a

small shallop. His face was long. "You've heard, sir? The battle?"

"Yes. It's all over, Tom, the whole mad business."

Tom frowned. "I wouldn't go that far, sir. I mean to say, the British troops drove the rebels off a hill at Charlestown, but the rebels shot the British regiments to pieces in the business. They killed or wounded well over a thousand redcoats. Two of the New Hampshire rebel regiments were in the fight, and some of the lightly hurt men have come home. Gage has crawled back into Boston, so they say, like a wounded bear. And the rebels are still outside the town, stronger than ever."

Johnnie stared. "But that's impossible! Aside from anything else the rebel army was so short of powder that. . . ."

"Ah! D'you know what saved 'em, sir? The powder from here. Yes! The hundred kegs they stole from this fort! That's what Paul Revere was after from the first. Our rebels hid the stuff upriver, and I guess there was some squabble before they agreed to part with it. But after the New Hampshire militia marched for Cambridge there was no more quibbling. They sent off the kegs in ox carts a few days ago, and the powder was just arriving at Charlestown when the shooting started. Old John Demeritt's cart got up Bunker's Hill with the first load just as the rebels were shaking the last grains from their powder horns. Oh, I tell you, our Portsmouth Whigs are crowing over that—even some that frowned on stealing the powder in the first place."

"Umph! To change an ill subject—what are my Council doing?"

"Going on with ordinary business of the province. The Sons of Liberty won't molest 'em so long as they keep to that. Old Mr. Atkinson remains in charge, as senior member and Secretary, and he has all the public records stowed away at his house. Priceless, those. Without 'em nobody in the province can prove they own a property or anything else. How long things will continue like this no one knows. The out-and-out Tory gentlemen have lost heart since the later news from Charlestown. They can't do any business—they can't even get servants any more. Mr. Parry and the rest are taking passage to Boston in one of Parry's ships, with all their furniture and household goods. It's an exodus."

"And Peter Livius?"

"He's off, too, but the other way, a sloop to Quebec. Thinks he can get a post with the government of Canada. Says his friends in London will see to that, and he never did like Portsmouth anyway."

"The fox and the grapes. He may find sweeter ones in Canada at that. What news of Colonel Fenton?"

"Safe and cheerful in the jail at Exeter. Everyone thinks they'll let him go before long. The rebels feel sure of 'emselves."

"And my house in town?"

Tom shook his head. "Ah, that's a sorry tale, sir—I was wondering when you'd ask me. When those ignorant spalpeens found us gone they made for the wine cellar, and after that there wasn't much they didn't do. They stole everything they could carry, smashed the mirrors, the chinaware, the chandeliers, tore down the hangings, even battered the parlor mantel carvings and the keys of the harpsichord with their clubs and gunbutts. Finally some drunken fools went to the stables, fetched all the horses across the road and turned 'em loose in the lower rooms. A sight the next day—dung everywhere, and the floors all splintered and scored by the horseshoes. Well, all that. Even the most ardent Whig gentlemen were shocked. Your father came and gathered up your private papers and letter books, and he'll send 'em off to the fort here at the first chance. The Committee of Safety's taken charge of the house and what's left of the furniture, and that's about all I know."

The hot-weather days went by slowly. Johnnie occupied himself with letters, Fannie with her baby and her tambour frame. Several pine chests of the Governor's private papers were put ashore at the landing place one night, by some silent men in a gundalow. Food came to the little garrison in the same way—as if they were lepers whose very friends were fearful of their touch.

It was a strange existence. Over the water on the Kittery shore stood the big house of the Pepperells, the home of old Sir William, dead for years but a living legend in the province, where old men still talked of Louisburg. As a small boy Johnnie had seen the ships and men of New Hampshire set forth on that famous expedition and heard the tales when they came back, listening eagerly on the wharves and at the tavern doors when he should have been at his schoolbooks. Everyone in those days was proud to call himself a soldier of the King. What a transformation now!

And yet the scene remained the same. Each day he climbed the steps of the squat wooden lighthouse and gazed as if it were something he must fix in his mind, like that other view below the pine on Mount Delight. The broad shining mouth of the Piscataqua, the tides sweeping in and out, the cluster of islands great and small, the green pastures and dark woods, the small cottages of the fishermen, the stony shores, the acres of fish flakes and the split cod drying in the summer air. At low tide the outer rocks emerged, like the heads of drowned men, streaming with their swarthy tangled locks; and gravel shoals where the mussel beds shone blue in the sunshine; and long muddy flats where the eel grass drooped in pale green masses like an uncut hayfield after a country flood. And there was the summer sky—Fannie's favorite blue—and the landscape shimmering in the distance with the heat, and everywhere the white flicker of gulls. In the seaward mirage the Isles of Shoals loomed like mountains and shrank to dots. Like this mirage of politics, Johnnie thought, an illusion of the eye, something that must pass with a change of wind or another hour's march of the sun.

The garrison of the fort consisted of Cochrane and his five men, Johnnie and his three servants, Tom Macdonogh, and young Benning. They divided themselves into watches and stood guard day and night, for most of the fishermen on Newcastle Island were Sons of Liberty, and frequently an armed party of them hovered among the rocks, watching the fort and the *Scarborough* offshore.

News came fitfully, by letter, often by unsigned notes, carried down the harbor in small fishing boats for a price. Early in July a sorry tale came all the way from Wolfeborough. A party of backwoodsmen had pillaged Wentworth House, and only the stout will of two Wolfeborough Whigs had kept them from burning it down. A few days later a note from the Chief Justice said that the provincial records were no longer in his hands. An armed group had come to his house, polite but determined, and removed every book and document to Exeter.

The news from Boston was no better. Gage's army remained idle inside the defenses. Food and fuel could be had only at outrageous prices. Fourteen thousand people had quitted the town for the country. Whole streets were empty. Less than seven thousand people remained, even including the hundreds of Tory refugees from the rebel districts outside.

"We're better off here, Fan," Johnnie observed. She made no reply.

Toward the end of July he described his affairs in a letter to Tristram Dalton, and added in the stately prose that flowed from his pen in solemn moments, the mingled product of a Harvard education and much reading of Addison and Steele, "This at present is our case, confined on the ocean's edge and experiencing the inconveniences resulting from the misguided zeal of those upon whose gratitude and affection I rejoice to have the justest demand. I will not complain, because it would be a poignant censure on a people I love and forgive. For truly I can say with the poet in his Lear, 'I am a man more sinned against than sinning.'"

So far Captain Barkley had agreed to let the fishing vessels alone, on a shrewd condition that the town butchers must sell him fresh beef, and this Johnnie had arranged by notes to the leading merchants. But in August the sailor broke the agreement and seized a vessel laden with fish. The next time he sent a boat ashore for supplies it was greeted with musket shots. He was furious. Indeed he was preparing to bombard the town, when Johnnie put off in a boat and talked him out of it.

"Very well," the captain grunted. "But since I can't get vittles in this nest of treason any more I must go to Boston for my supplies."

"How soon?"

"Some days afore the month's end."

"You realize, of course, that the rebels will overrun the fort as soon as you're gone? I couldn't hold it with my few men, the place is not defensible."

"I've seen to that, sir," with a dour smile.

"Then you leave me a poor choice. We must go with you— my men and my family—or resign ourselves to capture and insult by another armed mob."

Captain Barkley was in no sympathetic mood. "If you'd had any thought for your child and lady you'd ha' left here long ago and saved me a fool's errand all these months. I don't understand you, sir, damme if I do. They kick you out of your home like a dog, yet you beg me not to loose off a few cannon at their warehouses. This is war, sir, war, and the sooner you recognize that the better." A pause, and then with a stiff politeness, "I'll prepare accommodation for you and your party, if that's your wish, and I'll let you know when I'm to sail."

The day of departure came on the twenty-third of August. Fannie boarded the *Scarborough* with relief, even a smile, the first sign of happiness she had shown in months. Johnnie went gloomily. As the ship spread her canvas and drew away he stood aft, with a borrowed spyglass, and saw tiny figures swarming about the fort. The Liberty boys of Newcastle had not lost a moment. Then a last look at Kittery, and on the other hand, between the islands, a fleeting glimpse of Colonel Michael's house at Little Harbor. The town was hidden. Long after they passed the Isles of Shoals, with their flash of breakers, Mount Agamonticus stood blue in the distance.

To Fannie, the view of Boston, whether from one of its hills or from the sea, was the finest on earth. And it seemed like Heaven now. The tall hump of Castle Island, the long fringe of wharves, the familiar town draped over its low hills like a patchwork quilt over three or four stools, the steeples rising out of it, the thin blue wisps from hundreds of chimneys blowing away on the breeze. His Majesty's warships lay in the anchorage, a picture of sea power with their rows of gunports, their heavy masts and yards, their British ensigns fluttering in the breeze. There seemed to be a good many merchant ships at the wharves, too, in spite of Johnnie's talk about the end of Boston's trade.

She and Johnnie were still wearing the clothes in which they had escaped from the house on Pleasant Street. Fortunately she had stuffed the baby's things and a supply of underlinen in the portmanteau before they left, but washing facilities at the fort were poor, like everything else there. Her gown was shabby and stained, and so were Johnnie's coat and waistcoat and breeches.

"When we land," she said to him, "you must get a hire-coach and take us off to Mama's house right away. I won't have any of our Boston friends see us looking like this."

She was impatient to get into the familiar Boston shops, that catered to moneyed folk, and to her own mantuamaker in Middle Street. What fun, after all, to be choosing a whole new wardrobe, and all at once, like a bride! Johnnie, too, must set the tailors to work. It would be a fortnight at the very least before they could appear in public.

The captain's gig landed them at the Long Wharf and after some searching by Johnnie's grooms they found a hire-coach, a rickety thing with a wheezing rack-o'-bones in the shafts. When they reached Sarah Wentworth's house Fannie flew up the steps, while Benning picked up the baby and Johnnie paid the coachman an astounding fee that took most of the coins in his pocket. The widow greeted them with an outburst of exclamations, smiles, and tears. So it had come to this at last! Fannie's letters from the island refuge had told her a good deal of the tale, and their present attire and meager baggage told the rest.

Away went a servant with a note, and before long a carriage brought Fannie's sister Mary Brinley with her husband. From childhood Fannie and Mary had been much attached to each other, perhaps because they were nearly alike in face and figure and in their attitude to life, a sprightly pair. They fell into each other's arms with a happy squall of feminine cries. George Brinley, a prosperous merchant when the Boston troubles began, shook Johnnie's hand solemnly and drew him aside to the smaller sitting room.

"So New Hampshire's now in the rebel camp?"

"Say in rebel hands," Johnnie said. "Most of our people don't know what to make of these affairs. I was driven out by the lower orders, you understand—the lower orders. The Whig gentlemen had nothing to do with it."

"You could go back then?"

"I'm afraid that depends on what happens here, Brinley. When the British army has broken the rebels a lot of us will be able to go back to our proper places."

"That may take a long time," Brinley grunted. "You've come from frying pan to fire. We're in a state of siege, Mr. Wentworth, just as you were in your little fort at Portsmouth. The rebel army bars all the roads outside. There's no trade with the country. There's not much by sea, for that matter. The whole coast of America is pretty much in rebel hands, as far as I can judge, and their 'privateers'—call them pirates, for that's what they are—infest all the waters north of New York. Any Tory merchant who tries to send supplies to Boston takes a risk of ship and cargo and probably his life. The vessels you see here at the wharves are mostly English storeships for the army and fleet. My business is ruined, like every other in Boston, except of course the shops and taverns that cater to the army people—they seem to get all the supplies they want. There's little to eat for the townspeople and less fuel. And here it is fall, with winter just around the corner."

"What does General Gage intend to do?"

"General Howe commands the army now. A better soldier than Gage, his officers tell me. That bloody business at Bunker's Hill gave 'em all a shock and cost Gage his command. So Howe won't risk another bowling match of that kind. He's thrown up defenses on the Neck and wants the rebels to be the ninepins in the next game. They won't, of course. They've mustered about twenty thousand fellows, of all sorts and all ages, from graybeards to boys not as tall as their muskets, but they've got no artillery to speak of. The position seems to be that the rebels can't break in, and Howe's not inclined to break out."

"How are things in the town?"

"Bad. Three quarters of the people have gone away into the country. The rest, including most of the refugee loyalists from outside, are slowly starving. All that keeps 'em alive is a supply of fish caught in the bay and at the wharves. In another two months the fishing will be at an end, and they'll start to freeze as well."

"How do you manage yourself?" Johnnie asked.

"Oh, I do some business for the army commissaries—picking up odd lots of meat and vegetables from the more venturesome coasters." He paused and stared out of the open window into the street, where in the hot summer air a mingled throng of shabby civilians and smart redcoated and black-gaitered soldiers wandered aimlessly up and down.

"Something tells me this war's going to last a long time, Mr. Wentworth. Possibly for years. And no chance for a loyalist in private business till it's over. I don't know what influence you may have, but if you could put a word into the right quarter I might get an officer's post on the Army commissary staff for the duration of the war. I could do good service there, and frankly I need the pay. It would have to be arranged through London naturally."

"Um. I don't know anybody at the War Office. But there are other means of approach—I'll see what I can do, Brinley."

Johnnie said this airily, as if his connections were on the right side of London's politics. He was beginning to wonder about his own finances. He owed thousands of pounds to his father and others. The property at Wolfeborough, his only asset, which had swallowed so much money, lay at the mercy of any wandering lout with a tinderbox. His salary from the Assembly was cut off. No chance of collecting a penny there until the end of the rebellion—which might take years, as Brinley said. His sole income now was the £800 a year from London as Surveyor General of His Majesty's Woods. And how long would that be paid, when he could not set foot in the woods and no deputies would dare to serve him?

"What do you think of the rebellion?" he murmured.

George Brinley sucked his lips in between his teeth. He was a brisk and capable Bostonian with a wide trading acquaintance in the colonies.

"As a loyalist I detest it, if that's what you mean. I signed the farewell address to Governor Hutchinson; I signed the address of welcome to Gage in his place; and everyone who signed those papers is a marked man to the rebels now. It's no use blinking at facts, in business or war. This rebellion's no longer a scattered eruption of town and village mobs, my friend. That congress in Philadelphia seems to have got capable men together, from all the colonies, and they've taken charge. Oh they're smart—smart! See how they chose a Whig gentleman from Virginia to come here and command the rebel army. He's set up his headquarters at Cambridge, just over the river. Name of Washington. Nobody in these parts ever heard of him before, but he seems to be a soldier of some experience, and he's taking a stiff hand. Our Yankee rebels don't like that. I'm told John Hancock nearly had a fit. But you see the point? A man from the south in command gives this rabble outside Boston something of a continental flavor. It means the southern colonies won't mind sending troops this way. In fact some companies of riflemen have arrived already from Virginia. They'll be flocking up here if Howe doesn't do something decisive soon."

"What if Howe attacked them now?"

"I don't know—I'm no soldier. I didn't think the rebels had a chance at Charlestown—and look what happened! His Majesty's generals don't seem very smart to me. What I see is this swarm of men the rebels have got now and Mr. Washington busy making soldiers of 'em. If Howe sits here much longer he'll find the rebel army too big to lick, as my father found when he tried to thrash me at seventeen. And here's something else—for what it may be worth—something a tipsy naval officer pointed out to me. Howe hasn't got a single post on the Dorchester ridge, just across the harbor from the town, because, forsooth, it's at long range and the rebels have no siege artillery. Suppose the rebels occupied those heights? Suppose they conjured up from somewhere a battery of heavy guns? According to this man a few long twenty-fours would serve the turn. They could force the fleet out of the anchorage, whether their gunnery was good or bad, just by being there. And mark this: if the fleet has to leave, the army will have to leave, and so, my friend, will we. I wouldn't care to be the loyalist left in Boston—man or woman—if the rebels got in here."

The next day Johnnie went to a banker in Cornhill, with whom he had done some business in the past. The man greeted him effusively but with a shrewd glance at his shabby attire. His mouth was pursed to refuse a loan. The story of Governor Wentworth's flight was all over Boston. But he was quite agreeable when Johnnie mentioned his post as Surveyor General and asked him to cash a draft on the Treasury in London. He drew £200, which went almost entirely to tailors and shoemakers and milliners and mantuamakers in the course of the next fortnight.

Now he and Fannie could venture forth to look up their friends and join in the whirl of card parties, dinners, dances, and *conversaziones* that circulated about General Howe and his staff. People in this enchanted Boston circle addressed Johnnie as Your Excellency or Governor, as if he were merely on a social visit from Portsmouth with no unpleasantness involved, and Fannie basked in their attentions as his lady.

They were all of the old colonial upper class, which was now split so widely between Whig and Tory, and to them the Whigs were now "those rebel miscreants," while they were a strange new word, "loyalists." Many of them were spending their last guineas, determined to keep up the old appearances and trusting in Howe's army to put things right again.

Johnnie himself was determined to return to Portsmouth, with a warship or two, and to re-establish himself in the fort as soon as possible. He urged it on Admiral Graves, declaring his absolute need of a foothold in New Hampshire, however small. The admiral was unimpressed. He did not mention Captain Barkley's report, but he had no intention of sending ships back to that precarious anchorage in the Piscataqua, and he said so. He added, "Besides here's the autumn, and time for most of my fleet to make for the West Indies for the winter. I'm keeping three ships at Boston, and that's all. The rest won't be back till next May or June."

"Then," said Johnnie desperately, "at least order an armed vessel, however small, to take me to the Isles of Shoals. The New Hampshire Assembly will be meeting in late September unless I prorogue it beforehand, and I can do that from, say, Gosport on the Isles."

The admiral squinted a sardonic eye. "What good will that do? Your Assembly's under the thumb of the rebel group, by all accounts. They'll meet, with or without your permission, and no doubt they accede to all the rebels' demands."

"But without my knowledge or consent! I must keep clear before them the fact that I'm their Governor, supported by His Majesty's law, and that someday I shall be able to demand an account of all their proceedings."

At last Graves provided a small armed schooner. Appropriately her name was *Hope*, and she carried Johnnie and Tom Macdonogh to Gosport on September 25. From the rocky hump of Star Island they could see with a spyglass the lighthouse and the ruined fort very clearly in the golden autumn sunshine and the white dots of Kittery, the rolling woods and fields of Newcastle, and the far blue smoke of Portsmouth itself. In a fisherman's cottage Johnnie dictated the document of prorogation to Tom Macdonogh, addressed it to old Judge Atkinson as Secretary of the Council, and sent it off by fishing boat in the darkness of night to Little Harbor. The next night the boat went ashore again for the reply, but none came. None ever came. At the end of the month the *Hope* carried them back to Boston. As soon as she had gone a force of armed rebels descended on the Isles of Shoals in sloops and gundalows, gathered up hundreds of fishermen with their families and small belongings, and carried them off to the mainland, never to return. The Isles were not to be a base for Governor Johnnie, that was clear.

By the time the first snow whitened the Boston streets Fannie was absorbed in a new delightful life, where there was always wit and music and good food and wine, where sprigs of British nobility in handsome uniforms, like the gay Lord Percy, kissed the hands of pretty loyalist ladies and demanded their company whenever the dancing began—where, in fact, every day was a holiday and every night a feast.

She slept every morning until noon. Grandmother Wentworth was delighted to look after the baby. The child had been weaned, and there was no more need of those sleepy awakenings and suckings. Fannie could admire her figure again. Indeed her looking glass told her it was better than ever, and so did the eyes of the gentlemen at routs and balls, following her about the room. Whenever some jealous miss at the dance (and there were not a few) remarked aloud, "Thirty, if she's a day," the gentlemen did not care a rap. Johnnie himself, proud of her popularity, had a pang now and then. Time and trouble seemed to pass Fannie by. She retained the clear eyes and skin and the vivacity of nineteen, flitting about the drawing rooms and ballrooms of Boston with her mysterious little smile, as if she had the secret of youth and proposed to keep it to herself, and Johnnie could not help thinking with a queer dismay that next year he would be forty.

He met General Howe at many of these affairs, a swarthy man with a heavy lip and the eyes of a codfish. The commander-in-chief could be convivial when he wished, and in conversation Johnnie found him intelligent despite his looks. Some refugees, chafing over his inaction, called him a fool and a rake. It was notorious that a pretty American woman, Mrs. Loring, the wife of one of his commissaries, served as his mistress; indeed he flaunted the fact, or she flaunted him, at many a dinner and ball, and any hostess who wanted the General's presence at her party was wise to invite Mrs. Loring first. The general was not alone in such amiable diversions. Military gentlemen were not subject to the moral rules of other folk, it appeared; an indulgence went with their profession, posted hither and yon about the world, with hardship and death always in the offing somewhere. One had to keep a broad mind, Fannie laughed; the officers were pleasant fellows with such elegant ballroom manners, whatever they did outside.

The giddy round did not appeal to Johnnie as it did to his wife, however. There was a monotony about these affairs in which the same people were always doing the same things and passing the same idle talk. He was too anxious about the loyalist cause, perhaps. He wondered sometimes if there were any truth in what some dour loyalists were saying; that under General Howe's red coat and powdered wig lived a political knave; that he was a Whig himself, with all the cutthroat attitude of English Whig-and-Tory politics; that he despised his own government at home and had no intention of fighting hard for a Tory cause in America.

When the winter deepened Johnnie began to see another side to Boston life, the plight of the poorer townsfolk and refugees. As cold and hunger increased there was a sharp increase of crime, in spite of Howe's street patrols; indeed soldiers and sailors were involved in nightly robbery along with the desperate civilians. They broke into the houses left empty by people fleeing the city, and stole silverware, clothing, bedding, pots, teacups, anything that could be sold for food or drink. Then they were back again in a quest for fuel, breaking up furniture, tearing down cupboards and wainscots and panels. The time soon came when hardly one of the hundreds of abandoned houses remained intact. In many cases the very houses disappeared, board by board and post by post, until there was nothing but a cellar and a scatter of rubbish.

By Christmas people were eating the meat of starved horses that fell down in the streets. Dogs and cats mysteriously vanished, as if some Pied Piper had called them away. And the smallpox appeared, as a final misery, and worked its way with ease among humans huddling together for warmth behind the frosty panes. Death carts made their rounds and took the daily harvest to the graveyards. The funeral tolling of church bells became so frequent that it seemed a continuous sound of doom, and at last General Howe forbade it. The town, with its mass of misery and its thin crust of pleasure, seemed to Johnnie like nothing so much as a gilded chamber pot.

The British soldiers and sailors, unused to the cold and snow, weary of idleness all these months, an ocean away from home, loudly cursed the climate, the country and the people. Americans! Johnnie stirred unhappily whenever he heard these objurgations; and sometimes there was another feeling, the one he had confessed to Fannie long before and put away as if it were the voice of treason. *We're not the same people. We Americans are another race, with another destiny. We know it and so do they.* And again he put it away.

The new year came, the first stormy day of 1776, with drifts in the streets too deep for visiting by coach or even afoot. Fannie, hoisting her skirts to warm her legs by the stove in her mother's parlor, cried a murrain on the weather. There was to have been a grand ball tonight, with the General and most of his officers there. Johnnie was busy dictating letters to Tom Macdonogh in the next room. He seemed to do nothing else. As if, now that he couldn't be dashing about the woods of New Hampshire, he must send at least some part of himself hither and yon, if only a scrawled signature.

He came out to the stove and warmed his hands, while Fannie, with gown and petticoats high, exposed to the glow the full length of her flimsy cambric drawers. Johnnie wondered if she knew that Tom Macdonogh, pausing now and then to blow on his cold fingers, could see her plainly through the open doorway.

"You should wear flannels in this weather," he remarked.

"Flannels!"—as if he had said bearskins.

He wondered how to begin. After some moments he said, "Fan, I've been considering our position here."

"Oh?"

"I've drawn my London salary almost to the limit, and we can't keep staying here on your mother's hospitality—she has little enough money herself, the way things are. D'you realize that small leg of mutton yesterday cost a guinea?"

She gave him the look of blank unconcern about money matters that made him wonder sometimes if she would ever grow up. In this new glittering substitute for the old Portsmouth winter pleasure she had no room in her mind for anything so dull.

"It isn't just pennies or guineas," he said, almost with apology, as if he had uttered something obscene. "I'm alarmed at the look of things here in Boston. I've been talking to . . ."

"George Brinley, I suppose—poor gloomy man. Mary tries to laugh away his vapors, but it does no good whatever."

"I've been talking to George, yes, and some other sensible loyalist gentlemen," he replied deliberately. "And some of Howe's officers, the kind who spend most of their time at their posts and don't have much leisure for dancing."

Fannie gave him a dark under-glance. There was an irritated edge to his voice. She turned her back, shifting her hands and flipping up her skirts behind.

"A man came through the lines last night with a rumor that could be true. The rebels have begun to haul siege cannon here from Ticonderoga, away up on Lake Champlain, now that there's snow on the backwoods roads. That's what they've been waiting for—good sledding. It's a long way, but they can cover it in the next month or two while the frost holds. I've seen our mastmen hauling spars heavier than any cannon through the woods in just this kind of weather."

"And what of it?"

"When they're ready they'll knock the fleet out of this harbor, and the army will have to go with the ships. The troops can't live a week without stores that come by sea."

"Now you're at your fancies again; I wish you wouldn't, Johnnie, you only upset yourself."

There was something contemptuous in her voice and in the attitude of that exposed cambric bottom.

"I'm fully awake—to a lot of things," Johnnie snapped. "And I intend to act upon them now. In fact I've arranged passage for you and the baby to England in the *Julius Caesar*, which sails in two or three weeks' time. No—don't argue. You must go. You'll have nothing to worry about over there—I had letters from Lady Rockingham and from Paul Wentworth, by the store-ship that came in yesterday. They're much concerned with my last to them from the old fort at Portsmouth, and both urge that you come and stay with them until this trouble's over."

"And may I ask what you intend to do yourself?" she said. She had dropped her gown and petticoats in the shock of this explosion, but she remained with her back to the stove and him.

"My duty's here, and I must remain."

She folded her arms and turned around. His jaw was set and so was his gaze, with no more hint of compromise than Wolfe-borough granite.

"Johnnie, you stupid thing, are you jealous?"

"Of whom?"

"Oh, of Captain Beaumont and Colonel Ward and those other silly men who like to dance and flirt with Mary and me. I suppose you've overheard some of those spiteful she-cats at the parties. Is that it?"

Fannie's eyes met his boldly. Johnnie's tongue coiled on an angry outburst. It was some time before he spoke. "All I have to say is what I've told you already, Fannie. I'm writing to Lady Rockingham and to Paul, accepting their hospitality on your behalf. Paul will advance any money you need, and you can live very comfortably in Yorkshire as a guest with the Rockinghams until all this trouble's over."

She tapped a foot. She had always been able to twist him round her finger, and she wondered which approach was best now. An angry storm? Or tears and outraged innocence? Or just her coaxing mood, teasing him into laughter with some pert bit of wit at the right moment? At the present moment approach of any kind seemed difficult. He was staring across the room like that Great Stone Face he had told her about, up in the mountains.

England? She turned this astonishing new prospect in her mind. At Johnnie's urging she had penned long letters from the summer idleness of Wentworth House, prattling to Lady Rockingham of the woods, the lake, the horses and cattle and dogs, like a true countrywoman. Naive letters, reflecting her own awe at the notion of addressing nobility, even at a distance of three thousand miles. And now a chance to meet nobility in the flesh, to mingle with their well-bred visitors, of whom Johnnie had talked so much in days gone by, and actually to live for a time in that great Yorkshire palace with all the fabulous luxury of the wealthy English! It would be something to talk about when she returned to Portsmouth with Johnnie at the war's end. She could hear herself mentioning famous names, with an elaborate casualness, while the Portsmouth ladies sat agog.

"Well," she said, after a long silence. "If you say I must go, I must." Her voice was so meek that Johnnie was taken by surprise. He had expected a tempest.

SIXTEEN

On the choking cold morning of the nineteenth of January, 1776, the storeship *Julius Caesar* cast off her lines, set her big fore-topsail, and moved away from the Long Wharf. Fannie's mother had taken a tearful farewell at the house, but Johnnie, young Benning, Tom Macdonogh, and the Brinleys made a little group huddling in the lee of a shed and waving handkerchiefs from the wharf's end.

The snow on the town's roofs and the harbor slopes glittered in thin sunshine. Wisps of vapor writhed upward from the harbor in the bitter air and hung a canopy just above the mastheads of the shipping. Ice had formed about the shores in the night and broken away with the lift of the morning tide, and the big bluff-bowed transport moved in a broken trash of it, tinkling and crackling along her sides. At first Fannie could look up the short length of King Street to the Province House and King's Chapel. Then the ship veered, and that view was lost. The *Julius Caesar* fired a departure gun, and in reply there was a white puff and a bang from the South Battery below Fort Hill. For some minutes Fannie remained on the deck, shapeless in a fur-trimmed cloak and hood and with the icy breeze blowing up her legs. Her eyes wept, partly from emotion, partly from the cold, but still she gazed glassily toward the town and the small human knot at the wharf's end.

Sailors aloft were edging along slippery footropes, like chicka-dees in the bare branches of a winter maple, casting off the gaskets of sails that sparkled with frost. The canvas was so stiff that it would not fall from the yards until the men below began to yo-ho and heave away on tacks and sheets, and as each sail finally caught the wind and filled, it did so with cracklings and squealings as if in protest at such work in such weather. The sailors made their own protest, out of the master's hearing, as they came with pinched faces down the ratlines. But once on deck they were cheerful enough, skipping about at their tasks, bawling jokes in their English accents and heaving away, with their hands wrapped in old wool stockings for want of mittens. They were glad to be leaving this dull, starving, and frostbitten town; and who cared about the perils and hardships of the North Atlantic passage when good roast beef and English ale and the sluts of London lay at the end of it? One of them, coiling a rope on a belaying pin near Fannie, turned for a look at the town, a stocky figure in linsey-woolsey trousers so wide and so short that they might have been a petticoat, a striped woolen jersey, and a thin gray surtout bought or purloined in Boston. He had a broad red Devon face and a clubbed pigtail as thick and black as a junk of oakum. With an impudent wink at the lady passenger he put a thumb on his broad nose and waggled the fingers at the shore.

"That for 'ee, Boston—ay, and all Ameriky. Let the rebels have 'ee and be damned." And off he skipped to another task. Johnnie would have been outraged. Fannie, in spite of the cold, in spite of everything, felt the imp in her awake. She had a whim to thumb her own nose at Ameriky, thinking especially of Portsmouth, of those Portsmouth ladies who considered her no better than a whore, and of the rabble in the streets who had cried the word aloud. I don't care if I never see the place again, never! And Johnnie? A twiddle of fingers for Johnnie. Packing me off like a kitchen maid caught with a coachman in the hay, because forsooth he couldn't bear the sight of me having pleasure in the midst of other men. Dreaming all sorts of things, no doubt, with that fanciful mind of his. Well! We shall see.

And she went below, shivering but strangely exultant, as if she too had slipped a mooring, like the ship.

At some prodigious price Johnnie had engaged for her the great cabin at the stern, the captain's own quarters; and he had secured as traveling maid a young loyalist woman, penniless and anxious to find a refuge in England. And because passengers had to supply their own provisions Johnnie had obtained—only God and George Brinley knew how—boxes and hampers of bread, butter, sugar, cheese, salt, and smoked meats of half a dozen kinds (no fish, thank heaven!), jars of fruit preserves from Mama's own cellar cupboards, cold roast turkeys and chickens, pickled beef tongues, potatoes, turnips, a keg of salt cabbage, dried beans and peas, white flour, corn meal—enough, it seemed, to feed the whole crew on a three months' voyage, instead of two women and a very small baby for surely not more than three weeks.

And there were several bottles of cordials, a case of port wine, a casket of medicines, a vast bundle of sheets, blankets and quilts, a basket crib for the baby, a set of Mama's silver knives, forks and spoons, a teakettle, and some pans. All this besides two portmanteaus, half a dozen bandboxes, and six cowhide trunks full of clothes. Most of this had to be stowed below somewhere, but even so the big cabin and its lockers were so crammed that she and Prudence Latham had barely room to move. Over all loomed the captain's stove, a tall foreign thing, sheathed in white porcelain and looking like a headless heathen god.

All these signs of Johnnie's care mollified her a little. The stove glowed with a fire of Nova Scotia coals, from the army's fuel bins undoubtedly. The cabin was warm, heaving a little but not uncomfortably in the seaway. The baby, well wrapped, lay in the crib, with Prudence crooning him to sleep. And Fannie thought now of those last moments at the wharf end, when Johnnie took her in his arms. The strange brusque manner of the past few weeks had fallen from him like a mask unfastened. He was the lover again, holding her fiercely, kissing her lips as if he could never get enough of them in the time that was left. She had stood limp and indifferent, to punish him as she had punished him ever since he announced his intention of sending her away. Not once in these weeks had she allowed him an intimacy, even though they shared one bed; at his slightest attempt she had turned a rigid back as if to say, If I can't have my pretty gentlemen Your Excellency shan't have me.

Silly, she thought now. But he'll be all the more eager when we meet again. A good sauce, hunger. Whenever he came back from those long journeys in the woods he could never get me to bed quick enough, nor love me enough when he got me there. As for me, there's England and enough wonderful new things and people to occupy me a twelvemonth.

As the voyage went on, day after day, she found this blithe outlook hard to hold. For some days there was fairly smooth sailing, as if the sea itself were numbed by the frigid air drifting off the continent. Then came a storm for three whole days and nights, then a lull and another gale. And another. She came to know why seamen spoke of a winter passage of the North Atlantic as if it were a passage through hell. There were many days and nights when all the hatches had to be battened down. A heavy deadlight had been closed over the stern window long ago. There was no light in the cabin but that of a single whale-oil lantern swinging and reeking in gimbals overhead. The air became dead and foul. The ship leaped and swayed and swooped like a runaway gig on a mountain road. The sea smote its decks and hull prodigious blows, as if in that progress from time to time it fell right in the path of a moving cliff. The space below decks was filled with the boom and shock of these collisions, with the squeaks and cracks and deep groanings of timber, under stresses that were never two minutes the same, and the thudding of sea boots and the shouts of seamen overhead.

The captain knocked and looked in from time to time to assure his passengers that all was safe "in spite o' this an' that." He was a lean man of dark aspect with a long red nose, from whose end a gleaming drop continually hung. Johnnie had paid him well for his accommodation and his services, and he made these appearances as part of the bargain. "This and that," he did not explain, included various sails that carried away, a fore-topmast that snapped, sundry ropes and stays that chafed and broke. In addition a longboat on mid-deck was swept away in a boarding sea, together with three live pigs and a sheep that had been kept in it. The hen coop vanished. So did a seaman one bad night. And another slipped from the main topmast crosstrees in broad daylight and perished in one single horrid thud on the deck.

The "westerlies," as the captain called these howling winds, were "fair for England but a mite too boisterous." He frequently spoke of "running under bare poles," whatever those were. Fortunately the cold eased as the *Julius Caesar* thrashed its way toward mid-ocean, but the ship was never comfortable; there were whole days when no seaman appeared with a bucket of coal for the cabin stove, when no food could be cooked or even warmed; and in every storm there were thin trickles of water through the planking overhead. Through it all the baby lay content, rocked in this almighty cradle, with the crib wedged between a bulkhead and a pair of lashed trunks. If omens mean anything, Fannie thought, the child should be an admiral.

There were times when the wind swung ahead, with a storm of snow, and the ship lay hove to, the bow slowly coming up toward the blast and falling off again. Sometimes a helmsman let the bow fall off too far, and the hull tipped to a frightful angle, with everything below sliding and banging and huge seas pouring over the decks one after another.

There were days when the fickle weather calmed, when Fannie and Prudence took turns on deck, when even Fannie sucked in the cold fresh air as if it were some delicious and half-forgotten perfume. Sometimes there was a sun in the sky, when the sea was no longer the evil gray of a witch's hair but a deep blue, smooth and gleaming, like the steel of Johnnie's dress sword, stolen by the Portsmouth mob.

But these halcyon days were few and wide apart. In the rough weather the girl Prudence suffered wretchedly from seasickness, and Fannie, putting aside her own qualms, took care of her and the baby as well. Whenever nausea came she clenched her teeth and fought it back, as she had fought it in those mornings of her first pregnancy, with Theo dying and then dead and with the watchful women all about her. And all this in the cramped prison of the cabin, with its queer mingled smells of urine and boxed cheese and rank butter and unwashed female flesh and the stink of the whale-oil lamp.

More than four weeks of this purgatory crept past; and then one afternoon, toward sunset, the captain sent a hand to present his compliments and call Mrs. Wentworth to the deck. The sky was overcast except where the sun peered through at sea level, far astern. The air was mild, and here and there a fine drizzle of rain drifted across the sea's face. The captain pointed an unclean finger at a dim shadow on the horizon to the east.

"The Scillies, ma'am. Land's End is just beyond."

He was pleased with his navigation and his luck and expected a compliment, but the names meant nothing to Fannie. Sillies? Land's End? Her knowledge of English geography was confined to a few vague memories from a Boston dame school and Johnnie's talk of Yorkshire and London and Bath. What I want is the Sensibles and a Sea's End, she thought; we've gone far enough to fall over the edge of the world.

"What are they?" she said.

The captain snuffled. He was a patient man. "Tip o' Cornwall. Falmouth just around the corner, like. I'm goin' to hold her off for the night—nasty place, the Scillies—an' tomorrow I'll put into Falmouth for fresh water an' provisions. May be a long haul up the Channel an' round to the Thames if we git a spell o' weather from the east. I've see a fleet o' ships held in the Downs a fortnight or three weeks, awaitin' a fair shift."

"Then I shall leave the ship at Falmouth," said Fannie promptly.

"On t'other hand," said the captain, with the air of a man who does not trust the land very far, "it's a mortal long haul by coach from Falmouth to Lunnon, ma'am. Matter o' two hunnerd an' fifty, mebbe three hunnerd mile, an' the roads at their wust arter the winter rains. Rough goin', that, fer two women an' a babby."

"Falmouth," said Fannie resolutely.

"I mean to say, your husband paid your passage to Lunnon if ye want to keep on wi' the ship."

"No, we'll go by road," she said, and thought, *If we have to crawl to Lunnon on hands and knees.*

She was too excited to sleep, with this tremendous knowledge in her mind. She roused Prudence, and they spent most of the night packing the trunks and portmanteaus in the cabin, as if they would set foot on good solid earth by morning light. But it was far into the next afternoon before the *Julius Caesar* approached the Falmouth entrance. The wild rocky shore and the wooded slopes above looked utterly familiar. Why, it's like home, she thought; it's like New England after all; all it wants is pine and spruce and hemlock instead of all those bare hardwood trees.

And the town lay on a peninsula, somewhat like Portsmouth, with shipping at anchor in the roads. The streets were narrow and higgledy-piggledy, too, although nothing else was the same. Not a wooden house to be seen. Everything of brick or cut stone and looking as if it had stood there, with the rain pelting on its dark slate roofs, since Noah's time.

Fannie put up at an inn for the night. She wondered what to do next. Send a letter to Paul Wentworth and let him arrange to fetch her to London? Johnnie had given her a purse of guineas and London bank notes amounting to £120, all he could scrape together in Boston at the time of sailing. Pshaw! Why wait?

And so the next day she bargained with a wagoner to bring on the mass of heavy baggage to Paul's address in London, a fortnight's journey and a fat fee. She then set off in the Falmouth stagecoach with Prudence, the baby, and the portmanteaus. It was early March, with a gray wet sky and the trees bare, like late April at home. As the coach climbed up the cobbled slope out of Falmouth town they had a last glimpse of the *Julius Caesar*, seaworn and shabby, lying off the quay.

"Thank God that's over," Fannie cried. "I tell you, Prue, I'll not cross that ocean again in a year of Sundays, not while I keep my right mind. If my husband wants to see me again he shall make the voyage himself."

The road wound along a tidal river that ran far into the land and crossed the head of it at Truro, where at low tide the small ships lay heeled on the mud. The grass in the fields was a softer green than Fannie had ever seen in New England, and the farmhouses all had a solid ancient look that was charming even in the rain, but the Cornish countryside seemed stark and drear. She had thought of England as a land of milk and honey, and it was a surprise to see yokels at the wayside farms looking poorer than any but the poorest of backwoods folk or fishermen in America.

The roads were another. The coach bumped and swayed dangerously, on what seemed more like a stream bed than a highway, and often became mired in a slough-hole as bad as any on the road to Wolfeborough. At each posting inn, where the horses were changed, the hostler had a long list of warnings about the road ahead, and everything he said was true.

At Tavistock the coachman put his head in the door and jerked his head toward the east.

"We're coomin' to a baad bit nao. Twenty moil o' stwuns an' bogs. Dartmoor, we call 'un." And in a few minutes they were reeling and plunging in a wilderness as wild as a fire barren in the New Hampshire hills, a brown waste of barren rock and swamp, with patches of scrub oak here and there, all watched by rugged granite tors that stood over the dreary landscape like brooding giants.

At last they came to Exeter, a name with ominous memories for any New Hampshire loyalist, but a town very different from the one at home. Again the solid houses and shops, the cobbled streets, and here a tall and ancient cathedral, like nothing in America, and her first sight of a castle, dim in the rain.

Here they changed to another stagecoach, a ponderous thing with six powerful horses. It was like changing from a schooner to a frigate in mid-sea, for the road ahead was as deep in mud as the road behind. As the miles and the days went by, the journey became a blur of fields and villages and towns, all drenched in rains that paused at times but never ceased. And the nights were a succession of inns with hearty food but chambers as cold as charity, where the two women wrapped the baby carefully in its basket and then crept into one bed, clasping each other for warmth. Accustomed to the fires and stoves of New England, rarely extinguished before June, they found the damp of an English March as raw as a winter wind. The towns were merely names, shouted in talk at the inns, each a succession of narrow streets, muddy, or cobbled and merely wet, with the grim houses and slate roofs sliding by like cliffs on either hand. Salisbury, Andover, Basingstoke, Bagshot, Stanes, Brentford, all meant nothing.

It seemed to Fannie that she had been shaken and bruised for an eternity, first in the ship and then in these lumbering coaches, with no great difference. She had lost all knowledge of time, except that it was drawing on toward mid-March.

Then came Hammersmith and not far ahead, someone said, London. Magic name! She came out of the daze of the journey, peering eagerly through the door glass. The melancholy sky had cleared at last. The sun appeared miraculously, as if to prove that England had such a thing. And now in this warm light she saw dairy farms, and small clusters of houses, and great mansions, standing aloof in bare trees beyond acres of sheep-cropped lawns; and then the houses coming closer together, with gardens instead of fields, and taverns at frequent intervals; and then houses continual, and cobbled streets and flagstoned walks that went on without end. And now, in the fine weather, the sight of people in fine clothes, going in and out of shops or carriages, or pausing to chat with each other in a passing throng of common folk.

Johnnie had spoken of London as something fabulous in size alone, as big as all the cities and towns of America put together, and now she saw that it was true. The stagecoach, spattered with mud to the roof, seemed lost in a tide of carriages, chaises, hackney coaches, drays, carts, and gentlemen riding a-horseback. Somewhere in this maze the stagecoach stopped and discharged them, and they changed with their baggage to a hackney coach. They rode past Hyde Park and at last turned off Oxford Street into a small side street and stopped a few houses down.

"Poland Street, lady," the hackney coachman said. "And this

'ere is Mr. Paul Wentworth's 'ouse. Five shillin', ma'am, if you please."

For a moment, as he drove away, Fannie felt lost and faint. Prudence had the baby in her arms, and there at their feet were the portmanteaus and the baby's basket. The house was like any other in the row, a tall and narrow thing of gray cut stone, with large curtained windows and a short flight of steps to a massive door. A forbidding house, somehow. Nevertheless she went up the steps and jerked a white china bellpull. After some moments the door opened, and a stout footman in yellow plush breeches and a brown livery coat looked her up and down. She realized how worn and tired and bedraggled she was. His eyes went to Prudence and the baby.

"I've come to see Mr. Paul Wentworth," Fannie said timidly.

"Now, look 'ere," said the man. He had a cynical face, as if all this had happened before and he knew just how to deal with it. "Mr. Wentworth don't see gals that come to the door, ever. Besides he's out. So get along with you."

"But . . ."

"No tales, *if* you please. I've 'eard 'em all before."

The door slammed in her face. She was so nervous and weary that she felt she must drop to the step and weep. But now a smart brown carriage and pair clattered down the street, with a brown coachman in a cockaded hat on the box and a brown cockaded footman standing on the step at the rear. It pulled up outside the house. The footman sprang down and opened the door, and out came a short brisk pink-faced gentleman in a blue suit, a tiewig, and a cocked hat with heavy gold braid. He had a cane in his hand, and he indicated the portmanteaus, the basket, the women, and the baby in a single flourish.

"Whoever these creatures are, Jackson, get 'em away."

The footman approached them at a trot, and Fannie pulled herself together. Her back was one indignant line, as straight as a musket.

"Jackson, if that's your name, stay where you are. As for you, Mr. Wentworth, is this the way you receive a woman in distress?"

Up went Mr. Wentworth's brows. The American voice was unmistakable. So was the manner of a lady accustomed to freezing a servant with a word.

"Eh—I beg your pardon, madam—there seems to be some mistake. May I ask your name?"

"My husband's name," said Fannie coldly, "is John Wentworth, His Majesty's Governor of New Hampshire."

"Good God! I—Jackson, what the devil are you standing there for? Ring, man, and let us get inside." He trotted up the steps, stick under arm, and took Fannie's hands in his own. "Madam—Frances, isn't it?—Johnnie's written so much about you that I should have recognized you of course."

The door opened, and the hall footman, very obsequious now, bowed deeply as Paul swept the women inside.

"Get the ladies' things in here, quickly! Now my dear—is this your maid?—and your child of course. Well, bless my soul—come in here and sit down, my dear, sit down."

Fannie found herself in a long parlor furnished with gilt-legged and brocaded chairs, a pair of elegant sofas, side tables, a handsome Persian carpet, and rich velvet window hangings. Portraits of three or four elegant gentlemen looked down from the walls. And among them was Johnnie, the first copy of that Copley painting—Johnnie of the handsome head and the whimsical sidelong glance. Suddenly she found tears in her eyes and wished with all her heart that her good kind darling could step down from the frame and take her in his arms. A coal fire glowed under a white mantelpiece with elaborate carvings. The air had a faint mingled scent of elegant people who had sat in that room, and Fannie noted at once the scent of women. She had heard Johnnie's tales of Paul.

Wine came and some delicious sweet biscuits, and while Prudence followed a portly major-domo toward the servants' quarters Fannie gave Paul an account of her adventures since the revolt began in Portsmouth. As she talked she regarded her host carefully, seeing under the smart tiewig a short blond man of fresh complexion, with twinkling blue eyes, in the middle or late forties. He had an air of activity about him, even when sitting like this in a parlor chair. Johnnie had described his mind as brilliant and no doubt it was. He spoke with an intonation in which she could detect only a faint trace of the Yankee he once was. Years in the West Indies, in England, and on the continent, learning to speak French and Dutch and probably other tongues useful in his cosmopolitan trade, had given him an English speech that defied analysis. His questions were shrewd and pointed. He seemed to know a great deal about matters in America, including the present condition of Boston and Howe's army. She had a feeling that Johnnie was only one of many correspondents who kept him informed, but she knew, too, that he had a particular regard for Johnnie, begun all those years ago when Paul was a young merchant in Portsmouth and Johnnie a student home from Harvard. During those after years in England Johnnie had made his home here in Poland Street, and it was Paul's money and Paul's influence that had got him so many useful friends.

After a time he said kindly, "You're tired, my dear, after your long journey. Go to your chamber now—one of the servants will show your maid where it is—and rest yourself. I must dine out tonight, I regret to say, but I'll see you in the morning. Remember, this house is yours—dear me, it seems only yesterday I was telling Johnnie that, and it must be a good ten years and more."

"I must write to Lord and Lady Rockingham," Fannie said faintly.

"All in good time, dear lady, all in good time. Indeed I'll drop a line to Rockingham myself and save you the trouble. You must recover from your journey before you even think of setting out for Yorkshire. Roads—abominable, abominable, and York's as far from here as Falmouth. Gad, you won't want to face that in a hurry, eh? Nunno! Besides, you must see our London—which can't be done in less than a week—and I want you to meet my friends. It isn't often our London society sees a pretty American woman. I only wish Johnnie could be here to show you off."

And so began a very pleasant week that stretched into three

with surprising ease. After a few days the Falmouth wagon came with the baggage and for the first time since leaving Boston she could feel properly dressed. Nevertheless she was piqued to find that all her clothes, so smart in Boston, were at least a season behind the London mode.

Among the many gay and fashionable people she met at Paul's dinners and *soirées* was a Mrs. Phyllis Barradale, who had a house in Wardour Street not far away. She was a beautiful creature, about Fannie's own age, with smiling blue eyes and a tall figure. There seemed to be no Mr. Barradale, but the lady was well endowed, for she dressed expensively and kept a phaeton with four dashing gray ponies. She was never absent from Paul's parties and frequently came alone. On first introduction her manner to Fannie was cold, even hostile, but after that she seemed reassured about the pretty American in Paul's house and took her out a good deal.

It was Paul's own suggestion that Fannie add to her wardrobe in London before going on to Yorkshire, and for the wherewithal he took out a morocco leather pocketbook and slipped some bank notes into her hand. It was done with the finesse of a conjuring trick and the even flow of the conjurer's voice to cover the transfer.

"When that's gone, my dear, merely mention the word. I played Johnnie's banker in those old happy days, and it's like a new measure of life to play the part again. Tut! No questions. I promised Johnnie to look after you. Mrs. Phyl will be happy to show you where to shop and—if you like—what to buy. She moves with the best people and knows the mode—sometimes I think she sets the mode."

"But I can't . . ."

"Pooh! Johnnie'll wish you to dress well, meeting all these fashionable people, and don't forget you'll be staying with the Rockinghams in Yorkshire. They'll expect the best appearance of Governor Wentworth's wife. It's your duty to Johnnie, and you owe it to yourself."

When he had gone she looked at the notes in her hand. The

few slips of crisp paper amounted to £300. Well! Why not? The man was as rich as Croesus. She set off with Mrs. Barradale the very next day, in the phaeton with its spanking gray four and her coachman in a livery to match, and there followed a whirl of shops and milliners and mantuamakers beyond anything she had dreamed. For a week she lived in a haze of velvets and tiffanies and Cantons and Florentines, of moreens and crepes and satins and lutestrings, of buttons and ribbons and silver lace and gauze, of silken shoes and morocco shoes, of clocked silk stockings, of hats and bonnets and caps and plumes and bows and fichus and bandeaux.

Mrs. Barradale seemed well and favorably known. The mere sight of her ponies pulling up outside brought shopmen and milliners to their doors with smiles and bows, as if she were royalty. When she bought things herself—and she was fond of expensive trifles, especially in jewelers' shops—no money passed at all. She merely nodded, the shopmen smiled and scraped, a servant carried her lightest purchase out to the phaeton, and that was that. Once, in connection with a diamond brooch, there seemed to be a faint hesitation on a shopman's part, but in an instant a neat suave super-shopman appeared from nowhere, there was a whisper in which Fannie caught only Paul Wentworth's name, and all hesitation vanished.

At Paul's *soirées*, where he moved about like a busy pink cherub in the garb of a London dandy, Mrs. Barradale usually appeared as one of the guests, and he gave her the polite and cheerful attention that he gave them all. They were fastidiously dressed people and included women of all ages, from hatchet-faced dowagers to lovely creatures like Phyllis Barradale, and the gentlemen too were all ages, not a few with titles, and as elegant in dress and manner as the women.

They talked almost entirely of the *ton*, which meant themselves, it seemed. The word was constantly on their lips, as if nothing else existed in the world. Their speech was flavored with startling words and phrases never used in Portsmouth drawing rooms, although Fannie had overheard them in the army circle in Boston, and in their easy languid voices the most exquisite ladies and gentlemen exchanged gossip and jests that might have come straight from a barracks. Some of the prettiest ladies smoked thin little segars with all the nonchalance and the exact whiffs and gestures of the gentlemen. Sporting was a favorite word, and the sport of the *ton* seemed to include dogfights, cockfights, prize fights, horse racing, gambling for fantastic sums at faro or hazard at White's and Brooks's and a dozen other clubs or private houses whose names Fannie could not catch or remember, and the theater, the opera, dances, dinners, masquerades, the afternoon parade by horseback or in carriages in Hyde Park, and fine evenings strolling and flirting and sipping in the gardens at Vauxhall, in the Pantheon, or under the rotunda at Ranelagh. If she could believe her ears in these casual conversations, the most popular sport was that of hopping into bed with members of the other sex at every opportunity, and the most amusing part was the game of seducing one another's wives or mistresses. In this talk the *ton* made much use of nicknames, so that they talked in a kind of cipher, and it did not dawn on her for some time that a dashing female known as The Filly was in fact Mrs. Phyllis Barradale.

When addressing themselves politely to Paul's guest, they drawled one question about America; it always had to do with forests and Mohawks. It irritated Fannie sometimes. In spite of her London gowns and a new powdered coiffure as tall and majestic as one of the White Mountains, she felt awkward and provincial. She had none of the small talk of the *ton,* and she resented their condescension. When she said that she had never seen a Mohawk in her life and spoke of a genteel life in Portsmouth and Boston, they gave her a vague look as if she were talking of *Gulliver's Travels* or some other fantastical book of which they had heard but had not read, or they laughed very pleasantly, as if the notion of an American *ton* were a very witty one indeed.

Occasionally Paul gathered a much different company. The guests were entirely male, and they talked of business or art or politics or poetry with none of the languid foppishness of the *ton.* Fannie was introduced to some of them. Their names meant nothing to her, and on the whole their conversation was no more comprehensible than that of the others, but sometimes Paul would relate to her, the next day, a few things about them, and she realized that she had been for a time under one roof with some of the most famous men in London. A few remained in her mind. David Garrick as a short man, getting fat and closing sixty, with an easy jovial manner and a pair of bright clear eyes that seemed to see into the back of her head. Richard Sheridan in contrast was in the middle twenties, a lively nervous young man with a long nose in a sheep's face.

Paul said of them, "Garrick's about at the end of his stage career. Ready to sell out and rétire. Remarkable fellow, best actor England's ever had. Dick Sheridan had him off in a corner most of the evening. Wants to buy Garrick's half of the Drury Lane Theatre, a matter of five-and-thirty thousand pounds. Preposterous on the face of it. I mean Sheridan has a little money through his wife, and they've set 'emselves up in great style in Portman Square, but all he's got really is his brains. Brought out a play called *The Rivals* last year, and then *The Scheming Lieutenant,* and all this winter he's been doing a comic opera kind of thing called *The Duenna*—the rage of London. He'll find Garrick's price, I think. Borrow most of it on mortgage probably—I don't think he could raise a thousand pounds himself. A hot Whig and a friend of Rockingham's. Very eloquent against the present measures in America. Make a very good parliament man if he turned his mind that way."

And again, "Did you mark the man with big eyes and the nose like a bowsprit and the touch of Paddy in his speech? That's Burke, Edmund Burke. Best mind the Whigs have got, and a great friend of America. Made a remarkable speech on conciliation last year—everyone still talking about it. Bold gambler at the tables. Poor Burke can't keep away from 'em—worse than drink by a long shot—and the fella should. No luck, no luck at all. Rockingham's lent him thousands of pounds. Of course Lord Rockingham's got an interest in Burke apart from friendship.

Rockingham's an amiable well-meaning fella, head of the Whig party—or one faction of it I should say—and very anxious to unite 'em against North and the King. But, truth to tell, he's much too amiable for his own good. Weak, I mean to say, weak. Burke looks like the one man who could pull 'em together if he set his mind to it, and Rockingham knows it."

For a time it seemed to Fannie that Paul entertained nobody but idle fops and busy Whigs and a very odd collection of both. But one evening there was still another group, with another conversation, full of harsh words for the Whigs, both in England and America. Fannie was presented to them, but when she retired to her chamber to write a letter to Johnnie she could not remember a single name except the most important one, Lord North. He was a set-looking man in the forties, with a broad face, a great pug nose, an absurd little pointed chin; a very ordinary creature to be head of the government.

Apparently Paul played the political game from both sides. Or was it simply that he played no politics at all and marked his neutral position with these separate entertainments? It was all very puzzling, and she gave it up. It was much easier to write about the marvels of London, of her visits with Mrs. Barradale to Vauxhall Gardens and Ranelagh, of her rides through Hyde Park in the daily throng of the *ton*, an evening at the play, an excursion in a handsome eight-oared barge to Windsor in the bright spring weather, stopping for refreshments in charming little inn gardens at the Thames-side. Paul had been very kind. She had all the money she wished, and the baby was thriving. She'd had a very gracious letter from Lady Rockingham, and she was leaving in Paul's coach-and-four for Yorkshire in another week. Your affectionate wife, Frances.

Now that the move to Yorkshire was before her Fannie had a queer little dread of it. She remembered Johnnie's talk; his discovery that England and the empire were ruled, not so much by the King or Parliament as by the great Whig families, most of them immensely rich, who lived like kings in the countryside, and of his own astonishment and awe on visiting the Rockinghams and setting foot in fabulous Wentworth Woodhouse. She felt ignorant and *gauche,* afraid that in any word or step she might betray a lack of breeding in the English sense, so different from the little colonial aristocracy she had known.

She had got used to Paul's easygoing household in the heart of London and the blithe companionship of The Filly. Never a dull day, not even a dull hour, and still so much to explore in this exciting city where pleasure was the rule. But of course she must go, for Johnnie's sake. The horsy gentlemen who came to Paul's house were always saying that if North's government came a cropper in this American affair, or even faltered at a fence, damme, the Whigs would come into their own and take both saddle and reins again. As Paul explained to her, that could mean Rockingham as Prime Minister, with all the favors he might cast Johnnie's way—and God knew Johnnie needed favors now, with his position thrown down by the rebels and his whole future in doubt, eh my dear?

SEVENTEEN

*F*OR JOHNNIE the winter passed slowly, in pangs of cold and
doubt. As gale followed gale in the weeks after Fannie left he
fretted about her and the baby, haunted by visions of the old
transport foundering in the winter sea. He regretted sending her
now. A frightful risk. But when March came with its warmer
sun it brought some inner cheer. With God's grace she must be
safe by now, enjoying that lovely countryside in the soft English
spring. She would write at once, of course, but in the bluster of
the March westerlies the mails from England would find heavy
weather. A passage of six weeks at best, and probably more. He
could not expect to hear from her before mid-April, and he resigned himself to that.

Meanwhile, what with smallpox and slow starvation and
cold, Boston had become a combined pesthouse and almshouse,
much of it ruined. Scores of empty houses had been pulled
down and burned for fuel. So had old wharves and stables, even
the old North meetinghouse. Every old boat and wagon, every
empty cask in the fish sheds, every fence had vanished. So had
most of the trees that once shaded the Boston streets, the notorious Liberty Tree first and then the others. Even the row of
handsome sycamores by the church on Brattle Street had gone
up in chimney smoke.

The ships in the harbor swung at their icy moorings with
the tides and winds. The troops huddled in their barracks and
billets or behind the defenses at the Neck. The giddy whirligig
of parties and balls in the army circle faltered sadly, as if its
clockwork ran down.

George Brinley had got a posting to the regular army com-
missariat. Mrs. Loring's complaisant husband was at the head of

it, wearing his golden horns. Every day Brinley grumbled at the work thrust upon him and the other junior officers, but he clearly enjoyed work, throwing himself into it with all the astute energy he had used in his own business before the siege. On the side he was able to see that Sarah Wentworth's household, as well as his own, had food and fuel enough. And from time to time he brought news.

Boston seemed to be the only place still flying the King's colors in all the colonies. Even Canada was mostly in rebel hands. Benedict Arnold and an army of daring Yankees had crossed the wilderness to besiege Quebec, another rebel army had captured Montreal and swept down the St. Lawrence to join Arnold, and there the last British garrison was merely hanging on by its teeth, like Howe in Boston.

One frosty evening in early March George Brinley came with a solemn face, drawing Johnnie aside and shutting the door.

"Well, it's happened!"

"The rebels are in Quebec?"

"Quebec! The rebels are up on Dorchester Heights, right here across the harbor! In force! Howe can't attack 'em now—it'd be ten times worse than Bunker's Hill. He wouldn't bother about the Heights all winter. Said nobody could dig earthworks with hard frost in the ground and snow on top of it. But there the rebels are, and they're not digging earthworks. They're piling up ramparts of baled hay, soaking 'em with water and letting 'em freeze hard enough to stop a round shot. And now they've got dozens of oxen at work, sledding siege cannon up to the crest— guns brought all the way from Ticonderoga, just as we suspected. In a few days they'll be tossing shot down into the anchorage like ha'pence into a hat."

"Can't the fleet shoot back?"

"Bah! Most of 'em are transports and storeships. Only three are proper men-o'-war, and they can't elevate their guns enough to reach the Heights. They'll try, no doubt. But once they've had a shot or two about their ears you know what those Navy men will do. Howe may be high cockalorum ashore here, but the admiral's his own master, and he won't risk his ships for this blundering army—d'you blame him? So, Johnnie, look out for a chance to get yourself and Tom and young Benning away when the time comes. God knows where Howe will go, but all the refugees will have to follow him, that's sure. There's no safety for 'em here."

"What about you and your family?"

"The Commissary Department will look after us, and old Mrs. Wentworth and her servant if they want to go with us." He paused. "If you want to join Fannie in England there's a dispatch brig leaving for London in a day or two. That young friend of yours, Ben Thompson, is going in her to seek a position in England."

"I'd sacrifice my posts by running over there," Johnnie said. "I'm staying in America, whatever comes." He considered a moment. "I'll write a dispatch to Lord Dartmouth, explaining this new predicament, that's all."

When the dispatch was written he put it in the hands of Benjamin Thompson.

"I wish you to deliver this to Lord Dartmouth in person, Ben. And here's a letter of introduction. I've recommended you as a most capable young man and asked him to find you a secretarial post in the government offices in London. He'll do what he can, and I know you'll make the most of any opportunity he may put your way. You're bound to do well, with your brains and energy. Good-by, my friend. I hope someday we can meet again at Wolfeborough and make that survey of the mountains with the proper instruments."

On the fifth day of March the first rebel gun fired from Dorchester Heights, a sharp crack that sent echoes booming through the town and along the snowy slopes. It fired at irregular intervals throughout the day, all ranging shots, all short, and the warships hastily manned their frosty guns and thundered back, with no better effect. On the next day the rebel cannon fired slowly from first light until dark, and there were one or two ominous splashes in the anchorage. According to Tory spies the rebels would need another fortnight to get all their heavy guns in place and fully ready.

Now General Howe came out of his snug hibernation in a rush. There was furious activity in his headquarters and in the streets, and the word sped quickly through the populace. The fleet must leave the anchorage within ten days, no later, and the army would go with it. Johnnie made straight for the wharves, looking over the moored merchant ships, the fishing vessels and coasters of all sizes and rigs that lay along the water front. He was not alone. Other refugees were there, seeking passage. At last, after some hopeless bargaining—the skipper named a stiff price and stuck to it—he chartered a small coasting schooner for himself, Benning, Tom Macdonogh, old Dr. Caner the rector of King's Chapel, and various other loyalist friends of his too destitute to pay a penny. She was a grubby thing, with badly worn rigging and sails, but her name was *Resource*, a good enough omen. For the next ten days and nights the army marched, regiment by regiment, down to the Long Wharf to embark. The Light Dragoons, with their white death's-head badge, made an especially fine sight, although their horses showed the effect of many months on meager forage. Toward the end the town became a madhouse. The loyalists of Boston itself joined with the refugees from outside in a rush to the waterside, like frightened animals fleeing a forest fire, demanding, asking, finally begging and praying for passage in anything that had a deck and sails and would float. Many of them brought all their belongings, by cart, by sled, even by handbarrows. The rich and quick found room in a ship for all they had; others had to settle for a few choice pieces, or found no room at all. Toward the end the whole harborside from Windmill Point to the Charles River ferry was an amazing sight, piled with tables, chairs, beds and bedding, sofas, mirrors, pictures, carpets, and hangings rolled up and corded for a journey they would never make. At the very last, on the night before departure, groups of soldiers, seamen and refugee men went about with axes, smashing the abandoned furniture, setting it afire, and hurling the rest of the litter into the flames. Nothing must be left to the rebels.

The nocturnal looting of houses, which had gone on all winter, changed boldly to daylight in the last week. Thieves were inside and busy as soon as each family of refugees quitted a home for a ship. Long before the last of Howe's soldiers withdrew from the Neck defenses under cover of night most of the town had been thoroughly pillaged. Only those Whig citizens who had stayed during the siege and still remained were able to keep some part of their properties intact.

On the day of departure the warships sent a final futile roll of thunder along the harbor hills, and the great flock of shipping drifted on a light wind down the bay, just as Washington's army entered the town by the road along the Neck.

When the flagship reached safe anchorage in Nantasket Roads, eight miles from Boston, she fired a gun for attention and hoisted a flag signal. The whole queer assemblage came to anchor, one after another, until the Roads were a floating city of hulls and spars. More than one hundred and fifty craft of all kinds, from a three-decker to the little fishing pinkies, lay sweeping their masts back and forth under the hard March sky. The transports held more than thirteen thousand army people—soldiers, wives, children, and camp followers. The smaller craft had something like two thousand civilian refugees, male and female, old and young. Some of the refugees, like Johnnie, had been well-to-do before the war, but many more were of the middle class and the poor. They were exiles not so much because they loved the King as because they disliked the mobs and had been bold enough to say so. Their only hope now was in the King's army and a victorious return, and it seemed a faint one as they floated away.

If the past ten days had been bad, the next ten were worse, for during the whole of that time the ships wallowed idly in Nantasket Roads with their crowded and seasick freight. General Howe seemed unsure where to go. Rumor crept about the ships. New York was the favored destination—a loyalist town by

239

and large. Some thought the West Indies, where most of the North American squadron had gone for the winter. Some declared England. On March 17 the flagship fired a gun, hoisted sailing signals at last, and led the way to sea. The course was eastward. England? It was some time before the refugees knew. They were bound for Nova Scotia, that far wild outpost of New England, the only American colony that had not sent an agent to the Congress.

To troops and refugees alike it seemed a journey to the Pole, four hundred miles at the very least, and at the end of it, according to all report, a bleak peninsula of rock and forest, tenanted by Indians and a few thousand fishermen. Johnnie himself had only seen the town of Halifax and a few river mouths along the south shore, where he had cruised with Captain Harry Bellew in the *Beaver* years ago. The inhabitants seemed to be mostly seafaring New Englanders, who had moved there after the last French war to be nearer the cod banks. The country was said to be so cold in winter and so muffled in fog the rest of the time that the humorous Cape Codders called their down-East cousins Blue Noses.

The voyage was rough, and Johnnie thought often of Fannie and the baby, tossed on this cold gray waste for God knew how long on the way to England. The fleet was a fortnight merely getting from Nantasket Roads to Halifax, overcrowded and poorly provisioned, and most of the refugees were starving by the journey's end. The *Resource* proved herself a fair sea boat in spite of her decrepit hull and gear, and she sailed into Halifax harbor with the first division of the fleet on March 30. The rest straggled in two days later.

The harbor itself was magnificent, a deep fiord running between low wooded hills for miles and opening far beyond the town in a broad salt basin, like the Piscataqua at home. There was even a big island sitting in the harbor mouth, as Newcastle Island sat below Portsmouth. But there the resemblance ended. The town was a small wooden huddle on the flank of a sugar-loaf hill, with a fringe of rickety wharves and warehouses at the foot. A few officials and merchants had mansions of two stories, ornamented and painted in the Portsmouth style. The rest were more like the simple hovels of the Isles of Shoals fishermen, shingled or clapboarded, sharp-roofed to shed the winter snows, all weathered to the tint of the rainy sky. Rude batteries of logs and earth pointed a few guns over the anchorage, and some distance farther up the harbor lay a small naval dockyard.

As soon as the *Resource* dropped anchor Johnnie hurried ashore to seek lodgings for the refugee families who had come with him and for Tom Macdonogh, young Benning, and himself. The choice was poor, he found at once, but he wasted no time in renting rooms. The price of everything would leap to the sky as soon as that homeless multitude began to pour ashore.

With this done he called on the Governor in his painted wooden residence at the corner of George and Hollis streets. His name was Legge, a fat scowling personage, a former major in the British Army who had got the post through his relative Lord Dartmouth. This worthy gave Johnnie a few minutes. He was overwhelmed with the sudden descent of the army and all the demands that went with it, and he could offer no accommodation for the vagrant governor of New Hampshire. Johnnie mentioned casually his own friendship with Lord Dartmouth, but it made no difference. General Howe, it seemed, had sent one of his brigadiers in a swift vessel ahead of the fleet, and the best available housing in the town had been reserved for the General, his staff, and their numerous appendages, including his own pretty appendage Mrs. Loring.

As he tramped away through the stained slush and a winter's accumulation of flung slops from the houses Johnnie reflected dourly on his position. It began to dawn on him that a mere civil governor, in flight from his own province, had no claims at all in the train of an army at war.

All through the dismal April rains he chafed at doing nothing, at the absence of any word from Fannie. Some of the leading merchants, finding that the Governor of New Hampshire was in their midst, politely invited him to wine and dine. They regretted that they could not offer him a bed—every spare chamber in their homes was given over to officers of the army—and they seemed chiefly concerned with his post as Surveyor General of the King's Woods. Now that the mast supply of New England was in rebel hands, His Majesty's Navy must look to Nova Scotia, eh? A chance for some business in that line! Johnnie confessed himself too preoccupied with other matters to give much thought to masts, or to the Nova Scotia forest at all. It gave him a qualm to think that this wild corner of the coast was the only part of His Majesty's Woods still under his authority. He changed the subject, insisting that present conditions could not last.

Meanwhile the great migration had settled in and about the town. The army had marched up the steep narrow streets, a long red snake winding around the flank of the sugar-loaf hill, and across a swamp to what was called Camp Hill; and that low rise in the pastures behind the town was now covered with their tents. Every house in the town was crammed with officers and camp followers, male and female. Refugees with enough money had been able to bribe their way into lodgings; the rest huddled miserably in deckhouses removed from the ships and set up in empty spaces along the streets, in torn and discarded army tents, in mere wigwams of poles and brushwood in the fields.

Dispatches had arrived from England, but the General and his staff kept remarkably mum. Johnnie's only source of military information had vanished. In fact, George Brinley, that shrewd Yankee merchant in army scarlet, was now in his element, scouring the countryside for supplies. Weeks passed before he turned up on a galled cavalry horse and rejoined Mary and her children in their small rented cottage at the edge of the town. Johnnie went there to dine on the following evening, walking the whole way in the muddy lanes.

After dinner, over a bottle of excellent brandy ("some of Howe's own, I assure you, but don't mention it") the commissary captain lit a segar and held forth.

"Nothing to be had but timber anywhere on the seaward side of Nova Scotia, and we don't want that. The army's under canvas, and I'm assured there's no need of barracks. No winter quarters, d'you see? Mark that. Well, the land over on the Fundy side is quite another matter. Good red soil, fat grass in the marshlands, all kinds of cattle, hogs, sheep, and fowls. Scrubby breed of horses on the whole, but some good enough for cavalry mounts. Forage of the finest kind in the marsh meadows—the Light Dragoons have gone across to Windsor to make the most of it. These merchants here, a sharp lot, all at loggerheads with Governor Legge. Best of 'em's a man named Francklyn, Michael Francklyn. Knows everyone in the province and knows how to get things done. We're putting a lot of business his way, hence a few favors, like this house."

None of this interested Johnnie in the least.

"The army," he said impatiently. "What's the army to do here?"

George Brinley leaned back and blew smoke rings at a cracked and soiled ceiling that twelve months ago he would have scorned to sit beneath. He had the air of a man who knows something tremendous and intends to enjoy the possession for some time before parting with it.

"At the moment," he said cheerfully, "the army's presence is all that keeps the Nova Scotia Whigs from open rebellion. This Governor Legge—a fat noisy fool—has managed to quarrel with everybody in the province, as far as I can see, Whig and Tory, high and low. Most of the people are transplanted Yankees that came up here after the French war. Their friends and relatives are all in Massachusetts, Connecticut, Rhode Island—and you know what the sentiment is there. At the head of Minas Basin there's a busy colony of Scotch-Irish. Levelers to a man. As these people see it, all Canada's now in the hands of an American army, except for Quebec town. When Quebec falls some of the rebel forces will be free to come this way. Meanwhile Massachusetts is promising arms and reinforcements if the Nova Scotia Whigs rise, and Mr. Washington's sent agents to sound 'em out. A pretty picture, eh? Rebel armies marching from Boston and Quebec, the provincial Whigs up in arms, and Howe caught again between the devil and the deep sea, just the way he was in Boston. Observe, he's been here a month and hasn't even put a cannon on that sugar-loaf hill, which looks right down the Halifax chimneys. Dorchester Heights all over again. So he'd have to sail away again—his last foothold gone—and the whole continental seaboard in the rebels' hands. If you think that's purely fanciful, ask Governor Legge. He keeps an armed guard about Government House, day and night, there in the heart of the town, for fear the Halifax Whigs will cut his throat."

Johnnie thrust his fists into his breeches pockets and leaned back patiently. He did not care a rap about Nova Scotia or the people in it, Whig or Tory. And George Brinley was obviously enjoying himself with these fancies.

"On the face of it the rebels have a mighty fine applecart in North America at this moment, haven't they, Johnnie? The whole continent within their grasp. Ha!" Brinley took the segar from his teeth and pointed it at Johnnie like a fuming pistol. "Now, my friend, let me tell you what's going to upset it. It's something to be a commissary captain. If you can provide certain people on the staff with a nice tender round of beef, a prime shoulder of mutton, or say a case of fine old Oporto got no-matter-where, you hear the most interesting things. Johnnie, those gentlemen in the War Office haven't been asleep, it seems. They've been moving heaven and earth—England and half Europe anyhow. To be exact they're pouring British troops across the sea. Horse, foot, and artillery. A list of famous regiments as long as your arm. Even His Majesty's own Foot Guards, can you imagine that? And that's not all. They're hiring German soldiers by whole brigades in Hesse and Hanover and Waldeck and Brunswick. They're even trying to hire Queen Catherine's wild Russians by the thousand."

He paused, to let Johnnie savor this before going on. Johnnie was incredulous. "These informants of yours—I trust they were sober after all that old Oporto?"

"Cold sober, Johnnie. Cold and sober as these damned Nova Scotia rains."

"And who's to command these armies, and where?"

George Brinley took another whiff at the segar. Mary was upstairs putting the children to bed, and there was no one else in the house, but he dropped his voice to a tone just above a whisper.

"In the first place General John Burgoyne has sailed with an army of British and foreign troops for Quebec—they'll be there as soon as the ice is gone. They're to destroy Arnold's rebel army or chase it out of Canada. In either case they'll press on and take Ticonderoga. You know what that means. At Ticonderoga a British army, with a swarm of Canadians and Indians, can threaten the back doors of all New England or the Hudson Valley—the road to New York. In the second place Howe's to move his army by sea to New York, and another strong force from England will join him there, with a fleet commanded by his brother. By the end of June at the latest he'll be standing at the mouth of the Hudson with the biggest army ever seen in America."

He chuckled. "You know, Howe wasn't quite the fool we thought. Nor was Lord Dartmouth, over there in England. The trouble was, we couldn't see anything but Boston. They were looking at the whole map. Boston had no military value, except as winter quarters for the army, and once the spring sun began to shine it wasn't worth a rap. The proper place for the British army was New York, where they could strike at Philadelphia and send the Congress scampering. The plan was to move there this summer. When the rebels set up their cannon on Dorchester Heights they bustled Howe out of Boston before he was ready, that's all. There had to be time for those reinforcements and supplies to get across the sea. So he came up here to wait. By the first of June he'll be on his way to carry out the plan."

Johnnie shifted uneasily. His mind still clung to New Hampshire. If half this fantasy were true the army of Burgoyne might strike at Boston from Lake Champlain. In that case New Hampshire would be right in the war path. He traced the path in his mind, seeing a swarm of British and foreigners and Indians fighting the New Hampshire men in the familiar woods and farms. He could not help thinking of that autumn day under the pine on Mount Delight, when the whole scene had a bloody look.

He said in a hushed voice, "An invasion like that—it's monstrous. Every American, whatever his politics, would turn out to fight."

George Brinley smiled and tamped the stub of his segar into the bowl of a battered pewter candlestick on the table. "My dear Johnnie, don't you see the point? It means that once these British armies are in position the rebels will be offered a choice. They can have war at very bad odds, or they can climb down their Liberty poles and talk sense. Howe will offer 'em some sort of compromise. It's common knowledge in the staff that he doesn't want a war. And the Whigs in England, not least your friend Rockingham, are pushing the government for conciliation and all that. Well, there must be some peacable heads in the Congress too. I'll lay you ten guineas to five that the whole thing will be patched up by fall. The King's governors back again, on a guarantee of no reprisals. Take it?"

"Done! I'll be happy to pay you the money."

From this time Johnnie could bear idleness no more. It seemed to him that he must do something to earn his salary as Surveyor General, and there was the hint of the Halifax timber merchants about masts for the Navy. If George Brinley was right there would be a huge fleet in North American waters all summer. A gale or two, with masts and yards cracking right and left, and where were the new spars to come from?

He engaged a fishing sloop and set off along the Nova Scotia coast, looking into the rivers he had seen before, and then around to the Bay of Fundy. What he saw confirmed all his old impressions and added important new ones. There was a supply of first-rate spars to be had in a dozen places, and for good measure he had marked off whole blocks of timber at two points within easy reach of tidewater. It was refreshing to tramp the woods again—almost like going home. There seemed to be no cedar, but otherwise the trees were those of New Hampshire, and the forest had the same good smell of spruce and fir and pine. It was satisfying to watch his axmen blazing big pines again and carving in the clean white wood the King's broad arrow and his own JW. He returned to Halifax, examined the mast pond at the dockyard, and began a long report to the Lords of Trade and Plantations. He was busy at this one day with Macdonogh when Tom paused and looked up.

"I forgot to mention it, sir, but a dispatch brig came in from England yesterday with mails."

"Ha!"

"You'll have a chance to write by return, sir. She's leaving on the twelfth with Governor Legge—he's been recalled to England."

"Oh? What for?"

"Well, you know what these Nova Scotians think of him, sir. The merchants have been asking London to take him away before he goads the province into revolt—he's been trying hard enough. I venture General Howe's had a word to say too. Anyhow, Legge's going." Tom's Irish grin spread over his broad face. "A chance for you, sir. I hear the post is worth a cool thousand a year."

Johnnie smiled himself. "Nova Scotia? Tom, I wouldn't take it on a wager. D'you know what our refugees call this province? Nova Scarcity, and a damned good name for it. The only town of any size is Halifax—and look at it! The rest is a scatter of half-starved villages about the coast. Remind me to pay a call on Governor Legge on the morning of the twelfth—I must say Good-by to him if only for politeness' sake. And now, Tom, trot down to the post office and see if there's a letter from my wife. If there isn't I'll go melancholy mad."

When Tom came back he had a whole packet; letters from Paul Wentworth, from Lord Rockingham, from Lord Dartmouth, and two from Fannie—two! He opened hers at once, breaking the seals with such eager fingers that he tore the letter paper. The first was the simple note she had written soon after reaching Paul's house. He lingered happily at the foot of it—*Your affectionate wife, Frances.* Ah, my darling! The second letter was written two weeks later. She was settled and enjoying London.

She gave a list of places seen, of parties at Paul's house, of charming people she had met. She was going about a great deal with a Mrs. Barradale, a very well-bred woman and one of the *ton*. (What the deuce was the *ton*?) And she was leaving for Yorkshire soon. Give her love to Mama and Mary and dear Benning. What news from New Hampshire? *Your affectionate wife, Frances.*

The other letters now. Paul's was one of his usual brief scrawls. He affirmed that Mrs. Frances and the baby were well and happy and comfortable in Poland Street. Johnnie could be sure that their every want was attended. Lord Rockingham's letter said what Johnnie already knew, that the government was sending strong forces to America. He offered no particulars. He and the other Whigs were still pressing hard for a peaceable solution. He understood that General Howe was to offer the olive branch rather than the sword, but he feared too small a branch considering the size of the sword. He could only hope for Wisdom and Temperance on both sides. Meanwhile he and his lady had received a note from Mrs. Frances in London, and they expected her at Wentworth Woodhouse in a week or two.

The letter from Lord Dartmouth, busy man, was really from one of his secretaries. It referred briefly to the government's military measures. It hoped that the American troubles might be solved in the coming summer and Mr. Wentworth restored to his post and his provincial emoluments. In the meantime my Lord Dartmouth was sensible of Mr. Wentworth's difficulties, and he had arranged that the Pensions Fund should pay him, until further notice, £600 sterling per annum in place of the £700 provincial currency which Mr. Wentworth had formerly received from the Assembly in New Hampshire.

Johnnie put it down with a glow of relief. The money problem was solved, at any rate. He read the letters from Fannie again and again and rubbed his eyes and found them wet.

On the twelfth morning of May he put on his best silk breeches and scarlet coat and set out to pay his farewell call on Governor Legge. It was a bright warm day, with a few clouds drifting across the blue. The streets were muddy, stinking now with the winter's refuse, and churned to an evil mess by the wandering crowds of refugees and off-duty soldiers and sailors. Along the way, between the poorly stocked shops and roaring taverns, stood booths of boards and canvas and brushwood, like a sorry sort of fair, where hungry refugees offered their watches and trinkets, table silver, and other such objects for sale. The little town was glutted with such stuff, and a passer-by could have anything for a small amount in coin. Most of the refugees' customers seemed to be countrymen, up to town for the market with their oxcarts and driving hard bargains for their hams and potatoes and fresh beef.

Some of the trinket vendors Johnnie recognized as people once well to do in Boston and the outside towns. When their looks met, both were embarrassed; they that he should see them in this position, he that he could not spare them a shilling. In his offhand way he had been giving money all winter to friends in need, and now, even with the heartening promise from Lord Dartmouth, he knew the burden of his debts. In his pocket at the moment he had barely enough money to hire a vehicle at the coach stand by the Parade.

It was only a minute's walk from the Parade to the Governor's house, but he determined to call in proper dignity, as one governor upon another. The choice at the Parade stand was indifferent. The town afforded only two or three ramshackle coaches drawn by the poorest screws, and after a brief inspection he chose a newly painted sedan chair instead. In this, swaying over the mud of George Street in the hands of a pair of stout porters, he came to the residency. As he stepped out the grenadiers on guard said stiffly that the Governor had left, that, in fact, he was now at the King's Wharf about to embark. They pointed to the water front a short distance away.

At the King's Wharf he found a large crowd to see the Governor off. Most of them were poorly dressed townsmen, and Johnnie was surprised. Legge seemed to be more popular with the people than he had supposed. He paid off his chairmen in a hurry and began to make his way in the throng. When he reached the waterside he was too late. The Governor, a short fat figure in scarlet, with a black cloak and a high cocked hat, was sitting on a thwart near the stern of a man-o'-war's barge, and the boat was pulling slowly away from the stone steps of the landing place.

There was a strange silence. The people stood without a word, watching the departure. The white-wigged young officer in charge of a squad of redcoats at the head of the landing steps seemed uneasy, glancing now at the boat and now at the people. Suddenly a voice cried from the crowd, "Good-by, Governor—and good riddance!" At once the whole throng broke into cry. "Yahhhh!"—"Booo!"—and then a chorus of profane taunts and execrations. Someone threw a clod of mud. It made a bright splash in the water. In a moment others were stooping, and the boat's coxswain urged his crew to greater efforts. The young army officer did not seem to know what to do, except to murmur to his men repeatedly, "Steady! Steady!" They were standing at attention, with their musket butts on the ground and their bayonets sheathed. No doubt the memory of that old Boston affair still haunted the army's mind. None of Howe's staff seemed to have come down to honor the Governor with their presence. Indeed Johnnie could not see a single gentleman in the crowd except himself. The seamen in the boat were pulling heartily at their oars and grinning. As the boat drew out of clod range the squat figure of the Governor arose and turned about. He cried out something, lost in the uproar. His harsh jowled face was purple. He stood there, swaying at every jerk of the oars and shaking a fat fist at all Halifax.

Johnnie turned away. All the way back to his lodgings he mused on the crowd and that angry futile creature in the boat. The shouting reminded him of the Portsmouth affair, and he thought, Well, at least I didn't make a damned fool of myself. He slept uneasily that night, dreaming he was back in Pleasant

Street, with that uproar outside and poor Fannie cringing with her baby on the kitchen floor.

In the next few days Macdonogh fair copied the report for the Lords of Trade, and Johnnie wrote with a flourish at its foot,

> *Your Ob't Serv't*
> *John Wentworth*
> *Surveyor General of His Majesty's Woods*

He regarded the title with satisfaction. This, at least, was left to him. And now that he reflected on it he found that he was better off financially than before. With most of His Majesty's Woods in rebel hands there were no deputy surveyors to pay. The whole £800 a year was his, less the expenses of a simple cruise in a fishing sloop along the Nova Scotia shore. And there was the £600 in lieu of his salary as Governor of New Hampshire. If the rebels had deprived him of the post, they'd also cut off the drain of Wentworth House and the expenses of the Portsmouth house and servants and stables. And Fannie and the baby were in the care of Lord Rockingham. He would repay Paul for any money she required during her stay in England, but that wouldn't be much, after all. For the first time in his life he was in a position to save money. Who'd have thought it?

The next afternoon an orderly came to his lodging, a lank man in scarlet coat and breeches, long black gaiters and stiffly pipe-clayed crossbelts. A grenadier's cap stood up a good twelve inches like the miter of a bishop from his greased and powdered hair. He had a note from General Howe, requesting the honor of a call from Mr. Wentworth, at ten of the clock tomorrow morning, at his headquarters.

In the morning Johnnie went there, meticulously dressed, and in the same sedan chair with its gleam of fresh paint. Howe had made his quarters with the Governor since he came ashore, and now that Legge had gone away the whole residency was turned over to the business of his staff and clerks. The General greeted Johnnie with his soldier's grip, his cold eyes, a polite murmured compliment. And then, "Mr. Wentworth, I may tell you in confidence that I'm removing shortly with my army to the vicinity of New York. Just what will happen there I cannot say; I believe Mr. Washington will march there with his army, if he hasn't done so already. So he and I shall face each other again, in a much more important scene. My brother, Admiral Howe, has authority to make a peace offering to the rebel Congress. They may or may not accept it. In short we may have war at their choosing. I trust it will be peace."

"So do we all," Johnnie said fervently.

"Well, I tell you this because I have instructions from Lord Dartmouth to offer you and some other loyal American officials a passage in my transports. You may take two servants, no more. These unfortunate refugees from Boston will have to remain in Nova Scotia for the time being. My duties are entirely military. I shall afford you any further convenience that I can, but you must understand that in the event of war you will have to make your own arrangements at New York."

"I understand," Johnnie said. New York—who did he know thereabouts? Nobody but the Bayards, who had entertained him on that bygone journey home from Carolina, and they lived far outside the town at Weehawken. Also they were Tories. It was odd and painful to reflect that they, and all the other gentry whose hospitality he had enjoyed along that pleasant route from the far South, must have been driven from their homes long since, like himself.

"I may not see you in some time," the General said, putting out his hand, "so good-by, sir, and may we meet again in happier circumstances." He turned at once to a staff officer waiting with some papers in the doorway of a side room, and Johnnie took his departure.

In the early days of June, when the fogs and rains and peep-bo sunshine of May had turned to clear skies and an almost tropical heat, Mr. John Wentworth received his sailing instructions and boarded a transport with Tom and young Benning. George Brinley and his family sailed in another. As Johnnie and his companions watched the town disappear behind the dark woods of Point Pleasant, Tom Macdonogh shook his fist. "Nova Scarcity! If I never see the place again it'll be too soon."

Young Benning shouted with laughter, and Johnnie joined him. He had no love at all for this far northeastern outpost of New England, frozen half the year, wrapped in fogs the rest, and thinly peopled by a hungry folk. By the fourth noon at sea they were in the latitude of Portsmouth by the master's reckoning, and Johnnie gazed toward the west. Strange to be passing and repassing home like this, unable to set foot in it, unable even to see it, as if he were some sort of Flying Dutchman caught in an old salt's tale.

As the fleet surged on in the fair weather Long Island came in sight and passed slowly along the starboard side. Then Sandy Hook appeared. A few days later, as if by magic, another forest of topmasts poked above the skyline from the east, the fleet from England, its transports crammed with troops. A regimental band in Johnnie's ship began to play "Rule, Britannia." As the music crashed out he thrilled from head to foot. The power of that whole spectacle covering the sea! Nothing could stand against it—nothing!

EIGHTEEN

THE JOURNEY to Yorkshire proved much less of an ordeal than the dreary way from Falmouth to London. For one thing the showers of late April were nothing like the chill wet gales of early March, and when the sun came out between showers the air was delightful. For another, Paul had provided the coach-and-four that he used on his frequent flittings across the Channel and about the continent. It was a stout and roomy vehicle, well slung to ride the worst of jolts and with cushioned green velvet seats and padded panels. Fannie and Prudence rode on one seat, with the baby's traveling crib securely fastened to the other and their portmanteaus on the roof. As before the trunks and boxes were to follow by wagon. Paul's own coachman handled the reins, and a footman sat beside him, with a blunderbuss in a leather case close at hand. The fat little musket was to ward off highwaymen in the heaths outside the city, but Fannie did not know that, she had not even seen the gun, and it would have astonished her to be told that a traveler on the backwoods road to Wolfeborough was far safer than he would have been on any of the highways within an hour's ride of the royal palace.

On parting Paul said to her, "I'm sending one of my grooms, well mounted, to ride a stage ahead of the coach, my dear, and he'll secure the best accommodation at the inns. I've told the coachman to go carefully and make the journey in whatever time you choose. It's something like a hundred and sixty miles, and for your own sake and the baby's you shouldn't attempt more than thirty miles a day. The high roads won't be like Piccadilly, you understand, specially after the spring rains. The turnpike companies don't spend a ha'penny more than they absolutely have to, and in places where the road repair depends on

...es you'll find the going damnable. For
... a week on the way, resting a whole
...fway—Bedford, say."

...and put his lips to it in his brisk impersonal

..., my dear lady. I leave for the continent myself in
...onth, and I'll be gone until the late summer. Some—
...ew and most important business. You've enjoyed your stay
...London?"

"Oh yes, it's been wonderful, Mr. Wentworth—wonderful!
And you've been so kind, you and Mrs. Phyllis. How can we ever
thank you?"

"Tut! My dear, a pleasure. Whenever you return to town you
must consider my house yours. By the way, I'm changing my
abode when I come back from the continent. I find these
quarters pretty narrow for entertaining nowadays, and one must
jostle with all sorts of people here in Poland Street, not all of
'em congenial. So I've bought a house just outside the town to
the west, in Hammersmith. Brandenburg House to be exact, much
more commodious than this, and with quite pretty gardens—
you'll like it, I'm sure. Remember, Brandenburg House at
Hammersmith, any time after the end of August."

"You're too good," Fannie said, and fluttered a handkerchief
from the coach window as they drove away.

The days and the long miles to Yorkshire passed pleasantly
enough. The roads were little, if any, better than the one she had
traveled so often from Portsmouth to Boston, but they were far
more comfortable than Johnnie's track through the woods and
hills to Wolfeborough, and most of the inns were very good
indeed. Paul's outrider made sure that they got the best chambers,
and the mere mention of Lord Rockingham's name brought bows
and scrapes and leaping service from innkeepers, servants, and
hostlers all along the way.

The countryside was lovely now, with a yellow sprinkle of
primroses at the wayside and the soft greens everywhere that
New England lacked. There was no forest, as far as she could

255

see from the coach. The woods were scattered coppices, of beech and oak just breaking the bud, with bluebell and rose blooming underneath; nothing like New Hampshire's less mass of pine and hemlock and cedar, where Boston-b Fannie had always felt a menace lurking in the shadows. The English woods seemed purely ornamental, placed like neat green wigs on the rises of bald pasture and plowland. Often the gables and chimneys of a great mansion peered from their midst. And always the towns and villages had that ancient and everlasting look that came from brick and stone and slate instead of wood, with charming gardens and greens and venerable churches whose spires lifted above the landscape as if to mark the way from one village to the next. I like England, Fannie thought. It's all so—so arranged. Nothing wild.

The towns came and went; Bedford in the rich valley of the Ouse; Melton Mowbray where the coachman vowed you could find the best hunting horses and dogs in England; Nottingham of the huge open market place, the ruined castle on the hill, and the boys of the bluecoat school scampering past the inn like merry little monks; Sheffield with a sprawl of small manufactories smoking in the vale of the Don, and the Pennine hills and moorlands in the distance.

At last they reached the carriageway of the Marquess, winding through noble old woods where deer wandered and peered as tame as rabbits. At careful intervals the park opened into vistas of sunny green turf, smooth-shaven by flocks of sheep, with grottoes or small temples or bits of artificial Greek ruin standing lonely and romantic in the distance. Finally the mansion itself. Fannie gasped. Johnnie had often dwelt on its size, and she could hear him now—"The façade runs a good two musket shot from end to end, two hundred yards I tell you, not an inch less, as true as I stand here. And when you step in from the porch, you find yourself in a hall sixty feet square, with walls that go up forty feet. Forty feet!"

And now she saw it with her own eyes, like a sculptured cliff against the background of the park and the low hills. The great central block; the twin flights of stone steps converging to the majestic porch; the Greek columns of the porch soaring up to the massive carved pediment; the stone balustrades of the roof, each post topped with an urn as if to catch the rain from heaven, and the pediment itself crowned with great statues in picturesque attitudes that seemed to stand in the very sky. From this handsome and impressive center the wings of the house stretched out on either hand, each with its own pillared porch, a miniature of the main one, and each wing ending in a tall square tower with a belvedere that looked across lawns and trees to the hills.

Here again the outrider had performed his task, so that servants were awaiting as the coach drew up at one of the flights of steps, and as the coachman handed Fannie down she saw a pair of small figures coming out upon that tremendous porch. As she came up the steps, lifting her skirts daintily and mincing a little in imitation of elegant Phyllis Barradale, she was greeted by these people, a middle-aged pair with the neat aristocratic features she had come to recognize in the nobility she met in Paul's house, but with nothing else to distinguish them.

The Marquess evidently had just returned from an inspection of the estate, for he was in a plain blue coat and breeches and riding boots. The lady wore a gray dress of rich material that was, however, not nearly as smart in cut or fashion as Fannie's own. Fannie had an instant dread. Her pale blue lutestring gown, the clocked stockings, the dark blue greatcoat trimmed with silver, the dashing black-plumed hat, the powder, the rouge, and patches—everything seemed wrong. Her knees trembled as she approached. Again she felt as awkward as a tomboy in all her movements, and she hesitated to speak in her American accent and with her colonial expressions, which the *ton* had found so amusing. It was a frightful moment.

"My dear," said the Marquess, taking her hand, "we see now why our good friend John took so long in choosing a wife. How beautiful you are!"

Fannie flushed and made a little bob. He's nice, she thought, I won't be afraid of *him*. She turned and made another bob to the Marchioness. I am of her, though. Why is it I'm never afraid of men?

"Welcome to Wentworth Woodhouse," the lady was saying in a composed high voice. "Do tell your maid to bring the baby. I must see my godson." She's stiff, Fannie thought. But when Prudence brought the baby the face of the Marchioness melted. She took the child in her arms, smiling, touching her lips to the soft cheek, and Fannie saw in her eyes the hunger of a childless wife.

"Charles-Mary," the lady said. "Charles-Mary, oh you charming little compliment! Isn't he, Charles? Isn't he lovely? See, he smiles. He's pleased, the rogue. He knows he's lovely."

A warm delight shone in both of these well-bred faces, and Fannie felt a gush of relief. They had fallen in love with the child at sight. She could have stood on her head and uttered an Indian war whoop, and they wouldn't have noticed. What an inspiration of Johnnie's to name the baby after both of them!

And later, pen in hand, she was telling Johnnie so.

"I have a handsome apartment in one of the wings, and there is a special chamber for the baby, the very one furnished for my lord Rockingham when he was Charles-Mary's age. I see now why you called our place a Lilliputian Wentworth House. I smile when I think of that, and of *this*. How enormous it is. One could put our Wentworth House and all the outbuildings into my lord's stables alone. It is all very wonderful to me, as it must have been to you. I know I shall like it here. What a happy condescension they give to me, and how they *doat* on their godson, as if he were their very own."

And as she lay in her stately canopied bed that night, with Prudence and the baby sleeping peacefully in the next room, with the scents and sounds of the soft English night coming in the open window, she could not sleep for thinking how strange and marvelous it all was. Again she had those pleasant fancies of herself returning to Portsmouth and telling the story of her travels, of London and Paul's house and Paul's famous guests, and as a *pièce de résistance* her stay with one of the greatest and richest lords of England. What an adventure! And to think it had all come about because some noisy scoundrels ran about an American town and broke the windows of their betters! She could almost smile over that now. And she was quite happy to forego the return home for some time yet, whatever happened in America. Next year, perhaps. Johnnie shall come and fetch me. We'll sail the way he did years ago, by the warm and quiet seas to Madeira and Carolina. We'll come north as he did, visiting with the gentry all along the way, and we'll arrive in Portsmouth on a summer day, with all the people cheering in the square.

Why was I so afraid? Ridiculous! And I needn't have worried about my American accent. My lord Rockingham himself speaks in a Yorkshire accent, which is worse—and nothing like the *ton*. And I'm beautiful, he said. If you're a woman and beautiful it doesn't matter much how you speak, so long as you smile and keep your voice down. Still, I must watch and learn.

With a new world to explore in the following days Fannie began with the mansion itself. The great dim hall was like a church somehow and a little eerie. She felt the stern gaze of all those images as if she were a sinner coming unrepentant into a place of immense and ancient holiness. On one side of it doors led to dining rooms, huge and small, and on the other side lay the big drawing rooms, all sumptuously furnished and carpeted. Throughout these lofty chambers the walls were hung with portraits, of Rockingham ancestors, and landscapes, the work of foreign painters, notably Italian. Lady Rockingham mentioned the names of artists who were evidently important, and Fannie stored away in her busy little head the mental copies of these pictures with the names attached—Giordano, Guido, Titian, Caracci, Van Dyck, and the rest—for conversation pieces in the future. She was still in awe of the Marchioness. It rejoiced her heart to see the great lady unbend whenever she visited the baby's apartment, but it was not wise to presume on that. She never ventured a "Ma'am," but always called her My Lady with the utmost respect and was profuse with gratitude and little flatteries.

Somehow the Marchioness seemed to be part of the regal furnishings of the mansion, like one of those statues in the great hall, cool and aloof, to be admired and even approached, but never to be touched.

Fannie was more at home with my lord, a horsy man like Johnnie, never so happy as when he was in the saddle. When he found that she could ride he invited her to accompany him about the estate, mounted on one of his superbly kept hunters and ambling easily along the lanes from paddock to paddock or following the bridle paths through the park. She searched her memory for some of Johnnie's horse-talk, and when she mentioned "Rockingham, the greatest horse in England" the Marquess was delighted.

"My dear, that's a matter of opinion still. But I don't mind saying—with all due respect to your American horses, which I believe are very good—England breeds the best horseflesh in the world outside Arabia, and here in Yorkshire we breed the best in England. When I speak of Arab horses don't forget that the best Arabs or Barbs ever brought into this country for breeding stock were the Byerly Turk and Darley's Arabian, and both of 'em came to Yorkshire."

He went on at length, Fannie hanging on every word and getting him to repeat the names until she had them firmly in her mind. "I must talk over all this with Mr. Wentworth," she explained with her shy little smile. "He's so devoted to horses, my lord." But she was thinking of the *ton*, too, where the men rated horses next in importance to women, and a pretty woman with a stock of glib horse-talk could leave her rivals nowhere.

"Ah!" said the Marquess pleasantly. "D'you know, when I first met your husband he was betting on a horse of mine at Newmarket? In the coffeerooms of the Jockey Club, along with Michael Wentworth, I remember. When Michael introduced us I took to him at once. Handsome, you know, and with that frank and open manner of American gentlemen. I hadn't met many then, and I never met one quite like John. If you ever have princes in America he should be one."

The Marchioness preferred her carriage for transport, and Fannie went with her on afternoon drives about the countryside. Sometimes there were longer excursions to the rugged hills and moors, to York in its long low valley where the stately Minster raised its towers above the town, and to Doncaster, where on the town moor the country gentry raced their horses for fat bets, and where, according to my lord, they were starting this year an annual race that would make Doncaster as important to the turf as Newmarket itself.

There were stately calls at the mansions of other great folk in the countryside and frequently house parties filled Wentworth Woodhouse itself, where the gentlemen rode all day and supped hugely and sat long over wine after the ladies had withdrawn, talking horses and Whig politics. Everyone was charming to the pretty and modest American, so devoted to her infant, and so anxious about her loyal husband with Howe's army.

Yet nobody seemed to know much about America except Lord Rockingham himself. There was a good deal of wit about the pretty fix that the King and his creature North had got the country into, although most of the gentlemen were sure that Lord Howe could settle the matter without much trouble. Fannie found it all confusing. There were two Howes, it seemed, and brothers; one a general, one an admiral, and both good Whigs. The admiral was Lord Howe, otherwise Black Dick because of his complexion, and this sailor had been charged with the whole business of treating with the rebels because he happened to know Benjamin Franklin. How very odd!

Her first word from Johnnie came by young Benjamin Thompson, who sent the letter on to her after inquiring at Paul's house. It was Johnnie's hasty note written just before the army quitted Boston, saying he was departing with them, whither he did not know. Then came three letters from Halifax, with news of himself, of Benning, and the Brinleys. He sounded disconsolate and said he missed her very much, but he knew she was happy and in good hands. He was writing to Lord Rockingham, but meantime she must give him and Lady Rockingham his compliments and thanks. He intended to follow the army wherever it went, but what would happen he did not know. It seemed a long way from New Hampshire. Good-by, darling Fan.

At the moment when his darling Fan was reading the last epistle Johnnie was actually afoot on Staten Island, where the British army had encamped in the sultry July weather. Their white tents sprouted everywhere. Long columns of sweating redcoats and German bluecoats stirred the dust of the lanes and practiced maneuvers in the fields and woods, and the summer birds of this rustic paradise were silenced by a clamor of drums and fifes and trumpets from morn to night. All sorts of rumors passed over the officers' mess tables and through the tents and farmhouses. Johnnie had grown wary of them now. His only solid information came as usual from George Brinley, who had established Mary and the children in a farmhouse near Denice's Ferry, in full view of Long Island just across the water. Up the harbor, lost in the shimmer of the heat over Manhattan, lay New York, a mystery.

"The situation?" George said in his offhand way. "We're here, and Mr. Washinton's over there," pointing to Long Island. "He's got an army of sorts, but it's not more than a third the size of ours, and one of his generals is—guess!—that country lawyer from New Hampshire, your own Jack Sullivan. My Lord Howe's treating by letter with the Congress, but the rebels don't seem impressed with this fleet and army—not a bit! Why, as soon as we landed, the Congress issued that declaration of theirs—'these united colonies are free and independent states,' and so forth—you can read the whole fantasy in that copy of the *Pennsylvania Evening Post* over there if you've a mind. So they're not scared. I doubt if anything will scare 'em but a damned good drubbing in the field, and my Lord Howe might as well ferry his brother's army over the water and start the drubbing now. The rebel army's in a nice position for it—Howe's warships can block the Sound and coop 'em on the island like a flock of sheep for slaughter."

"Do you think he will?" Johnnie said.

"Mr. Washington's betting that he won't."

It was almost the end of August before General Howe transferred his army to Long Island. Johnnie moved with the British camp to Flatbush, and there he watched a battle for the first time in his life. It spread over too many miles to make a clear picture. What he saw were long columns of British and German troops tramping in various directions along the dusty island lanes, or moving in ranks of red or blue that disappeared in woods and reappeared on a slope beyond, only to vanish again. There was a good deal of distant musketry at times, like the running crackle of a fire in dry brushwood, and sometimes the heavier note of cannon, and whenever there was firing a gray vapor arose and drifted lazily across the distant fields, like the wisps that rise and merge over a New Hampshire bog on a frosty morning in fall.

After a time he was told that the rebels had been defeated, that most of them had run like sheep, that many had surrendered or were hiding in the woods. A staff officer explained, scratching with his cane in the dust of a road, how the British army had "amused" the rebels with false attacks at left and center, and stolen a march to their rear along the Brooklyn heights. It was quite simple after all. Mr. Washington and all his men were trapped. The war was over in one battle. Another morning would see the final surrender.

But when morning came Mr. Washington and most of his army had slipped away in boats to Manhattan. A naval officer said that General Howe had failed to close his trap at the last moment. An infantry major raged and swore that Black Dick had failed to send his ships to block the Sound. A wounded loyalist, serving as a volunteer with Howe's dragoons, declared to Johnnie that Black Dick and his soldier brother were just a pair of scheming Whigs, and they'd deliberately let the rebels get away—"The best officers serving the Congress in all America today."

It was all very queer. In his own charitable mind Johnnie could only conclude that my Lord Howe and his soldier brother still hoped to patch up a peace without much bloodshed, and he devoutly wished they would. The sight of American prisoners gave him an uneasy feeling, like the qualms of a sick digestion, whenever he passed a group of them shambling along between the British and Hessian bayonets on the road. He looked for New Hampshire faces, but saw none, although he heard that John Sullivan was wounded and a prisoner.

A fortnight passed before General Howe, in his leisurely way, moved the troops over to Manhattan, crossing to Kip's Bay above New York, where again there was a chance to catch and crush Mr. Washington between the British army and the fleet. Johnnie remained at Flatbush, writing hopefully to Fannie and Lord Rockingham, and he was there when Mr. Washington made good his retreat across the Hudson. With the other loyalists in the train of the army Johnnie took up lodgings in New York and stayed there through the autumn, filling his letters to England with great news. The British forces from Canada had reached Lake Champlain and destroyed Mr. Arnold's fleet. Next year they could strike at Boston or down the Hudson Valley as they chose. General Howe stood on the road to Philadelphia. The Congress were shivering in their shoes.

At Christmas he wrote to Fannie again by the light of a lone candle in his lodging near the Battery. The British army had settled in winter quarters in the city and round about—some of the officers were carousing below at this moment—but of course there were strong outposts in the Jerseys, and next spring would see the last march. Mr. Washington's army, according to all report, was down to a mere rabble, somewhere beyond the Delaware. He had talked to the latest refugee from New Hampshire, who assured him that his return with a force of fair size at his back would be welcomed by all, except the men most committed to the rebel movement. This he would do at the first opportunity. He understood that the British government were furnishing a few loyalist corps with arms and rations and pay, and he proposed to raise a force of mounted gentlemen among the New England refugees on Long Island, giving a preference to New

Hampshire men. This would be much better than British or foreign regiments marching into his province. The thing was to get there first with a brigade of loyal Americans and do away with such a necessity. *Next summer, my dearest, you shall return with our darling boy, and we may take up our life again as if this past two years had never happened. God bless you both, and may you have a happy Christmas, as indeed I know you will at Wentworth Woodhouse. Your affectionate husband, John.*

NINETEEN

*I*N SEPTEMBER 1776, as Johnnie rode with the British army into New York, Fannie and my lady rode by carriage to watch a pheasant-shoot on the Rockingham estate. To Fannie it seemed a dull and very noisy business of beaters and of gamekeepers loading fowling pieces for gentlemen in velvet caps and round jackets and breeches and gaiters. In a pause for refreshments some of the gentlemen stopped to chat beside the carriage. Fannie found them attentive to her, a little more perhaps than to my lady, in a polite way of course, and in side glances and remarks more than anything else, but it was somewhat embarrassing, and she turned their attention back to her hostess with a deftness that she admired in herself afterward.

It was pleasant to have that tribute of daring eyes, of course. It reminded her of those assemblies in Boston when the English officers were flirting with her under Johnnie's indignant nose. How silly he had been about that—as if there were any harm! Could she help it if men found her charming and told her so at every opportunity? Or could they?

She was sorry when after several days' shooting and convivial dining the sporting gentlemen departed. The mansion was like a vast deserted temple now, with the summer gone and all the parties over. Servants flitted like wraiths through the endless chambers and corridors. The figures on the pedestals and in the picture frames stared in their fixed attitudes, as if frozen in paint or stone at some moment in time beyond which they yearned to go but never could. The elegant furniture stood stiffly about the silent rooms, as if daring anyone to use it until another summer came. My lord had gone to London on political concerns.

My lady was kept to her rooms with a touch of fever and ague, seeing no one but her maid and her physician.

And now came the east winds and the autumn rains, driving in from the North Sea and across the farms and moors. The sky was dark, the chambers darker still. Day and night, but especially at night, the gales found every hollow and cornice, playing on the great pile as if it were an organ with an infinite variety of stops and keys. The very urns on the long roof balustrade gave forth a chorus of mournful notes at certain swoops of the wind, and the windows rattled, doors slammed, draperies filled and sank on the walls like a ship's sails in fluky weather, and in the halls the drafts were those of a winter cave. Even in Fanny's apartment, where the servants trudged with their scuttles and kept good fires of coal from morn to night, the dank chill of the sea could be felt as if the German Ocean were just beyond the park instead of sixty miles away.

And the rain! Fannie could not decide which was worse, the torrents dashing against walls and windows like a stormy sea at a cliff, or the dismal drip-drip-drip of the calm interludes, splashing on the flagstones outside, and from the drenched trees of the park, where my lord's deer huddled sodden and sorry. We had sea gales in New Hampshire, she thought, even up in the woods at Wolfeborough, and going on for days, but never like this. Give me a wooden house and a small one after all. There's warmth in a wooden house. The damp can't creep in, as it does through these stones. And in a small house you don't feel lost— you feel snug. She thought of the snug house on Pleasant Street across the sea, and for the first time felt a touch of homesickness.

As October dragged its days away she was lonely and rebellious. She had cheerful letters from Johnnie, full of Mr. Howe's great victory at Long Island and his own plans and hopes and politics. All very well for Johnnie, there with the army, in the midst of those merry officers who would sooner kill a dull moment than a rebel. Here I'm thrust away like a nun in a convent, in the middle of nowhere, and in a rain like the end of the world, forty days and forty nights. What a penitence! And why?

Why when there's London and Paul's house and all the fun of the *ton*? A week's travel at most. If Johnnie can enjoy New York why shouldn't I enjoy London?

At the end of the month she put it to the Marchioness—my lord was still away—after rehearsing every word and gesture a dozen times. She came to the subject in a shy faltering voice and with the most demure little hesitations. She'd enjoyed every moment of her stay; she loathed the very thought of parting from my lady, who had been so kind, and from my lord, who had been her husband's good, good, friend through all these years and would, she hoped, remain his friend and hers. But her John had told her she must not presume upon their kindness, and he wished her to spend the winter in the household of his kinsman in London.

Lady Rockingham protested in her hospitable way. Presume? Nonsense! Besides, it would be bad for the baby, bumping over those awful roads in the middle of the rains again. And now the ready tears came to Fannie's eyes, and her mouth quivered, although her chin was suspiciously firm. She knew all that, she said. She must confess a weakness, something selfish perhaps, but she couldn't help longing to see and talk with some of the other American refugees in London, to share their hopes and memories for a time. And, too, she couldn't help wishing to get her dear love's letters the moment they reached England. She was anxious about him, there with the army, and with fighting going on. He was raising a regiment among the loyalist gentlemen, and she knew how brave and reckless he was wherever his duty was concerned. She could only hope that it would all be over by next spring, and he could join her in England for a rest before taking up his labors as a governor again, and then perhaps, if my lord and lady were so kind, they could come with the baby to Wentworth Woodhouse for the summer.

And so, at last, she and Prue and the baby took the road again, in a fine blue-and-buff coach of my lord's, with six horses, a coachman, a footman and a pair of outriders, an impressive turnout, clattering through the villages like royalty itself. The

November rains dripped all the way, and the coach broke an axle in a deep slough near Higham Ferrers, which cost them an extra day and a night at a very bad inn. They saw the hanging smoke of London at last on a bright cold afternoon as they came through Paddington in the fields. Then a roll through the skirts of the town and a final three miles along the Great West Road to Hammersmith.

Fannie had scratched off a note to Paul by post some days before, and all was ready for her. Brandenburg House proved to be far larger than the old abode in Poland Street, handsome in a stolid fashion (all these stone houses looked like prisons), with tall drawing rooms wainscoted to the ceiling and furnished with a curious jumble of English, French, and Dutch sofas, tables, chairs, mirrors, paintings, and hangings, the mark of Paul's travels and interests.

Paul received her and the baby happily and declared with the air of a fond uncle producing a doll for a favorite niece, "I have a surprise, from your own Portsmouth." Fannie's eyes went wide. And in came old Colonel Boyd, who had sailed to England from Portsmouth when the troubles began. Her tongue flew with questions. But he had heard little from New Hampshire, and his eyes had a haunted look, sunk in the bony face and the frame of the long white hair.

"I near the end of my time," the old man said heavily. "I wish only to be buried in my own home soil. I've had my tombstone made. It shall go back with me when these troubles are over. If I die before that I've given instructions that my old bones shall be shipped to Portsmouth whenever it's possible. This is a pleasant country, my dear, but it isn't home—it isn't anything like home."

How gruesome, thought Fannie, who did not like to think of old age, let alone death, and she changed the subject brightly to memories of the old happy days, the dinners, the balls, the pleasure parties in the country, the people they both knew.

The old shipbuilder's mind wandered. Once he said, "That fellow Livius. Went to Quebec, you know. The rebel army nearly captured him when they attacked Quebec about a year ago. But now, if you please, he's Chief Justice of Canada. Fancy that. Influence of course. He always had that, eh? But a fox! And there's poor Johnnie wandering with Mr. Howe's army, without a post, not even a home. Sad! Sad!" And a little later, "I leave here tomorrow. I've taken a cottage at Bristol. Seems closer to America somehow."

He tottered away to his room. A servant came in with a tray of cordials. Prudence had gone off to put the child to bed. There was a swish of silk in the doorway, and Fannie turned with a greeting to Mrs. Phyllis on her lips, but it perished there. The woman coming into the room was quite unlike the tall blonde Filly; a petite creature in the twenties wearing a gown of emerald green, with a small dark face rouged and patched and a tight little mouth.

Paul said blandly, "Mrs. Wentworth, may I have the pleasure of introducing Mrs. Targill, a very dear friend of mine? You'll be seeing a good deal of each other here." Mrs. Targill's black eyes were hostile and wary, as The Filly's had been when Fannie first appeared. She gave the pretty American a nod and looked her up and down, as so many women did, trying to guess her age and intentions and ending baffled. And she sat with a sidelong gaze as Paul and Mrs. Wentworth talked about matters in America. Her attitude eased when Fannie began to prattle about her Governor, her dear brave love, and how she missed him, separated by this cruel sea. Soon the little brunette was smiling.

Paul passed the cordials, and in another minute the two women were in animated conversation about the latest fashions and gossip of the *ton*, exchanging a glance now and then with their host. They understood each other now. Fannie wondered what had become of The Filly. Evidently in changing his domicile Paul had decided to change his doxy too, and because Brandenburg House was outside the town it was more convenient to bed the lady here than in that rented place in Wardour Street.

On the next afternoon, when Colonel Boyd had gone, a little

procession of coaches and carriages brought a party for dinner and an evening of cards and wine. They were all of the *ton*, and many of them Fannie knew from her stay in Poland Street. The ladies were Mrs. This and Mrs. That, but as usual few of their names seemed to have any relation to the gentlemen who brought them there. Once again there was the gay banter and gossip, the camaraderie, the naughty wit, the whole air of easy pleasure that she had missed in the wilds of Yorkshire. From time to time one of the gentlemen whispered in her ear, and when she met Paul's quizzical eyes he smiled as if to say, *You can take care of yourself, my dear, I'm sure*—and so she could.

The winter's rains and snows had blighted the afternoon parades of the fashion in Hyde Park, but the belles and beaux still amused themselves at the theater, the opera, at balls and masquerades, as well as the round of private cards and wine that never ceased for weather or anything else. Paul and Mrs. Targill drove in quite often to these affairs, and Fannie went with them. They made an odd trio. With Paul, Mrs. Targill was like a devoted wife, joining the merriment, but giving her best attention to her husband always, and avoiding amorous gestures from other directions with disdain. When Paul was away on his mysterious business affairs she kept to herself at Brandenburg House and discouraged visitors; indeed to male callers she was ice itself.

She seemed haunted by the fate of The Filly and no doubt the long succession of others before Mrs. Barradale. In such intervals Fannie grew bored and a little contemptuous.

After the old year passed into '77 she began to go into town alone in Paul's pony chaise. There was no lack of company there. If their ladies were sometimes dubious the gentlemen of the *ton* were delighted with the pretty and witty American. They admired her person not only with their eyes but aloud, in the custom of the *ton*, complimenting her points as if she were a pretty mare at the races, and they were intrigued by her changes of temperament, the frivolity that let them go so far, the dignity that crushed them if they went beyond.

She had learned to recognize men with the magic compound of breeding and money and to distinguish from them the wastrels of one or the other and the sharpers living on their wits. And so it was with the odd melange of fashionable wives, mistresses, actresses, and dainty whores who formed the feminine half of the *ton*. She was drawn instinctively to people of breeding and, with conscious snobbery, to those of title, and she began to imitate their speech and manners, casting off her New Englandisms like garments out of style. In this her old gift of mimicry helped a great deal. It amused her to deceive the casual strangers she met in this fashionable whirl and set them wondering who or what she was, and soon she was no longer playing a part but actually living the role of a well-bred Englishwoman whose whim it was to mingle unescorted with the *ton*. Perfection in the role could only come with time, of course, although she could soon disguise her American origin quite well.

One evening at a masquerade in the Pantheon, where eight hundred people whirled, she became separated from her party in the crush. Tired of dancing, of sauntering or merely standing in banter with other masks, she found a small alcove and sank into a chair. It was empty except for herself, another chair or two, and a gilded vase in the window niche which doubtless held flowers at summer fetes. She was wearing a gown of pink satin and a brass-buttoned jacket of scarlet faced with blue, like those of officers in royal regiments, the latest feminine whim in the *ton*. The combined skills of Prue and Mrs. Targill had piled her hair over a tall frame of delicate basketwork and powdered it to the hue of snow, and a domino of pink silk covered her brow to the nose.

She was fanning herself languidly when a tall man in a black mask came by, returned, and stood in the frame of the entrance.

"View hullo!" he said. "It's the pretty *militaire*. Noticed you everywhere tonight, but hadn't a chance to speak. And nobody knew who you were. May I ask now—as one soldier to another?"

He wore the splendid uniform of a Hungarian hussar, but his speech was as English as roast beef and Burton ale.

"You may ask," she said lightly, "but I'll not answer—as one soldier to another. I know who you are."

"Ten guineas to one you don't!"

"Pooh! You're a captain of His Majesty's Horse Guards, you've just recovered from a bad cropper at a hunt last autumn, you're the heir to a title and six or seven thousand a year, and last month you celebrated your twenty-fifth birthday with a party at White's."

"Zooks! Anything else?"

"Yes. You enjoy the ladies, but you're very particular in your choice." She put out a hand. "Now, sir, pay up."

Without hesitation he drew a purse from a breeches pocket and spilled a yellow heap of guineas into that slim peremptory palm. Fannie turned and in the same careless way tipped them into the vase behind her.

"For the poor," she said.

He laughed. "How the deuce do you know all that about me?"

"Because I've seen you everywhere too, captain—and I had better spies."

He slipped off his mask. "This is no good, it seems." His face was lean, with the returning color of a healthy convalescent. A pair of lively blue eyes regarded her over a short roman nose. His mouth was pleasant, with a lazy strength about the lips that seemed to express all the rest of him.

"Well, since you know everything about me, pray take off that mask and tell me all about you. That's only fair, I think—seeing I've paid up."

"I'll do nothing of the kind. You may guess if you like."

"Very well. You're not an Englishwoman. . . ."

"Oh? What makes you think that?"

"Something in the way you speak. You're—um—well, at a hazard you're the daughter of a West India sugar nabob, you spent some years in England at school before you married, you're—um—three-or-four-and-twenty, and now you're visiting London alone because your husband's busy with sugar or whatever husbands are busy with in the West Indies."

"All wrong."

"May I sit down? I feel like a schoolmaster, standing over you like this propounding theories."

She made an indifferent gesture with the fan, and he dropped into the farther of the chairs. Beyond the alcove, in the blaze of lamps under the great dome, the costumed figures went by, some with masks and some without, in a hubbub of talk and laughter in which the music was lost. The Pantheon swam in the scents of wine and segars and perfume and warm flesh, the very breath of pleasure.

He tried again. "I had it wrong way round. You're an English girl who's been some years abroad, in one of the colonies. You're married, I feel quite sure. And of course I was wrong about the West Indies—ladies from those hot places always have a drained look, the musketos, I suppose. You—what I can see of you, specially those eyes—you've too much zest about you for a place like that. Your husband's an army officer stationed in—um—Canada."

"Wrong again."

"Am I getting warm?"

"You hunt the thimble no better than you hunt the fox. No wonder you fell off your horse!"

A rueful grin. "Well, I'm sure of this—you're the most charming creature I've seen in a twelvemonth."

"That's what every rake in London says to every morsel he fancies. Can't you say something new?"

He leaned back in the chair and pushed his hands in his breeches pockets.

"What's new since Adam met Eve? Tell me. I deplore my ignorance."

Through the mask her eyes considered him carefully. His looks, his manner, the discreet distance he kept, everything about him confirmed what she had heard in that continual and all-embracing gossip of the *ton*. A young officer, the son of an earl and of good manners, with a healthy interest in women and a taste in his choice. She felt the compliment of the whim that had noticed her "everywhere" and turned him into the alcove when he saw her sitting there. And she knew what it meant. Her instinct had never failed her in that since she was seventeen, as if she had in her flesh a harp string tuned to the male note, something always taut and never out of key.

"This is very far from Paradise," she said evasively. "It's more like the Ark—two of every kind and all in an uproar."

He nodded, with a contemptuous glance at the passing crowd. And then bluntly, "I have a closed chaise waiting in a mews across the street. In ten minutes we could be in my rooms, very quiet and much more agreeable."

"What for?"

"To hunt the thimble, shall we say?"

"My friends would miss me, and we're to sup together at twelve."

"I'll have you back by half past eleven at the most, 'pon my honor. Do come! We have an hour and a half. And time's such precious stuff."

The cord was singing hotly now. It was a pleasant music too. She arose.

"You make me curious. I must see how well you play this game. Bring your chaise to the east gate. I'll get my cloak and meet you there."

He took her hand, brushed the fingers with his lips, and vanished through the crowd. In five minutes she slipped out of the east gate, muffled in the cloak, and there he was, and there was the chaise.

At twelve, true to his promise, she was at supper with her friends. None had missed her in that madcap mob.

TWENTY

On an evening in January '77 Fannie's husband sat in a country house at Flatbush, busy with pen and ink. Outside the frosty window panes the landscape lay white and rigid under the light of a half moon and the stars. The snow was deep and the cold sharp. Even in his room, despite a fire on the hearth, the candle had a winding sheet. From time to time he had to take penknife and slice away the unmelted tallow for better light. The very ink was gelid in the little brown galipot and oozed slowly from the quill point, so that his usual free handwriting suffered.

Other than foraging patrols the British army lay quiet in winter quarters. Like many another loyalist refugee Johnnie had found New York too costly a place in wartime, and he had moved back to Long Island with the first cold weather. Most of the New England refugees had made their way there, even those who first went to "Nova Scarcity," and the island villages were filled with them and others from the Hudson Valley and Connecticut.

The letter was for John's sister Ann Fisher. Her Tory husband had been obliged to flee his customs post at Salem on a moment's notice, leaving wife and family to return to her father's care at Portsmouth. The quill moved in Johnnie's cold fingers.

I have prevail'd on a man, bound on a trading journey, to forward you this letter, and one to my father, with one from your husband . . . I have a box containing 16 pair children's shoes, 3 pair women's silk and 3 pair Calamanco shoes, 4 patterns of Calacoe and 4 handkerchiefs, which Mr. Fisher sent for you by Mr. Brinley.

He paused, thinking of George Brinley. Since forwarding the

box from New York that fearless man, seeking army supplies in the Jerseys, had ridden straight into a rebel ambush. He refused to surrender, indeed fought his way out, and galloped four miles to the British lines with two musket balls in his legs and one in his body. Now he lay between life and death in a New York hospital.

The pen moved again. Johnnie mentioned Brinley's misadventure briefly. He said nothing of the recent rebel successes at Trenton and Princeton. The letter, he knew, would be passed from hand to hand among his friends who remained in Portsmouth and it seemed better to keep his remarks in a high vein of confidence.

From dispositions and intelligence from Pennsylvania and southward it is more than probable that the present unnatural war is almost at an end. Be assur'd an army of 20,000 Russians and 12,000 Wirtembergers are engag'd and will be in New England by June next, unless prevented by Peace. Mrs. Wentworth and Charles are very well. The latter is taken under the wing of his noble sponsors and namesakes, who are incredibly fond of him . . . Pray remember me kindly to all my loyal steadfast friends, the time of their rejoicing is at hand. I am in good health and will not leave America until peace is restor'd. Those that love me and that I love will be good to Prisoners and Captives— I would sell my all for their comfort. Our worthy parents will accept my most cordial and attach'd salutations, and all will oblige me in their continued affections, which are inestimable to,

Your affectionate Brother,

J. Wentworth.

He sealed the letter and rode to put it into the hands of a furtive skipper bound "down East," along with a packet of mail from other New Hampshire refugees.

Returning to his quarters half-frozen he went to his feather bed for warmth and to read by the light of a dip on the chest of drawers. He had started to recruit his regiment among the New Hampshire refugees, under the title of Governor Wentworth's Volunteers, but nothing could be done about training and organization until spring weather opened the countryside. Meanwhile he had borrowed from British officers some books on the military art, most of which were translated from the German. The British regular army seemed convinced that only the Germans knew the art of war. To Johnnie it all seemed stiff and foreign and worthless in the American landscape, but he read on dutifully.

His Volunteers were really the old notion he had cherished so long for the militia at home, a regiment of American horsemen armed with sword and pistol and light musket, men who could move fast and far, and in woods and broken country could dismount and fight as infantry. This did not chime with the notions of the British army staff. They had an irritating air of contempt for American soldiery, loyalist or rebel. A few regiments of loyalist infantry had been authorized and placed on the army establishment, but only two mounted groups, both under the command of British officers.

When April came Johnnie began to train his men in the Long Island fields. It pleased him at roll call to hear familiar New Hampshire names like Rindge, Meserve, Lutwyche, Hale, Trail, Peavy, Stavers, Starke. Captain John Cochrane, late of the Portsmouth fort, was second-in-command. Fannie's young brother Benning had a cornet's rank, and Tom Macdonogh served as adjutant. The rank and file were pitifully few. The able-bodied New Hampshire refugees were few in any case, and only those who had brought away a good sum of money could supply their own horses and equipment and serve like this without pay.

One day at his Flatbush headquarters there was an unexpected visitor. Johnnie shook Benjamin Thompson's hand fervently and drew him into the farmhouse parlor, calling over his shoulder for rum and hot water and sugar.

"Tell me about Fannie," he said eagerly.

"I didn't see Mrs. Wentworth, sir, I'm sorry. I sent your letter on to her in Yorkshire, and I suppose she's still there. In London I'm so busy quill driving I don't get about much."

Johnnie's face fell. "Well, tell me about yourself."

Thompson wore a sober clerkish dress, and except that his red hair was now powdered and drawn in a neat club queue he seemed very much the same young man who had visited at Wolfeborough and planned those scientific surveys in the mountains. The same clear gray gaze, the same promise of energy and efficiency in everything he did.

"There isn't much to say, Governor. I delivered your dispatch concerning New Hampshire affairs to my lord Germain, and he was good enough to offer me a clerk's post in his department, so I took it. Nobody there seemed to know much about America, except from reports—least of all my lord himself. I've managed to make myself very useful. In fact I'm now in my lord's confidence, and if this government stays in office I have a good prospect of becoming Undersecretary of State for the Colonies. Meanwhile, in my private hours, I amuse myself with odd notions as I used to do at home. Just now I'm trying to devise a system of signaling for ships at sea and an improved kind of musket and a better sort of gunpowder to use in it." He laughed. "So you see I keep myself out of mischief."

The grog appeared, steaming in a jug, and Johnnie poured the cups full.

"What are you doing over here?" he demanded.

"A leave of absence—and some duty. I wanted to see a few old friends like yourself and to get a firsthand view of things over here. I've spent some weeks in New York, and I sail back to England soon. But tell me about yourself, sir. I was the deuce of a time finding where you were. What are you doing?"

"Trying to raise a regiment of horse amongst the New England refugees. A matter of some difficulty—unless I can get on the army establishment. D'you think you can do anything for me there? I haven't been able to impress General Howe."

"Then you need much better influence than mine," Ben said bluntly. "The Secretary of State for the Colonies is directing the war in America, of course, but he's busy quarreling with the generals, and the generals have a poor opinion of my lord. Between ourselves, I don't think Lord Germain's got the military capacity of a corporal, and I wouldn't rate the generals' much better. However that's not my business and not the point. Lord North is head of the government, with the King's hand firmly twisted in his coattails. Have you any influence in that direction?"

"My great friend and patron over there has always been Lord Rockingham."

"Never mention it. The King hates Rockingham and his Whigs like poison."

"There's Paul Wentworth," Johnnie said hopefully.

"Um! Paul's got some influence with one or two ministers, but I'm afraid His Majesty has a low opinion of the man himself. You've got to stand well in high quarters if you want anything in London."

"You mean I can't fight for the King because Howe doesn't like me, and His Majesty doesn't like my friends?" Johnnie blazed.

Thompson gave him a curious smile. "The British army are quite sure they can beat the rebels. That being the case they don't care to see too many loyal Americans trained and armed. They might get notions after the war. Much better to hire clodhoppers all over Germany. The change in the wind will come perhaps when Howe marches into the country. He'll find a need for American light troops, horse and foot, in the kind of fighting he'll meet in the Jerseys and Pennsylvania. I recommend patience, Governor."

"Patience!" Johnnie took a pull at his grog. "You say His Majesty has a low opinion of Paul Wentworth. Why?"

Thompson glanced at the door. "Can one talk freely here?"

"These people are loyalists. There's no one in earshot anyway. You sound as if you had some dreadful secret."

"It could be that, in the wrong ears," Thompson said mysteriously. "I suppose you know the rebels have sent a commission to Paris?"

"I've heard something of the sort."

"It's there now—Silas Deane, Arthur Lee, and shrewd old Benjamin Franklin. And they're up to mischief. In fact they've persuaded the French king's ministers to let 'em have great quantities of arms and money and supplies. Not openly of course. It's all being done through Beaumarchais."

"Who's he?"

"A man of parts. A gambler, a writer of plays—there's a comedy of his called *The Barber of Séville* quite popular in Paris at the moment, I believe. But his main activity is something else. He's head of the French secret service. To cover the movement of this war material to America he's created a trading firm called Hortales et Compagnie, with offices in various ports and no less than forty ships. It looks like a busy trade."

"How do you know all this?"

"In my department a secretary learns all kinds of things. How well do you know Paul Wentworth? What he does, I mean."

"Paul? He's a speculator on the money markets in London and abroad. He does a lot of business on the continent."

"Quite so. And a speculator on the continent must have good sources of information. Would it surprise you to know that Paul Wentworth maintains a clever little lady in Paris, another in Antwerp, and another in Amsterdam?"

Johnnie laughed. "Knowing Paul, no."

There was a twinkle in Thompson's eyes. "Each of these ladies has a wide acquaintance and a sharp ear for information that might be useful to her patron—and of course she provides him with a comfortable *pied-à-terre* whenever he makes his rounds. Business and pleasure in one pretty bundle. The man's a genius! But to be serious, a system of that kind could be useful in other directions, eh? This rebel commission in Paris, for instance. Or the activities of Hortales et Compagnie in the ports of France and the Low Countries."

"I'm dull at riddles," Johnnie said.

"I mean Paul's enlarged his—um—facilities and placed 'em at the disposal of the British government. He reports through Sir William Eden, who's connected with my department. In other words Mr. Paul Wentworth, late of New Hampshire and Surinam, is now the chief agent of the British secret service on the continent, with a crew of spies in Paris and the chief ports. He travels back and forth under a dozen names; he's well supplied with money from the Secret Service Fund, both for pay and for bribes; he speaks French fluently and Dutch and Spanish and German fairly well; and of course his best agents have the universal language, a pretty talent for the bed."

"Well?"

"An American secretary with the commission in Paris has a weakness for ladies' beds. Another is in Paul's pay. In short everything done by Benjamin Franklin and company—or shall we say Hortales et Compagnie—is very well known in London."

Johnnie frowned. "What's London doing about it?"

"Not a thing. Paul reports to Eden, Sir William reports to Lord North, North reports to the King—and the King refuses to believe that his fellow monarch across the Channel would assist a pack of rebels. In fact, His Majesty says that Paul's just 'a dabbler in the Alley'—that he wants to throw the London exchange into a panic and make a financial coup."

"What does the government think?"

"As I understand it the fleet's in a rotten state—neglected ever since the old French war. They haven't ships enough to blockade the American coast, and they daren't try to blockade the French. They won't risk a war with France while they've got this American affair on their hands. So Hortales et Compagnie can pursue their busy trade."

"What do you think, Ben?"

"These arms and supplies are just what the rebels need. By next summer you'll see the effect. And if the rebels can give the British army one good thrashing in this year's campaign I'm afraid you'll see something else."

"What?"

"The French coming into the open—fighting on the American side. The French want revenge for the last war and this is their opportunity. That's what our mutual friend keeps telling London." Thompson grinned suddenly. "I wouldn't put it past Paul to plan a coup on 'Change, mind you. It would be just like Paul. But that doesn't alter the facts."

Johnnie twitched his shoulders irritably. It seemed farfetched, all of it, in spite of his respect for Thompson's alert mind. The story of Paul's new role was fantastic, and he said so. Thompson chuckled.

"My dear Governor, if you think that's fantasy, hear this. The rebels themselves have a secret agent in London. His name is Edward Bancroft, a Massachusetts schoolmaster with a scientific turn of mind. He spent some years in South America—in Surinam to be exact—studying tropical botany. Then he moved to London. Gives scientific lectures there, and so forth. Highly respected. I've a scientific bent myself, as you know, and I've found the man very interesting. Franklin also has that bent, and I suppose that's what drew Bancroft to him when the old fox turned up in Paris. In any case Silas Reade was one of Bancroft's pupils in America. So they all got together. In no time Bancroft was up to all sorts of mischief in England—even hiring some mysterious fellows to set the royal dockyards afire. He travels back and forth to Paris, sits in the most secret councils of the rebel commission, and then slips back to his lectures in London. Have you guessed anything from all this?"

"Nothing."

"Surinam! Surinam! Bancroft wasn't the only Yankee to wander there. Years ago Paul Wentworth met a rich widow on a trading voyage there and married her and lived in Paramaribo till she died. That was when he moved to London—like Edward Bancroft. In fact, they're old friends and thick as thieves. There isn't a thing that Bancroft wouldn't do for Paul. So when Paul undertook the British secret service, Bancroft was in his pocket from the start. You see? Bancroft keeps up his meetings with the Franklin commission in Paris and tattles every word to Paul Wentworth. And, Governor, those tattletales confirm everything we've learned from Paul's own spies there—book, chapter, and verse. D'you still think it's a fantasy?"

"I don't know what to think," Johnnie said gloomily.

"Mind you, the war in America can be won this summer if our generals use their heads. And there's an end to the whole conspiracy, both sides of the sea."

"What if it isn't won this summer? What if the French come into the war?"

"That'll change everything. In the long run I wouldn't give tuppence for our chances here."

The even voice, the cool gray gaze, the memory of Thompson's uncanny insight even as a boy in the teens, all gave Johnnie a chill. He lowered his gaze to the lees in his cup and sat silent.

"Well," Ben Thompson said, rising suddenly, "I must be off if I want to see General Clinton in New York tonight. He's a hard man to catch away from his duties and his pleasures, and I have some matters to discuss for the information of my lord Germain. While I'm there, sir, I'll put in a word for your regiment if you like, though it won't do much good. Good-by, Governor. It's been pleasant seeing you again. Like old days at Wolfeborough. Let's hope we can shove our knees under a table at your mansion there before another year rolls by."

A short hard grip and he was gone, the shrewd young Yankee in the councils of King George, and leaving that strange impression of a wizard with the knowledge of ages concealed inside a man of twenty-four.

For Governor Wentworth's Volunteers the spring and summer passed in military exercises according to Johnnie's books, carried on doggedly in all weathers and with the poorest of equipment. Sometimes there was a bit of action, usually at night, when parties of rebels crossed the Sound in boats to raid the loyalist farms; a business of sudden alarms and long wild gallops in the dark, a flurry of pistols and muskets, a few shadowy figures melting away, and then silence and no more.

Late in August came a rumor of fighting in New Hampshire, but no detail except that Burgoyne's German troops had clashed with the rebel militia there. Again Johnnie had that dismaying vision of his own people at mortal strife with a swarm of foreigners and Indians among the familiar farms. It was a relief when word came that Burgoyne's main march was down the Hudson after all.

In September he scratched off an excited letter to Fannie. Wonderful news! General Burgoyne had reached Saratoga Springs and would soon be storming into Albany. General Howe had defeated Mr. Washington and captured Philadelphia. The Congress had fled, nobody knew where. The end was in sight. Next spring he would be riding into Portsmouth at the head of his gentlemen Volunteers. She must sail at the first news of Mr. Washington's surrender, which was bound to come before the winter's end. She must join him in his happiness.

The hardwood trees turned color with the first frosts, and skeins of wool went sailing over the island sky and out to sea. By mid-October some of the red maples already were dropping their leaves. A week later Governor Wentworth's Volunteers, riding back in the dark from a long day's maneuvers, saw along the horizon a bright flicker of northern lights.

"Like home," someone said, and Johnnie thought of crisp nights when those wildfires danced in the sky beyond the hills of Wolfeborough.

At the Trider house he and Benning tramped stiffly, spurs a-jingle, into the light of fire and candles. Old Trider and his wife stood by the hearth with somber faces. He sensed something wrong at once.

"What's the matter?"

They were silent. Then the woman spoke. "It's bad news, sir. The rebels have taken General Burgoyne and his whole army."

"A lie of course," Johnnie said easily.

"I don't think so, sir. It's what they all say in New York."

"Ha! New York's always a-buzz with some wild thing or other."

But the next night there was a note from George Brinley.

My dear John,

My thanks for the basket of apples, which Bannister brought me safely. I keep him waiting for this brief note, and then he

*shall be off to you. By this time you must have heard the sorry
news from Saratoga. Burgoyne was cut off and oblig'd to surrender, bag and baggage, on the seventeenth. Clinton here could
do little for him—General Howe holds the main army in Philadelphia. This will raise the rebels' tails, I fear, and we shan't see
peace for a long time yet. I mend well, can limp about on a
crutch, and hope to report for duty by spring. My compliments
to you, and to Mrs. Wentworth when you write.*

"Well?" young Benning said, watching his face. The boy was
nineteen now, impatient to be fighting in the war.

"It's true," Johnnie said. "Burgoyne is taken with all his men."

"Then the war will go on?" The boy seemed more pleased
than sorry.

"Another year. More than that, perhaps."

After supper Johnnie went up to his chamber and sat heavily
on the bed, head in hands. The long days in the saddle put a
rheumatic ache in his bones by nightfall now. He was forty-one.
His "regiment" was still no more than a hundred men, and some
of them had begun to slip away, seeking service in one of the
authorized loyalist battalions. Those who remained were New
Hampshire men, clinging to him out of personal loyalty, and
gentlemen from various other provinces, who preferred the
dignity of riding to war instead of marching on their feet. He
realized now that he could never build the little troop to a respectable strength, and without that there was no hope of getting
it on the army establishment, whichever way the wind blew.

Three months had passed since the last letter from Fannie,
and that just a brief scribble with the usual things: she was well
and happy, the baby thrived, a rainy summer, my lord and lady
Rockingham sent their compliments. Johnnie longed for her
sadly, and for a sight of little Charles. It would soon be two
years since he saw them last, and it seemed half a lifetime.

He was tempted to sail for England. Training was over for
the winter. The Volunteers were quartered in a scatter of farmhouses about Flatbush, where their horses could be stabled at
the least expense. And he was his own master, after all. No need

to ask leave of some lofty British officer. Come back in the spring.

But still, the whole rebellion might collapse before the winter ended, Burgoyne or no Burgoyne. General Howe had beaten Mr. Washington and sat in Philadelphia now, the very seat of the Congress. Besides, all the rebel merchants must be pinched with the lack of trade and money. Men out of work everywhere. You can't eat a liberty pole.

For Christmas he crossed over by wherry from Brooklyn to New York. All was gay in this city where living was too dear for the poorer loyalists, but where well-to-do refugees seemed to be thicker than wild pigeons in a summer forest, and where Clinton's officers were in town for the cold weather. No one seemed to care about Burgoyne; indeed some of the British officers declared he had no business where he was caught, and serve him right.

George Brinley was out of hospital, convalescing in a Tory merchant's home in the Bowery, and Johnnie had his Christmas dinner there. It was a noble feast, and afterward, sitting over old brandy and whiffing segars fresh from Santiago, they talked of absent wives and of the happy days before the war. It was Johnnie who turned the subject to the future. With the talk of the past and the warmth of the brandy he was beginning to see everything in a mellow light. He spoke of "riding home before the next campaign is out."

Brinley's wounds had made him testy. "That's nonsense, Johnnie, and you know it."

"If I rode into Portsmouth tomorrow the people would welcome me back."

"Ha! They'd shoot you and your Volunteers out of your saddles as quick as they did those Germans of Burgoyne."

"What makes you think so?"

"Oh, stop spinning fancies, Johnnie. You still think it was only a mob that turned you out—that the better people wouldn't have done such a thing. Any man in New England could give you an argument on that. But you're ignoring something else—what's happened since. When Burgoyne came blundering down from Lake Champlain he sent his foreigners on a side raid to New Hampshire. They were supposed to collect horses and provisions, but in fact they pillaged every farm they came to. That brought your old friends the Green Mountain boys flocking down to fight. And the affair at Bennington was just a beginning. The whole of New Hampshire set off to war; every man and boy that could walk and carry a musket, heading west over those roads you cut in the wilderness, indeed every path or trail that would take 'em toward Burgoyne. And when they got to Burgoyne they fought like wildcats, along with Morgan's Virginians and the New York militia and the rest of Gates's army. Your old friend John Starke, your old friend Seth Warner—they could tell you a whole lot about that."

"May I ask how you know?" Johnnie said stiffly.

"Firsthand, my friend. When I was in the hospital a wagonload of rebel wounded came. They'd got astray from their army and blundered into one of Clinton's detachments lower down. I talked to 'em, naturally. Some were from Massachusetts, some from New Hampshire. Countrymen, mostly. Quite simple manly fellows, no ranting, just saying what they knew—and what I'm telling you now. One of 'em had been a mastman on the Piscataqua in the days gone by. I asked him how he felt about Governor Wentworth. 'Johnnie?' he says, pleasant enough. 'Oh, I never had anything agin Johnnie. A real gentleman from the word Go, and a mighty good woodsman too.' So I said, 'How if he came back to New Hampshire?' He thought about that a minute. Then he said, 'They'd never let him back. He's for the King—like Burgoyne.' You see? Like Burgoyne. They'll never forget Burgoyne. And you're tarred with the same brush."

"Damme, I'd nothing to do with Burgoyne!"

"Nor did I, but I was for the King, like you and Burgoyne, and in my case I've got some pretty scars to show for it." George grinned sourly at his segar.

"Suppose His Majesty's forces win this war. They'll have to remain, to keep the people in submission. I wonder what it would be like, back in Boston, walking about amongst a conquered people that used to be old friends. Have you ever thought of that?"

"Not in that way," Johnnie said.

"Ha! They hate a Tory now as they hate an Indian. Specially Tories like you and me that went off with the King's army. The Congress has decided that all Tories of that kind must be banished forever. They're leaving the detail to the provincial bodies, and every Committee of Safety is making a list. You know what that means, surely? They intend to confiscate the lands and properties of every Tory refugee, whether he served with the King's army or not. I tell you I've seen a copy of the Massachusetts list, sent to the army here by a secret agent. I'm on it. So is my brother. I could name you dozens of other Tory refugees you know, including invalids and old men who couldn't fight for the King if they wanted to."

"That's Massachusetts."

"I suppose New Hampshire rebels are different?"

"They were never like your ranting Sam Adams and his crew," Johnnie snapped.

All the way back to Long Island he reflected on George Brinley's words and his embittered face. Of course George was a cynic now. Those painful wounds. And that ruined business left behind in Boston. Nothing to come back to. His only hope for the future was the British Army, as a career after the war. He'd done well in the Commissary Department. Even General Howe had noticed him. And when it came to promotion his wounds in action would count for a lot. It wasn't often that a Commissary officer had a chance to show his courage under fire. All very well for George. My case is different.

Late in January '78, in the chill monotony of his winter quarters in Flatbush, he received what appeared to be a letter from New York. The outer fold was addressed in his brother-in-law's hand, but when he broke the seal he found a printed sheet with a scrawl in a strange handwriting at the bottom: "Be assur'd that this will be passed at the spring session, and as it stands." It was a copy of an Act to be placed before the assembly of New Hampshire, listing seventy-five Tories who had left the province. It forbade them ever to return. Any who did would be deported and warned. For a second offense the punishment was death. Peter Livius was on the list, and so were famous old Robert Rogers of the Rangers, John Cochrane, Colonel Fenton, Samuel Holland the surveyor, Bart Stavers, Benjamin Thompson, John Fisher—Anna's husband, ever Fannie's brother, young Benning.

And the first name on the list was his own.

TWENTY-ONE

*F*OR MRS. FANNIE the year '77 had passed like a dream, a somewhat naughty dream in parts, but none the worse for that. Among the *ton,* where Paul had introduced her simply as Mrs. Wentworth, some thought her his latest mistress, although the watchful presence of the little Targill creature made that a puzzle. Fannie had never told her captain who or what she really was, even in their most intimate moments in the rooms off Berkley Square. Once, when he demanded her real name—"because I love you by Jupiter!"—she answered, laughing, "If I'm loved by Jupiter he should know."

From that time he called her Juno and knew no more about her except that she seemed well-bred, that she lived in the outskirts of the city somewhere, and that she had a complaisant husband, or at any rate someone who kept her well provided and let her go her ways.

Fannie favored him with these hours in his apartments at discreetly chosen intervals. When he saw her with her friends at the theater, in the Hyde Park carriage parade, at the Pantheon, in the Ranelagh gardens at Chelsea, or across the river in the bowers of Vauxhall, she gave him a faint smile in passing and that was all. He was piqued, naturally, and Juno kept him so. By the time summer came she was a little tired of her Jupiter. There was a sameness about him, the nymph in her no longer tingled at caresses that followed a too-familiar order, and even his nobility had lost its flavor. There were other noble fish in the stream of London fashion quite ready to jump at a pretty fly.

The move to Yorkshire in June made a refreshing break in the affair. The Rockingham mansion was another world, as far removed from the captain's arms as Yorkshire from America.

Again the Marquess and his lady made her welcome and lavished their affection on Charles. Again there was the dignity of being waited on by a swarm of liveried servants, of moving about those stately rooms as if she belonged there, of meeting the friends of my lord and lady as one of the family, and altogether enjoying the queenly side of herself instead of the romp.

It amused her to compare all this with the life of the *ton* and with Paul's *ménage*, where the little Targill woman alternately glowed and sulked with the master's appearances and disappearances. Lord Rockingham made an occasional call at Brandenburg House on his brief visits to London, but he never discussed Paul with Fannie except to say once, "Curious feller, that. Known him for years, but never knew quite what to make of him. Does anyone, I wonder? Likable, of course, and most obliging with advice in money matters. Knows a lot about stock-jobbing. I don't have much to do with those people on Change Alley—or is it Sweetings Alley now? Not a gentlemen's society. No reflection on Paul of course."

At the Yorkshire dinners and balls and whist parties, where the society was so much more sedate than the fashion of London, there was also more serious talk about the war in America. Often Fannie was asked for her views, and she could only give her invariable reply that it was all very strange and terrible, and that she prayed every night for it to end soon and let her join her dear Governor again.

When September came she was quite ready to leave, and she did, over the protests of my lord and lady as before, and with the same excuses. At the end of a hard and dusty journey she rejoiced to see once more the hanging smoke, the forest of chimney pots rising out of the fields, the dark sea of roof slates, wave behind wave, and then the streets thronged with vehicles and people. At Hammersmith she found Brandenburg House wrapped in the austere quiet that it always had when Paul was away. Mrs. Targill looked lonely and glad to see her back with Prue and the child. Paul had been absent most of the summer.

"Abroad," Mrs. Targill said with a shrug. Fannie suspected a woman abroad, and obviously so did the little brunette. Sometimes Fannie wondered how much Mrs. Targill suspected of her own excursions, especially those jaunts to town in the past spring, when she returned so often with the sunrise casting long shadows on the road before the chaise and horses. But, la, who was a kept woman to suspect or judge Mrs. John Wentworth? As for Prudence, that good plain creature lived up to her name and devoted herself to the baby. If she thought Charlie's mother a rather frivolous woman she gave not a sign. The only person of whom Fannie had any misgivings was the coachman at Brandenburg House. Lest he tell a tale she had paid him well for the nights when she kept him so late in town. To make doubly sure she had never driven directly to Berkley Square, but left chaise and coachman in a mews off Piccadilly and took a sedan chair with drawn curtains to the captain's rooms. In the same cautious way she had refused the captain's chaise on the return, sending his manservant out for a chair and departing for the mews as mysteriously as she had come.

A few days after her return from the country she ventured forth to Ranelagh. The *ton* were back in town after their summer scatter to Bath and other country resorts, greeting each other with the hubbub and preening of pigeons who have all arrived back at the cote together. It was a usual Ranelagh crowd on a fine night, with a concert in the tall Rotunda to which nobody listened, and the gardens alive with gay blades and women and with small colored lampions glowing like fireflies in the shrubbery. Once she had a glimpse of her late lover, the captain of Horse Guards, but she slipped aside in the crowd.

In the bleak rains and sleet of the new year she retired to the seclusion of Brandenburg House and determined to remain away from the *ton* until it was time to go to Yorkshire. She took up her music again, played with little Charles for an hour at a time, and wrote long letters to Lady Rockingham and to Johnnie across the sea.

She felt quite virtuous about her little fling. It was Johnnie's fault, sending her off to live with strangers thousands of miles away and with all this temptation about her. Where were his senses? Far wiser to have kept her with him, following the army, no matter what he thought of those roistering officers. And she went on thinking of herself as a neglected wife, thrust away into this silent house of Paul's where the Targill girl moved about like a mournful ghost. By February of '78 she was dying of *ennui*.

March began with its rough winds through the streets and died away into the languid airs of an English spring. Driving back to Brandenburg House in the dark hours of a morning in the third week of March, Fannie saw lights in the drawing room and guessed that Paul was back at last. The night footman opened the door as the chaise wheels rasped up to the steps, and she passed him her cloak as she stepped into the hall. The drawing room door was open.

She heard Paul's voice saying, "King Louis received 'em officially two weeks ago, the full trio—Franklin, Deane, and Lee. Truth is, they've succeeded in getting a treaty of alliance with France. The French have even named a minister to the Congress. Sometime soon they intend to seize all English shipping in their ports. Then puss will be out of the bag, all teeth and claws. It means open war with France by summer at the latest."

She did not know why she paused in the hall. It was only Paul rattling on in his positive way to some visitor, a member of Parliament probably, staying late over pipe and port. She was drowsy after a night's dancing and a late supper with her newest whim, an avid young conqueror of nineteen. She would show herself in the doorway and exclaim, "Paul! How good to see you home again," and then fly up the stairs to bed. She moved to the drawing-room entrance, noiseless in her silk dancing slippers. The greeting was on her lips, but instead she gasped. The other man, sprawled in a deep armchair, with his chin on his breast and his legs thrust out before him, was her own Governor.

Johnnie! What the devil was he doing here? She was in a fever of guilt, in a moment perspiring even to her upper lip. How had he found out? Prue? Targill? They didn't even know where he was. She pictured vaguely an officer of the *ton*, gone to

America and prattling over the mess tables of a dashed fine piece who called herself Mrs. Wentworth, and Johnnie there, the visiting colonel of American volunteers.

Paul's back was toward her. Johnnie remained frowning at his shoe buckles, with his fine lips thrust out in the familiar way when he was troubled. Fannie drew herself together. Courage, my dear. He won't say anything in front of Paul—Johnnie's nothing if not a gentleman. And once in the bedroom—pshaw! A husband's a man like any other.

She ran into the room crying, "Johnnie! Johnnie! Oh my darling love what a wonderful surprise!" And as he sprang up she threw herself on him, arms about his neck, kissing and weeping—weeping actual warm tears that made a ruin of her powder and touches of rouge. She was reassured at once by his own arms, clutching her so hard that the top buttons of his military coat were cruel to her breasts. Quickly she put her head back for his kiss. It was long and passionate.

Paul sat watching with his bright curious eyes, as he watched everything in his world, and with the pursed smile of a man who has had too much to do with women ever to believe this little scene. Mrs. Targill, like all his other clever little ladies, had kept him well informed.

Fannie was conscious of that gaze and of the pale blue crepe so deeply *décolleté*, the dress panniers at her hips awry from sitting in the chaise, and her white coiffure with its plumes and lace and pearls all tousled as if she had walked from London in a gale. Johnnie was holding her off now at arms' length, feasting his eyes after two long years of nothing but letters and memories. There was only admiration in his gaze, but lest he find awkward questions she rattled out quickly, "Oh, don't look at me, love, I'm a fright. A dance with some of Paul's friends, and then nearly upsetting in the chaise, and now blubbing my eyes out. You must come upstairs. Paul's had enough of you, haven't you Paul? Come, love, tell me how you came, and why, and—and everything. I vow I won't sleep till you do." Already she was sweeping him out of the room. Johnnie walked in a trance, with

295

Paul's port and the voice of darling Fan singing one song in his head.

It was noon when a polite tap on the door and Fannie's drowsy "Come in" brought Prue with a tray and breakfast. Johnnie awoke then and insisted on Prue's bringing little Charlie to him, and he sat up in bed playing with the child and his toys, oblivious of the food.

Fannie smiled over her teacup. "Haven't we taken good care of him, Prue and I? See how he's grown. And so strong, the little rogue—I can hardly hold him when he squirms. And isn't he handsome? You all over again, except the mouth and chin. He gets those from his mama, don't you, love?"

The child had one of those sunny natures that accept all the world as playmates, and after the first strange moments he was quite at ease with this gentle and humorous new creature in the household. And Johnnie could not get enough of him. When Fannie commanded Prue to take the boy downstairs to play, her Governor was out of bed at the close of the door, dressing quickly and hastening down to join Charlie on the drawing-room floor. Lazing for another hour, Fannie could hear faintly the little boy's shouts and laughter.

She mused on this unexpected twist of things. For the best of reasons Johnnie had not talked much in the night. All she knew was that he had arrived at Paul's house by coach from Falmouth, after a passage of only twenty-four days from New York; he had turned over the command of his little troop to Captain John Cochrane; they had fought in no battles at all; and her young brother Benning, impatient boy, had gone off to one of the established loyalist regiments. It all sounded paltry and dull. She had pictured Johnnie leading charges of cavalry, with a splendid flashing of swords like the Horse Guards, and driving before him a cowardly rabble who had exactly the faces of the Portsmouth mob.

When she came downstairs after an elaborate toilet she found that he had gone into town with Paul and would not be back until night. They returned at dark, bringing Benjamin Thompson with them, and there was long and serious talk over tobacco and wine behind the closed doors of Paul's library. Fannie went to bed in a nettled mood and pretended to be asleep when at last Thompson's carriage drove away and Johnnie came to bed. In the later hours of the morning she forgave him and again they lazed until noon.

But the rest of the day was a repetition of the first. He was away in town until dark and again sat late in talk behind shut doors, this time with Paul and a swarthy whiskered man in a round blue jacket and trousers of some coarse stuff like canvas, very wide in the cut and short in the leg, exposing a pair of thick shanks clad in striped woolen stockings.

"Who the deuce was that?" she demanded pettishly when Johnnie came to bed at last.

"A sea captain, a friend of Paul's."

"He looked more like a fisherman. What did you find to talk about with such an oaf, and so late? I feel quite put out. Wouldn't you rather talk to me?"

"Of course, love. But I've a lot of business to do. I must go into town again tomorrow."

"What for?"

"Um—well, I have to see various gentlemen about my affairs. My lord Sackville, and so forth. For one thing I've got to find how I stand with regard to my pensions as Governor and Surveyor General, now that I've left America."

"You mean you're not going back? What about your regiment?"

His sober gray eyes looked away evasively. "I'm afraid my poor little regiment is about to disband. The gentlemen are tired of no pay and small prospects."

"You should buy yourself a commission in the regular army, as the gentlemen here do."

He was silent. In the two frugal years away from Fannie he had saved roughly a thousand pounds. In that time, he discovered from Paul, she had spent more than double the sum.

"The army seems to get along without my services quite well.

In any case I've no great desire to fight against—to fight in a British regiment."

"Because you don't like the morals of British officers!"

"It isn't that, Fan. Don't ask me to explain. All I can say now is that a lot of things have changed in the past year."

"Have I?" she asked archly. He seemed in no hurry to join her in bed, sitting on the edge of it in breeches and shirtsleeves and with that brooding look.

His tight lips parted slowly in a smile. "Yes, Fan, you too. You're a different woman. Not just the way you do your hair and all that kind of thing, but the way you move, everything you do, even the way you speak—like an Englishwoman. Like a woman of the London fashion."

"Is there anything wrong with that?"

He put out a hand and touched that soft skin of a girl who could never be more than seventeen no matter how time went by.

"Not at all. You're more charming than ever—and younger. I myself—I just seem old."

"At two-and-forty? Stuff! You're my handsome Governor, the very one who set me aflutter the moment I saw him that day in the Parade at home. You were the man of London fashion then, remember? And I was the simple country wife. Now do stop dawdling with your clothes and come to me."

A week later she found him choosing some clothes and stowing them in a pair of portmanteaus. He said casually, "I'm going away for a few days, Fan, a week perhaps."

"Where?"

"With Paul. It's a confidential matter, love, and I'm bound to tell no one, even you."

Fannie sniffed. Her eyes searched his face. His voice was odd. There had been something odd about him ever since he came. And now going off with Paul, that devious wanderer.

"You're up to something, Johnnie, I can tell. You and Paul. And it can't be respectable, or you'd tell your wife."

But the mouth was set in that stubborn jaw. He kissed her

briefly and stepped into the coach where Paul was waiting. Away they went. Fannie turned and found Mrs. Targill watching from the doorway. They exchanged a look.

"Where are they going?" Fannie said.

The brunette stood with folded arms for a moment and then turned into the house. Over her shoulder she said coldly, "Who knows where men go?"

For ten days the two women sat about the house, passing the time at books and backgammon and needlework and peering forth quickly whenever there was a sound of wheels in the carriageway. Usually it was a tradesman's cart with milk or meat or greengroceries, and once or twice a messenger came from Whitehall with a heavily sealed letter for Paul.

Then the big coach returned. Paul sprang out briskly, and Johnnie followed, greeting Fannie with a heartiness that she knew was false. It was eleven o'clock in the morning. He was unshaven, and his plain blue coat and buff breeches had a rumpled look as if he had been out all night. As soon as he got indoors he commanded a decanter of brandy and gulped at a glass of it as if his life depended on getting it down as quickly as possible. Fannie watched him with a quite unaccustomed feeling of dismay. Johnnie? She had always been so sure of him in all ways. And now she was a betrayed wife. He had been off with Paul, that smiling rake, enjoying the devil knew what debauchery for ten whole days—the coach had come from the direction of the town. Memories of the *ton* floated before her, filled with pictures of the women and their ways with men. Paul was an intimate in that half-world of course; it was he and The Filly who had introduced her there. Johnnie had changed in these two years away from her. In New York with those rakehell officers. She could see it all now, and she was outraged.

He went upstairs to wash and shave. When he came down in fresh clothes he made straight for the decanter again. Paul said casually, "Isn't it early in the day for so much eau de vie?" But Johnnie did not answer. He remained silent and morose through the day, eating little and drinking much. By evening he was drunk, staggering up the stairs and throwing himself down fully clothed on the bed. Fannie undressed him with angry jerks and lay awake most of the night hearing his sodden snores.

The next day was like the first, except that Paul said nothing now, merely running a quick glance from Johnnie to herself and busying himself with letters. She was tempted to snatch the decanter away and demand to know everything, but in the presence of Paul and Mrs. Targill she held her tongue. Her chance came on the following afternoon, when Paul took carriage with the brunette, all smiles now, and went off to town for dinner and an evening at the play. Fannie ran upstairs. Johnnie was just arousing from the long stupor of last night. He sat up and groaned, putting his hands to his head. In her anger she seized him by the shoulders and shook him.

"Wake up! Wake up, you—you sot! If you only knew how disgusting you look!"

"Brandy," he begged, and she rattled him again with a strength that surprised him. In another moment she snatched a ewer from the marble washstand and dashed a cascade of cold water over him.

"Are you awake now?" she cried. "Are you?"

He stared at her with bloodshot eyes, as if she were a phenomenon.

"Fan?" And then, "Get me a dram of brandy, quick!"

"Where do you think you are—in a public house?" she said furiously. And then, thinking better of it, "I'll get you a dram at a price."

"What?"

"That you tell me where you've been and what you've been doing. I demand to know."

He blinked slowly and regarded her again.

"Very well." He sank back on the pillow as if the effort of sitting up were much too painful.

She ran down to a sideboard in the dining room and found a decanter with a pint or more left in it. When she entered the bedchamber and closed the door she placed the brandy where he could see it, out of reach, and poured a small dram. She faced him with folded arms and watched him drink it.

"Now," she said.

TWENTY-TWO

Johnnie put his tonguetip out and slowly moistened his lips.

"I'll have to go back a way," he said thickly. And then in a stronger voice, "Back to Portsmouth, when people began to turn against me, even my friends. I couldn't believe it. Even after those rioting fellows drove us out. Even on Long Island I still thought I could go back. With a turn in the war, I mean. Everybody coming to their senses. I'd ride back with my gentlemen—no British soldiers, you understand—and everyone would welcome me."

He closed his eyes.

"Well?" she said irritably.

"Another dram," he begged. "Just to loosen my tongue a bit."

She hesitated. Well, why not? Men and their drams! The looser their tongues the more you heard. She poured him a big one and watched him drink it down.

"Where was I?"

"Dreaming of Portsmouth," she said contemptuously.

"Ah! That's all I've dreamed about these two years. The old province and the old friends and the old times. I never had an enemy but Livius, and he wasn't a New Hampshire man. Even when the trouble came I was still Governor Johnnie. There were hard feelings, but nobody hated me. Not then."

Fannie eyed him suspiciously. The second dram seemed to be whipping his wits together. He was talking quite rapidly, almost feverishly now. Did he think he could put her off with this garrulous talk about old times?

"When the trouble turned into a war," he went on, "there was just one hope. A short war. The whole mad business over and done with in a battle or two about New York and Philadelphia. That, and cool heads and a wise policy afterward. The shorter the war the better. No chance for hard feelings to settle into something that couldn't be mended. And—it was selfish, I suppose—no fighting in New Hampshire or anywhere near. I wanted the war to stay well away from my province and people."

He closed his eyes for a time and then stared at the ceiling again. "Burgoyne ruined everything. That affair at Bennington set all New Hampshire ablaze, all New England for that matter. Like a fire in the forest. Every man and boy scrambling through the woods to fight. That was the first consequence. No middle minds any more. Everybody up in arms. Then Burgoyne got trapped and captured with his whole army. That brought the second consequence. Ben Thompson had warned me. The French were watching across the sea. If the Americans won a big battle against the King's armies the French would make up their minds. They'd choose their moment and join the Americans in the war. And they're considering the moment now. It'll come before this spring is out."

"How do you know?"

"Paul."

"Him! All he knows is money. Money and women."

Johnnie lifted his head and looked her in the eyes. "I'll tell you something—something you're not supposed to know. You must keep it mum. Paul is the chief British spy in France. He has eyes and ears everywhere. He knows everything that goes on in Paris and in the ports. Make no mistake about that."

"Humph! Well, I'll believe anything of Paul. Go on. It's you and Paul I want to hear about."

"The French can't beat the British in Europe—they never could. They've got a strong fleet, so they'll send their troops to America. A mighty useful battleground, half a world away, and not so much as a broken windowpane in France itself. So the war's to be fought out on American soil, God knows how long—probably for years. You see what that means? Every American taking his stand on one side or the other and blood and ruin everywhere from Maine to Florida. And the black hate setting in between Americans, Whig and Tory. It's setting in already. I didn't realize how far it had gone till about two months ago. I saw a list of Tory refugees, compiled for the new Assembly in New Hampshire. They're all to be proscribed—forbidden to return, you understand. On pain of death. All their property will be confiscated when the act is passed this spring. They're to be rubbed off the face of the province like an old sum from a slate. My name is at the top."

He paused again, watching her with that red and somber gaze as if she must be stricken at this news.

"Were you surprised?" she blazed at him. "After all they did to us in Portsmouth? Bah! I despise them all. I hate them all. I wouldn't want to go back there, ever." She paused, and recollecting herself, "But that's got nothing to do with you and Paul. Tell me what I want to know and stop this stupid talk of America."

"Do be patient, Fan. I can't ask you to understand, I suppose. Just hear me. As soon as I saw that list I went to New York and took the first ship out for England."

"To see me of course?"

"You and the baby, yes."

"Not Paul?"

"I had to see Paul and some other people in London," he said guardedly. "And one or two in Paris."

"Why Paris?"

He turned his eyes away. "I suppose you know the American Congress has a commission there. I heard that my old friend John Adams had been sent to join them."

"So you went to see him?"

"Yes."

"That Boston rascal—the worst of all rebels!"

"You're thinking of Sam Adams, perhaps. John's a leader in the rebellion, yes, but he was never like Sam. He's honest, whatever one may think of his opinions. We were classmates together at Harvard College, we were like brothers, he and I, and we kept our friendship after we graduated in '55. I went to see Adams whenever I was in Massachusetts, and as you know he visited me when his law practice took him down East."

"Oh, I remember well enough. That cold clever fish! A leveler even then—looking down his nose at what he called our 'little pomps and vanities' at Portsmouth."

"He used to twit me about that, I admit, but our friendship had nothing to do with positions. Not for twenty years."

"Well, go on. You went to see him. How?"

"Paul has ways of getting to Paris quietly and easily. We crossed to France by night in a Channel lugger, with that smuggler you saw here. At Boulogne we avoided the public conveyance. Paul had a coach waiting. And in Paris we stayed at a grubby little *pension*, using false names. One of Paul's spies has a connection with a quill driver in the American party, and we found that on a certain night Mr. Adams would attend the piay at the Comédie Française. So I went there and saw him enter a box near the stage. I lingered about the entrance to the boxes. I don't understand French except a few words, and the play seemed to go on forever. When it was over and the people arose I stood in the box entrance and seized John's hand as he came out. For a moment he didn't recognize me. I suppose when you're in a foreign country you don't expect to meet anybody you know. I said, 'Governor Wentworth, sir' and shook his hand. He knew me then of course. And he was taken aback. He was cold and suspicious. Maybe he knew something of Paul's activities. He certainly knew I'd made my home with Paul when I was in England before. I'd often talked of that. Perhaps it was something else. The French themselves have secret police watching every move of the Americans in Paris; they don't trust anybody, and now that they're planning to enter the war they're watching for any sign of the Americans backing out of it. They know the British Whigs, especially Lord Rockingham, are eager to patch up a peace with the Americans. And Adams knew he was watched. So when a loyalist American governor turned up in Paris, shaking his hand in a public place like that, he may have sniffed a plot to discredit him. The meeting would be known to the French ministry in half an hour. That's what Paul says anyhow."

Johnnie dragged himself back to a sitting position, shook his head as if beset by flies, and passed a hand slowly over his face.

"Whatever it was, my old friend looked at me as if I were a snake he'd met in the woods. I sought to put him at his ease, asking for news of my father and various other relatives and friends in New Hampshire, and he told me very civilly what he knew of them. Then I asked after the health of Dr. Franklin and said I must come out to Passy—he lives outside the city—and give the old gentleman my compliments. I said I shouldn't dare to see the Marquess of Rockingham on my return without having paid Franklin a visit. My lord and Franklin are old friends, you understand, from the time when we were all in London fighting the Stamp Act, back in '65."

"Yes, yes—go on!"

"I could see Adams was embarrassed, standing there talking to me with the French people brushing about us. So I said I hoped to see him at Dr. Franklin's house in Passy. I said I'd come in two days' time, in the morning. And with that we tipped our hats and parted. Two mornings later Paul got a carriage for me, and I went out to Passy. I found them in a small château, a queer pile of stone towers and turrets and gables, a worse jumble than Uncle Benning's house at Little Harbor, but comfortable and very prettily situated in gardens on the bank of the river Seine. The old doctor peered at me over his spectacles. He wore a homely snuff-colored suit, with his hair straggling about his shoulders. Adams was in broadcloth. He had his son with him, a bright little fellow of ten or eleven, and Franklin had two of his grandsons there. The boys came into the room as I was introduced, and to break the ice I talked with them for a time, asking them how they liked Paris, and so forth. But I couldn't break any ice with the two men. I talked about America, of course, nothing of political matters, just polite and pleasant trifles, and they responded in the same way."

Johnnie threw out both hands and splayed the fingers. "I was like a blind man fumbling at a wall! I couldn't get to them. I couldn't say what was in my heart. They were suspicious, they were hostile. I was an enemy—that was in their faces all the time. As if—as if I'd come there with a pistol hidden under my coat-tails. Oh, they were polite, you understand. But behind all that genteel conversation I could feel them saying, 'For God's sake go!' And so, at last, I went. Paul had some business in Paris. I had to remain in that damned *pension* like a lost soul in perdition till he was ready to return. Then we took private coach to Boulogne and crossed the Channel as before, in the night."

He turned and thrust his face into the wet pillow as if he wished to drown.

There was a long silence, and then Fannie spoke. She was still in a frigid attitude, arms folded, tapping a silken foot.

"What was it you wanted to say to them?"

A muffled voice from the pillow. "You wouldn't understand."

"Oh yes I do! You think they'll win their war now that the French are on their side, don't you? And you can't bear the thought of being shut out of America forever. You can't think of anything but your precious New Hampshire and your precious friends and relatives on the rebel side and your precious estate up there in the woods at Wolfeborough. So you went to ask John Adams and old Franklin to intercede for you. You went to ask those rebels for mercy—and they wouldn't let you."

He did not answer.

"Look at me!" she demanded. "There, that's better. You can't hide yourself in a pillow. What a child you are after all! Do you realize what you've done on this foolish whim? You've risked the only real position you had left, your pensions and everything else. Hadn't you any thought for me? You know perfectly well what would happen if the Secretary for the Colonies learned what you were up to—calling secretly on those Americans in Paris. They're watched all the time, you admit that yourself. And you actually got Paul to arrange it. How far can you trust Paul, this wonderful spy as you say? How do you know he won't report the whole thing to London, just to keep his own skirts clean? Why, you must be mad!"

Johnnie made no answer. He lay like a sculptured image of despair, with the nightshirt ruckled about him in quite classical folds, and looking indeed what he was, a man who has lost his last illusions. She was so angry that the image filled her with contempt. He had abandoned the neat London wigs, which were now going out of fashion, and wore his own hair long, and now in spite of the queue it was tangled and hanging in untidy bunches about his temples, with most of the powder shaken out of it and natural gray hairs showing among the brown. There were sacs under his eyes from the drinking and long hours of stupor since he got back from France. He looked old enough to be her father.

She was scornful, and yet, as she stood there contemplating him, she felt pity too. She could not love him in the old way any more. Not with the reflection of a fresh young woman in the twenties which her own mirror gave her every day. But in the other part of her, the second woman, the calm and regal self which was so utterly separated from the romp, she could not help thinking of all he had meant to her in days gone by, and her mind turned to the future, with Johnnie as her partner in the business of making a way in the world. The weaker partner now, because his mind was still rooted in New Hampshire and his old small round. Her mind was free of all that. London— London was the heart of the world, America or no America. The home of the King, of Parliament, and an empire where there were always good posts for those who knew the right people and could pull the proper tassels. If the King's armies won the war in America, well and good. But she had no wish to go back to Portsmouth. If Johnnie could get the governorship of New York, say, or one of the southern provinces where the gentry lived and entertained like lords, on great estates with swarms of servants, that would be satisfactory. They could visit England from time to time, and when the time came they would retire in England where her spirit belonged. It was only an accident that she was born in America. She spoke and thought and lived as an Englishwoman now, and she wanted to be nothing else. If only Johnnie could get a good position here! Surely he could do it with a little influence in the right places. Young Benjamin Thompson had done it with no influence at all. The only shadow was this Paris escapade. She would say no more about it. Let it be forgotten as quickly as possible, and pray that my lord Sackville never heard a whisper.

And so she left the wretched man in the bed and walked slowly down the stairs. Paul was still at his letters in the library. She had a notion to confront him with the whole affair. Had he fallen in with Johnnie's whim merely to oblige an old friend? Or had he used Johnnie deliberately in a stupid little plot against Adams and Franklin, under the suspicious eyes of the French? Paul was a ruthless gambler, capable of anything. But she chose to keep her peace. She even permitted herself a hard little smile, thinking, We can't quarrel, any of us; we all know too much about each other.

She turned her thoughts to the future. With Johnnie here things would have to be different. No more little peccadilloes. A harmless flirtation now and then perhaps, just to assure herself that she was losing none of her charm. But from now on she would be unmistakably the lady of Governor Wentworth, with Johnnie at her side, no longer a shadowy presence across the sea. A pair of brave loyalists in exile, with every claim to the best of English hospitality. A man and wife could make their way in good society where a lone woman couldn't, even with such powerful patrons as the Rockinghams. Especially in that powerful and sedate society which lay outside the *ton*, dimly seen but solid as a pyramid, with the royal family at the top. As Whigs, the Rockinghams and Johnnie's other titled friends were all on the wrong side of royal favor. It was time to cultivate a few on the right side as well. One or two of her lovers were slips of the Tory nobility, but that was not the same thing as being received in their family drawing rooms. Well, we shall see.

For a few days Johnnie remained subdued, and by a little conspiracy with Mrs. Targill and the house servants Fannie kept the brandy from him. He had always enjoyed food and drink, but never to excess; his pride of person kept him from drunkenness. Gradually now he recovered himself, he could even laugh sometimes, especially when romping with little Charlie, and whenever Fannie permitted him he was the uxorious and grateful husband again.

They went to the plays, they dined with Johnnie's old friends, they rode together in Hyde Park. Fanny led him boldly to the Pantheon and the other evening haunts of the fashion, introducing him to her friends in a clear voice as "my husband, Governor Wentworth," and clinging to him at the balls and masquerades very prettily and possessively, as if she feared some naughty creature might run off with him if she let him out of her sight. When occasionally she encountered one of her former indulgences she met his eyes with a blank chill stare, and for their part they glanced at Johnnie ironically, wondering how long this handsome middle-aged successor could hold his elusive prize.

The weeks rode by, and when June came they went off with Prudence and the baby to spend the summer at Wentworth Woodhouse. In these rural scenes, astride my lord's magnificent horses, Johnnie was in his element. The shadow passed from his face and then from his eyes. He seemed happier than he had been at any time since the old days on his own country seat in the New Hampshire hills. Fannie herself found it a little too much like the Wolfeborough days. He was gone from morn to night, often beyond the estate altogether, roaming the country, quizzing the farmers about horses and cattle and sheep, inspecting the woolen mills on every stream, even going down one of the shallow coal pits. What was worse he talked about these things at dinner and in the evenings, as if they were all of immense importance, as if he would use this knowledge somewhere—presumably in America—after the war.

The Marquess and his friends joined in this talk with the sure knowledge of landowners. It was all very dull. She was relieved whenever my lord turned the subject to the war, even though the news was bad. In June word came across the sea that the secret alliance between France and the United States of America —that strange new term which Fannie refused to utter—had been announced by the Congress. Within a few days British and French warships were at hammer and tongs in the Channel, and all through England there was a scurry of militia, drilling and marching, wearing their uniforms very badly, and looking as fierce as if French invaders would arrive at any moment.

Toward the end of July, in a week of soft persistent rain that drenched the lawns and park and kept the ladies indoors, the post arrived with a London newspaper. Over the dinner that night my lord had a whimsical look and Johnnie looked dour as death. There were more tidings from America. In view of his new dangers, with a French fleet on the sea and possibly a French army as well, General Howe had abandoned Philadelphia and retreated to New York, with Mr. Washington in hot pursuit.

"Good lack!" Fannie said as they undressed for bed. "One would think the world was coming to an end, to see your face."

"My world is," Johnnie said.

"You heard what my lord said. The war's not over. It's just beginning."

"Yes," Johnnie said. "So it is."

TWENTY-THREE

*A*s FAR as Fannie was concerned the war could go on forever. Life had never been better. If Lord Germain ever heard of Johnnie's rash visit to Paris nothing came of it. The Board of Trade and Plantations went on paying his pension, of £600 a year as Governor of New Hampshire and £400 as Surveyor General of His Majesty's Woods, and raised no question whatever about his living in England until the American trouble was settled and he could go back to his posts.

In Paul Wentworth's hospitable home, with his staff and stable and carriages, they were able to live grandly without a penny of household expense, leaving a clear thousand a year for clothes and amusement. That was only a pittance in the fashionable world, of course, but with clever management and a cunning dressmaker Fannie was able to stretch it far. With these contrivances and a few hundred guineas now and then from the generous Paul they could always be seen with the right people in the right places. When the country was the thing they stayed with well-to-do friends, acquired in Bath and other resorts of the fashion, and always there was the princely hospitality of Wentworth Woodhouse in the north. Altogether they were able to follow the fashionable cycle as if they had a fashionable income, including a journey across the Channel in summer for the pleasures of Brussels and the medicinal waters of Spa.

France had been joined by Spain and Holland in the war at sea, and there were even rumors of daring American privateers off the British coast. But the war in America was like a shadow on the moon's face, too far to be felt at all and only vaguely to be seen. Johnnie watched the newspapers with a keen eye, but Fannie only knew that General Clinton still hung about New

York, and that the hero now was Lord Cornwallis, winning victories all over the southern colonies. London was buzzing with these and especially the exploits of his young English cavalry officer, Colonel Tarleton, who commanded a brigade of loyalist dragoons. Whenever there was news of Tarleton's Legion, Johnnie would exclaim, "There! I always said there was nothing like a regiment of Americans, moving everywhere on horseback and trained to fight on foot as well as in the saddle. That's what I tried to raise, but they wouldn't listen to me."

London had another hero, present and visible, in the spring of 1780, when little Prince William came home in his midshipman's uniform, straight from the wars. He was only fourteen, and he had actually served with Admiral Rodney in a sea battle near Gibraltar. Everybody was toasting "our intrepid Sailor Prince." Fannie commanded her husband to make sure of seats at Drury Lane one night in March, when the King and Queen were taking the small hero to see *The Tempest*.

Nobody paid much attention to the play. William sat with Prince George and Prince Frederick in a box, facing his father and mother in another. Before the play could begin at all there was tremendous ovation to the little middy, everybody tossing up hats and waving handkerchiefs and clapping and shouting "Huzzah!"

"What a manly little fellow," Johnnie said, between the acts.

"Homely," Fannie observed. "A very red face and that odd shape to his head. He looks like a coconut scraped down one side and painted scarlet for a curio. And how pleased with himself! A brat, I venture; I'd much rather look at the Prince of Wales. He's eighteen and handsome enough for a picture. See how he keeps glancing toward the curtain. Perdita's not on the stage tonight; she's not well, it seems, and he misses her."

"Who's Perdita?"

"Don't be stupid. Mrs. Robinson the actress. He's madly in love with her; it's the talk of the town, and that pimp Lord Malden's wooing her desperately on the prince's behalf. Everyone's betting she'll give in, too, before the month is out."

"How the deuce do you know all this, Fan?"

"Oh, we ladies are quite interested, naturally."

"Lord Malden should be horsewhipped," Johnnie growled, "and she too."

"Come now, darling! She can't help being the handsome creature she is or enjoying the attentions of a prince. She's really a very intelligent woman—she actually writes and publishes poetry."

"Where's her husband? If she's really got one."

"Living with her of course. I'm told he's very accommodating where her lovers are concerned. Don't look so scandalized! This isn't New Hampshire, darling. How often must I tell you that?"

"But a boy of eighteen!"

"Pshaw! All boys of eighteen must learn about women, and she may as well teach him. Much better Perdita than some common little strumpet, I say. Ah! There's the curtain going up again!"

News came from New Hampshire in devious ways. Bit by bit Johnnie learned the fate of his property. When the state congress moved to confiscate it, his father put in a claim of £13,000 for money advanced on the estate at Wolfeborough. But a swarm of other creditors appeared, with claims for thousands more. Grim old Mark had been able to rescue nothing but the family portraits and what remained of the furniture in the house on Pleasant Street. The contents of Wentworth House at Wolfeborough, even to the books from Johnnie's library, had been sold at auction and so had the timberlands.

For a long time there were no bidders for the big house and farm, so far from Portsmouth and so costly to maintain. But at last, in 1781, the state trustee sold them to a Massachusetts man. "Andrew Cabot," said a mysterious letter, "who has made a pretty fortune in privateering since this war began. You will smile at the price, £354,470 Continental paper currency, which is worth no more than £9,000 sterling. All goes to the creditors of course.

The state gets nothing for its trouble. And you see what a pickle our Sons of Liberty have got their money in."

When this news came in the autumn of '81 Johnnie and Fannie had settled down for the winter at Brandenburg House, after another summer spent about the English countryside and on the continent. The war had shut off France and Holland and Spain to English travelers, but Belgium remained open and was now more popular than ever.

Governor and Mrs. Wentworth had traveled there in July, leaving little Charlie in the care of Prudence and the Rockinghams. A fast packet sloop took them from Ramsgate to Ostend, braving the danger of small French privateers dashing out from Dunkirk. But none appeared, and they traveled in a hired *diligence* through the flat green Flanders landscape to the Belgian capital. There they tarried a fortnight, dining and wining with fashionable English visitors, attending the Opéra and the *Comédie,* riding in the Parc, or merely driving in an open carriage about the streets of the handsome old city.

The merry Belgians did not seem to mind their Austrian rulers; indeed they were celebrating, with days and nights of high festivity, the arrival of a beautiful Austrian archduchess as their governor. Once, pressing close in the throng, Fannie saw her go by.

"I could have put out my hand and touched her!" she said, thrilling. "Just think, she's a daughter of the Queen of Austria and sister to the Queen of France!"

"What an abject royalist you are!" laughed fat amiable Lady Derby, whose husband was one of the great Whigs.

"You mustn't forget," retorted Fannie, as she did on every possible occasion, "that we have suffered cruelly and lost everything, my dear Governor and I, for our own King."

"Let us hope then, my dear, that His Majesty will someday put out a hand and touch you both." The lady settled back in her carriage and drove on.

"Someday," murmured Fannie to nobody at all, "someday he shall."

They moved on to Spa, the little town in the wooded slopes of the Ardennes, where again they found the *ton*. Fannie had tasted the famous waters and found them horrid. It was far better to sip a light Rhine wine in the shade of the trees before the hotel, watching the livelier young men of the *ton* at cricket on the green, or riding with them in the shady woods, or dancing with them in the evenings, while Johnnie lay long hours in the baths and sipped faithfully at the nauseous waters for the good of his rheumatism.

He was getting a paunch now, and a settled fat began to show in his silk-stockinged calves and in his face, the result of these idle years in England. His old restless energy and the hard muscular figure had been left behind in the New Hampshire woods. In the mornings, before his hair was powered, the gray showed increasingly in the straight brown locks.

At thirty-six Fannie could look at herself in the glass without a qualm. There was not a line in her face. The satin skin, the wide-set dark eyes, the slender tilt of nose, the mouth with its sensuous little pout, the high cheek bones, the wilful chin—nothing had changed. People often spoke in her hearing of "the American governor and his pretty young wife," and some, observing her English accent and manners, assumed that this middle-aged man had married a girl of some well-bred London family since he fled across the sea.

From Spa they had moved on to Antwerp for a week and then returned to London. Prue had brought young Charlie down from Yorkshire, and Paul was there, stocky and nimble and smiling, and darting his sharp blue glances. Mrs. Targill had gone long ago. She had not lasted more than two years, and she had not been replaced. Perhaps Paul found the immediate presence of a mistress a little embarrassing after Johnnie came to join the household. Probably he was satisfied now with his ladies on the continent, where he spent so much of his time.

He was French in his dress, even to his coiffure, and his conversation bubbled with French phrases that came fluently and naturally, not like the self-conscious bits of French that Fannie, with so many of the *ton*, put into their speech like plums in pudding. He seemed to have slipped into a French way of life with the same ease that enabled him, long ago, to change so quickly from a young Yankee merchant into a fashionable Englishman.

When Paul was at home there were almost nightly dinner parties, with cards or talk or music afterward according to the taste of the company. Often there were distinguished American refugees like young Sir William Pepperell of Kittery and old Governor Hutchinson of Massachusetts and Copley the painter, late of Boston and now a huge success in England. Benjamin Thompson came sometimes, slipping off his scientific hobbyhorses as well as his post as Undersecretary of State for the Colonies. And once Robert Rogers came, an old, untidy, ugly caricature of the famous Indian fighter who had led the New Hampshire rangers in the old French war. Since then he had spent most of his time in England, living on his reputation, his half pay, and his wits, and slowly becoming the unlovely sot he was now. At the start of the American war he had gone to Boston to raise a corps of rangers for the King's service. For that his native New Hampshire proscribed him, like Johnnie and the others. Eventually he had recruited a small corps among the loyalists on Long Island, but he was too old and too drunken a man to command it in the field, and Howe had dismissed him as worthless.

"He kep' my men though," Rogers grumbled. "Put a young sprig of an English officer in command and calls 'em the Queen's Rangers."

"I saw them on Long Island," Johnnie said. "They've done well in the fighting since." But all this reminded him of his own failure with the Volunteers, and he turned the subject to something happier for them both, their memories of the New Hampshire mountains and the mountain men.

"What a disgusting creature!" Fannie said when he was gone.

"I enjoyed him," Johnnie said mildly.

"The way he kept talking of 'us loyalists'—ugh!"

Johnnie cocked a whimsical brow, but he said no more, and Fannie went to bed still indignant. She liked to think, indeed she always spoke, of the loyalists as a superior class, the better part of American society. It was outrageous to suggest that there might be common and even vulgar creatures in their ranks.

Late in that autumn of '81 Johnnie met Benjamin Thompson riding in Pall Mall. They pulled up knee to knee, and Johnnie said, "Hello, you look very serious."

Ben gave him one of his clear cool looks. "So will you when I tell you what I've just heard. It'll be all over London tomorrow. Lord Cornwallis and his army have surrendered, just like Burgoyne."

"No! Why, Cornwallis has beaten rebel armies all over the South!"

"Small armies—his and theirs. He made the great mistake of marching north where the big armies were and expecting Clinton to support him from New York. You know Clinton. He just sat where he was. So Mr. Washington slipped away with the whole of the American and French forces and sent the French fleet to block any escape by sea. They caught Cornwallis at a little tobacco landing called Yorktown. And that was the end of him."

Ben paused. "The end of this government, too, I think. North and his cabinet can't survive this blow, even with the King behind 'em. You'll see the Whigs in power again by spring—and your humble servant out of work."

"A Whig government," Johnnie mused. "Who'll head it?"

Thompson smiled. "Your friend Rockingham probably. Of course there's Lord Shelburne, who's ambitious. And there's Charles Fox, the best of all brains amongst the Whigs—but he's erratic, no one ever knows what Fox will do. I think it will be Rockingham. You'll be all right, sir."

When Johnnie told all this to Fannie that evening she reflected a moment and said, "That means you can get your pay increased of course. You should be getting the full £800 as Surveyor General, and they cut you down to half. You might even ask my lord for an addition to your pension as Governor. You could say your expenses now are much more than they were at home."

"I'd better leave well enough alone," Johnnie said. "I'll be lucky if they keep on paying me a thousand pounds a year for nothing."

"Pooh! Get along with you! You're always looking on the gloomy side of things."

Johnnie gave her one of his patient looks. "England can't go on fighting one nation in America and three in Europe. My lord Rockingham's told me not once but many times that this war must be stopped; if necessary it must be ended on the Americans' own terms. What then becomes of posts like mine?"

"Well," she said quickly, "what if England does give up America? There are good posts to be had in London if you'll just assert yourself a little with Lord Rockingham. Zooks, I wish I were you and you were me. I'd assert myself, I assure you!"

He nodded resignedly and said no more. What was the use? Poor innocent Fannie. She thought that posts and money grew on bushes as most women did. When you were lucky they said I told you so. When your luck was out they said it was your fault.

All through the winter, London's drawing rooms and clubs and coffeehouses chattered over those tidings from America. In March of '82 the result came. Lord North resigned, and out went the government, with all the sins of the American war upon its head. In came the great Whig lords again, to the disgust of the King, and to the delight of Governor and Mrs. Wentworth. Their good friend and patron Rockingham was head of the new cabinet.

But Paul, hopping over from France to London at the news, offered Johnnie some shrewd comment.

"I daresay this means the end of my interesting—and lucrative—work for the late government. Charlie Fox is Secretary for Foreign Affairs, and he'll throw out everyone connected with North. Heigh-ho! As for you, my dear Johnnie, don't be too sure of things. Your friend Rockingham's a charming man, but weak for what he's got to handle. He has one faction of the Whigs behind him, but Lord Shelburne has another just as powerful. Shelburne despises Rockingham and everyone connected with him. And, my dear Johnnie, Shelburne is now Secretary for the Colonies—your department."

"What's your drift, Paul? I don't see. . . ."

"Johnnie, Rockingham wants to end the war, but on some sort of honorable terms for England. Shelburne's quite cold about that. It's no secret that Shelburne would throw everything overboard in North America—tomorrow if he could. Scratch the whole expense off the ledger and have done with it. He won't even wait till the war can be brought to an end. He and Burke— a sharp devil—have had their heads together for weeks on immediate economies. They're planning a bill to cut away all sorts of posts and salaries, at home and abroad, from the King's household to the Board of Trade and Plantations. D'you see what I mean?"

"I begin to see. But you're a pessimist."

"If I were you I'd see Rockingham as soon as possible. He daren't oppose Shelburne's group. All he can do for his friends is to grant pensions in other directions before the new bill can go into effect."

Johnnie hesitated for a week. Lord Rockingham's town house, which he had used so little in the long years out of office, was now buzzing with cabinet ministers and messengers, and besieged with supplicants like Johnnie himself.

At last Johnnie wrote a polite little note requesting an interview, but there was still no answer by mid-April when the economy bill was placed before the Commons and the Lords. As the debate went on Ben Thompson called at Brandenburg House.

"I've come to say good-by, Governor. I'm off to America."

"What for?"

"To fight," said Thompson calmly. "It seems the only thing to do now. Our generals haven't learned much in the past six years, but at least they've learned to equip loyal American regiments and give 'em encouragement in the way of rank and pay. As for the war, there's still a chance. The rebel armies are just as weary as the British, and the Congress is bankrupt. One resolute campaign this coming summer, redcoats and loyalists together, and we'd end the whole affair before another snow."

"How do you propose to fight?" Johnnie's tone was quizzical. It was hard to picture this ingenious civil servant as a soldier.

"I have a commission to raise a mounted regiment among the loyalists—d'you know there are thirty thousand loyalist refugees in New York alone? I'm to call it the King's American Dragoons."

"Ah! That's what I tried to do. I always said. . . ."

But Thompson cut him short, with a tolerant smile. Poor Governor Johnnie had been saying that for years. It was his defense for waiting through the war in England. He had been eager to fight the rebels wherever they might be found, but the general would not listen. Johnnie really believed it now. He talked sometimes as if his naive little troop of "gentlemen" could have won the war singlehanded in '77.

"I'm afraid I must be on my way, sir. I met Mr. Paul Wentworth in town and took my leave of him there. Will you give my compliments to your lady?"

He put out his hand and Johnnie shook it fervently. What it was to be young! No doubts—no doubts about anything.

It was nearly noon, and Fannie came downstairs in a morning robe of pink silk and lace, yawning and tapping fingers over her mouth. She had been in town late the night before, and Johnnie looked up fondly. How many men his age had wives who could look so charming in the mornings? In the past two years he had begged off many of those evening trips to town. Fannie was tireless, but he found it hard to keep up the round, especially the dancing, and because he was a serious player he found the chatter at card parties irritating. It was easier and much more satisfying to sit at home playing *écarté* or cribbage with Paul, or with some neighboring crony when Paul was not there; or merely to sit alone by a good fire, reading a book or the latest newspaper, with a bottle of prime port at his elbow and now and then a segar in his teeth. He did not enjoy these Cuban things, which Fannie, like so many ladies and gentlemen of the *ton*, affected nowadays; he preferred Virginia in a long cool clay, but tobacco of that kind was hard to get, especially now that His Majesty's forces had all but abandoned the southern colonies.

Fannie came over and kissed him on the forehead. "Who was that you were talking to?"

"Eh? Oh! Young Ben Thompson. He lost his post when the government fell, so he's off to fight in America."

"That's silly, isn't it? I thought you said—or was it Paul—that this new government intends to end the war as soon as possible."

"So they do. But there'll be months and months of negotiating, you may depend. And it'll all be so much easier for our side if His Majesty's forces can improve their position in the meantime. It's like a game of cards. You need a trump or two in hand. And speaking of cards, did you enjoy your party last night?"

An indolent gesture of Fannie's hands. "*Comme ci, comme ça.*"

"That sounds as if you held bad cards. You always play so well."

"I've held better cards, but I think I played quite well." The faint smile passed over Fannie's lips. "The company complimented me."

That afternoon there was a sound of carriage wheels, and Paul came bursting in, with eyes round and gleaming like the blue china buttons on his French coat.

"Well, it's passed," he shouted, "and the town's in an uproar I can tell you. Burke got the bill through the Commons, and Shelburne's sure to pass it through the Lords. They've slashed right and left, like a pair of mad hussars in a shop full of plaster images. The principal officers of the Great Wardrobe, the Jewel Office, the Treasurer of the King's Chamber, the Cofferer of the Household, six of the Board of Green Cloth—all must go! I'm told the King actually consents, imagine that! And of course they took a particular slash at the Secret Service. They've cut the fund to a pauper's ransom, and henceforth the Secretaries of State must take a solemn oath on every penny they spend. Which means I'm on the heap with all the rest. And I've told you nothing yet."

He seemed almost happy in a devil-may-care way, but now the grin vanished and he looked at Johnnie with concern.

"Go on," Johnnie said stolidly.

"It's bad."

"I've heard bad news before."

"Well, they've as much as admitted America's gone. I mean they've cut away dozens of the old American posts and salaries in one swoop. You'll begin to see what I mean when I say they've abolished the Lords of Trade and Plantations. Your office as Surveyor General of the King's Woods won't exist any more."

Johnnie looked up at Fannie. "There goes four hundred pounds a year."

"I'm afraid it's worse than that," Paul said grimly. "You see, they've slashed the Pension List too. Those that remain will receive not more than £300 a year; that's the limit; and their names and pensions are to be laid before Parliament at each session in the future. So even that won't be certain."

Fannie stared. She was at her full height, straight and rigid as a marble pillar, and clutching the robe about her like an outraged Boadicea.

"Are you saying we're to be cut off with a miserable allowance of three hundred pounds a year?"

"If that," Paul said.

"But it's impossible! How can we live on that? You know what a pinch we've had to get along on a thousand."

"I'm afraid we're not expected to live on it," Johnnie said quietly. "I shall have to find something to do."

"Do! The thing for you to do is to go and see my lord Rockingham at once and put an end to this nonsense!"

Paul glanced at Johnnie. "Your friend Rockingham's in a bad

323

position for that, I fear. Just before the bill went through he awarded fat pensions to his good colleagues Barré and Lord Ashburton. Both Commons and Lords are boiling over that. He couldn't grant another penny to anyone. Your best chance is to approach him later in the year, when things have simmered down, and see if he can get you a post in the West Indies, or somewhere like that."

"Fever and mosquitoes and black people," Fannie cried.

"It's not as bad as all that," said Paul slowly. "I once lived in Surinam—still have an estate there. At the moment it's one of the few assets I have left."

Johnnie looked at him. Paul had always been so affluent that this hint came as a shock. They stared at each other for a moment and looked away. It was true, then. These years of war involving America and half Europe had ruined other speculators, why not Paul? And now his rich Secret Service income was gone too.

"How much do I owe you?" Johnnie asked, still gazing across the room.

"I've told you before. Nothing."

"But you've lent us thousands, besides giving us a home all this time."

Paul grimaced. He made an odd figure, sitting with nonchalance in the chair, in the foppish French coat, rich lace at wrists and throat, elegant white breeches and silk stockings, shoes with enormous gilt buckles curving over the instep and almost touching the floor at each side. His hair, once the color of good New England hay, was pink with the pomade and tinted powder in vogue among the *beaux* of Paris and London, with the pigtail clubbed in a pink silk bag. And yet there was the long pointed nose, thrusting into the air before him for all the world like the bowsprit of a Piscataqua sloop, and the blue eyes that had in them all the worldly wisdom of fifty-one and yet shone with the adventure of a Yankee boy's.

"My dear Johnnie, we're friends and kin. Your father gave me a start in New Hampshire many years ago. That put me on my curious way to fortune. If there's any debt it remains mine.

Say no more about it. The war's ruined many more than you and me. We'll have peace soon, I feel it in the air, and then we can recoup our fortunes one way or another. *Courage, mon ami, courage!*"

TWENTY-FOUR

*E*ARLY in May Johnnie sought in person an interview with the Marquess. As he approached the big town house he was startled to see straw laid thickly in the street before it, and at his knock a stout footman in the Rockingham livery and plush breeches appeared, recognized him, and said in a broad Yorkshire voice, "M'lord is very ill, sir. He can see no one, sir, the doctor says."

Johnnie murmured, "Please convey my deep regrets to His Lordship."

"I'll speak to the doctor, sir. Will you step into the drawing room if you please?"

He dropped on a chair. A pair of women-servants swam by on tiptoes. The house had the atmosphere of death. Rockingham? He was barely turned fifty and as hale as a hunter. Some passing fever perhaps.

The man appeared again. "M'lord wishes to see you, sir. Will you come this way?"

They passed up the stairs. A soft tap on a door, a murmured "Come!", and he was inside a large chamber where the velvet window hangings had been drawn against a bright spring sun. In this semi-gloom he could see a stout man in broadcloth standing by the foot of the great bed, the doctor of course, and as he advanced a dim head turned on the pillow.

"John," it said cheerfully.

His pupils were widening to the shadow now, and he was startled by Rockingham's appearance. The healthy Yorkshire pink had gone from his features and left a mask of drawn tallow. The eyes glittered with something more than fever.

"Come near," the Marquess said. "Whatever I've got is not contagious, John. A pain inside. I daresay it'll go away in a few weeks. Did before. What did you want to see me about? You sent a note, but I've been so busy with Parliament."

"Oh, sir, my concerns are too small to inflict upon you here. Another time."

"I think I know, my dear fellow. It's that bill of Burke's. Shelburne was bound to have it, y'know. Nothing I could do. Have to keep peace in my party or down we go, the way we did before. North and the King would be delighted. Can't have that."

The physician spoke. "I can allow you only five minutes, my lord."

"Very well. We must come to the point, John, eh? You're cut off with a pittance like so many others. And America's gone, we must recognize that. No hope for you there now. Sad, that. Very sad. We must find a post for you somewhere. Nothing here, nothing at all, with all these economies. Have you ever seen Nova Scotia?"

"Once or twice, sir, yes."

"Burke has a poor opinion of the place. Calls it a worthless expense to this country, and so on. But it's something—something. Anything's better than nothing in these times, eh? I have in mind the post of Governor. About a thousand pounds a year. The post came to my attention with a lot of other things when we were considering Burke's new bill. Present governor's a feller named Legge, appointed by the Earl of Dartmouth years ago. Had some trouble there with the people in '76. Legge was recalled to England but allowed to keep his post. Odd situation, very. He's been here ever since, drawing his full salary and paying some part of it to a lieutenant governor in Halifax. That's the capital town of the province, I believe. D'you follow me?"

"Yes," Johnnie said.

"Well, we can't let that go on. Cut off this useless Legge—there's a pun for you—I can still laugh, you see. Appoint a new governor and send him out to Nova Scotia with full powers and pay."

Johnnie was silent for some moments. His memories of Nova

Scotia were not attractive. A poverty-stricken patch of rock and forest at the tag end of New England. The province of Canada was much bigger and better, but of course Livius was Chief Justice there; he could never get along with the man, and the old intrigues would begin again at Quebec as they had in Portsmouth. In any case my lord hadn't mentioned Canada. Nova Scotia then. Beggars can't be choosers.

"I think I'd like the post," he said, wondering what the deuce Fannie would say. The place was just a poor caricature of New Hampshire, with everything mean in scale. New Hampshire at the wrong end of a spyglass.

The voice of the doctor broke in sharply. "I think your visitor should go now, my lord."

"Tush!" said the Marquess. "Another minute or two won't kill me or you, my dear Parkinson. Now, John, there's just one thing about this Nova Scotia post. Shelburne has a man in mind, a friend of his. A veteran of the old French war named Parr. At present he's Major of the Tower of London, a snug little post, and besides, mind you, this Parr draws full pay as colonel of a regiment. He should be satisfied with that, but he's got his eye on something more. Well, I mentioned your name strongly to Shelburne as a deserving loyalist and an experienced Governor. The matter will be decided this summer, so that the new Governor, whoever he is, can make the voyage in good weather. Remind me early in July. And now Parkinson's looking daggers at his watch and you. Good-by, my dear feller. My compliments to Mrs. Frances and my love to the boy."

Back at Brandenburg House Johnnie found Mrs. Frances quite unpleased. "Nova Scotia! Why not go to the Pole? All I've heard of the place was fogs and ice and snow. You know what the Yankee skippers call the people there. Blue Noses!"

"Well, the thing's not to be decided now. Lord Shelburne's got another gentleman in view for the post, and Rockingham must have time to talk him out of it."

"Is the Marquess very ill? I must write a note to Lady Mary."

As the weeks went by the Marquess remained very ill, able

to see no one but his ministers. With the approach of warm weather the physicians advised country air, and as the journey to Yorkshire was too rough and far Lady Rockingham had him moved to a small estate nearby in Surrey. At polite intervals Johnnie and Fannie drove to Wimbledon in Paul's carriage, to pay their compliments and leave a message for the invalid.

Fannie refused to talk of Nova Scotia, sure that something better would turn up, but by the end of June Johnnie found himself eager to go.

"The residency's fairly large and comfortable, Fan—a good ballroom, you'll like that. And I confess I look forward to being an actual Governor again, with work to do, and of course enjoying what John Adams used to call our little pomps and ceremonies."

"And because it's in America and something like New Hampshire," Fannie said, amused. "You'll never get New Hampshire out of your mind, my poor darling, will you?"

Two days later a mounted groom in the Rockingham livery delivered a note at Brandenburg House. Fannie glanced at Johnnie's face as he opened it.

"What's the matter now?"

He seemed unable to speak, as if his mouth had been clamped by lockjaw in a moment. At last he said hoarsely, "Rockingham—he's dead! Yesterday. I—I can't believe it."

Fannie put out a faltering hand for a chair. She sat down and burst into tears, and Johnnie wept with her. Their whole world seemed to be tumbling about them.

With Paul, and in Paul's big traveling coach, they took the long road north to Yorkshire, traveling day by day in a solemn little procession of carriages led by a black-draped wagon carrying the coffin. They wept again at the funeral service in York Minster, seeing the last of that kindhearted gentleman disappearing into a tomb beneath the church. It was not until they were on the road back to London that Fannie spoke a word on the practical side of things.

"Who will inherit the Rockingham estates?"

"Everything goes to his nephew, Sir William FitzWilliam. Lady Rockingham's provided for naturally. I thought you knew," Johnnie said.

"Oh! We've met Sir William and Lady Charlotte there a good many times of course. About my age and very nice too—such charming condescension. I'll send her a note as soon as we get back. And be sure you write Sir William."

Paul was looking out of the coach window at the rolling dust. "D'you think FitzWilliam will cut anything like the figure in Whig affairs that his uncle did?" he asked blandly.

"I wasn't thinking of that," Fannie said quickly.

"Of course not. Still, one must be practical nowadays, eh, Johnnie?"

Johnnie frowned. There were times when Paul was a little too sly. But he met the barb with dignity.

"We'll keep up our friendship with Lady Rockingham, and with the FitzWilliams, naturally. And it's quite possible that Fitz-William can do something for me later on. At the present time I'm only too well aware I've lost my patron."

"Are you also aware that Lord Shelburne now becomes head of the government?"

"Shelburne!" Fannie cried. "God forbid!"

"I'm afraid neither God nor FitzWilliam can do much about it," answered Paul. "Shelburne is the devil himself to those he doesn't like. And he's got his own friends to look after. Even the devil has friends."

Less than a fortnight later Johnnie knew the truth of that. A pair of Whitehall quill drivers, chatting in a coffeehouse, remarked that "a little strutting cock sparrow of a man" had lately got an appointment as Governor of "some Godforsaken place called Nova Scotia in America."

His name? Mr. John Parr, a friend of my lord Shelburne's.

Paul merely screwed his mouth at this news. "You're probably well shut of the place, Johnnie. I have some news myself. Shelburne sent another friend of his to Paris some months ago, as soon as the Whigs came to power. Richard Oswald, who's never seen America. And this naive gentleman was charged with opening peace talks with wily old Franklin and your sharp friend Adams. I hear he's gone a long way toward agreement. The Americans want His Majesty's troops and rule withdrawn entirely from North America—including Canada and Nova Scotia. Shelburne's quite willing to give up everything, but some of the cabinet insist on holding those last parts. Just what will happen is on the under side of the cards, but I still have sharp-eyed friends in Paris and some pretty little ears. I'm told the preliminary peace terms must be signed not later than this autumn. Neither side wants to face another winter in the field."

Johnnie said, "I'm told there are thirty thousand loyalist refugees behind the British lines at New York. What's to happen to them?"

"They'll have to get out with the British troops, I suppose, some time next year. They could remove to Nova Scotia in the fleet—if Nova Scotia's left in British hands by the treaty. If not, God only knows where they'll go."

Johnnie was silent, thinking of that hurried flight from Boston, and the misery of the Tory refugees put ashore in Halifax. And they were only two thousand. He tried to picture thirty thousand stranded there. If that happened the little cock sparrow was going to find his post a nightmare.

I'm well out of that, he thought. And so it's all over and the rebels have won!

It was just over seven years since he and Fannie fled to the old fort at Portsmouth harbor mouth and heard the news of Bunker Hill. What a deuce of a time!

With their last prospect gone and their income a mere shadow Fannie put a brave face on it. No more of the *ton*. No more of Bath and Tunbridge Wells and Brussels and Spa. Paul still kept his style at Brandenburg House, and with his carriage and horses she and Johnnie drove on fine days in the nearby countryside or about the town. Sometimes they stood in the Hyde Park throng like any cockneys to watch the stout popeyed King out for a ride with some of his boys, and Fannie dropped a curtsy and Johnnie swept off his hat as they went by.

On fine Thursdays, when His Majesty allowed the public to roam about his gardens at Kew Palace, they went faithfully for a peep at the royal family. The King apparently disliked Buckingham House, the small brick mansion in the town where he and Queen Charlotte had spent the early years of their marriage. The royal family now lived most of the time at Kew and Windsor. They were an enormous brood. Fourteen sons and daughters and, as Fannie noted with a perceiving eye on Her Majesty one day at Kew, another on the way.

There was something magical about the aura of royalty. When the lively royal tribe was at Windsor the Wentworths drove there frequently and walked outside the Castle and about the sleepy little town and admired the lush green view from the hill.

"When you retire," Fannie said once, "this is where I'd like to live. A nice little estate where we can see the Castle and the royal family sometimes; and somewhere by the London road, so we can have an easy drive to town whenever we wish."

Johnnie shook his head with a melancholy smile. "Ah, Fan, you're the dreamer now. What could we retire on? Three hundred pounds a year?"

"Let's see." She turned her pert nose toward the Castle tower, as if consulting an oracle. "You'll get an appointment to be Governor—of Jamaica—that's the rich part of the West Indies, isn't it? We'll live there in a huge stone mansion with palm trees all round it, and hundreds of black servants to wait on us. . . ."

"And to fan us in the heat!"

"And beat off the mosquitoes. And then at last you'll retire, and you'll condescend to accept a pension of five thousand a year from the grateful planters, and we'll buy ourselves the nice little estate. Over there somewhere. Sunning Hill, say."

"And what if the planters aren't grateful?"

"Charlie will have to marry an heiress and buy Sunning Hill for us."

They both burst out laughing, and Johnnie patted her hand affectionately. What a dauntless creature she was!

November brought momentous word from Paris. The British and American peace commissions had reached agreement and signed their names. The formal and final document would be made next year, when the last British soldier left the thirteen colonies. Britain was to recognize the independence of the United States. His Majesty would retain only the two provinces in North America which had never joined the Congress, Canada and Nova Scotia.

It was black news to the great host of anxious loyalists in New York. Some had expected it, however, and sailed away. London seemed full of refugee Americans. Ben Thompson turned up in the uniform of the King's American Dragoons and talked of going off to join the Austrian army against the Turks. Fannie's brother Benning came, a bronzed captain, veteran of four years' fighting in a loyalist regiment, and talked of studying for a degree at Oxford University. Her merry sister Mary came with her family—George Brinley remained at his Commissary duties until the army left New York. Even that hearty sailor Captain Harry Bellew, R.N. appeared with his wife and her grown-up children, the young people all looking very much like their father, Johnnie's brother Tom.

Brandenburg House became to all appearances an American club, with these and other relatives and friends coming every day to exchange greetings and news and tales of the war and to chatter over prospects for the future. The house was in an American hubbub all through the winter and the spring of '83.

In May Johnnie wrote to Captain John Cochrane, "My destination is quite uncertain; like an old flapped hat thrown off the top of a house I am tumbling over and over in the air, and God only knows where I shall alight and come to rest. We are all looking for something to do."

A month ago, surprisingly, Lord Shelburne's government had gone down to defeat. The Whigs seemed doomed by their own quarrels, and brilliant Charles Fox had actually gone over to the enemy. Lord North was back in power again, with Fox of all people at his side and both of them using the convenient figure of William Bentinck, Duke of Portland, as the head of their government. Fannie rejoiced at the downfall of Shelburne, "that hateful creature," but Johnnie could see nothing else to be happy about. Yet now, in his darkest hour, came one small ray of light. A few days after writing to Cochrane he had a card from Lord FitzWilliam inviting him to call at the Rockingham town house.

Rockingham's heir greeted him pleasantly, and they chatted for a time about affairs at Wentworth Woodhouse. At last Fitz-William murmured, "I mustn't raise your hopes too much, Mr. Wentworth, but it's possible the new government may have something to offer you. Nothing of great importance, you must understand, before I go any farther. I've kept in mind what you told me of your present unfortunate situation, and I've made some careful inquiries. I know Billy Bentinck very well—Lord Portland. A friend of my late uncle's in Whig party affairs, and by an odd chance now the head of the government. Truth to tell, he's quite under the thumbs of North and Fox, but he's in a position to recommend some favors here and there."

"My pension," Johnnie began hopefully, but FitzWilliam cut him short.

"I'm afraid nothing can be done about that. Economy's the watchword in Parliament now, especially with this disastrous end to the war. No, what I have in mind is your old office as Surveyor General of the King's Woods in America. Shelburne had it abolished on the ground that His Majesty no longer had woods to survey in those parts. Now it seems we're to retain Canada and Nova Scotia. In fact I believe thousands of loyalist refugees at New York have already sailed to Nova Scotia on the promise of lands there. The Crown Lands office in Halifax is overwhelmed. There's also the matter of masts for His Majesty's Navy. The fleet now hasn't a good haven on the whole coast of America, except at Halifax. I understand there's a fair amount of mast pine in Nova Scotia. Do you see?"

"I think so," Johnnie said.

"I've been talking to one or two gentlemen from the Colonial Office, who furnished me with these details. In fact they had one of your old reports on the pines in Nova Scotia. It's clear that the government should send out, this summer, some competent gentleman to direct the surveying of lands for the loyalist settlers and to explore the woods and reserve a supply of mast pines for the Navy. In short, another Surveyor General of His Majesty's Woods. Would you be willing to go?"

"Of course, my lord."

"The matter of—um—pay is a bit uncertain. As I understand it the former honorarium was £800 a year, but of course that covered all the colonies. Now there's only Nova Scotia to consider—Canada's too far back from the sea, and I believe the approach by water is frozen six months in the year. The Colonial Office is prepared to pay only £400 a year."

"I see," Johnnie mumbled in dismay. He could hear Fannie now.

"With your present pension that would give you £700 a year altogether, not a princely sum I admit—it wouldn't go far in London, eh?—but I understand life is much simpler and cheaper in the colonies. As you can see I've explored the matter at some length. D'you still feel you'd like to go?"

The dismay was plain in Johnnie's face. He recalled the cost of bare necessities in Halifax in '76. And now, with all these new refugees pouring into Nova Scotia, bidding against each other for food and a roof overhead—God!

Lord FitzWilliam read his look with sympathy. "If I can find a better post for you later on, you may be sure I shall do so. At the present time the government's besieged with people wanting posts of every kind. Next year, with the fleet and army discharged and so many loyalist officers flocking over here, the outcry will be worse. Pandemonium. How would Mrs. Wentworth feel about going to Nova Scotia?"

"She'd much rather live in England, my lord."

"Well, we can sympathize with her, my dear fellow, can't we? Could you put it to her as a temporary affair, something that may last only a year or two? You might even go out alone and leave her and the little boy in comfort here. But naturally she'll decide on that—the ladies always do. And now I fear I must be off to Tattersall's. Some excellent horseflesh coming up for sale, and I want to look it over for my stable. Shall I suggest through Portland, then, that you'll take the post in Nova Scotia if it's offered?"

"Yes, my lord. You've been most kind—all this trouble."

"Tut! Not a word. Good-by, Mr. Wentworth. Be sure to see me again before you sail."

Johnnie shook his hand and departed quickly. In the street he slowed his pace, preparing himself for Fannie. He would have to put this carefully.

TWENTY-FIVE

*F*ANNIE received the new turn in their fortunes in silence, sitting with knees tightly crossed and arms tightly folded, the attitude of a woman on guard against all the maneuvers of mankind and watching mankind's face. Her gown was a simple sprigged muslin. She wore neither rouge nor patches now, even on evenings when fashionably dressed people came to Brandenburg House for cards and talk. She dressed her hair low and wore becoming but cheap laced caps made by a sewing woman in the neighborhood. In fact, as she said to Paul, she had introduced a bill of economies just as drastic as Mr. Burke's and carried it through both sides of her parliament.

Her quick mind soon grasped the main points of Johnnie's tale, and while he went on with his careful discourse she was calmly making her decision. When he stopped at last she gave him her answer at once, and it surprised him.

"How you beat about the bush! You must take this post, of course. And I shall join you. We'll show FitzWilliam that we're ready to make any sacrifices for a living, even the barest, in the worst of places. Our fortunes depend on his interest with Lord Portland now, and we must hold his sympathy. After we get there you shall keep him informed how we fare on this poor crumb, and for my part I'll ply my pen in the direction of Lady Charlotte and of course dear Lady Rockingham, who knows the Portlands even better."

"Fan, you're a trump. I was afraid you wouldn't want to come." He smiled broadly in his relief. "We'll probably sail about midsummer, a passage of five weeks or so, which takes us there before the autumn gales."

"Not so fast, love," Fannie said. "You may have to launch into

337

your new work at once. Indeed you will, for I know *you*, my jockey. You'll be riding off to the woods as soon as you land, and gone for weeks. After that you'll set about finding a house for us, and furniture, and servants—we can't manage without a cook and a housemaid at the least. You mustn't expect me to stay in some horrid little lodging while you're doing all that. No, I shall wait here, and you can write me when all's ready."

A shadow crossed his face. "But Fan, that'll mean a passage in the stormy weather for you. I mean to say, the hurricane season begins about the middle of September, and by the time that's over it's cold weather and a long rough voyage against the westerlies."

"Very well, then I shall wait till the next spring. I crossed the ocean once in the rough season, and I'll never do it again. Certainly not with a nine-year-old boy on my hands, and into mischief all about the ship."

"You'll have Prudence," Johnnie suggested weakly. "She's always so faithful."

"Prue? When we crossed before, Prue was seasick the whole way from Boston to Falmouth, and I looking after her. No, my dear, there's no way out of it. You must go this summer, and I'll wait over the winter here."

He nodded slowly and resignedly. It was the sensible thing, naturally. And he was lucky that she'd come at all.

He notified Lord FitzWilliam the next day, and after a slow grind of government machinery the appointment came in June. He set off at once for the London docks to seek a passage to Nova Scotia. He returned somewhat downcast. "It seems the only ships making dependable voyages to Nova Scotia go just once a year. They accommodate some passengers, but chiefly they carry the annual supplies for the garrison and merchants of Halifax. And they sail at the end of August. That means I probably wouldn't get there till October, on the edge of winter. There may be naval vessels going to the Halifax station, but I'm not important enough to get a passage of that kind."

A few days later Paul Wentworth, who could always discover

things, anywhere it seemed, had the solution. "Johnnie, I learn there's a brig at Bristol loading for Halifax with whaling supplies. She's to sail in a few days' time. The accommodation will be on hard lines, but I'm assured you can get a berth if you leave at once."

A great flurry of finding everything he would need, from stockings to one of Paul's saddles, and packing and boxing, and roping the boxes, and stowing them all in Paul's big coach. It was a dismal day. London lay smothered in one of its fogs, dark with the soot of Newcastle coals, and a faint air from the east whirled it slowly about Brandenburg House and along the Great West Road. Johnnie took a solemn farewell of little Charlie, sitting in a chair with the boy before him and his hands on Charlie's shoulders.

"You must be a good boy, and mind your dear Mama for me, and pay attention to your spelling and arithmetic. I'm going over the sea, a long way, more than two thousand miles—three perhaps, I'm sure I don't know. Next year you and Mama will follow me, and you'll be in a new country, nothing like this, but very exciting for a boy. You'll see Indians, wild from the forest, walking about the streets; and soldiers and sailors, and lots of fishermen, and all the houses made of wood, and deep snow in the winter time, and ice to skate on—I've told you how I used to skate when I was a boy like you. It's very like Papa's own country, and you'll enjoy it."

The boy stared at him with round eyes. Tears came into Johnnie's own, and to hide his emotion he jumped up, kissed Charlie hastily on both cheeks, and turned to darling Fan. Fannie was tearful herself; it was such a long way, she cried, and the ocean so wild and a ship so small; she sobbed in Johnnie's arms and kissed him again and again before she let him go.

At the end, remembering for the first time the cautious custom of sea travelers, Johnnie stepped into Paul's library, took paper and quill, and scratched off a will. He did not enumerate his poor possessions; he merely left everything to "My dear wife Frances, regretful that it is not what she deserves, and I humbly

339

ask my Maker to have pity and protect and care for her and my little son in the event of my death."

Paul came out to the coach with him, and Johnnie pushed the folded paper into his hand, mumbling, "I leave this in your care. God bless you, Paul, for all you've done for me and mine. If there is anything that I can ever do for you, count me your servant."

"As it happens," Paul said in a musing voice, "there's a little something, Johnnie. I learn that many of the American refugees going to Nova Scotia are from the southern colonies, and some are taking their household slaves. Now, in the nature of things in a raw country like Nova Scotia, and with no great means to support 'em, these people must find they have to sell their slaves for what they'll fetch. In short, my nose tells me that good sound Negroes, male and female, might be had at a bargain in Nova Scotia by the coming winter's end. Watch the chance then, Johnnie. Buy me a score if you can, and ship 'em to my plantation in Surinam. That's my great asset now, and there's a fortune in it waiting to be developed. I'll repay you to the penny, and with a good interest, you understand. Pish! No argument. You must keep an account and let me know. And now good-by and good luck to you, and a short safe voyage. I shall look well after Frances and the boy, you may be sure, and see 'em off to you next spring. I'll expect to see you back in two years—no more, mind—and taking over the post of Secretary for the Colonies, nothing less!"

The coach rolled away into the murk, with Johnnie leaning out and waving a handkerchief at the dim figures of Fannie and the boy in a window and Paul in the stable yard. When he was gone little Charlie piped, "Mama, what are you crying for? Next year we shall see Papa. And there will be Indians and fishermen."

"Yes," Fannie said truthfully, "and that's why Mama cries."

It was autumn, the stormy autumn of '83, when the first letter came from Halifax. As Fannie had foreseen, John had been swallowed up by his duties from the day he landed. The refugees from New York and the southern colonies were pouring into Nova Scotia; some of them well to do, many destitute, all clamoring for land. Ten thousand of them—"I do not exaggerate" —in one spot alone, hewing away the forest on a wild part of the coast in order to build a city laid out like New York. A place without an acre of good soil, indeed nothing to support a tenth of them, a veritable Utopia. "And my dear they are so stupid as to name it Shelburne, after the very wretch who threw them to the wolves."

In Halifax itself everything was in a turmoil. Such a little town, and loyalists, male and female, and discharged British and German soldiers all tumbling over themselves for want of room. Rents and food prices fantastical. Impossible to buy a house except for a fortune. People with money renting the merest hovels for as much as £200 a year. People without money huddling in churches and warehouses, in brushwood wigwams and old army tents pitched on the town common—"a mere swamp"— even in deck cabins torn from the ships and set up in vacant lots along the streets.

He had written a full account to Lord FitzWilliam and could only hope that amiable gentleman would appreciate his situation. Meanwhile he was striving to get a house, even a small one, so she and little Charles could come to him in the spring. A thousand kisses to them both.

The next day Fannie called on Lady FitzWilliam, dressed in a modest little gown of brown lutestring, with her hair neatly done but unpowdered, and a small chip hat perched on it at a brave little angle. She took Charlie with her, and poured out her sad story with the greatest humility and deference. Johnnie's poverty in the midst of all these frightful expenses. Her longing to join him in the wilderness—quite impossible because he could not afford the merest hovel to house her and their darling boy. She had been separated from her husband two long years of the war, when he was fighting bravely for his country, and now it seemed they must be torn apart again, for Heaven knew how long. Fitz-William came into the room in the midst of it, and she went on

341

with a catch in her voice and at the last with tears in her eyes. They were kindly people and much affected. His Lordship declared he would see Portland at once, and off he went.

In November darling Fan was able to write triumphantly that the old full salary of £800 had been awarded to the Surveyor General of His Majesty's Woods. "With your Governor's pension this will give you £1100 a year, as much as you ever got in New Hampshire and all sterling money. There for you! What would you do without your clever wife?"

And now another winter came. It was not so dull as those former days when the Targill woman moped in Paul's absence and the house was like a crypt. As the favorite calling place for American refugees in London it was lively now from noon to night, and in spite of his financial reverses Paul seemed able to keep up the round of dinner parties and card parties without cease.

After her habit Fannie lay abed through the morning, and drank tea there at eleven over the *Morning Herald*. It was the liveliest of all the London sheets, and in its pages she could read the latest gossip of the *ton*. The pace was madder than ever now, with the war over and so many new and old bucks out of the army and back in town. The leading belles at the moment were known in the *ton* as the Blue-eyed Nun, the Bird of Paradise, the Farrenelli, Dally the Tall, and Perdita. The fascinating Mrs. Robinson was still the talk of them all. Her scandalous affair with the young Prince of Wales had lasted no more than a year, but Perdita had a rich choice of other lovers, and now she had been swept off her own pretty feet by Colonel Tarleton, the handsome hero of the campaign in Carolina.

What a career! thought Fannie. Of course it's vulgar, parading her amours like that; still they say she's very genteel in her manners and talks like a well-bred woman. If I were in her shoes I'd play the game a little more discreetly, to be sure. Perdita's shoes would fit me very well. I don't look a day older than she, for all she's in her twenties, and I've got exactly her shape, which is what gentlemen most admire. I made note of that when she was on the stage, wearing her gowns half down to her waist, or showing her legs to the last inch in trunk hose as Viola and Rosalind. She liked those parts where she could display herself as a woman and then a man. I don't doubt I could have been as good an actress too. Sheridan taught her all she knew, and slept with her to boot.

What a list she's had! Robinson, Sheridan, Charles Fox, Sir John Lade, the Prince of Wales, that French duke—what was him name, Chartres?—and that other one, Lauzon; and Lord Malden, of course, and now this devastating Tarleton—and the deuce knows who else between acts. How strange it is; whenever I've seen her at Drury Lane, or dashing about the town in her pony phaeton or at Ranelagh with the crowd on tiptoe for a look at her, I've wished that could be me. And I'm not a bad woman. Half the wives of London wish that. Heigh-ho! A pretty conceit, my dear. You're bound for Nova Scotia in the spring. Who shall you charm there? A savage in feathers or a codfisher in boots and a tarpaulin jacket?

As the days drew on toward Christmas she had some news that shattered all reverie with a fact. Paul came from town one afternoon, threw off a wet greatcoat and hat, and in the drawing-room doorway announced, "My dear, you got your extra £400 for Johnnie just in time. The government's gone down on the India Bill. Your friends are out."

"Again? I don't believe it!"

"Fact! Young Billy Pitt's to form a new cabinet—at the age of five-and-twenty. He was one of Shelburne's followers, you may recall."

Fannie wrinkled her nose at the mention of that name. "Does this mean another Shelburne government?"

"Not at all. Pitt's playing his own game now and choosing his partners in the Tory camp. Naturally the thing's not settled yet. There'll be a general election in the spring."

"Ah! Then our Whig friends may win again."

Paul cocked his head knowingly. "My dear, they haven't a chance. From all I hear, Billy's Tories will win by a mile—

what's more they'll probably keep office the deuce knows how long."

"Oh pish! The government changes every year as far as I can see."

"Not quite. But the country's sick of everlasting chop-and-change. That's why I'll bet on Billy and his Tories for a good long run, with the King behind 'em all the way. His Majesty's delighted to be rid of the Whig lords. He hates 'em all."

"Including Lord FitzWilliam?"

"Naturally."

Fannie nipped her lower lip in her neat white teeth.

"How shall I ever tell poor Johnnie?"

Paul shrugged and walked away, whistling the air of "Man's Life's a Vapor."

In March of '84 she had a happy letter from her Surveyor General. He had secured a small house in Halifax at £150 a year, and she could sail in April or May, when all the rough weather was past. He missed his darling Fan very much and could scarcely wait to take her in his arms again. The only cloud on his mind was little Charles. The boy's education was most important, and there was not a proper school for the sons of gentlemen in the whole of Nova Scotia, nor a college of any kind. What did she think? Would it be wise, perhaps, to leave Charles in some such school in England until FitzWilliam could find a post there? He would leave the matter to her.

And she would inform Paul, please, that he had bought nineteen Negroes at auction in Halifax and sent them off to Surinam in a lumber ship, consigned to Paul's plantation agent at Paramaribo. All good healthy creatures, and Christians—he had had them all baptized by a Church of England clergyman before they sailed. The prices ranged from £60 to £100, excellent bargains, and he had given his note for £1520 in payment. Tell Paul, please, to regard this as an investment in the plantation.

Fannie passed the letter to Paul. When he had read it with his quick blue gaze she said, "Poor Johnnie! He hadn't my last letter when he wrote of course. He still has such hopes in Fitz-

344

William. When I think of having to live in that awful place indefinitely—ugh! I'm sure I don't know what to do."

"My dear lady, there's just one course for you." For once the bland note had gone from Paul's voice. It had a steely sound. "Place the boy in the Westminster School and sail to join your husband. He needs you. Go to him as soon as you can, and face the world with him. There aren't many good men in this world. He's one."

Fannie lifted a haughty stare and met the gaze of a man who had no illusions about the world or her, and it was she who looked away. That evening she wrote to Johnnie. She would sail for Nova Scotia as soon as a ship could be found. As for Charlie, she would not think of bringing the boy to such a place. She wished him educated as an English gentleman, and it was time for him to go to a proper school. She would place him in the Westminster School, which was very genteel.

In May she wrote that Paul had been unable to find a ship with decent accommodation for ladies. A month later she wrote that the only prospect was in what Paul called the annual ships, and she and Prue would be sailing in either the *Saint Lawrence* or the *Adamant* toward the end of August.

To her sister Mary, and to brother Benning when he came up to town from Oxford, she said repeatedly, "My last summer in this country for heaven knows how long. I feel as if I were going to my death and had just these little months to live."

At the end of June she journeyed with the Brinleys to spend a few days at Bath. A good many of the *ton* were there, including Perdita and her gallant colonel, driving about the town in her splendid scarlet-and-silver carriage with its white satin seats and the famous chestnut ponies in their silver-mounted harness.

One afternoon Fannie sat alone in the gardens while George and Mary Brinley attended the baths. Two army officers strolled along the path among the throng. She noticed the younger one first because he uttered a loud "Gad!" and gave her the bold look of a connoisseur among petticoats. He was only twenty or so, a short pert fellow, wearing his cocked hat with an air, and with a sword cane tucked beneath his scarlet arm. She was more amused than indignant. Her eyes went to the taller man. The Horse Guard! He stopped at once and swept off his hat.

"Juno, is it really you?"

"Good afternoon, Captain." Fannie was conscious of being well dressed for the first time in many months. On the assurance of Johnnie's increased pay she had been gathering a new wardrobe, and at the moment she wore a paduasoy gown with a snug bodice in the fashionable long points and the skirt modishly bunched and flounced and looped. She was dressing her hair high again and powdered, and upon it sat a wide black hat with black ostrich feathers sewn along the brim and about the crown. The loops of the gown exposed a scarlet flash of petticoat at the front, and from the petticoat hem peeped a very neat ankle in a clocked silk stocking. She ran over all these items in her mind as she met Jupiter's gaze, and she was conscious of something else about herself—a singing note from the mysterious harp string in her flesh.

The younger officer had his hat off now. He was still giving her that bold appraisal. An annoyed look passed over the captain's face.

"May I beg your leave for a few minutes, Dyott? I'll rejoin you farther on."

Dyott gave a knowing grin. "Of course, my dear fellow." He bowed to Fannie, replaced his hat, adjusted the cane, and strutted off.

Jupiter turned to Fannie with an apologetic voice. "A lieutenant of the Fourth. A very devil with the ladies." And then eagerly, "How handsome you look! Are you here for long?"

"Only another day or two. I'm with married friends." And casually, "I expect them here at any moment."

"So you wish me to go in a moment. How cruel you are! D'you realize my heart's been broken ever since you jilted me?"

"You look extremely well, dear Jupiter."

"A mere shell, I swear. I've thought about you all this time—I really have. What did I say or do wrong? I've gone over every-

346

thing a hundred times, and I still can't understand. You were my idol, Juno. You know that. I worshipped you from head to toe."

Fannie wore her little secret smile. How well she knew that! And now the notion of him seemed quite pleasant again. The *ennui* had gone. He stood there beseeching with his eyes, and from a corner of her own she perceived Mary Brinley coming toward her, with George a few steps behind.

"That's very easy to say," she declared invitingly.

"I'll prove it again whenever you choose." She did not fail to note the familiar deep tremor in his voice that came always when he was aroused.

"You still have the same chambers in town?"

"Yes, of course."

"Be there next Saturday evening at eight, and see what the gods may send. Now be off with you!"

"Who was the handsome officer?" Mary Brinley said as she came up.

"A gentleman I met in London—a mere acquaintance."

Mary looked at Fannie's eyes and that betraying mouth. The sisters had always understood each other perfectly. She uttered her hearty laugh, the laugh of a good-natured matron in the presence of a naughty but enchanting child, and gave the child a light tap of her fan.

"You!"

TWENTY-SIX

*T*HE STOUT SHIP *Adamant,* veteran of many annual voyages to the wild coast of America, found her way to the chief harbor of Nova Scotia on a September afternoon in '84. With the blessing of fair winds she had made a remarkably quick passage, and after the first two days even Prudence had suffered no sea sickness. *Adamant* fired a signal gun, as she passed abreast of a long wooded island in the Halifax entrance, and was answered after some minutes by a puff and a bang from a small island far ahead, a mere green hump that seemed to be anchored like a ship just off the town.

Fannie, standing with Prue on the after deck, gazed about her with an odd feeling of recognition. It was so like coming into New Hampshire's Portsmouth. The spruce and pine woods more blue than green on the low hills; the patches of turf and cod-drying flakes and small hovels of fishermen by the shore; the streets of the little town flowing in wooden waves down the slope; the bristle of schooner masts at the wharves; the harbor shining beyond the town and far into the land like the broad water of the Piscataqua itself.

The captain peered through his spyglass at a bare hill that stood like a fat green wigwam at the town's back door.

"Citadel Hill," he said to Mrs. Wentworth, pointing with the spyglass. "They've got our signal on the blockhouse staff for all the town to see. Oh, they watch pretty sharp for us here, I tell ye, ma'am. There'll be a crowd on the wharf. And in a day or two, when the merchants have hauled the pick of their stuff ashore, you'll see the ladies flocking the shops to see what's new from London."

Fannie sniffed. All she wanted to see was Johnnie with a

decent carriage to take her away from the dock. It would be just like the jockey to be miles off in the forest somewhere. Under shortened sail the ship eased in slowly, and a boat took off a cable end to the wharf. There was a crowd indeed. Apparently the whole town came down to welcome the annual ships from London. She noticed a number of redcoats among them. There was a garrison, then.

Seamen stamped barefooted about the capstan, singing one of the slow tunes they used for this sort of work, and in a key doleful to Fannie's ears. She liked much better their halyard chanties, especially the ribald and lively ones they sang when they were giving short quick pulls to finish a job. It took a long time to warp the ship in, and *Adamant* was almost alongside before she noticed Johnnie waving a frantic hat from the crowd. He was smiling and calling out something she could not catch in the uproar. As soon as the gangway was in place he came bounding up the thing like the spry Johnnie of the old Portsmouth days, and beaming all over his face.

"Oh Fan! Fan!" For a moment she had a dread that he would set to hugging and bussing her there in front of all these staring people—she could see some well-dressed gentlemen among them, but he remembered his manners, caught her hands and kissed them, and then touched his lips to hers quickly and lightly before taking her arm and leading her ashore. Behind them his hired wharf porters waited to pick up the baggage. On the way up the wharf, in the jostle of the crowd, he said apologetically, "I've hired the best carriage in the town, but it's not much. Naturally this isn't London."

No, it isn't, thought Fannie. There was a strong reek of split codfish drying on the flat roofs of the warehouses. The carriage was a faded thing from some hackney stable, drawn by a pair of nags more suited to a London night cart. And as they swayed along the muddy water-front street, past shabby wooden houses and small slopshops and boozing dens, the reek of fish was mingled with viler smells.

"One would think they all emptied their chamber pots in the

street," she gasped, and drew a scented lace handkerchief from her *étui* and held it to her face.

"They do," Johnnie said. "You'll see a better quarter when we turn up the slope."

She did not take the handkerchief away until they turned into an open square, lined with quite handsome wooden houses and shops, gleaming in white or yellow paint, and two or three large coffeehouses. A gambrel-roofed mansion of two white stories sat on a garden terrace in the midst of the square, with a pair of tall-capped grenadiers beside their sentry boxes at the entrance.

"Government House," Johnnie said.

"Oh? Where we should be!"

He gave her a rueful grin, "Never say that near Governor Parr, my dear."

They turned again at what he called the Mall—"or as some say, Barrington Street"—and he pointed out the parade ground. "That's the Ranelagh and Vauxhall of Halifax. No shrubs and flowers though. The garrison guard musters in Grand Parade every evening in summer, and all the beaux and belles of the town saunter up and down, and an army band of music plays till dark. I must take you some fine evening—it'll all be over for the season in October."

She gave it a glance. "What's the church?"

"St. Paul's. We'll attend Sunday service there. Governor Parr always goes with his family and staff—and the troops. It's the garrison church. A lot bigger than our chapel at Portsmouth, eh? You'll be surprised when I tell you this. It was built with timber from our own Piscataqua, fetched here when this town was founded thirty-five years ago."

"Is this where the gentry live?"

"Yes, round about here and the governor's square, and during the war quite a few of the most prosperous merchants built mansions up there on Argyle Street, where you see the willows."

The carriage was still bouncing on—away from the genteel quarter, she was quick to notice, although the plank walk of the Mall continued beside the road and far on into the distance. They passed the town burying ground. The houses were few and smaller and shabbier, and there were stretches of stony pasture, although here and there a mansion stood in shrubbery and young ornamental trees, well off the road. The worn planks of the Mall ended, and now the muddy road went on alone, a mere track.

At last Johnnie said, "Ah! There's our house. That one! And this part's called Pleasant Street. You see? We're right back home!"

A small wooden cottage of two unpainted stories, with all its shingles weathered gray, and a chimney at each end. A fence tottered about a neglected garden patch, half-seen behind it, with one or two apple trees. As they went inside Fannie's heart sank into her shoes. A dark little hall divided the lower floor into two chambers, furnished as sitting and dining room. The kitchen was in an ell at the back, like a rickety afterthought. A steep and narrow staircase led to a pair of bedrooms above.

Everything had been recently swept and well scrubbed—Johnnie had seen to that—and he pointed out with pride the furniture, the carpets, and window hangings.

"Some of those New York refugees brought beautiful household stuff in the ships and had to sell it, for any price at all. They'd nowhere to store it, and they needed money just to keep alive. I'm ashamed to tell you what I paid for all this. They spent a terrible winter, most of those people. One of these days I'll take you up to the town common and show you how thousands of 'em spent the cold weather. Their brush huts and wigwams are still there—falling down now of course. Most of the refugees moved away in the spring to the Saint John River or to Upper Canada. But that's a sorry subject. Now that you see our abode, what d'you think of it? I can tell you I was deuced lucky to get it for £150 a year—to get it at all, the way things are."

"There's not a speck of paint, inside or out," she said coldly. "Let alone wallpaper. We had a better house for our gardener at Wolfeborough."

"I got the lease of it last winter, when I wrote you," he said unhappily, "but I had to wait till spring for the other tenants to

351

move out—they were refugees going to Montreal. Then I had to be off about my work, at Shelburne and up the Saint John River, a dozen other places. I had a fatiguing summer; it's all rough country, and I find I'm not so tireless in the woods as I used to be. I didn't get back here till about a fortnight ago and—and, well, I've done the best I could."

"Two bedchambers, one for us and one for Prue. There's no room for servants." And on a sudden thought, "You *have* engaged servants, I trust?"

"Oh yes, love. I told 'em to wait in the kitchen while you looked at the house. The housemaid's a girl from down by the harbor—it's not far, down that way. She'll sleep out of course. So will Juno."

"Juno!"

"The cook, a black woman. She was one of twenty I bought for Paul. The rest were field Negroes and quite cheap, but Juno's been in a genteel family in New York for years and knows how to cook and serve every kind of food in the best manner. So I kept her. I'm very proud of Juno, though she's ugly as sin to look at. I had to give my note for £200. The gentleman who sold her said I could search the kitchens of the best people from one end of the town to the other, including Governor Parr's, and not find a better. I've arranged to bed her with a free black family that live at the edge of the Common."

Fannie sank down on a green sofa in the sitting room.

"Will you order me a glass of wine, please. I feel faint."

There was no bellpull, not even a hand bell. He had to go to the kitchen and speak to the housemaid himself. The girl came with a tray, an awkward young slattern in brown cotton gown and apron, broken shoes, and upon her head a vast mobcap sprouting ribbons of all colors like a flower bed gone mad.

When she had vanished again Fannie sent Prue upstairs to prepare the bed in the larger chamber—"I wish to lie down for a while."

Johnnie sat beside her and put a solicitous arm about her waist. He had dressed for this great occasion as soon as a running messenger carried him word of the *Adamant's* signal flying on the hill. The exertions of the past year had pared his fat to something like the old figure, and he wore his London clothes with the distinction that came to him so naturally. A green coat of fine cloth with silver buttons, scarlet waistcoat, ruffled shirt, lace cravat, and tan silk breeches. The combination of green and tan was the mode among the fashionable gentlemen of London, copied from dashing Colonel Tarleton, who wore it on every occasion as the uniform of his late regiment. Johnnie, thinking of his own Volunteers, had adopted it in something of the same spirit. Among the American refugees there was a sharp distinction, very important in petitions to London, between loyalists who had borne arms for the King and those who had not. Except that his face was as brown as a carter's he would have looked well in any English drawing room, and Fannie's sidelong eye approved.

He took his arm away as Prue came down.

"I turned back the bedclothes, ma'am."

Fannie drained the glass of wine. "Thank you, Prue. You had better come up with me." She went up the stairs slowly. In the chamber Prue quickly slipped off Fannie's gown, bodice, and petticoats, and unlaced her stays.

Prudence was now well into the thirties, a lean and somewhat grim creature utterly devoted to her mistress. After young Charlie passed his baby years she had become Fannie's handmaid entirely. In her own way, like gallant Captain Jupiter across the sea, she worshipped the beautiful mistress from head to toes, and took the greatest pleasure in dressing and undressing her as if Fannie were a doll grown in some marvelous way into a woman. She was deft and usually silent, although with the privilege of her kind she made free comment on anything that affected her doll's welfare.

As Fannie lay down Prue covered her with a light quilt, at the same time jerking her head toward the stairs and saying, "It's not much, this place, eh?" Fannie closed her eyes. "It's miserable. But it will have to do till he can get something better.

And he shall, mark that. I don't care what it costs. Meanwhile we'll have this ruin improved as far as paint and paper can make it."

"The furniture's quite genteel," Prue said, "and the carpets and hangings. A lot better in some ways than all that queer stuff in Mr. Paul's house."

"Yes. Those New York refugees apparently had taste. Paul had everything in the world but that."

"D'you really feel faint?"

"Naturally not. I just wanted to get off by myself and think a bit."

"I thought so," Prue said. "D'you want anything more before I go down and see what that blackamoor's cooking for dinner?"

"Just untie my garters so my legs don't swell, lying here."

When Prue was gone, her mistress lay very still with her thoughts. There must be some sort of society to this place. Like Portsmouth, probably, a clique of purse-proud merchants and their wives. And some of the moneyed refugees must be able to do themselves well. And of course there's this Governor Parr and his officials, the garrison officers and their ladies, and the naval staff at the dockyard down the harbor. We shall call and leave cards as soon as possible. Governor and Mrs. Wentworth. Let them see we're as good as anybody in this wretched town. Johnnie shall have the house properly decorated and get some decent silver and china and glassware. We must entertain if we want to be entertained. Keep a good wine cellar no matter what it costs. If this black woman's cooking is what he says we should be able to offer a first-rate dinner. That means a lot. Better to have good food and wine in a hut than a damned poor meal in a palace—how often I've heard Paul say it, in that poky house in Poland Street. And think of the people who used to come there. Some of the best in London.

For the next two weeks the little house was in a flurry of painters and paper hangers and carpenters, and it assumed a fresh appearance. Meanwhile in a hired carriage Governor and Mrs. Wentworth called on Governor Parr, on the Admiral, the

Commissioner of the Dockyard, the Chief Justice, and other officials, and upon the chief merchants and their wives. Johnnie was well known to them after a year in the town, and most of them called him "Governor" out of courtesy to his former rank.

But alas the courtesy ended there. Fannie received no calls in return. In the past twelve months the little town had been flooded with such people as themselves, once-prosperous Americans looking for hospitality in this northern wilderness, and hospitality was exhausted. What was worse, the provincial society now had a jealous eye on the newcomers. The loyalist exiles in Nova Scotia were demanding every sort of post and privilege as a reward for their faithfulness to His Majesty in the other colonies, and His Majesty's government was inclined to indulge them as much as possible. Johnnie's own appointment in the Nova Scotia woods was an example. The native settlers already were calling themselves "the old inhabitants" and the loyalists "those damned refugees."

Fannie was scornful. "What is this Halifax society but a little parcel of provincial snobs and smug officials from England like that absurd little rooster Parr? And Mrs. Parr, how she looked down that big nose of hers whenever anybody called you Governor in her presence. And that simpering girl of theirs who thinks she's a beauty—just because the young officers have to make themselves agreeable to the Governor's daughter! What shocking frumps, all these Halifax women! Did you ever see such sights in your life? They stared green with envy at my London modes, and all jealous because I've got a shape and they haven't."

Fannie leaped up, struck a pose, and cried in an affected voice, "After all, who's she to cut such a figure here? The wife of that Wentworth man who runs about the woods and still likes to call himself a Governor. Why, they can't even keep a carriage, my dear, and live in a hovel in the edge of the Point Pleasant woods."

And springing down again to her own self, full length on a sofa with one leg thrown out and a foot on the floor, "Johnnie, the only well-bred people I've seen in the town are Lieutenant

Ayer of the 17th and Captain Bentinck of the *Assistance* frigate. I discovered in conversation that they're both relations of the Duke of Portland, and I lost no time in inviting them to dinner, you may be sure. They're coming next Sunday. As for these so-called Halifax gentry, what have they got to be snobbish about? I'm told the town was founded by criminals sent from England thirty or forty years ago. . . ."

"Oh, that's hardly true, Fan. I believe the first settlers were simply poor people from London; I daresay they had a proportion of absconding debtors, but they also had a number of gentlemen amongst 'em like old Mr. Bulkley, who's told me a good many stories of the early days. What's more they were joined by a lot of New England merchants and fishermen—even some from New Hampshire. And since the late war, they include a good many loyalist refugees and disbanded soldiers and sailors."

"A mongrel crew, one and all," said Fannie, and nothing could change her mind. She conveyed her impressions in her first long letter to Lady FitzWilliam, when Johnnie had gone off to his woods again.

Halifax
Oct. 5, 1784

My dear Madam,

I feel myself separated from everything (except Governor Wentworth) that my heart holds dear. I have scarce reason to except Gov'r Wentworth, as he has been absent on his duty more than two thirds of the time since I arriv'd. Seven long months I was endeavouring to get to him, and he had to leave on his surveys after a fatiguing summer.

During his absence, which Your Ladyship will readily conceive must have been dreadfully dull, I confess I felt my change of fortune with a poignancy almost insupportable. We pay £150 a year for the house we live in, which has an eating room and sitting room on the lower floor, and divided into bedrooms above, without any accommodation for servants, not one room prepar'd or painted until we came into it. I must secretly own to you that there are other things more humiliating. The returning to a Country where for years I knew myself the first in it, with a competence and I may justly add affluence to aid the station I possess'd, makes it hard for me to meet and mix, and be looking up to, many who a little while ago were in a situation too inferior for common acquaintance.

This Province was first settl'd by Vagrants and wretches who escap'd the law and were exempted from debt by being here, a method adopted to settle this part of America as being convenient for a Dockyard, but otherwise held very cheap, as a soil not worthy of improvement. It requires a century before such blood can be purify'd, and the contamination remains.

I plumed myself with hope that a short exile, for so I hold my present situation, would enable a better arrangement. The dreadful change of Ministry backens all my views. The time will come when you can, by a word, make us happy. It's quite impossible the present young Minister can hold the reins of that important country long, they must be return'd to abler hands, and the guidance rest with or about you. Bear in mind, then, the solicitation I have ventur'd to suggest to you. I trust it does not wear the face of impertinence.

I keep to the house and entertain only a few friends. We gain more satisfaction in the company of Captain Bentinck and Mr. Ayer, because they are relations of the Duke of Portland, than from everyone else. Governor Wentworth and myself consider Captain Bentinck as one of our family.

My dearest Madam, adieu. Accept Governor Wentworth's best respects to you and Lord FitzWilliam. From your Ladyship's most perfectly attach'd and devoted servant,

F. Wentworth

Fannie surveyed this screed for some minutes, brushing her nose gently with the feathered end of the pen. She liked the long roll of the sentences and the carefully chosen words. It was really excellent, all of it, and a neat beginning to her campaign for "a better arrangement." She sealed it for the post with Johnnie's monogram and wrote the address on the outer fold with a flourish.

Captain Bentinck was the best of company, with all the bouncing spirit of the Navy, and Fanny was sorry when the *Assistance* departed with the rest of the squadron to spend the winter in the West Indies. However the young *militaire* Mr. Ayer remained, and at her suggestion he brought one or two companions to her dinners throughout the autumn. Not always the same companions. Word of the Wentworths' food and wine, and of the gay and beautiful hostess, soon passed in the officers' messes of the garrison. Where else could a man of taste find such a combination in this dreary colonial outpost? Mrs. Wentworth had the speech, the manners and dress of a fashionable Englishwoman, something they had not seen in a long time, and she had all the latest gossip of London, the very last word of the *ton*. They roared at her little tales of Perdita and the Farrenelli and the rest, all told with a spicy wit, while she sat in a negligent attitude after dinner, blowing wisps of smoke from one of her amusing little segars. And they in turn regaled her with tales of Halifax society, those purse-proud merchants and their underbred wives, all so anxious to play the genteel in the presence of English officers and all so naive and so unaware as the officers tittered up their sleeves.

Johnnie was away most of the time, even after winter came. The part of Nova Scotia that lay toward Canada had been split off by a recent London decree and was now a new province called New Brunswick. This obliged the Surveyor General to send a capable deputy there and to pay the man out of his own salary. There were times when his mounting debts at Halifax frightened him. In his need for money he had been levying fees from every loyalist who got a grant of land, and this had brought a storm.

The refugees were bombarding Governor Parr and the new governor of New Brunswick with their complaints, and some with important connections had written to London. In short Johnnie was in hot water, and it was not the soothing water of Bath or Spa. He told Fannie nothing of this. Except that she never had enough of it, she was not concerned with money. She was determined to show her contempt for the ladies of Halifax society and to outwit them all, and already she had accomplished both. The most eligible young officers of the garrison and fleet, whom the provincial snobs were dying to get into their drawing rooms, were calling on every opportunity at what Fannie gaily described as "our shabby little cell in the edge of the woods."

Nevertheless Johnnie was uneasy. In his own polite way he got along very well with the provincial people, and his experiences in New Hampshire had taught him to be chary of making enemies. Fannie seemed to be making a lot. When one makes enemies one must be careful about one's armor, and Fannie in her spirited way cared nothing for armor at all.

At Christmas when he came home from one of his long journeys he ventured cautiously, "Fan, you mustn't think I'm criticizing, understand, I'm merely thinking of what other people might say. I mean about entertaining these young gentlemen night after night when your husband's absent. D'you think it's wise?"

"Odds fish! Are you being jealous again? Fie on you!"

"I'm not, dear Fan, and never shall be. I understand you, and these people don't. I've heard some whispers, even as far away as Shelburne town, and scotched 'em very quickly. But there it is. You know how tongues wag in a small society, specially where a pretty woman's concerned. Don't misunderstand me, darling Fan. My whole thought is of you. You're goodhearted and hospitable, and you like to entertain. I wouldn't have you any other way. I'm only jealous of your good name."

"My good name in what?" Fannie cried. "In this trumpery little Halifax society? Who are they to censor me? There isn't a well-bred man or woman in the lot—including that smug old Parr. Pooh! Their town stinks to my very nose! Where in God's world would you find so many low taverns and boozing dens in a small population? They blame that on the soldiers and sailors, of course, when everybody knows half the business of Halifax is to sell rum and the other half to drink it. They have the same excuse for all those bawdyhouses on the upper streets and along the harbor front. Why, those precious snobs on Argyle Street can hear the whores laughing and shrieking up the hill whenever they open their back windows. And from the other direction so can Governor Parr, down there by Hollis Street. My young officers jest to me that Halifax is garrisoned with one regiment of artillery, two of infantry, and three of whores— they've never seen such a place for debauchery in all their travels. If the truth be told the women of this town are just a little huddle of prudes in a crowd of common sluts. And because I'm neither one nor the other they dare to roll their eyes at me! Well, that for them!"

She snapped her fingers under Johnnie's nose as if he were all the prudes in one. For the rest of the day she would not speak to him. When they went to bed she turned her back and kept apart as if he were leprous. And his punishment continued until he went away once more to his precious woods.

TWENTY-SEVEN

*T*HE TIME of ice and snow, of storm doors and early candlelight and the daylong glow of stoves and open fires, which she had always loved in New Hampshire, went merrily enough for Fannie in Nova Scotia. On days when there was no wind and the sun was bright she fared forth with her ponies in the sleigh, a red *cariole* of the Canadian kind with a high front curved inward like the crest of a breaking wave. She went well wrapped in furs, with a hooded scarlet coat to match the sleigh, and a little cap of fox fur at a jaunty angle with the tail dangling down her back. Many of the officers and merchants had smart sleigh turnouts, and pretty Mrs. Wentworth often fell in with a jingling procession through the streets and along the Windsor road as far as the Blue Bell tavern, where everyone stopped for hot grog or negus or coffee, and sweet cakes and sillabub. Although some feared her, the military wives had a kinder view of Mrs. Wentworth than the ladies of Halifax itself, and the more lively ones admired her, so that Fannie did not lack feminine companionship when she chose. But her choice was for the gentlemen, and when the severe weather came in January she stayed close to her fires and let them come to her.

Eagerly the young officers followed the white lane to her little house, riding if the snow was not deep, often walking the whole way from their quarters on snowshoes and bursting in, cheerful and glowing from the cold. Sometimes their careless chatter mentioned dinners or dances given by the elite of the town, to which she was never invited, and she burned within, but she never revealed these fires except to Johnnie. Her guests saw only a blithe hostess lending her beauty to a delicious dinner, playing a clever hand at whist or *écarté*, singing gay little songs to her own tunes on the harpsichord, or reclining on the sofa in those careless charming attitudes that never seemed posed, while the young gentlemen drew up hassocks in the firelight and talked of their experiences in the late war, of life in England, of Halifax, and of her. Mostly they talked of themselves and her, admiring both like all young men, and adroitly Fannie led the conversation back and forth.

The scattered dwellers along the track called "Pleasant Street" noted sometimes that one or another of the military gentlemen came alone, and that he stayed very late; and whenever this happened, by a coincidence, Mr. Wentworth was away. Their comment passed idly from kitchen to kitchen until it reached the town, and there it took wings and flew from drawing room to drawing room, gathering spice and color as it went. Before winter was over the virtuous wives of Halifax spoke of Mrs. Wentworth as a veritable Messalina, with a husband playing Claudius to the life, and apparently the whole garrison performing the other roles.

As for Johnnie, that uxorious man spoke no more about the danger of appearances. He was afraid to provoke another furious outburst and another long sentence to silence and a frigidly turned back. At forty-eight he did not seek a husband's privilege as often as in younger days, but now when the desire came to him he found that if he had not displeased her in other matters she awarded her person as prettily as ever, she was generous, even ardent, and he fell asleep with all shadow of doubt brushed away.

At the frosty turn of the old year into '85 there appeared a sudden lift in his hill-and-dale fortunes. Since the end of the war hopeful rumors had buzzed among the outcast loyalists that His Majesty's Government might repay them for the property they had lost in the United States. Johnnie and some others in London had even submitted hopeful claims, making them modest for fear that Parliament might reject the notion. Nothing had come of them. But now came a letter from Paul Wentworth saying that His Majesty's Government had decided to be generous. A sum of £150,000 was to be set aside for a loyalist fund—and this was merely a beginning, a payment on account. The plan had yet to be completed, but he believed that commissioners would arrive at Halifax late this year, and they would set up an office to consider the claims of loyalist refugees in Nova Scotia.

At this news Fannie leaped to her feet, plucked up her skirts and danced a shepherd's hornpipe of her own invention on the moment, knees high, kicking out her legs, and humming the tune of "A-hunting We Will Go!" At last she pranced up to Johnnie, snatched the letter from his hand, and waved it over her head.

"Three cheers for Billy Pitt! Huzza! Huzza! Huzza! Who'd ever have thought it! And now—now, my Johnnie—we can show these Halifax *canaille* a thing or two!"

"How?" he said.

"What a silly question! For one thing we can get a decent house in town."

"But, Fan, you can't rent a decent house in town for any money. You can't even buy one."

"Then build one! There are vacant lots to be had not too far from Saint Paul's or Government House if you want to pay the figure for 'em. I don't care where you build, so long as it's under the noses of those prigs."

"It would cost like the devil, Fan. Wages, lumber—everything's so dear in this place."

"I don't care a fig what it costs! Go and look out a suitable lot, and buy it. And start to build as soon as the snow's off the ground. I want a house finished by mid-summer at the latest—stable, coach house, and all!"

"But Fan!"

"Don't Fan me, Johnnie! Think of those creatures and the way they've snubbed your wife. So we live in a tumble-down cottage, eh? We can't afford a carriage, eh? They shall see!" And away she went again, a whirl of legs and lifted petticoats.

Johnnie watched her in a mixture of amusement and dismay. Some fairy gift in the cradle had abolished the laws of nature for Fannie and decreed that she should be forever young. She was one of those rare creatures that the world produced from time to time for the envy of all other women and the admiration of all men. He had heard Paul speak of such a one, a French-woman called Ninon something, who captivated men till she was sixty—though of course one never knew how much to believe from Paul where French ladies were concerned. He watched this giddy flying creature with a growing sense of awe. Nobody, and certainly none of those young officers, could have guessed her age within a dozen years. Even the spiteful gossip he had overheard avowed her to be "nudging thirty, if a day," exactly what spiteful she-gossips had said in that Boston winter a good nine years ago. And Fannie would be forty next September!

Dutifully, as the winter waned, he searched for vacant lots within the magic circle about Saint Paul's and Government House. None satisfied Fannie. Then an old mansion on the Mall went up in flames one stormy night in March, together with the elderly merchant owner and his wife. Johnnie bought the ground and a cellar full of ashes from the lawyer in charge of the estate. When it came to planning the new house he was relieved to find that Fannie wanted nothing big.

"After all," she said shrewdly, "we won't be here forever. As soon as FitzWilliam can get you a post in England we'll be off like wild swans in the fall. And it isn't as if we had a crowd to entertain. Just twos and threes, as I've done here. What I want is just a neat little villa, with a fair-sized sitting room and eating room, and say four bedchambers above. There must be an ell for the kitchen and rooms over that for the servants. At the back a stable and coach house combined. We won't need much in that; a good carriage, a smart sleigh for winter, a riding horse for you and one for me, and a matched pair of ponies for the carriage of course. You might as well send to England for a phaeton now. I want it green, with your monogram and a circle of roses painted on the doors, and the seats done in white satin like Perdita's. And look about for a pair of good chestnut ponies like hers too."

Johnnie set about all these matters with his native energy, and his close knowledge of the province proved most useful. He knew a sawmill on a small river down the coast that could turn out most of his building material at a reasonable price, considering the times. He found a coasting schooner willing to move the stuff to Halifax at a reasonable freight. He even got his chimneys built of bricks that came from England as ballast in a timber ship. His heaviest expense was in wages to the Halifax workmen, accustomed to fat pay during the war and refusing to take less now. To finance all this he gave his notes wherever possible, and for the rest he borrowed cash from a Halifax moneylender.

As soon as the snow was gone a crew of carpenters and masons began to work on the new house. It might have been finished in mid-summer as Fannie had decreed, but her own changing ideas about the interior finish delayed matters until fall. They moved into the villa in September. The furniture they had was almost sufficient for the downstairs rooms, and for the rest Johnnie again was able to buy excellent stuff from refugees moving off to Canada. From an army major transferred to India he bought a pair of handsome and nimble carriage ponies of the proper chestnut hue, and with his eye for a riding horse he soon picked up a pretty little bay mare for Fannie and a fine black hunter for himself. Indeed all went fortunately, for the new phaeton arrived in one of the annual ships just as they took up their residence under the noses of "those prigs," together with a fresh wardrobe of gowns and hats in the latest mode from Fannie's own dressmaker and milliner in London.

Now the merchant aristocracy of Halifax were permitted to see, indeed they could not avoid seeing, every day, the beautiful and wicked creature of the tales, so long withdrawn in the mysterious little house toward Point Pleasant. In the golden autumn afternoons, when the harbor lay like a blue sword blade in the folds of a tufted and many-colored quilt, Mrs. Wentworth drove her pony phaeton up and down the Mall and around the Government House square each morning and each afternoon, always accompanied by two or three scarlet-coated gallants well mounted and trotting at her side. Sometimes her husband sat with her, but usually he was away somewhere, swallowed in His Majesty's woods.

All of the well-to-do young officers in the garrison had light carriages and fleet-footed ponies of their own, and often there was a merry challenge and a madcap race with Mrs. Wentworth down the Mall, while staid folk cautiously drew their carriages to one side, or if afoot took refuge on the long plank promenade and shook their fists. At band concerts in Grand Parade, when the whole area by Saint Paul's was thronged with people, and "those snobs" stood in their accustomed groups or sat in their carriages nearby, naughty Mrs. Wentworth was sure to be there, beautifully dressed, sitting easily in the phaeton. And a cluster of young naval and military gentlemen was always about her, even taking turns at holding her ponies' heads like common grooms, and all chatting away and laughing at her sallies. And when she departed, always before the concert's end, they escorted her to her very door, as if music had no charms without her, and as if in that short passage along the Mall she might be insulted by footpads or assailed by Indians.

The ladies of Halifax society, especially the mamas of marriageable daughters, were in fury and despair. The ships of His Majesty's squadron sailed in and sailed out; the regiments came and went in the regular process of garrison reliefs; and it made no difference. Within a day or two of each new arrival the most eligible young officers, the ones with family and money, the most handsome and dashing, were drawn to Mrs. Wentworth's phaeton wheels and to her house as if by royal command. It was of no use to denounce her, to invent and spread the worst of tales about her and make sure that they reached the proper quarters. The more the young gentlemen heard, the more they were intrigued.

As for cutting her, the ladies of Halifax had cut her long ago and flung their only weapon at her pretty head. They were defenseless now. Whenever she met her enemies Mrs. Wentworth looked through them as if they were not there at all. They might take what pleasure they could in the fact that she was never invited to their balls and parties and suppers. The young English officers who went to those affairs had an abstract look, as if something were missing. They were inclined to be contemptuous of provincial society, joking to themselves about this gown and that headgear and yonder shocking-bad pair of ankles, and quoting hilarious little bits of provincial *gaucherie*. And more than one of them, when the scarlet woman was mentioned in provincial accents, declared coldly that he considered Mrs. Wentworth a gentlewoman and one of the few to be found.

Everybody, and especially her young courtiers, would have been astonished to see the other Mrs. Wentworth—the Fannie who sat down in quiet hours and penned long obsequious letters to Lady FitzWilliam and Lady Rockingham, bewailing the loneliness and monotony of her life in the wilds, separated from her dear husband for weeks and weeks, and longing to see her dear friends and her own darling boy Charles-Mary far away across the sea. And there were the pleasant homely letters she wrote to brother Benning, now married to the daughter of an English squire; and to sister Mary Brinley, whose oldest girl was to be married soon to a London merchant, with the wedding at Paul Wentworth's house. "You'll be a grandmother, dear Mary, before you know it. How strange that seems to me, tho' I'm—no, I've forgot how old I am. Is it true that George might be posted here?"

Johnnie himself was busy with pen and ink whenever he came home. A snow of letters fluttered across the sea to Lord FitzWilliam, Lord Portland, and a score of other people of importance, and letters no less important to young Charlie at Westminster School. The boy was doing well at his studies—his masters had written commending his progress in Latin and Greek—a prodigy at ten years old. To Paul Wentworth he wrote cheerfully, "I hold no connexion with New Hampshire now but I confess a part of my heart lies there, and I was much gratified to learn last year that you had, at your own expense, published in London the careful map of that province which Mr. Holland made in my time as Governor. What a paradox it is that Mr.

Holland was proscrib'd along with me and many others who had labour'd so long for New Hampshire's welfare.

"My duties still take me all over Nova Scotia and give me little rest. A wise and industrious Governor could make something of this country, which has portions of good soil for cultivation as well as the forest and the fishery. The present Incumbent is content with his comfort and emoluments at Halifax. As for the town itself, it is beneath contempt, as I suppose any garrison must be in such conditions. The chief money income of the town is from the troops and fleet, with what results you may imagine. I have never seen such depravity. In a small town of twelve hundred people we have whole streets and parts of others given up to bagnios and drinking dens, with every crime from theft to murder. This year no less than fifteen criminals have been tucked up on the gallows in George Street. There are many good sound people here, however, and I think if Nova Scotia could enlarge a natural commerce this dependence upon the army and fleet would shrink away, and these evil conditions with it."

November came, and with it the English commissioners on loyalist claims, a thin-faced lawyer named Jeremy Pemberton and a bustling Colonel Thomas Dundas. They set up an office, and Johnnie was one of fifty-three American refugees who favored them with a complimentary address. He went over his own claim carefully, with Fannie at his elbow, and stated it before the commissioners and their clerk one afternoon as Christmas approached. For Fannie's benefit he obtained a rough summary of their submission to London.

"Governor Wentworth had 4,387 acres in Wolfeborough, New Hampshire, with a new mansion house and offices, with gardens, park, etc. He estimated that in House, Gardens, Mills, and Improvements he laid out £10,000 sterling. He lived upon the Estate, had between 300 and 400 acres highly cultivated, and a garden of 47 acres walled in. He valued it at £20,000, which sum he would not have taken for it. The claimant had other lands in New Hampshire, purchased or inherited, at

Portsmouth, Barrington, Lyman, Thornton, The Gore, Lime, Dorchester, Cockermouth, etc. The claimant was oblig'd to flee to Boston in 1775. Has recovered no part of furniture, stock, carriages, or plate. A mob broke into his House and destroy'd a great part. Thinks some part was sold. Mr. Nathaniel Ray Thomas bears witness that claimant had a most magnificent house, the best in the four provinces of New England. The house was almost furnish'd. A Park fenced in with deer, and a large Garden. His carriages and horses were very handsome."

Fannie read the sheet quickly. "What d'you think you'll get?"

"I don't think the government will pay the full claims. When you stop to think of all the refugees, some of 'em very wealthy people in their provinces and bereft of everything, the sum would be enormous. I may get ten thousand."

"Ten thousand pounds. That's not bad."

"Of course I still owe a good deal of that, for money advanced me on the Wolfeborough property."

"To whom? That canting pack of rebels? They took everything you had!"

"I'm thinking of my father," Johnnie said slowly. "When the other creditors filed their claims on my estate he set his own aside. In the heat of the times it was the only wise thing to do. He kept out of political matters himself, but as father of the Governor he had to be careful."

"But your father's rich! He can afford it!"

"I wonder. You must remember his main dependence was the mast business, and that was ruined during the war. I feel it's a debt I must pay if he should ask me for it."

"As if you hadn't other debts!" She frowned at him, but she said no more. Within a fortnight her mind was eased. Mark Wentworth would never ask a penny in this world. He had died five days after Johnnie placed his claim before the commission.

The return of warm weather enlarged Fannie's world again. The ponies took her phaeton to all the usual places in town, including Grand Parade for musical evenings and the wide expanse of the Common for garrison reviews, and when the mud had gone from the country roads she began to fare forth a-horseback in her favorite blue habit, with a wide hat and plumes, or in breezy weather a cap fashioned like a little cavalry helmet with a strap under her chin. With her cavaliers she ambled through the wood paths to Point Pleasant, or to the narrow blue fiord called North West Arm, or along the Windsor road past the Blue Bell to the shores of Bedford Basin.

Johnnie came with her quite often when he was in town. His presence did not discourage her little entourage, who were always very polite to Mr. Wentworth, calling him Governor and deferring to him in all manner of ways. Indeed they irked Johnnie with their very deference; there was something about it—as if he were a nice old gentleman attached to their goddess in some way like an uncle or even a father. His hair was quite gray now, and he never powdered it except for a call on Governor Parr or some other official of importance. It made a handsome contrast with his sunburned face and neck, and even the ladies of Halifax who pitied him as a cuckold never failed to remark his distinguished looks.

Fannie sensed his irritation, and to soothe it she sometimes begged off her cavaliers and rode with him alone. It always made him happy to ride with her, and on the wooded roads outside the town he could almost fancy himself back on the Governor's Road, heading for Wentworth House and another summer in the sunny peace of the woods and fields. Once in that fall of '85 they rode as far as Birch Cove on the Bedford Basin shore, six miles from the town, where they paused to refresh themselves at the small wayside inn.

"Before we turn back, Fan," Johnnie said, "there's something I want to show you, over there by the mouth of the cove." They rode along the road through the rustling birches for a short distance, and Johnnie jumped down and gave her a hand to dismount. He tied the horses to trees at the roadside and led her afoot through a grove of pine trees to a small steep knoll. On the crest of it they stepped forth on a slate ledge, and Johnnie swept an admiring arm about the scene. The knoll had a hand-some view. Behind them and just beyond the road the land rose in a bluff covered with white birches in yellow leaf. Before them the ripples of Bedford Basin danced in the sunshine, with dark-wooded hills far across the water and the shore at their feet run-ning away to the right and left, a long arc unbroken by any sign of habitation. Only the exposed olive and yellow sea wrack marked the existence of salt water or a tide. This expanse at the far end of Halifax harbor, like a broad mirror at the end of a slender handle, was so completely enclosed by the hills that to all appearance it might have been a lake in the heart of the continent.

"It's four miles long and a good two wide," Johnnie said. "They say the whole of the King's Navy could ride at anchor here, with room for every ship to swing and shelter from every wind."

"It's pretty," Fannie said, wondering why he had dragged her through those trees to look at a great patch of water.

"But doesn't it remind you of anything, Fan? Don't you see, it's our lake in the New Hampshire hills—without the islands of course. The same size and much the same shape, and the same woods on the hills. I daresay there's another Mount De-light and a big pine on the shoulder of it, if we climbed back over that birch bluff and went far enough."

"What's in your mind, Johnnie?" she said suspiciously. If he had some wild notion of starting another Wentworth House out here, miles from the town, she would have to scotch it quickly.

"Just a little summer house, love, here on this knoll. A hut, a mere cell, a place where we could come in the hot weather and stay for days and nights, just we two." He put his arm about her. "We could lie here and look out on the water and dream we're back in New Hampshire."

She stiffened at once. "That," she said, "would be a nightmare as far as I'm concerned. If you want to have a summer villa, build one where the Halifax merchants have theirs, on the Dart-

371

mouth side of the harbor, or at North West Arm, or even on the tip of Point Pleasant like Colonel Fanning."

"But I've already bought the land here, love, a hundred acres. Oh, don't be alarmed. I got it for a mere trifle. And it'll just be a little hut, as I said."

She stepped away from his arm and shrugged. "Build your cell if you must play the hermit. But I won't promise to join you, except now and then, perhaps. I haven't your love for solitude, Johnnie. I never did."

And she began to walk down the back of the knoll toward the horses and the road. He followed her with a downcast face. Perhaps if he built a comfortable little cottage here, next year say, and made a proper carriageway from the road, she would see it better. At forty-nine he began to feel odd pangs and yearnings, as if the best of life were slipping away, as if he must do something now to recapture that old sweet time with Fannie, when they were first in love and before the troubles came. Impossible to find it in the house in town, where they never seemed to be alone. But the yearning was more than that. What he sought was Fannie and the New Hampshire scene in one. The lake at Wolfeborough and the smell of pines, and the daylong creak of saddle leather and the pleasure of her arms at night; and in the dark the loons calling and the waves lapping on the shore and the treefrogs cheeping for rain in the summer weather. All that. Soon, too soon perhaps, FitzWilliam would find him a post in England—and he would never find that in England, ever.

They rode off toward the town in silence. The road was dusty and scattered with droppings of cattle and sheep that the drovers brought through the forest from the farms of Windsor. The horses picked their way daintily. After a time, to bring a happier mood in her, he remarked, "In another week or two—three at the outside—George and Mary will be here."

She smiled at once. "It still seems incredible. How did George Brinley do it? He must have influence that poor you haven't got."

"Oh, I don't know. George has got along well in the Commissary Department ever since he was attached to the army at

New York. He showed his worth there, I tell you Fan. And he's got a good head for business—always had. Influence is all very well, but even the British army has to have some men who can stand on their own worth."

"What's his new rank again?"

"He's to be Deputy Commissary General to His Majesty's Forces in Nova Scotia. Which means the garrisons at Halifax and Windsor, Fort Cumberland and Fort Anne. He'll make his headquarters at Halifax of course. So you and Mary will be company for each other."

"Yes," Fannie said, a little dubiously. Her isolation in the town had a pretty advantage that she was reluctant to give up. But on second thought she was reassured. George would be busy at his duties always, and Mary—Mary would understand, with a sisterly wink and a nod. Mary was that very rare creature, a virtuous woman with a sporting view of life.

TWENTY-EIGHT

*W*HEN George Brinley arrived at Halifax he took up his residence in Hollis Street a few doors from Government House, as became an official of his importance, and Fannie welcomed not only her sister but the presence of a house always open to her in the heart of the town's elect. Although Mary was only two years older the birth and upbringing of five children had left their mark on her. She retained the lively temperament of Sam Wentworth's girls, but she was now thoroughly the comfortable middle-aged matron who let out her stays and enjoyed her food and her nips of cordials and was never without her little bundle of segars. She gave Fannie her family news with a cheerful air of insouciance. One son had died, one was in the army, another was studying for the law in London, and her daughter was now well married there. She had with her only the youngest boy, a hobbledehoy of fifteen.

"Very different from your boy, Fan. We went to see Charlie now and then, as you know. What a delicate creature he is, so mannerly and soft-spoken, and so dainty in his movements, more like a girl than a boy. Reminds me of you at that age, even to your mouth and nose, though he's got Johnnie's eyes." Mary gave one of her deep chuckles and a knowing look. "He'll have none of your *diable au corps*, as far as I can judge, and a good thing too."

"What a thing to say!"

Another chuckle. "You always had a lot of that, Fan, why deny it? How is John?"

"Still madly in love with trees."

"You don't see much of him, I take it."

374

"He comes home often enough."

"So you don't find it dull, eh?"

They looked at each other, and Fannie made a mouth. "This is a damned dull town, my dear, as you'll soon discover. For myself, I confess my *diable* helps me pass the time. Now tell me all the London gossip. You may begin at the top—the Prince of Wales."

"Ha! Georgie's amours alone would take a twelvemonth to tell you. Perdita gave him the first taste of a woman, and he liked it so much he's gobbling his way merrily down the whole London *menu*. A pretty example to his young brothers. But of course they're all full of the Old Scratch, and everyone takes an indulgent view—a sign of good health and spirits in a young man, after all. Well, to begin with Prince Georgie. . . ."

The Brinleys kept a good table like the Wentworths, and they dined often together, back and forth. For his other guests Brinley preferred officers of the garrison and fleet and made a point of inviting one or two sprightly young subalterns to give a sparkle to the conversation and afterward to sing with Fannie at the harpsichord. A few favorite officers, the best of all company, appeared at both boards. It made an intimate little cycle, and if Mary sometimes winked at her husband, guessing how matters were, Johnnie remained oblivious, and Fannie did not care.

There was another feature of this new turn of affairs which amused Fannie herself. As the chief Commissary officer George Brinley was a man to be cultivated by the town merchants, whose best profit came from supplies to His Majesty's forces. He and Mary were flattered on every hand and showered with invitations from the very people who would not give Mary's sister a nod in the street. And when in turn the merchant-aristocrats received a card to dine at the Brinleys', they often found themselves at table with the naughty Mrs. Wentworth and obliged to be polite to her.

And Fannie had no mercy. It was they who had to address themselves to her, to scrape their noddles for thing to say, and to smile throughout, suffering her cold gaze and the subtle barbs of her wicked little tongue in reply. They could still punish her, as they thought, by keeping their own doors closed to her. And she was never to be seen when they entertained abroad at the Great Pontac, the Golden Ball, or Roubalet's, or the new and elegant British Coffee House where three hundred people could dine and dance together. But Mrs. Wentworth remained indifferent, letting it be known that she herself would not associate with such a pack of bores and flaunting her own choice of company in the face of everyone.

What scandalized the critics as much as anything was her regular appearance with Johnnie, or in his absence with one or more of her courtiers, at the Sunday morning service at Saint Paul's. It was always the great show of the week in the fortress town. The regiments marching down behind their bands, infantry in red and artillery in blue, and forming up before the church. The gentry arriving in their carriages and coaches. The Governor, the Commodore, the General, and the Chief Justice stepping down with their families. The Governor taking the salute of the troops and passing inside with his brilliant staff, all scarlet and blue and plumes and gold lace. The soldiers filing to their places upstairs in the long galleries. The officers and gentry settling themselves in their pews. The fops taking snuff and sneezing and making a great display of silk handkerchiefs. The common folk jostling at the back—and halfway down the center aisle the Wentworth pew notably empty.

And then, just before the first boom of organ notes, Mrs. Wentworth sweeping in, a morocco-covered prayer book in one silk-gloved hand, and the other tucked in Mr. Wentworth's arm or in her muff—for she never touched her other gentlemen in public. She was always dressed as handsomely as any woman there, and better than most, including the somewhat dowdy ladies of the Governor, but with her looks and figure and that bearing of an empress she could have looked better than most in an Osnaburg sack.

She never wore paint or patches on these religious expeditions.

And standing, kneeling, or seated as the service went on, she never glanced to right or left. With her chin high she kept a steadfast gaze on the altar, offering friends and foes alike the pale chiseled profile of a saint in plumes and velvet. In all that colorful and self-important company she was a cynosure from first to last, when she sailed out in the same manner, like a royal yacht in a crowd of codfish schooners.

Johnnie was never so proud of her as at these times. He saw nothing but admiration in all those staring eyes. And in that unwavering mystic gaze at the altar he saw a revelation of the true Fannie, the woman essentially pure under all that weekday façade of mischief. She was good, really good, and he was ashamed of the doubts that crept upon him from time to time.

The rush of American refugees had subsided in Nova Scotia like a tide that pours into a sea pond and then drains away, leaving only a few small pools here and there. The work of the land surveyors had drained away with it, and Johnnie no longer had to keep an eye on them. He was now able to devote himself to his proper duties, searching out mast pines in the forest and marking them with the King's broad arrow and his own JW. As in the old days in New Hampshire he had orders to reserve such trees anywhere they might be found in reach of tidewater, even on private land, and as in the old days he had to make frequent rounds of his wide domain, watching the marked trees and the loggers.

He truly loved these living wooden giants and hated the notion of cutting them at all. Trees were like people. Here and there among them, rooted in the same soil, under the same suns and rains, one grew straighter, stouter, taller than all the rest, and free of all the common flaws. As if certain trees and men were born to stand over the others, and no more to be disputed than any other fact of nature.

In this train of thought he could not think of Governor Parr as a monarch pine. The man was too small in all ways and not even native to this soil. A petty creature on the fringe of Lord

Shelburne's favor, and so granted this post in the wilds. Johnnie got along well with him as he got along with most people, but he could not help feeling a contempt for His Excellency. The vulgar little man loved ease and food and wine, and had no interest in the province whatever. He seldom went farther into the country than the head of Bedford Basin.

Once, in the fall of '83, at a dinner to introduce the new Surveyor General to some of his officials, Parr had confided himself to Johnnie at his elbow. The Governor had done well at the wine and was talkative, but Johnnie could still remember every word.

"My dear feller, some people in London wondered why I gave up the Tower to come away here to this rude place. But you'll find it's not so rude after all. In my own case I enjoy my position as head of the government, with the greatest civility and attention from all ranks of people. The government provides me with a most excellent mansion and garden as you see. To get away from the heat and smells of the town in summer I have a farm of seventy or eighty acres, at a distance of two miles, with a snug farmhouse on it, a beautiful prospect and good fishing. In town I enjoy plenty of provisions with a very good French cook to dress 'em for the table. I've a cellar well stocked with port, claret, Madeira, rum, brandy—and of course plenty of Bowood's strong beer. Ha! As you know, I've reserved an estate for myself in this new town of Shelburne down the coast. And what d'you think I call it? Bowood! Bowood—that's very good, don't you think?

"But as I was saying, I'm well off here. I draw full pay as colonel of a regiment that I never see, and the Governor's salary besides—a neat income of £2200 a year, far beyond my expectations in London. London! In London they shudder at the very notion of a winter here. What do I care? I've got warm clothes, damme, and plenty of wood and Cape Breton coals to stand off the cold. I tell you, at fifty-eight I'm as happy and comfortably seated as anyone could wish to be, and I intend to live a hundred."

Johnnie heard him with a polite smile. All that, he thought, should have been mine if Lord Rockingham had only lived another month. What a business it all was—a man's fortune hanging, not on his worth, but on the whim of a few lords jostling each other for power in London! You felt so damned helpless. There was nothing you could do but write cadging letters to people who might be of importance, and at regular intervals send them little gifts—a well-spiced and smoked bear ham, a pretty bauble of amethyst from Cape Blomidon, a carved walrus tooth, an Indian *bijou* case of birch bark ornamented with dyed porcupine quills—anything at all to catch their eye for a moment and remind them of their humble servant, off there in the wilderness.

Meanwhile dear Fan was keeping up her own valiant little campaign by pen to Lady FitzWilliam and other wives of useful Whig lords. As she kept saying, "That upstart Billy Pitt can't hold the government forever. One twist of affairs and the Whigs could be in again. And Whigs, like all men, listen to their wives."

Darling Fan! How anxious she was for his success! He thought often of that time, long ago at Wolfeborough, when they heard the news of Uncle Benning's will. And Fannie flinging her arms about his neck and crying, "Never mind, I'll bring you fortune yet, I vow I will!"

He rode into the town of Shelburne on a gray afternoon in October '86, admiring the site, a long low slope beside a harbor that ran deep into the land like the one at Halifax. Four years ago the first crowd of loyalist refugees from New York had come here, cleared away the woods, and laid off an ambitious town with wide streets, crossing at exact right angles, from the ridge crest to the water. Within a year they were joined by the final exodus, including many British and loyalist soldiers of disbanded regiments. In all, more than ten thousand people had built here one of the greater cities of America, with a bristle of wharves, handsome shops and stores, and street upon street of painted frame houses extending over the crest of the ridge. Many of them spent every penny they had in creating and furnishing as fine a mansion as the one they had fled in the United States.

And then the bubble shattered. What was here to support a city? A worthless hinterland of rock and thin clay hidden under the forest. A thin river that led nowhere and dwindled to a brook in dry weather. The only hope of a living was in the codfishery, and few of the refugees were fitted for that. Their claims for property lost in the United States were still in the slow government machine. Not a penny had been paid, and all the signs from London indicated a delay that might go on for years. And so they drifted away, first in hundreds, then in thousands. They were still going, seeking lands in the Annapolis Valley, on the Saint John river, in the savage reaches of Upper Canada.

Johnnie rode past whole streets of good houses, nearly all empty and silent, the paint already beginning to peel, a broken window here and there. An occasional chimney smoking, a few children playing outside a door, the rattle of a well windlass or the sound of an ax splitting firewood at the back—except for these it might have been a city of the dead. It filled him with melancholy. As if the American loyalists were a race accursed, doomed to wander like the Jews in the wilderness, without a home and without a hope. How had it all happened? And why? After eleven years of exile he still could not understand.

It was a relief to pull up at last outside the big clapboard residence of Captain Gideon White. The captain was from Plymouth, Massachusetts, a descendant of the first child born to the Pilgrims in America, and with the spirit of the Pilgrims he had determined to remain in Shelburne, finding what business he could and living in his accustomed style, come what may. A Negro servant ran out to catch Johnnie's reins, and he entered into the welcome of the house. It was a typical New England mansion; the wainscoted walls, the sturdy but elegant furniture, the Turkey carpets, the family portraits, the fires blazing under well-carved mantelpieces.

And in an hour he was seated before a good New England dinner of roast turkey, potatoes, squash, corn, and beans, with pumpkin pie and coffee to follow, and a decanter of well-traveled and matured Madeira at his elbow. The talk was of old times of course. That came first whenever refugee met refugee. Then it drifted to woodland matters. Finally, after a lull, when the port was passing at the dinner's end, the captain said, "When did you leave Halifax?"

"A week ago."

"Then you didn't see the *Pegasus* frigate?"

"No," Johnnie said, with indifference. The movements of His Majesty's ships to and from the Halifax station did not interest him much.

The captain laughed. "I guess your Halifax society will be bowing and scraping all over the place. Her commander's young Prince William Henry, fancy that. Came out from England by way of Newfoundland and plans to stay a time before going on to the West Indies. Our little cock Parr will be all of a fluster—royalty right on his doorstep—bang!—like that."

Johnnie sipped his wine in silence. It was easy to picture the fluster. The military parades, the levees, the dinners, the balls, the fetes, the firework displays, the nightly illuminations. And the problem of invitations. He could see Parr scratching his wig over that minor official, the Surveyor General. How to invite Mr. Wentworth and not to invite Mrs. Wentworth—the social problem of Halifax for the past two years. And the relief to hear that Mr. Wentworth, as usual, was off in the woods.

He put up his chin. "I'm well away from all that, Gideon. I confess I'm not much of a man for formal entertainment nowadays. I suppose I've got out of the way of it since I left New Hampshire." And with a shake of his head, "How strange it seems, that boy commanding a warship. I saw him in a London theater not so many years ago, a middy of fourteen or so. But of course he must be, what, twenty or one-and-twenty now. How the time flies! A sign of age, they say."

"Not in you, Governor. Why, you're just in your prime."

"I'm fifty," Johnnie said. "Fifty and creaking at the joints, like an old ship that's seen too many storms, and as far from harbor as ever. It isn't just the years that count, my friend. It's the weather."

TWENTY-NINE

THE LITTLE DINNER was one of Juno's best. Turtle soup, partridge, and woodcock, a noble round of the best Windsor beef, a golden-brown crusted prune pie, tarts, and coffee. For the wine Fannie had chosen some of Johnnie's special claret. The guests were three of her favorites, Captain Jack Hoskins of the 60th Regiment, Lieutenant Catesby of the 57th, and Lieutenant Broadhurst, R.N. of the Dockyard staff. Their uniforms made a gallant show of blue and scarlet about the table, and Fannie showed no less gallantly in a white gown whose bodice was tipped with Limerick lace like the foam of a breaking wave. The foam, as the sea officer noted to himself, came barely to the neaptide mark. A modest wisp of gauze was draped loosely about her shoulders, and she wore on her powdered coiffure a bandeau of navy blue—"especially for you, Broadhurst." She had a small round necklace of pearls at her throat, and her favorite pearl earrings. Her hands were bare. She seldom wore rings, except on her wedding finger when she appeared at church. She had found long ago that at dinner or cards the whole art of a woman's appearance was in what showed above the table, and rings spoiled the grace of the white hands, nervous and slender, playing about the cloth before her, an exact foil for the serene display a few inches above.

The window hangings were drawn against the curiosity of passers in the street, candles gave the softest of light, and below the mantel a fire of maple logs sent out a comfortable glow. Juno's son, a neat and silent Negro youth in green livery, attended the table, and as he removed the soup Fannie said, "Now, dear boys, let's hear all about Our Sailor Prince. You start, Broadhurst, you're the naval man."

A dark grin from Broadhurst. "Our Sailor Prince is a card, in fact he's the deuce. He celebrated his twenty-first birthday on the voyage out, and I'm told it was no mere splice of the main brace but a general souse, at his command. At one stage a gang of tipsy seamen carried him about, shoulder high and cheering away, and nearly knocked his head off against the deck beams. In fact Our Sailor Prince, his officers and half his crew were so completely drunk for hours that His Majesty's frigate *Pegasus* was in charge of the midshipmen. As one mid put it to me, it was a case of 'Reel, Britannia' and chorus of 'All in the Downs.'"

A roar of laughter. "Mind you," Broadhurst went on, "it could have been merely a case of sorrow to drown. It's whispered that His Highness fell in love with a young girl over there somewhere"—a jerk of Broadhurst's black head toward England—"and he actually proposed to marry her, so his royal papa got him packed off to the North American station. If that's the case we may see quite a bit of Sailor Billy in the next year or two. Nothing like time and Canadian winds for a hot head."

"Have they ever chilled yours?" Fannie asked with a meaning little twinkle. "But tell me, what's he like?"—instinctively not mentioning that she had seen the Sailor Prince a remarkable number of years ago.

"Well, in the Navy they call him Coconut Head."

Another roar. "Fact! His noddle goes up to a peak just like that. Indeed he's not what you'd call impressive. Stands about five foot seven or eight, straw-colored hair, face the color of a ripe red apple and about the same shine. Very brisk, very nautical—talks like Jack Tar. Free and easy in many ways—he passed the word to our officers here that they're not to make a princely fuss, that he's plain Captain Guelph of the Royal Navy, and so forth. Just the same I'm told it's not wise to overstep the mark with him. Not when he's sober, at any rate. Speak when you're spoken to, hands off and all that, else you find yourself brought up with a round turn."

"Very well," Fannie said. "Now you, Jack, tell me about the

formal landing today. By some oversight His Excellency didn't invite my presence." They laughed again. Fannie made no secret of her private war with Halifax society.

"My dear lady," Hoskins chuckled, "he merely wished to spare you. It wasn't much, I vow. His Royal Coconut landed at the King's Wharf under a full royal salute from the *Pegasus* and the batteries. . . ."

"And what a din that was!" said Fannie, making a face. "Enough to wake the dead."

"Quite so. Well, the 57th lined one side of the way to Government House, ours the other. The General and little Parr were on the dock in full fig to receive him. Swarms of people everywhere. They never saw a prince before—mad with curiosity. Hard time keeping 'em back. The bands struck up 'God Save the King.' We presented arms and all that. They walked up to Government House between our lines, and then our officers and the town bigwigs were presented to him there. Fussy business. I could see he was impatient. As soon as that was over he took a quick look around the younger officers, caught Catesby's eye— and well, go on with it, Jeff."

Lieutenant Jeffery Catesby rolled his eyes at Fannie comically. "You won't believe this, dear ma'am, but here goes. He beckoned me over and said he wished to take a walk about the town with me. And off he started, at half a run. He seemed dam' glad to get away. So I steered him up to Grand Parade and along the Mall—a wonder you didn't see us, but naturally the streets were crowded. Showed him inside Saint Paul's on the way back, and thought that'd be the end of it. Sailors, you know, ain't got the legs for a long march," with a grin at Broadhurst. "But then, deuce take it, he said he wished to view the town from the top of Citadel Hill!"

Catesby leaned back in his chair and uttered a hoot. "We never got up the hill. When we reached Albemarle Street, where the better dolly-shops are—the sixpenny ones are further up the slope on Barrack Street—lo and behold the ladies were just up and washed for the day's affairs. This was about half past two in the afternoon, and of course the best-lookin' merchandise was in the windows, as usual. I said this was the bawdy quarter, but we'd be out of it in a few more minutes. And by the great Jove if he didn't insist on goin' in and talkin' with the gels! Said they were His Majesty's subjects, damme! the same as you and me. What's more he knew their language, make no mistake—laughin' and jokin', discussing their, um, points—and they lost no time showin' 'em, you may be sure. You've no idea, my dear lady, no idea. And this went on right along the street from one place to another, wherever a pretty baggage caught his eye—Madame O'Hara's, Hogg's, the Sultana's—the whole brigade."

"He seems to have chosen a most knowledgeable guide," chaffed Fannie.

"My dear ma'am, you wrong me. We have to pass and repass those places—we run the whole dam' gauntlet every time we come or go from the barracks. Ain't that so, Jack?"

"Never mind," Fannie said. "Go on."

"Well, he called it 'inspectin' the larboard watch,' making sure that everything was properly unrigged and coiled down and well cleared for action. That's the way he talks. It was deuced comical, you know, but still I was a bit nonplussed. I mean to say, it's one of the sights of the town for new officers on the station and other visitors, like takin' a new boy to the Punch and Judy show, but—well, I couldn't help thinkin' I might get into hot water for takin' him there, and all that. I hinted at it, but he shut me up; said he was his own master on this side of the Atlantic, and nobody was goin' to tell him what he should or shouldn't do."

"Well," said Jack Hoskins, darting a grin at Broadhurst, "we all know what sailors are of course. It comes of being shut up aboard ship too much, and not enough saltpeter in the beef. Besides. . . ."

"I think," broke in Fannie, in her most imperial tone, "we shall talk about something else. After all, who are we to discuss the idiosyncrasies of princes? Besides, I'm not the least bit interested. Do you like the partridge, Jeff? Mr. Wentworth sees I get a constant supply of game—I expect a haunch of caribou very shortly, and if you're very good and mind your manners nicely you shall taste it, all of you."

His Majesty's frigate *Pegasus*, twenty-eight guns, remained in the anchorage day after day. Prince William seemed in no hurry to join the squadron in the West Indies for the winter. There were formal dinners and balls of every kind. There were carriage drives, each a long procession of smart turnouts filled with officers and gentry, while the Prince inspected the woods in their autumn color along the Bedford Basin road and about Dutch Village and the shore of North West Arm. The garrison staged sham battles for his benefit on the Common and Camp Hill. There were London plays, acted by young officers and gentlemen of the town in the theater on Argyle Street. There was, indeed, every polite entertainment that the town could offer.

The Prince appeared to enjoy them all, but he enjoyed his odd private entertainment no less, and he often cut his formal evening engagements for the purpose, to the great chagrin of the tufthunting ladies of town society. Again and again he was to be seen, accompanied by one or two gay young officers, visiting the ladies of the larboard and starboard watches on the upper slope. The gentry were shocked or merely puzzled, according to their temperament. Even his officer companions hardly knew what to make of him. His whims were uncertain. He seemed a young man full of zest who does not know quite what to do with it. He was a frequent guest at regimental dinners, where a redcoated band played softly in an anteroom and the grenadiers were lined up outside, in the frosty dark, to fire volleys in honor of the main toasts. At these affairs the wine always flowed freely. Sometimes he drank himself into a stupor and was carried off to bed, or at a late hour was led down the hill, with a staggering escort of officers, to the half frozen crew of his barge, waiting at the quay. At other times he drank nothing, but took a mischievous delight in calling a long list of bumper toasts in quick succession and walking off and leaving the company swaying in their chairs or sliding under the table. When the Governor and the General were present it made no difference. Their dignity had to go down with the rest. If he saw anyone nursing a half empty glass he would cry in his tops'l yard voice, "I see some of God Almighty's daylight in that glass, sir—banish it!"

Word of all this came to Fannie through her own young officers, who often arrived with headaches and notable tales from the night before. She could almost hear the agitated whispers in the tight little circle of Halifax society, those prudes who lived so far from the London *ton* and knew nothing of what wagged the world. It was impossible for them to believe that good King George and plain little Queen Charlotte had produced such a wild young man.

At four o'clock on a dark afternoon she sat in her drawing room awaiting Captain Hoskins. It had been raining for the past two days, and now under the dull October sky a cold wind swept along the Mall. The curtains were drawn, the candles lit, and the fire crackled pleasantly. She had just finished one of her plaintive letters to Lady FitzWilliam when the knocker sounded in the hall. She sanded the last sheet hastily and slipped the letter into a drawer. Prue went to the door, and there was a sound of two male voices in the entrance. So Jack had brought a guest. Why? They were to dine and spend the evening together *à deux*. And now, having parted with hats and cloaks, the two men came into the drawing room.

She hardly saw Hoskins at all. Her eyes went at once to his companion, a stocky young officer in naval blue and white, wearing a pair of muddy Hessian boots. His eyes were blue and very large, they seemed to bulge in the florid face, and his yellow hair was gathered in a short queue with a blue ribbon.

"Mrs. Wentworth," said Hoskins, "may I have the honor of presenting you to Captain Guelph, of the Royal Navy?"

For a moment her knees shivered, and her face went hot. What did this mean? They had been on what Prince Billy called a "cruise," that was obvious from their boots. Did Sailor Billy think she was part of the "starboard watch?" If so, what had Hoskins said? He was a gentleman, all her chosen companions were gentlemen, not the sort to bandy a lady's name about where a favor was concerned. But where a prince of the realm was concerned, what then? Would they feel obliged to mention her as a particular sort of confection? If Jack Hoskins had even hinted at such a thing she could kill him.

The flush left her face, and her knees were firm again. With a cold dignity she dropped a curtsy and murmured, "Your Highness," looking at his boots.

"Stuff!" said His Highness, stepping forward. He seized her hand as she arose and kissed it with a jerky little bob, like a boy at his first dancing lesson.

"Call me Captain, ma'am, if you please. That's a good fire you have over there. Mind if I warm my flippers?" And without waiting for a reply he strode to the fire and held out his flippers to the heat, tossing over his shoulder, "This is a very nice little house you have here. Everything snug—and elegant, of course, very elegant. Hoskins tells me your dinners are the best in the town. Eh? Eh?"

Captain Hoskins cast her a mute gaze of apology, embarrassment, and a faint tinge of despair. Her own eyes were frosty. She would never forgive him.

"Your Highness," she began.

"Captain!"

"Captain Guelph, you mustn't believe everything Mr. Hoskins says. He's most unreliable, I find. As it happens my servants have prepared a dinner, nothing extraordinary, and if you'll do me the honor you shall have a chance to judge."

"Ah! Well, that's most kind of you, Mrs.—Wentworth, is it? Have you any Madeira? I always drink Madeira when I can—nothing like it."

Fannie rang the bell and ordered a decanter and glasses.

"I'm afraid you'll find it a little ordinary, Your . . . Captain."

"It'll be very good, I'm sure."

When the decanter came the Captain attacked it thirstily.

"Not a bad little wine, this, eh? Eh? Tomorrow, my dear lady, I shall send up some Madeira of my own for you. Magnificent stuff, eight-and-twenty years in bottle, I give you my word. A gift from Sir Archibald Campbell just before I sailed."

By the time they sat down to dinner the Captain had imbibed the amount of a full bottle, and he drank as much again during the meal. He became very talkative, rattling on about his ship, his officers, his crew, his seven years in the Navy. Hoskins sat silent over his food, avoiding Fannie's eye.

"You're an American, I understand," Prince Billy said, interrupting his own long discourse in the abrupt way he had.

"Yes, Captain. My husband was Governor of His Majesty's Province of New Hampshire. Before that terrible war, of course, which ruined all the loyalists, as you know. I lived some years in England after, with Lord and Lady Rockingham and other friends. England was a home to me, and seems so still. I shall never be quite happy till we can get back there."

"Husband's got some sort of post in the woods here, eh? Eh?"

"Yes, he's at his duties now."

"How long d'you expect him to be away?"

"A month or so."

"Um! Well! A man must go where his duty is, eh? That's what I have to do, damme."

At the dinner's end Fannie ran her fingers over the keys of her new pianoforte, and discovered at once that Captain Guelph liked to sing. He had a loud unmusical voice, but he commanded a variety of songs, especially drinking songs, and bellowed them with tremendous gestures as if he were on the Covent Garden stage. As the evening wore on Fannie lit one of her little segars, and the Captain took snuff and launched into another long straggle of talk about his nautical experiences. He knew every rope and plank aboard a ship and the duties of every man, whether in storm or battle or in harbor, and he seemed anxious to display his knowledge, as if to convince his hearers that he was a captain, not through royal influence, but because he had, as he said, "Come aboard by the hawse, not the gangway."

Fannie's heart sank in *ennui*. It was a relief when Hoskins murmured something about going. The Captain jumped up at once, saying, "Yes, by Jove. It's late, eh? Eh? You must see me to my barge, Hoskins. Good night, ma'am, and thank you for an excellent dinner and a most pleasant evening. I may come again, eh?"

"Of course, Captain Guelph."

"With or without Hoskins, eh?"

"As you choose." Her voice had a faint contempt. He was so absurd, like an overgrown schoolboy, blustering and stumbling over himself in his eagerness to be a prince and a man at one time. Prue helped the gentlemen into their cloaks, and they departed. When the door closed Prue folded her hands and said, "Well! A prince in our house! I can't believe it even now, but there he was. And you—you deserve it, ma'am, after all the nasty things these people have said about you. I always said the best was none too good for you."

"That," Fannie said, making a mouth, "remains to be seen."

THIRTY

*T*HE NEXT MORNING a handcart and a party of seamen arrived with half a dozen cases of prime old Madeira, and a polite young lieutenant handed Mrs. Wentworth a card scrawled, *With my Thanks and Compliments. William H.*

On the following afternoon she noticed him walking along the Mall with the General and another officer, but he did not give the house a glance. She did not see him for another two days. Then he came in the forenoon with Hoskins and would drink nothing but tea, because he said the sun was not over the yard-arm. They stayed half an hour, and diffidently Fannie offered an invitation to dine. She knew he was beset with invitations on every side and that Governor Parr was holding a ball in his honor tonight. To her astonishment Captain Guelph accepted at once, and added, "I'm to dance at the Governor's later. D'you mind if I dress here? Eh? Eh? I always come ashore in boots, and so forth."

"Captain, if you'll give this poor little house the honor, please consider it your *pied-à-terre* at any time."

She extended the dinner invitation to Hoskins, but in such a cold voice that he looked away miserably and said he had duty.

So it was a dinner *à deux*, and she wondered what would happen. A naval servant brought a portmanteau with the Captain's dress clothes, and Prue placed it in the best of the spare bedchambers. Her guest drank little, in view of the ball to follow, and at dinner talked of nothing but his midshipman days in the Navy, full of little anecdotes that he seemed to think very funny indeed.

"Is New Hampshire far from New York? I was in New York once, during the late war. Some of the rebels planned to kidnap me, I believe—a compliment, that, eh? They wouldn't do that for the admiral, eh? It was wintertime, devilish cold, but I enjoyed it. Just a boy then. Snow on the ground, ice on the ponds. Some of the fellows put a chair on runners and pushed me about a pond, scattering the skaters right and left and yelling, 'Make way, make way for Prince William!' Ha-ha-ha, what a lark! Whenever I think of America I think of that. Nobody in America would make way for me now, eh? Would they, eh?"

"How soon must you leave for the West Indies?" Fannie asked at last.

"Oh, that. I m putting it off as long as I can. I'll stay three weeks altogether. Then I must be off. I'll come north again with the squadron in the spring of course. Look forward to that. I like it here in Halifax. Very jolly place."

The hour came for him to go "aloft," as he said, to dress for the ball, and Mrs. Wentworth was kind enough to lend her carriage for the muddy passage down to Government House. His servant had been lurking outside, and now carried off the portmanteau with his "boots, and so forth."

As William took his leave, in full dancing fig, from powdered hair to silk stockings and pumps, he gave one of his jerky bows and kissed Fannie's hand. He held the slim fingers for a time.

"Did you really mean what you said about making this my *pied-à-terre?*"

"Of course I did, Captain."

"I mean to say, Hoskins mentioned to me that you're always very kind about putting up a guest or two on wet nights, and so forth. I could bed at the Governor's or any of a dozen places, but they're all so deuced stiff, those people. I mean to say, I have to be my rank with 'em all the time—all Prince and no Billy. I like it here. Feel like myself here. Don't like a crowd. And you're such pleasant company."

"How very good of you to say so, Captain," Fannie murmured, and paused. And then deliberately, "I should warn you that—outside of the garrison circle—I'm not considered good enough company for the ladies of the little society in Halifax. They don't call on me—are you sure you should?"

She watched him carefully, and he looked away. He had heard, then. Old Mrs. Parr probably, very conscious of her responsibilities, setting forth the people to meet and those to avoid. His large blue eyes came back to hers. He sucked in a great breath that turned his hearty pink face almost purple. Then he exploded. His voice was just short of a scream. "I go where I wish and do what I please! Who are these people to tell me who's acceptable and who's not? They're all in trade, the lot of 'em. That's why I don't accept their private invitations. That's my rule. Why should I hobnob with tradespeople? I choose my own friends. No one shall do that for me—not even my father!"

Fannie waited for this eruption to subside. "Thank you, Captain. Then you may come to my house as often as you wish." She waited again a few moments, with a cool straight stare into those bulging blue eyes. "You won't be breaking your rule. As Captain Hoskins has surely informed you, I am *not* in trade."

In return for the formal hospitalities ashore the Prince gave a few dinners aboard the *Pegasus*, with his own staff of cooks and confectioners and a magnificent array of china and silverware. His guests were ferried to the ship in his handsome eight-oared barge, with oarsmen dressed in white trousers, short scarlet jackets and black velvet caps. The coxswain wore a cap of gold cloth which (as the Prince informed everybody) had cost fifty guineas. Fannie's chief enemies received cards to some of these affairs and were delighted to see she was not there. But it was a hollow triumph. In his brisk way the Prince declined all private invitations. It was his rule, he said, to accept entertainment only from the chief officers of His Majesty's government, fleet, and garrison. And in the following days they saw him keep his rule in every direction—except one.

Each morning His Highness came ashore to take his pleasure for the day. And no day passed without a visit to Mrs. Wentworth's house in the Mall. Sometimes an army officer came with him, sometimes he came alone. He drank tea there in the mornings, he dropped in for a glass of wine whenever he passed in the afternoons, he dined there often, and when he did he stayed the evening. He used her carriage, but alone—she was never to be seen with him in public. Her foes drew what satisfaction they could from that. The worst feature was that he sometimes stayed the night at Mrs. Wentworth's. He was even known to keep clothes there, and whenever he appeared at a ball to which the merchant aristocracy were invited, it gave the ladies a pang to know that he had dressed for the occasion at that wicked woman's house.

At hard-drinking dinners where the guests were all male, at the Governor's, at the Commissioner's, at the three barracks on the hill, and whenever he was too far gone to return aboard, he would mutter, "Take me to Mrs. Wentworth's," and a group of fuddled officers took him there. When he came down red-eyed in the morning his hostess awaited him, smiling, always immaculately dressed and groomed, and always ready with a silver pot of hot black coffee for the dry mouth and the queasy stomach. He would never know what a sacrifice it was for her. Fannie had always loved to lie late abed, and it was good for the complexion; she felt she needed every possible hour at rest.

One evening when she knew he had gone to dinner with the officers of the 60th, a notably hard-drinking crew, she decided to retire early.

"Catesby tells me the Prince is sure to bed at the barracks," she informed Prue. "So I'm off to bed for a nice long sleep myself." She went upstairs and Prue undressed her, loosed her hair from its pins, and plaited it for the night. She was asleep almost as soon as she touched her head to the pillow, but it was not a nice long sleep. She wakened to the banging of the door knocker. It was hard to see the bedroom clock in the wan light of the nightcandle, which for safety's sake Prue always stood in a saucer of water on the dressing table. She sprang out of bed and saw that it was only half past eleven.

She threw a chintz *peignoir* over her little night chemise, thrust her feet into slippers, took a quick searching look at her face in the glass, and hurried downstairs. Prue was there with a candle, a shapeless figure in flannel.

"It's him again," Prue grumbled. "And drunk again, without a doubt, and a crew of those foolish young officers, fumbling and stumbling up the steps." But when she opened the door Captain Guelph was alone, and although his breath smelled of wine he was far from drunk. He wore a black boat-cloak over his uniform, and Fannie saw from the mud on his Hessians that he had walked all the way down from the barracks. Pausing on the way no doubt for a chat in Albermarle Street, or perhaps even that shrieking slum on Barrack Street.

He offered no apology for this unexpected call. "Those fellows of the 60th," he said, passing his gold-knobbed malacca to Prue and tossing off hat and cloak. "They pride 'emselves on their heads for wine, but I saw 'em all scuppered before I left. Drank a few glasses myself but gave 'em no mercy—called the toasts myself. The Royal Family, one by one—that's seventeen counting me. And bumpers all, with just time for breath between. Ha! Well, I walked off and left 'em there with their heads spinning, and here I am, stranded and looking for a bed."

He uttered his braying laugh, but there was no pleasure in his face. He seemed excited and restless and unhappy.

"You may go, Prue," Fannie said coldly. "The Captain can light himself to bed."

She took Prue's candle and from it lit another on the little table in the hall. The woman vanished into the shadows toward the servants' quarters. Captain Guelph picked up the second candle and followed Mrs. Wentworth "aloft." She had the chintz clutched about her with one hand and held forth her candle with the other. She was vexed, and she showed it in the rigid line of her back and head. From the first meeting with him she had held herself armed against any familiarity, guessing that he had come to see her as he went to see the women of "the hill." She had determined to show him she was not to be rated in that class, and indeed was far more a lady than he was a gentleman. And she had succeeded. Aside from his awkward little courtesies he had not made the slightest advance.

But he carried his hands-off policy much too far. She resented his failure to invite her to dine and dance with him at those affairs aboard the *Pegasus* and to demand that Governor Parr invite her to the Government House affairs, as he might easily have done. He was always ready to use her carriage but never asked her to drive with him or be seen with him anywhere. He used her home exactly as she had offered it, as a *pied-à-terre*, convenient to the center of the town. But what right had he to treat her as the keeper of a common lodginghouse? Coming at any hour of the day or night, and more often drunk than sober! In the face of the Halifax snobs it was a satisfaction at first to have a prince of the blood under her roof, but now the satisfaction had gone with the novelty. What was he after all but a stupid and drunken young bore? Jack Hoskins with his dark good looks and pleasant manners was twenty times the man.

On the landing at the top of the stairs, where her chamber stood open in the small glimmer of the night light, he paused as if to say Good Night, and she turned to face him. With the candles held up before them they inspected each other like two night-faring strangers meeting suddenly in an alley.

"Ma'am," he said morosely, "there's something I want you to understand. I only drink because it cuts me adrift from all the cursed restraints that have been put upon me since I was a child. And because it excites me of course."

"And is that why you go to see those strumpets up the hill?"

He blinked. And then in the same voice, "Yes. They're so different from the ladies I meet in drawing rooms and the like. They don't put on airs. They don't expect airs from me. They talk to me as if I was just a man."

Into Fannie's mind poured that scene at Drury Lane, the happy and excited boy in the box, the young hero home from the wars. And the older youth beside him, the Prince of Wales, gazing at the painted scene on the curtain and longing for Perdita.

396

What was it she had said to Johnnie? *Better Perdita than some common little strumpet.*

Without hesitation she touched her candle to his and blew out both in a puff. Only the faint glow of the chamber light remained.

"Come in," she said.

For ten days more the *Pegasus* swung idly at her anchors, and each of those days the Captain was seen passing in or out of the little white house in the Mall. There remained a good deal of official entertainment that he could not refuse, including bibulous farewell dinners at the various officers' messes of the garrison and the Dockyard. Again he was led, stumbling, late at night to the quay or deposited at Mrs. Wentworth's house, a fuddled lump, to be put to bed. But there were evenings enough when he could enjoy one of her quiet little dinners, her gay little songs and pranks and the comforts of her bed.

He was to sail on the twenty-fourth of October, and he took his leave of her on the afternoon before. "There's to be a grand farewell dinner and ball at the Governor's tonight, and I must be there, my dear. I'd stay another week if I could, but Schomberg says I must sling my hook tomorrow."

"Who's he?"

"My first lieutenant. Aged thirty-four, if you please, and an old West Indies hand. The Lords of Admiralty put him aboard to keep an eye on me, and damme he acts sometimes as if he were the captain. I've put him in his place more than once, you may depend, but I daren't carry it too far where the ship's concerned."

There was a long and tearful farewell in her drawing room. A few evenings before, in one of her romping moods, she had played for him her imitation of Perdita in a breeches part. And now, feeling the drama of this moment, she made her farewell as good as anything ever done by Mrs. Robinson at Drury Lane, to the very last, when she turned away flinging the back of her hand across her eyes as he moved toward the door.

She was still feeling pleased with this performance when he

walked in cheerfully the next night at ten o'clock, just as she was undressing for bed.

"William! What are you doing here? Go, Prue."

"Ha! The ship's wind-bound. Schomberg was bound to try beating out, but we had to come back inside the big island and anchor. So I came up to town in my barge. Promised him I'd come off again at the first sign of a fair slant. And here I am."

And there he was indeed, with the greedy look, as if he had been gone a twelvemonth.

Hours later she awakened and heard the town watch passing along the Mall and their hoarse rum-tuned voices bawling, "Three o'clock. Three, and all's well." The tired blond coconut was heavy on her shoulder. She moved for comfort, and he stirred and wakened. He lay silent for some minutes. Then he said, "You know, there's something I can't fathom about you. I don't know what it is exactly. You're clever, and I'm stupid of course. All I know is you seem to be two or three women all in one."

"Well?"

"I like the one you are now. You—you content me. That's the only word I can think of. I never feel wild and angry when I'm with you like this—and I do whenever I'm away from you. I'm not putting it very well, I s'pose. But you do understand me, don't you?—you always do."

"Of course."

Another pause, and then, "Your husband—when d'you expect him back?"

"About the end of the month."

"He sleeps with you, eh?" There was such jealousy in his voice that she smiled at the ceiling, where the last flicker of the night-candle played before guttering out in the water saucer.

"Naturally."

"Are you like this with him?"

"My husband's a handsome man in his way and much older than myself. In fact he's past fifty, and you're twenty-one. Does that explain what you want to know?"

"Ah! You know, you seem a very young girl sometimes, specially now, with your hair down in a thick plait like that, like a—like a dark rope on a deck that's all polished white from the holystones. 'Course I know you're older than me. How much?"

"I've forgotten."

"Tell me how old you are!"

"Hark!" She sat up and gazed toward the window. The candle had gone out, but the moon was up, and its light shone through the panes.

"What is it?" He threw an affectionate arm across her lap.

"The wind—there's a wind blowing."

"Let it blow."

She threw off his arm impatiently and sprang out of bed to the window. The wind was hissing in the eaves, and in the moonlight she could see fallen leaves blowing along the Mall.

"It's straight down the street—that means a fair wind down the harbor, doesn't it? Get up, quickly! You must get to your boat at once."

He was still inclined to linger, but she would have none of it. In twenty minutes he was bullied into his clothes and down to the door. There he halted.

"You didn't answer my question, did you?"

Fannie kissed him, opened the door, and thrust him forth.

"Save your questions for the ladies in Jamaica and Antigua— and try to remember me."

"I'll count every day till next summer."

"Your Schomberg's counting minutes now—go!"

She stood for a moment watching him run down the moonlit street, with the cocked hat jammed down to his ears and the boat-cloak blowing out behind him. It was cold there in the new north wind. She shivered and went back to bed.

THIRTY-ONE

FANNIE had no illusions about her royal lover. There would be royal drinking in the naval ports of the Caribbean, a thirsty part of the world, and he would call the roll of larboard and starboard female watches wherever they might be found. And he would find no lack of ladies like herself, willing to be flattered with the royal embrace. For she was flattered enormously, in spite of her first coolness. She did not realize how much until he had gone. Whatever the sailor prince was counting in the West Indies, she found herself counting weeks if not the days until he came north again.

It was odd to think of those London days when the magic air of royalty had drawn her again and again to Kew and Windsor, merely for a peep in the distance. How awed she had felt as the King and his sons rode by in Hyde Park! And now here in the wilds of Nova Scotia, of all places, that mystic presence had been laid upon her in person with the rollicking captain of the *Pegasus*. It was like being touched by a god in a Greek fable. One of the odder gods perhaps, but nevertheless she felt transfigured. When Johnnie came home she asked him to sleep in another chamber, pleading the delicacy of her health and her need of unbroken sleep. "You snore so, love, and the doctor insists."

For Fannie the winter and spring went well enough, but May crawled and June was a torture. Would he never come? The month had almost gone when the quiet of a hot afternoon blew apart in gunfire from the batteries and then from the ships. The long and seemingly endless thunder of a royal salute clapped along the harbor hills and rumbled about the wooded slopes of Bedford Basin. Johnnie was busy at a mast report for the Commodore, seated at the little writing desk in the sitting room. He looked up.

"That must be His Highness back again!"

"Yes," Fannie breathed. She glanced at the papers on the desk. "How long will you be on that report?"

"Another two or three days."

"And then you go to Cape Breton?"

"Well, I have various other matters here. I shan't be able to leave for a week or more."

She bit her lip in vexation. The slow scratch of Johnnie's pen was intolerable. She sent for the groom to harness the phaeton, and in fifteen minutes she was whipping her ponies up the hill past Saint Paul's, past the tall wooden mansions of Argyle Street, on through the harlots' quarter, and at last up the rough track to the peak of Citadel Hill. There she found the redcoats of the citadel battery running wet sponge-rods in and out of the hot guns after the salute. They paused to gaze at the phaeton and its beautiful driver, as she swung the blown ponies and sat looking down at the harbor.

It was the finest view in Halifax. Barrack Street, straggling along the shoulder below, marked the uppermost fringe of the town, and from there the jumbled cascade of wooden roofs went down steeply to the water, broken only by the open space of Grand Parade and the spire of Saint Paul's. In the strong sunshine the harbor flickered like brandy afire, a hot blue flame in the long trough between the hills. Several ships lay in the anchorage, but only one thing in the whole scene had importance, the small black frigate furling sail inside the knob of Georges Island. Already a speck detached itself from the side of *Pegasus* and moved in toward King's Wharf. The Prince's barge of course. His first call on the Governor—the formal debarkation would take place tomorrow. She pictured William receiving the Governor's smug little courtesies, impatient to be off to the house in the Mall.

At once she lashed the startled ponies, and away went the phaeton down the hill. It seemed to touch the stony track only here and there, flying through air like the car of Aurora herself. The soldiers gaped. At the house Fannie gave Juno a volley of instructions for dinner and ran to her chamber, calling for Prue. For months she had been creating a new wardrobe for this important season, and now she chose an afternoon gown of light brown, with sea-green silk bows and Bruges lace. She sat long at the mirror, with Prue at her back busy with her hair. Any moment now the knock would come.

Slowly the afternoon waned, and no knock. At five o'clock she had Prue powder her hair for the evening, changed into *décolleté*, rouged her cheekbones, placed patches with care at her mouth corners and chin, and held up the dinner until Juno was frantic and Johnnie starved. And still no sign of the Prince. At last they dined alone, or rather Johnnie dined, while she pecked at food that had no taste and sipped wine that had no tang.

"Aren't you well, my dear?" he asked after a time, seeing her lack of appetite and the flush on her face.

"I'm perfectly well. I'm just a little put out, that's all. But I'm used to it. I've told you how the Prince is. One never knows when he will come, it may be any hour of the day or night, and one has to be ready for him whatever the hour may be. I'm not complaining, I'm sure. You realize what an honor it is for us, having him regard our house almost as a home when he's ashore."

"Of course."

"His officers say he'll be on this station for a year longer and probably more. So we have the chance to do a lot for him in the way of hospitality. When he returns home it means a friend at court, remember that—he's told me he never forgets a favor. Naturally I'm not thinking selfishly about any of this. I regard him as I do any of our young officer friends, so far from home in this horrible place."

Johnnie sipped his wine thoughtfully. "As an old loyalist I wonder sometimes about the gratitude of kings and princes. Prince William seems an erratic young man from what you tell me and what I've heard outside."

"What have you heard outside?"—with a sidelong glance.

"Oh, you know, drunken bouts night after night, and calling on those sluts up the hill, and so forth. I'm told the King sent him abroad to get him out of bad company—the boy's been his father's favorite ever since he went to sea as a midshipman. But it seems to me here, amongst these dissolute young officers. . . ."

"What a thing to say of our good friends in the garrison!"

"Fan, I learned long ago that military and naval gentlemen live at a faster pace than the rest of us; it seems to go with the profession, and I suppose one must accept it as one accepts the weather or the moon. Nevertheless I can't help feeling the officers here overdo it. Life's dull in a garrison in peace time anywhere, but need they go in for so much drinking and wenching and all those riotous larks? The older officers tell me Halifax now beats Gibraltar as the most disreputable post in the empire. It's notorious."

"Oh, stuff! You sound like the dissenters' preacher in the little meeting house down by Hollis Street. He's always preaching sin and damnation."

"I think he's got a good text."

"Bah! You never hear that kind of thing at Saint Paul's. That's what I like best about the established Church—it minds its own business."

"Maybe I'm just getting old," Johnnie said mildly. "Speaking of the Church, I'm told Nova Scotia's now an episcopal see, and our first bishop's to come in the fall. That means an improvement in all directions. Some of the gentlemen are planning a grammar school here. They even talk of a college—subsidized from London under the Church of course—in another year or two." He smiled suddenly and warmly. "Do you know, love, that means we can bring our own dear boy here in another twelve months?"

"Charlie?" she said, astonished. Swiftly she turned the notion in her mind. In chatter with her young gentlemen she sometimes mentioned a "child" at school in England. Charles-Mary would be thirteen next year, rather big for a child. In fact a boy at the awkward size and the inquisitive age—underfoot every evening. Impossible! She said the word aloud.

"Why?" he said sharply.

"Well . . . well, what sort of school could they start here? What sort of teachers could they get? Indeed what would they have, when all's said and done? A shoddy little backwoods imitation of something much better in England! Charlie's doing well at Westminster. In a few more years he'll be going on to Oxford. Meanwhile he's quite happy there, and he spends his holidays with the FitzWilliams, in the most genteel society anyone could wish. Do you really think I'd let him come out here, to this shabby end of the world—this notorious place as you say yourself—where the so-called ladies don't even speak to his mother? You must be out of your mind."

She was pleased to see that Johnnie looked properly dashed. He was foolishly fond of the boy, and for Charlie's sake she had put a wise foot down. He turned away to his everlasting documents and was silent. The clocks ticked on through the evening. At nearly midnight, just as they were about to go upstairs, there was a rattle of wheels in the street outside, a jostle of feet on the steps, and a sudden rat-tat-tat of the knocker that rang through the house like pistol shots. Fannie flew to open the door. A small curricle, driven by one of the garrison officers, was just turning under a street lantern in the Mall and heading back toward the barracks. And here was her Prince at last, swaying on the doorstep like his own *Pegasus* in a heavy sea. He reeked of wine. The fore peak of his cocked hat was tipped over his eyes. The gold-laced coat of navy blue hung unbuttoned and open, so did the white waistcoat, and somewhere in the course of a convivial evening he had spilled a glass over his white silk breeches and calves, which were spattered as if with blood. He pushed back the hat and lurched inside, thrusting out his arms affectionately.

"Ahoy there m'dear! Pegasus the winged stallion. Gad, you look marvelous!"

She was aware of Johnnie on the first step of the stairs, pausing on his way to bed, and she evaded William's clutch, crying at the same time, "Welcome—welcome indeed, Your Highness. May I present my husband, Governor Wentworth?"

"Another?" said William loudly. "Damme! The town's overrun with governors." And then, as her words penetrated the wine fumes in his head, he stared past her at the approaching Johnnie. And pulling himself together with invisible halyards he said carefully, "Good evening, sir. I hadn't the pleasure when I was here before." He shook Mr. Wentworth's hand solemnly, turned into the drawing room, dropped in a chair, and tossed his hat on the floor.

"I'm a bit far gone, as you see, sir. I've been well seen to, you may depend. Dinner with those devils of the 57th, and drink for drink after. For the honor of the Navy, you understand. Zounds! You never saw such a slaughter of bottles in your life!"

His head fell forward. He was far gone indeed. Fannie gave Johnnie a glance and a significant nod of her head toward the stairs. Prue appeared, and now she and Johnnie got the captain to his feet and up the stairs, Fannie leading with a candle. They deposited him on the bed in a chamber at the farther end of the hall, and Fannie modestly withdrew while they undressed William to his linen and covered him for the night.

She was sitting at her dressing table when Johnnie paused in her doorway.

"Does he come very often like that?"

"Oh, sometimes," she said calmly. "It's only when he's been to one of those mess dinners. When he dines here he takes a little Madeira, and that's all. He's really quite abstemious when he has a chance to be just himself. Tell Prue to come and do my hair—she can clean the Prince's clothes before he gets up in the morning."

And in the morning a very different prince came down the stairs. The hour was well on in the forenoon, and he sat drinking cup after cup of Fannie's coffee and talking volubly to Governor Wentworth. When Johnnie asked him about naval life in the West Indies he went on at great length. He was strict, sir, strict, and his officers didn't like it. Specially that watchdog Schomberg that the Lords of Admiralty had put upon him. In fact Schomberg and the rest had put in for transfer to another ship. Deuce of a row.

"I was supported, mark you, by my superior officer in the Leeward Islands. Captain Nelson. Just a young man, and very capable—though I confess I thought him a queer phiz at first. A very old-fashioned cut to his clothes and a regular old Benbow pigtail down his back. Ha! But we got along very well, very well indeed. I even gave the bride away at Horatio's wedding. Fact! A widow at Nevis. Handsome creature in a cold sort of way. Couldn't see the attraction myself. Besides, there's his career. A man in a profession like yours or mine, Governor, must consider his career before marriage or anything else, eh? How long d'you expect to be at home, eh?"

"I don't know exactly," said Johnnie evenly. "A week, perhaps two—it depends on the business in hand. I cruise the woods as you cruise the sea, sir, and we must both put into port for a refit now and then."

"Ah!" The Captain looked at Fannie and back to Mr. Wentworth. "That's true—and very neatly put, I must say. Well, I'll be off to my own business. No, no, ma'am, I can't stay longer. You've both been very kind, I'm sure." And suiting action to the word he rushed out into the hall, clapped on his hat, and departed at a brisk trot down the Mall.

The next ten days were purgatory for Fannie, listening for a familiar banging at the door which never came. Her hopes lifted at the end of a week, when Johnnie departed in a coasting sloop for Cape Breton, far to the east. But Pegasus had taken his wings elsewhere. There was the customary round of dinners and dances in his honor, and before long Fannie knew the topic whenever the ladies whispered together. His Royal Highness was cutting that creature in the Mall. She'd been one of his passing whims after all. And Fannie could picture the rejoicing. She would not stir abroad. She refused to expose herself to the knowing smiles and glances of "those prigs." Even her courtiers stayed away, in deference perhaps to that royal standard she had flown so long.

There were times when she lay on her bed through the silent evenings and wept in mortification. If only Johnnie had been in the woods! Why did he have to be here with his stupid papers just at the wrong time?

At last she could stand it no longer. On a warm evening she appeared at Grand Parade. The artillery band was playing, the beaux and belles of the town, the clerks, the fishermen, the soldiers, and sailors, and their girls, strolled up and down or sat on the grassy verge; the gentry and their ladies sat in their carriages along the Argyle Street side, where they could look down on the scene and enjoy the music in comfort. For twenty minutes Fannie sat lonely in the phaeton, conscious of stares and remarks, with her own eyes half closed, as if the flat notes of the bandsmen, well primed with beer in the summer heat, were the very music of the spheres. It was the spry little dandy Catesby who rescued her. He appeared suddenly at the phaeton wheel, thrusting his cane under his arm and sweeping off his hat. She did not waste words.

"Where is H.R.H.?" she demanded in a swift undertone.

"Dining at the Dockyard—the Commissioner's."

"Jeffery, you must get word to him for me. My Governor's gone away, and I'm alone. Do you understand?"

He gave her a comical look of reproach.

"You see my position, Jeff—I won't have these cats laughing at me. You surely know what this means to me."

Catesby looked down as she said this, sucking the knob of the sword cane.

"Well, my dear lady, it'll be a little difficult. I mean an army subaltern can't go barging in on His Highness with odd little messages. I'll have to do it through one of his friends, Major Linzee probably."

"Then go, as quickly as you can." And with her most intimate smile. "You'll be rewarded, Jeff, I promise you."

"Done!" He was off through the crowd at once, and Fannie turned her ponies and drove away slowly, with her head high, down the Mall.

The next day passed without a word or a sign. She was in despair. And then, just at dark, William came. Inside the door he bent over her hand politely.

"I'm sober, my dear, as you see. I find that Bacchus interferes with Venus damnably. Not to mention the presence of husbands. Is he really gone?"

"For several weeks."

"What a shame I've only got four more days! My orders are to sail for Quebec and, damme, spend the rest of the summer there."

"But then you'll come here again?" she said quickly.

"Oh yes. I purpose some weeks here, as I did last year."

"Bless you, William, for a moment you frightened me. You don't know how I've missed you, all this time. Come! Juno's prepared a little supper, all the things you like, and if you coax me nicely you shall have some Madeira—but not too much."

"And then?" The large blue eyes regarded her greedily.

THIRTY-TWO

*T*HAT SUMMER Johnnie's carpenters built his "cell" on the knoll near Birch Cove, a flimsy doll's house of pine boards and shingles, with two small rooms and a veranda. A corduroy track for the carriage led through the trees from the Windsor road, and a flight of wooden steps climbed the side of the knoll to the door. It was a charming spot, even Fannie admitted that now. Frequently in the hot August weather she drove out there with the Brinleys and one or two of her own cavaliers to spend the afternoon and evening. Juno provided a hamper of good things to eat and drink, and at low tide the gentlemen and the Brinley boy waded among the weedy rocks below, hunting for lobsters. Fannie and Mary themselves took off shoes and stockings and dabbled their feet like children.

"What are you going to call it?" Mary said.

"The Hermitage, I suppose," Fannie smiled. "John plans to spend a lot of time here with his books and papers."

"And you?"

"Oh, I like it well enough with company, like this. But he can have his precious solitude."

Captain Lingay looked up from the water. "I suggest you call it Friar Laurence's Cell."

"What for?"

"Because that's where Juliet came—and not for solitude."

Fannie waved a leg at him. "Well, why not? Friar Laurence's Cell. It sounds romantic."

"Which part shall Johnnie play, Romeo or the friar?" said Mary.

"The friar of course!"

When Johnnie came back in September he was delighted with

his new retreat and no less with its name. It was only a short ride from town. Here he worked away at his papers and maps in utter peace, and at the head of every letter he wrote with a flourish, "Friar Laurence's Cell." As October drew near he began staying there several days at a time alone. Fannie rode out once with her little troop to visit him, but he received them a little coldly, as if they were an intrusion, and they did not stay.

The leaves were changing color now. Already a company of maples stood like scarlet infantry in the grassy swamp beside the knoll. Fannie measured the days carefully. The Prince would be sailing from Quebec at any time and Johnnie showed no sign of leaving for the woods. As she remarked to Prue, Johnnie at the Cell was Johnnie neither here nor there, but just an easy forty minutes' canter from the town. By mid-October she was getting frantic. On the twentieth she drove to Birch Cove in the phaeton, climbed the steps, and found Johnnie sprawled in a chair and gazing idly at the water. She came to her point at once.

"Isn't it time you went off to the woods again?"

"I'm in the woods now," he smiled.

"Don't be silly. I mean your work. You've been in town six weeks or more."

"Oh, I don't know, Fan. I begin to feel I've been much too concerned with the woods and not enough with the town." He gave her a side glance and went on, "I mean of course I'm not a young man any more. Those backwoods' journeys are tiring, and my rheumatism gripes me hard sometimes. There are days when every step I take is torture, and every jolt in the saddle, specially in wet weather. Why should I suffer all that for £800 a year? So long as I can write a good report, on yards of paper, those men in London will be satisfied. I take example from Governor Parr. He thrives on paper."

"This doesn't sound like you," Fannie said uneasily.

"We all change, my dear."

He was in an old waistcoat and a pair of comfortable hodden breeches, the sort he wore in the woods. His stockings were ungartered and hung in loose wrinkles to his ankles, and a pair of worn Indian moccasins disgraced his feet. His jaws had not seen a razor for at least two days. An unclubbed queue hung down his back like a rope of tarnished silver. He might have been a back-woods' farmer taking his ease in some patch beyond civilized reach.

"You look and talk as if you'd thrown away all ambition," she said.

"Let's say better that I've thrown away my illusions."

"You mean you've got downright lazy!" Her voice was angry, and the careful English accent disappeared. The sound was that of a scolding Boston wife. "Oh, get up out of that chair, do, and take a look at yourself."

He did not stir. "Why are you so anxious for me to go away?"

"Because I haven't lost my ambition, and it seems I must find enough for both of us."

"You mean you expect the Prince now, don't you?"

"Yes, I do."

"And what is His Royal Highness to you, my dear?" He said it quietly, with that same dreamy gaze on the water. Fannie sat up very straight and drew in a breath, watching the calm profile of the man without illusions. "What do you think?" she said sharply.

Johnnie turned his head. "He's your lover."

"Yes."

"Does he, by any chance, know you're old enough to be his mother?"

"That makes no difference," she snapped, "to him or to me."

"Apparently. Is this passion on your part or mere tuft-hunt-ing?"

"You know very well what he can do for both of us."

"I doubt it very much."

Fannie leaped to her feet. To the slouched figure in the other chair she seemed to rise tall against the sky over Bedford Basin, like one of those majestic statues on the pediment of Wentworth Woodhouse, dressed as a fashionable mortal.

"You doubt! You doubt everything, Johnnie. Because you're

weak! Because you've lost all your purpose. Because you think of nothing but your misfortunes. And I'm your chief misfortune—that's it, isn't it? That's what you've always felt, inside, ever since you married me. Oh, I had my points as a woman, but as the Governor's lady I embarrassed you. I was the bride who set the tongues wagging all the way from Kittery to Wolfe-borough. I was the wife who cost you Uncle Benning's fortune. Oh yes! Don't deny it! And now I'm the scandal of every jealous prude in Halifax. Well, you've heard what they had to say. Now listen to me!

"Johnnie, when we first came together there in Portsmouth I was mad about you. Love-love-love, that's all I thought about. Love and nothing else. And of course you loved me in your fashion. After we were married I soon came to know what that was. Your wife was just something pleasant for a journey's end, like meat and ale and a good warm bed. All you really cared about was that crazy dream of yours—New Hampshire the biggest province in America, and John Wentworth the greatest man in it, the one everybody looked up to and admired. What was a mere wife to that? I was just something with your mark, like one of those mast pines in the forest. You could go traipsing off through the woods for weeks and months, and I didn't matter. Oh, you were Prince Bountiful to everyone else. They could have your time, your money, your smile, your influence, anything they wanted. But not me. You were selfish, Johnnie, after all. Selfish!"

She paused, as if for breath after this outburst or perhaps to see what he would say. Johnnie remained dumb, hunched in the chair.

She began again, but in a lower voice, very cool now. "When I tried to amuse myself in innocent little ways you paid me the compliment of being jealous now and then, but that was all. When I tried to help you in my simple way you brushed me off, as if I were a silly little black fly buzzing in your ear. I heard the way people were talking in Portsmouth. The grumbling about the favors you gave your friends. Then all that talk about liberty, that kept growing and growing and growing. Your friends begged you to take a strong hand, to crush those plotting busybodies while you had the chance. But you wouldn't listen. Then I tried to tell you, but of course I was only your wife, poor dear empty-headed Fannie! You stood like one of those precious mountains of yours, with your own foolish head up in the clouds and a forest fire running at your feet.

"So the trouble came, and we were driven out. We had to run away in the dark, like a pair of good-for-nothings flitting to Boston because they couldn't pay their bills. And still you wouldn't see that I was right. I was always wrong, in everything I said or did. Ha! Even in Boston. You shipped me off to England as if I were a piece of baggage that annoyed you underfoot, something you wanted out of the way. And for two years you left me there alone, in the midst of strangers. Well, my Johnnie, your baggage had time to do some thinking for herself over there. To see how big the world was, and how small New Hampshire after all.

"And at last you came to me—or rather to see those rebel friends of yours in Paris. And you came back from that meeting with your tail between your legs. All your wonderful dream was gone, wasn't it? What a picture you made then! How those Portsmouth villains would have laughed! From that moment I knew our fortunes were up to me. And I had my own dream by that time, mark you, Johnnie. We were never meant to be nobodies, you and I. I vowed that we'd be somebodies again, if I had to crawl and knock my head against the pavement all the way to the royal palace. Oh yes! And I've worked at my dream. I've put myself in the way of people that had position or title—anyone who might have any influence at all. I've hinted, I've cajoled, I've schemed—I've stopped at nothing. And all the time I've held up my head in public. I've let people see that I was somebody. Especially here in Halifax, where they tried to snub me from the first. I've made it clear that they were the nobodies. Any officer in the garrison of rank or family can tell you that."

Again she paused. This time Johnnie spoke. His voice was

dull, and he did not look up. "And where has it got you, all this?"

"So far, nowhere. We're still in this wretched hole. But now my chance has come. A way to the royal palace at last—and not on my knees!"

"Prince William?"

"Who else? I'm a good influence on him, the only one in Halifax—the only one he's ever met since he went to sea as a boy. In the time to come he'll be grateful to me—and to you, of course—and when we have a favor to ask . . ." Her voice trailed off. She was not looking at Johnnie. Her face was lifted to the sky over the Narrows, toward England, and she smiled into the distance and made a little open gesture with her hands.

Johnnie was still staring over the water. The smoky haze of Indian summer hung over the Dartmouth hills. A pair of savages paddled a bark canoe toward the Narrows and the invisible town. On the bright skin of the Basin it crawled like a sluggish ant.

"Those other gentlemen of yours," he said at last. "Captain Hoskins, say. Was that a matter of good influence too?"

"You can forget Hoskins. He went with his regiment to Quebec."

"Ah, of course! And, to be sure, the 4th Regiment came from England to take their place. The King's Own Regiment. The Devil's Own, as some carping folk in the town call them now. And young Mr. Dyott of the Devil's Own took Mr. Hoskins' place very quickly, didn't he?"

"I met Dyott in England, one day when I was at Bath with George and Mary Brinley. When he called on me here I couldn't be less than courteous."

"I see. And what does courtesy require toward the most notorious young buck in that regiment of rakehells?"

"Billy Dyott's the most popular officer in the regiment, and he comes of a good English county family. All those prigs in town would welcome him into their parlors, so I invite him into mine. To spite them. And that's been true of my other gentlemen visitors, ever since we came here, as you know very well."

Johnnie turned his head slowly and regarded her again. She made a handsome figure in the fitted blue riding coat with its silver frogs and huge military buttons. A blue sugar-loaf hat with a small curled brim was pinned at a jaunty angle on her hair. She stood with her gloved hands clenched on the back of the chair, and a small fur muff dangled from one wrist. Her dark eyes glittered. Tears? Anger? Both? He could not tell.

"My dear," he said heavily, "do sit down. As it happens I'm very glad you came today. I've wanted to discuss this matter with you, and in privacy, something we could never do at the house in town. I haven't been blind all this time, Fannie. I don't accuse you of deceiving me. I simply deceived myself. I wouldn't believe my own eyes and senses, any more than I believed the gossips. And please understand I'm not angry now. I'm getting old, Fan. I seem to have left you behind, in another world. Why should I care what happens there? Life's too short for that."

Fannie's eyelids closed to slits, and the movement sent a pair of tears sliding down past her nose. What did this mean? Was he being horrid, or was he really indifferent? Her lips moved as if she were about to speak, and he held up a finger for silence, as if he were in Council again and wished no one to interrupt what he had to say.

"The sum is this, my dear Fan. When I was younger, when we were in that other world together, I loved you very much, in spite of what you say. I had my work to do, of course, but I loved you—I enjoyed you, if you want to put it that way. I enjoyed my whole life then, and you were no small part of it. A very sweet time, that. Something to look back on. Something no one can ever take away from me—not even a prince. And now we're two other people altogether. Like a change of horses at a post-inn. It's the same coach with a different pair in the harness. And whatever we do, Fan, whatever our separate gaits may be, our marriage must roll along somehow at our heels. We've been too much to each other in the past to break the harness now—and we have our boy to think about. Very well. You go your gait, and I'll go mine. And if your gait makes the leather rub me here and there, well, the world has galled the old horse pretty thoroughly, the past ten years, and another gall or two won't make much difference."

Johnnie gave her a sad tired smile. "Horse talk—I can't keep away from it, can I? But you see what I mean."

Fannie returned him a long and careful stare with those half-closed eyes. There was nothing contemptuous or mean in his face, only that look of resignation and despair. For one wild moment she had an impulse to throw herself on her knees beside him, weeping, begging forgiveness as if she were a naughty child, but she crushed that with the hard grip of her hands on the chair back.

"Then you agree to go away into the country while the Prince is here?"

"If that's your wish." And then, in a cold voice, "May I ask when it might be proper to return?"

"Give me until the end of November."

Fannie's companion of the past summer, Lieutenant Dyott of the King's Own, was twenty-six, a wiry bundle of energy with brown hair, gray eyes, and a satanic arch of eyebrows. His regiment had arrived a week or two after Prince William's departure, as the warm weather began. In a hard-living officers' mess he was the boldest rider, the best shot, the most reckless player at cards or dice, the most valiant at bottle. He was foremost in every sport under the sky, from boat sailing on the harbor to coursing hares with a pack of terriers on the moorland behind Citadel Hill; and indoors it was the same, from ballrooms to bedrooms. There was no one in Halifax quite like daring laughing Billy Dyott.

Fannie, with her inevitable choice of the most admired men in the garrison, had awarded him her favor soon after he came. She had got over that absurd feeling of dedication which made the time so long between the Prince's visits. Dyott amused her in all ways. And she was not entirely surprised when, soon after

Prince William returned in the autumn, His Highness chose Dyott as the boon companion for his jaunts ashore.

Unfortunately their combined spirits were like the ingredients of a skyrocket, acting one upon the other in a fizzing spectacle of mischief. There was never such wild drinking. There was never such a visiting of the half-world on 'the hill,' and never such a commanding of wanton performances to be whispered about in Halifax drawing rooms. And there were never such other pranks. More than once, after a convivial dinner at the barracks, the Prince commanded the entire garrison to march to the top of Citadel Hill and fire a *feu de joie* in his honor, no matter the hour of the night. Once, after Captain Duvernet of the Artillery had provided a firework display from the hill, His Highness demanded something real, in fact a firing of live shells from the battery, and with a sublime disregard of ships in the dark anchorage the shells were thrown. In a short time the shibboleth of the whole town was *What next?*

In all this merry roistering Fannie had to content herself with her Prince's brief morning or afternoon calls, and those evenings when he came sober or sufficiently sober for a lover's enjoyment of her charms. She felt that she was the one good influence on him—hadn't he told her so last June?—and with every wile she strove to anchor him in her sensible little haven. The difficulty was—as he had also confessed to her—that he was rigged with too much canvas and no rudder. For nineteen days and nights the madcap round went on. Long before the end, everyone in the town but Fannie wished that Pegasus would take to his wings and fly away to his winter station in the Caribbean.

Fannie did not see him at all on the night before he left. That was spent in a last carousal with the officers of the King's Own, of which Dyott gave her a comical account the next evening.

"And finally," he chuckled, "I begged leave to give the superior toast, to be swallowed standing on our chairs and with three times three cheers. I tell you it was a laughable sight; old Governor Parr, the General, and the Commodore, all so drunk they could scarcely stand, and hoisted up on their chairs, each with a bumper in his hand. After that, while we were still on the chairs, I proposed a toast to His Highness and a fair wind on the morrow. He stood at the head of the table—he'd taken care not to drink so much as the rest of us—and I never saw a man laugh so. The old Governor asked if we'd any more toasts, because if he ever got down he'd never be able to get up again."

"And after all that?" Fannie said impatiently, piqued that her lover had not come to say good-by.

"He demanded that I take him for a walk—in fact what he calls a cruise."

"How could you!"

"My dear lady, when a Prince commands you don't offer objections, not when you're a humble subaltern in His Majesty's forces. Anyhow he went straight down to the quay and back to the ship." Dyott paused and regarded her carefully. "He's not sailing where he's ordered—to the West Indies. Did you know that?"

"No! Where's he going?"

"Home to England. Fact! He told me he'd had letters from his older brothers in the last mail. The Prince of Wales and Duke of York. They're going the pace in London, you know, and the King's quite furious; and now they've invited William to join 'em in the fun. There'll be the deuce to pay, you may depend. Apart from anything else, the older pair were given dukedoms, and so they get a fat grant from Parliament. William still has to ask his father for every penny. And of course he resents it, and he intends to make a row about it."

"So that's what was on his mind!" Fannie cried. "I saw he was more excited than usual, whenever he came to me. Did he say anything about me before he left you?"

"Not a word."

She was hurt and indignant. How ungrateful the creature was, after all! And now he was off to England, and she would never see him again!

Johnnie came home, polite and amiable, at the end of the month and settled down to his books and papers as if nothing had happened. The interview at the Cell had cleared the air between them so perfectly that Fannie wondered now why she had hesitated so long. Together they settled into the winter calendar, and the little cycle of dinners and whist parties at the Brinleys' and the Wentworths' in turn, sometimes with Dyott and one of his fellows as guests, sometimes with more ponderous colonels and majors. The town lay under snow, sleigh bells jingled up and down the Mall, the soldiers marched muffled in greatcoats and mittens to and from their posts; the harbor smoked in the frigid weather, and for a few days in February put on a skin of ice thick enough for people to cross on foot.

Spring weather brought letters from England, including a note from Paul Wentworth. Would Johnnie please procure him a schooner lading of good pine boards and scantlings and send it off to the Surinam plantation? And, please, add the charges to his account for slaves, et cetera. He had no news, except one or two of the latest tidbits of the *ton*. There were letters from the FitzWilliams and other friends, the usual family news, spun out in long stately sentences to make a decent packet for the mail. They did not mention Johnnie's hopes of a post in England any more, and their silence was eloquent. And finally there was a letter from Charles-Mary, written in a beautiful hand that did credit to his writing master. It recounted his progress at lessons and what he had done in the Christmas holidays, and how the King had come to see the boys of the school and patted him on the head. But there was no more of that touching longing for his dear Papa and Mama which had appeared in the childish scrawl of the first few years. The gap was growing as wide as the sea.

With the coming of summer Johnnie departed for a long season of timber cruising, leaving his wife to her own devices. Most of the town society had gone to spend the warm weather on their country estates about Windsor, forty miles away on the shore of Fundy. Even the garrison was dull. Since Prince William's departure the air of the town was like the silence and darkness after a display of Captain Duvernet's fireworks from the top of Citadel Hill. Fannie's courtiers found her listless. Even those excellent meals at her table lacked something. It was like taking food and wine in the presence of a widow newly bereaved, with the coffin in the next room. Their best efforts at a lively conversation fetched a faint smile to her lips that came and went like an illusion. There was no change in her eyes. Fannie's dark gaze regarded them in a way that made them uneasy, as if she were trying to see someone else inside the uniforms. One by one they fell away. There were other pretty ladies, after all.

Only Dyott persisted. The gay cockerel of the King's Own was a little surprised at himself, but he came faithfully to the house in the Mall and rode faithfully at Mrs. Wentworth's phaeton wheels whenever she went abroad. Perhaps she would be grateful by-and-by. After all, the gods came only once in a mortal life and never again.

On an August evening in that hot summer of 1788 he came to dine. The Wentworth cook, that black magician, had provided a meal fit for a prince, and as usual the wines were first-rate. When Dyott lifted his first glass and murmured politely, "To you, my dear lady," he seemed to detect for the first time in months a trace of that long-vanished interest in her eyes. With the skill of an accomplished hunter he kept his elation to himself. She was recovering, then. Was she ready to lower her royal standard at last? That remained to be seen. What a splendid game it was!

As the meal progressed, with the silent Negro boy gliding in and out of the room with the removes, and with due attention to those first-rate wines, the captain began to feel pleasantly sure of himself. The lady was there like a delicious dessert for the meal's end. He was only mildly annoyed when these happy anticipations were interrupted by a knock at the door. Prue answered it. Dyott heard a murmur of low voices and nothing more. Then Prue called her mistress out of the room. When Mrs.

Wentworth came back to the table Dyott had a rude shock. Her face was utterly changed. It had come alight. Indeed her whole person seemed to glow like a paper lantern at a ball, lit in a moment by some mysterious taper in the hallway.

"He's back!" this transfigured creature cried.

"What! Impossible! Who says so?"

"A seaman—a naval servant of the Prince. He says his master will be here in a few minutes. You must leave at once, Dyott."

His face was red and furious. "This is some trick of those devils at the barracks." He sprang up, but he made no move to leave.

"Not at all!" she answered. "He's here straight from England, in a frigate called *Andromeda*. Andromeda! Do you know your Greek mythology, Dyott? Wasn't she the girl who was chained to a rock for some monster to devour and delivered by a hero at the last moment?" She cried it out to him in a challenging voice, as if he were the monster.

And now there was a tremendous rat-tat-tat at the street door. Fannie destroyed the unhappy Dyott with a final look and ran out into the hall, just as the door burst open and Prince William's hearty voice rang through the house. He must have come hard on the heels of his messenger, for he was panting and the red face shone with perspiration. He was in his sea uniform, without cane or cloak, and carried in his hand a salt-stained hat with tarnished gold braid on its tall naval cocks. Dyott had followed his hostess into the hall.

William was in one of his excited moods. He noticed Dyott with a nod, turned into the drawing room, dropped in a chair and hurled the hat across the room.

"Sit down, everybody!"—as if the house were full of people. "Gad! I've run the whole way from the King's Wharf. Ring for Madeira and a tumbler, my dear lady, I'm parched. And I've got the deuce of a lot to tell you." He sat there panting until the wine came and then drank off a full tumbler.

"That's better! Well, I'm back, you see. And I've had a time of it, you may depend. Sailed home without orders. Lost my nerve when I got to Plymouth, I must confess. Dropped my hook in the Sound and sent off a note to George and Frederick in London. Down they came, hell for leather. Spent days there with me, egging me on to go to London with 'em and join the fun of the fair. Strolled about the Plymouth streets with me, arm in arm, and all the people cheering."

He poured himself another glass and drank that off. The wild smile left his face, and the voice turned querulous. "After all, why shouldn't I go home, hey? After all this time on foreign service. Eh? Eh? Home, and a title and a grant from Parliament like my brothers. That's only right, damme. That's justice."

A harsh laugh. "But no, not for William! The devil to pay. Father furious. Admiralty furious. Gad, those purple-nosed admirals, they'd ha' hanged me at the yardarm if they could! A mere frigate captain defying 'em in that manner! But they stuck to their course according to the chart. Consulted His Majesty. Took 'em some time to make up their minds. Meantime I was ordered to take command of a frigate in the home fleet—and stay away from London. Then it came, both broadsides—bang! bang! Father first. No title, no parliamentary grant. I must continue to look to him for every sixpence above my captain's pay, same as before. And, by gad, if I broke orders again I'd never get another penny. You see? That's to keep his hold on me. That's to keep me out of this quarrel between him and my brothers. Then the Admiralty. I must return to the North American station at once, in *Andromeda*. Barely gave me time to ship my stores. What could I do? I've been in the Navy since I was a child. Discipline! They put it in your bones. So I slung my hook, and here I am again, Captain Guelph of the *Andromeda* frigate, if you please, that and nothing more."

He addressed himself to the Madeira again, glaring at the decanter as if it were His Majesty and the Lords of Admiralty all in one. In the silence Fannie murmured, with a careful diffidence, "I suppose you must go on to Quebec and spend some time there, as usual?"

"No!" He rapped out the word like a gunshot. "Damme,

they've ordered me to the North American station till the snow comes, and then off to join the West Indies squadron for the winter. Very well! I've no great liking for Quebec. Halifax suits me better. So as far as I'm concerned, Halifax is the whole North American station. Here I am, and here I stay till the snow comes. Mark that, Dyott, and tell your friends at the barracks. We'll make a merry season of it."

William's face wore again that frantic and unhappy grin. His eyes lifted slowly from the decanter and met Fannie's gaze. Her mind was calculating rapidly. The snow never came—not to stay—until late November.

Three months. Three whole months!

THIRTY-THREE

THE SURVEYOR GENERAL of His Majesty's Woods, far away in the western parts of the province, did not hear of Prince William's return until late in September. He dismissed the news with a clamp of his teeth and went on with his work, cruising his own green domain with diligence, riding the rough bridle paths that passed for roads about the coast, exploring rivers and a maze of lakes by canoe with a silent Indian for companion, visiting many a lonely settlement and finding welcome wherever he went. Here and there he slept in a mansion, usually the home of a well-to-do loyalist. More often his shelter was a rude little country inn or the dim smoky log hut of a fisherman or a backwoods farmer; mostly he slept under the sky, or in rainy weather beneath a brushwood shelter thrown up for the night.

The American refugees had forgiven him that unfortunate attempt to levy fees on their land. They saw John Wentworth now as one of themselves, a man who had known better days and faced misfortune with courage. The Nova Scotians, inclined to look upon all the refugees with suspicion and dislike, saw a forester with a good sound knowledge of the country, a gentleman who could make himself at home with the poorest backwoods family, a lone Halifax official who actually gave sweat for his money. Fannie herself would have been surprised to see the man who fled, whenever he could, from the formalities of Halifax to the slovenly comfort of Friar Laurence's Cell. Here among the country folk he traveled the woods in rough hodden and linsey-woolsey, in moccasins, and buckskin leggings to the thigh, but he carried with him a suit of dress clothes, ruffled shirts, silk stockings, buckled shoes, along with the clean linen and soap and razor in his journey baggage. His hosts, whether well to do or poor, received a sunburned unshaven woodsman at nightfall, and in half an hour were entertaining another creature altogether.

There was a thin snow on the ground when he returned at last to Halifax and the house in the Mall. Fannie greeted him quietly by the sitting-room fire.

"You look well, Johnnie."

"Thank you, my dear. Did you—have a good season?"

"Yes." There was a look of ravaged triumph in her face, and he said no more.

In the idleness of winter Fannie was able to look back upon those three tempestuous months with the philosophy of a warrior after a hard campaign. During the whole of that time she had been mistress to a youth whose sole concern was his own whim and pleasure and whose appetites had no end. Her house was his. He came and went as he pleased, sometimes alone, sometimes with Dyott, sometimes storming in with half a dozen others of Dyott's stamp, demanding food and drink for all. Each day from morn to night she held herself poised, powdered, rouged, and beautifully dressed, and with her household drilled and alert like a quarter guard awaiting the officer of the day.

As always he refused to appear with her in public. Yet he would stop and strike up a conversation with any pretty whore he chanced to meet. When Fannie was bold enough to reproach him on that score he said loftily, "You must understand that I can't be seen abroad with the wife of one of His Majesty's officials in the absence of her husband. I have to consider your position as well as mine. These little baggages I hail when I'm cruising the streets have no position at all."

"But I don't see why I . . ."

"Madam, you have no right to question me."

"Forgive me," she said meekly.

"I may point out that I never appear ashore with any of my own officers—I choose my sporting companions among the army gentlemen. That's for the discipline of the ship. Do I make myself clear?"

"Yes, Your Highness."

So she was another of his officers, performing her duty in her own little ship, but never to witness his liberties ashore. Sometimes, waiting alone through evening vigils while the clock struck off the hours, longer and longer, she asked herself what he meant to her, just as Johnnie had. And there was no easy answer. William was anything but handsome, an absurd strutting cockerel in manner and appearance. He was a libertine and a snob. There were times when she despised him, when in her anger she was tempted to have the door shut and bolted in his face—and yet she craved the very sound of his voice.

What for? Her own *diable au corps*? Her determination to flout the pious snobs of Halifax? The magic touch of royalty? The hope that William's influence might be useful later on? Or just pride in her looks, the constant urge to prove that she was all she had been at five-and-twenty, the assurance that time moved for other women, never for Frances Wentworth? Something of all these. A curious sum.

As the weather softened into spring she began to look forward with eagerness and dread to the fourth season of her royal liaison. Each morning she inspected herself carefully in the glass. Her body was flawless still. So were the even gleaming teeth, something rare in married women over twenty—and every knowing gentleman looked a horse or a woman in the mouth. But there was no denying a small sag of flesh under the firm little chin, a slackening of that white skin at the throat, and lines beginning to show about the eyes that stared back from the mirror. Worse than all that, for the past year Prue had been finding and plucking gray hairs from that soft brown fall about her shoulders. One morning she wept.

"What's the matter?" Prue snapped.

"I'm getting old."

"Fiddle! You don't look half your age."

"I do, I'll soon look all of it—and I'm nearly forty-four!"

"Who knows that? Stop fidgeting while I brush this tangle out. You're thinking of your prince, I suppose."

"Yes."

Prue sniffed. "You're too good for the likes of him any day of the week. And that hell-gate Dyott too. What a pair! Come summer and the two of 'em will be bouncing in and out again, and ordering us about like chambermaids."

"They're just selfish. All young men are. It's something a woman has to put up with."

Another sniff. "Well, stop crying, do. It's bad for your looks. You've just got a fit of the mopes, that's all. You're as lovely as ever—you keep that in mind and stop adding up your birthdays. What men don't know won't hurt 'em. They're all fools anyway."

The remark came back into Fannie's mind on All Fools' Day, when there was a sudden rumble from the batteries. She tried to count the reports, but it was impossible in the jumbled chorus of actual guns and the *bang-clop-bang-clop* of echoes in the harbor. It seemed long enough to be a royal salute. The Prince? Impossible! He was not due from the Caribbean until June at the earliest. Two hours later Johnnie came in, with a sardonic glance, "I suppose you know the *Andromeda's* here?"

"What!"

"In fact I met the Prince himself, as I was stepping out of the Crown Lands office."

"What did he say?"

"He looked me up and down and said, 'Well, my dear Governor, you're in town, I see?' And then he asked me very politely how I was, and how my lady was, and passed on without another word. Unfortunate, wasn't it?"

She felt a chill at the heart. "What on earth's he doing here, at this season, when there's still deep snow in the woods? The squadron never leaves Jamaica till summer."

Johnnie did not miss the unconscious irony of that "deep snow in the woods," but he went on calmly, "There's a rumor in the street, from his boat's crew, I suppose, that he's on his way to England, that he had a squabble with his superiors down

427

there and sailed north on the spur of the moment. And something else."

"What?"

"This part's no rumor. There's news from England. The King's ill—in fact he's mad. If he doesn't recover, that means a board of regency, with the Prince of Wales at the head of it."

"What's that got to do with William?"

"Everything, my dear. He was sent abroad on his father's orders, to put him away from his brothers' influence. Now he can go home to join 'em. A board of regency's bound to include Prince Frederick and Prince William. And the Prince of Wales will see that William gets his dukedom and a grant from Parliament. So Billy can quit the Navy at last. He's always resented being shoved abroad like a naughty boy. I daresay that's what made him so wild and erratic on this station—if you'll forgive me. I refer of course to his other aberrations, not to you."

She was silent.

"Do you wish me to disappear?" he said. "This warm weather's made the roads almost impassable—the frost coming out of the ground—but I could remove as far as the Cell."

With a shrug that was almost a shiver Fannie said, "I'm afraid it doesn't matter, if what you say is true. His mind's full of England now. He'll be off as soon as he can get his ship refitted for the voyage."

A week passed with *Andromeda* lying at the dockyard quay. The Prince abolished all official receptions, dining privately with the Governor, the Commissioner of the Dockyard and no more. He made no appearance in his old haunts. Even Dyott had no word from him. But at the last, on the day before he sailed, a naval servant brought a card to the house in the Mall. It was written by William's secretary, and it invited Mr. and Mrs. John Wentworth to a dance and supper aboard *Andromeda* tonight at seven.

Half an hour after sunset the Wentworth phaeton drew toward the Dockyard in a little train of carriages. Their lamps flickered and bobbed like the eyes of drunken cats along the miry road from town. At the quayside, in the light cast by a cluster of lanterns, Johnnie sprang down and handed out his lady. He was in blue velvet, with his hair powdered and clubbed, and his erect figure and the bronzed face under the white hair gave him a distinction not to be missed. Fannie was proud of him. She took his arm and moved toward the ship's gangway with the air of a duchess.

She had been at her toilet without cease from the moment the card arrived. She had put on and discarded gown after gown, studying herself from every angle in the mirrors, walking away and coming back again. She had made Prue arrange her hair in various ways before the powdering, each of which took infinite care and patience. And so it was with shoes and stockings and gloves and headgear. She had nearly driven Prue mad. The dress of her final choice had a modest *décolleté*, a shimmering green silk body and train festooned with delicate lilacs, and the front looped to show a dark green tiffany petticoat. On the snow of her powdered hair sat a cap of small green feathers. Her pearls were at her throat and ears and in her hair. And on one finger, plain to be seen, was her wedding ring.

The Prince's carpenters must have been busy for days. *Andromeda's* quarter-deck was divided at the mizzenmast by a partition of hung flags. The deck from there to the mainmast had been prepared for dancing. Behind the flags were concealed the supper tables. The whole of this area had been covered by walls and a roof of wood and canvas, festooned inside with panels of white and blue cloth. Rows of borrowed sofas instead of cannon lined the bulwarks, and seven musicians were perched on a staging overhead.

Captain Guelph stood with his officers just beyond the gangway head, receiving the guests as his boatswains piped them aboard. He acknowledged Johnnie's bow and Fannie's curtsy with an easy impersonal smile and a nod, precisely as he greeted the others. As they passed into the canvas ballroom the glow of dozens of small colored lampions overhead made it like a little Ranelagh. Fannie looked about her carefully. Including the

Prince's officers about sixty people were chatting and circulating slowly under the lights. She beheld the cream of Halifax society in assembly at last. Apart from government officials and their wives they were all "tradespeople," merchants in fish, in lumber, in West India stuffs, in wines and spirits, in dry provisions, whale oil, and ironmongery. Some of the men seemed to be at ease in gold-laced coats and embroidered waistcoats and silk tights and stockings. Some of the ladies looked well in silks and flounces and laces of all the proper hues. But these were exceptions. Most of the men were awkward in ill-fitting finery, like lubberly boys obliged to wash and dress for church. And their ladies were amazing. What a riot of vulgar colors, of loops and bunches and ribbons arranged in what their dressmakers considered the height of fashion—the height of five years past! And what coiffures! Hair done in mountains, with plumes nodding and waving from the peaks, like the fume-clouds of impossible volcanoes, and the whole prinked with ribbons and beads and brooches as if a ped-dler's pack had been shaken over their heads!

Fannie looked them over with contempt and received their hard glances in return. A veritable muster of her foes. It had been deliberate, then. Had William invited her here, at this last mo-ment, for the humor of seeing her cut in public by the people she hated most? Or would he make a point of favoring her with his attention, to show them all—now that it did not matter any more—where she stood in his regard? He was capable of any-thing. The Brinleys were there, and the colonels and senior ma-jors of the regiments and their wives, with whom she was on friendly terms, but she was aware of female daggers right and left, and behind her smile she was tortured with anxiety.

After an hour of the general chatter the Prince gave a signal, and the musicians struck up. There was not room for more than one set to dance at a time. The tune was for "Country Bumpkin," his favorite, which he danced indefatigably with the prettiest ladies at every ball. He chose six now, a delighted Fannie among them, but casually he went on to select half a dozen gentlemen for the set and retired to watch. And so it went through the evening. William did not dance a step, but he saw that everyone else did. He was sober, smiling, courteous, the perfect host. And his alert blue gaze was everywhere. If anyone thought of cutting Mrs. Wentworth they dared not try it. Whenever the conversation on the sofas flagged, wherever there was a tendency to draw apart, Prince William was there with his hearty little quips and his commanding eye to set things right again. The dancers swept back and forth, and twirled and bowed, and one set followed another as the musicians went on from "Country Bumpkin" to "Tarleton's Delight," and "The Little Ploughboy," and "I've Kissed and I've Tattled," and the other tunes in their repertoire.

At one o'clock in the morning a pair of midshipmen pulled briskly on the halyards of the flag partition and drew it up to the roof, revealing the supper room. A yammer of Ohs and Ahs arose at the decorations, notably a large transparent painting of Saint George's Cross and the Garter, lit by a lamp behind, and another of the Scottish thistle and motto. The tables formed a horseshoe, with a feast of cold meats and fowl of every kind from joints of Windsor beef to platters of partridge breasts, of wines from hock to port, and a magnificent display of pastries and sweetmeats.

The Prince sat at the head of the horseshoe and called the toasts himself, a discreet little list with only one bumper, to His Majesty the King. And although many of the provincial gentlemen applied themselves thirstily to the wines thereafter, especially to the Prince's champagne, their host touched little of anything. His chief steward hovered behind him, and with curt little commands tossed over his shoulder William directed the crew of waiters, watching everything about the table, like an admiral directing a fleet in action.

In an hour he arose, and the company sprang up hastily and followed him to the dance again. By three o'clock, however, some of the gentlemen were showing signs of the champagne, and their ladies decided it was time to go. The Prince moved with his officers once more to the gangway head, and the company made their farewells. It was a long business. When the slowly moving line brought Fannie to her host he seemed a little weary of the whole affair, but his politeness was unshaken. Her eyes were bright with gratitude and something close to tears as she curtsied and arose. But she found his eyes impersonal, as they had been throughout the evening. He said exactly what he was saying to the rest, "Good-by, my dear lady, I trust that we may meet again." Then she was past, and Johnnie was making his bow.

It had been warm in the canvas ballroom, but the April night outside had a chill breath of the snows that lingered still in the woods. Fannie shivered all the way home in spite of her fur cloak, and once indoors she went straight to the fire, pulling up her skirts to warm her legs. She did not feel sleepy in the least. When Johnnie came in from the stable she said over her shoulder, "Did he seem strange to you—the Prince?"

"I'm afraid I haven't seen enough of him to judge. Unless you mean it was strange to see him sober and well-mannered."

"That's nasty."

"Well, I suppose he wanted to show everyone that he could play the proper Prince and gentleman, in spite of all his other antics. I daresay he's all right at heart. The trouble with him is his spirit and brains. He's got too much of one and not enough of the other. If he were in ordinary life he'd have had a lot of the nonsense knocked out of him before he reached twenty-three. As a prince of the blood everyone's been too eager to indulge and spoil him."

"Is that a thrust at me?"

"My dear, we settled that last fall."

"It was kind of him to ask us, don't you think?"

"You're the best judge of that, my dear. He owed you something, after all. Don't be offended. As I said once before, gratitude's not a common trait with kings and princes, and I suppose a little thing like this must mean a good deal to you."

She tossed her head, and Johnnie went off to bed. Now that the first glow of the evening had gone she was dissatisfied. William! It wouldn't have hurt him to give me some little recognition in front of those others—since he'd gone far enough to invite me. He could have danced with me. He could at least have held some talk with me. I wonder if that was why he didn't dance or talk with anyone especially? Because he didn't want to be put to the test?

She went up the stairs in a discontented mood, and lay awake going over it all again. It was long before she dozed away, and she did not awaken until the noon gun from the Citadel clapped over the downtown roofs. Prue brought her tea and bread and butter. She drank the tea and ignored the rest. Now that it was all over, the whole affair that began nearly three years ago, she felt drained in body and spirit.

"Draw the shades again, Prue, and leave me. I shan't get up today."

Late in the afternoon the long thudding of the guns began. He was leaving. Leaving forever, and picturing to himself, as she could picture all too well, the merry round of London's *ton* with his brothers. What was one woman in his madcap life? No more than a bottle tasted and pitched aside. She found herself sniveling and was angry that she could care that much. In the evening Prue tiptoed into the chamber.

"Are you awake? Lieutenant Broadhurst came."

"Send him away. I won't see anyone, least of all a man. If I don't see another of those ungrateful creatures in a twelvemonth it will be a happy year."

"I'll believe that when I see it. Anyhow, Mr. Broadhurst has gone. He just came to leave this package. Said he'd been charged to deliver it to you."

"A very stupid way of getting a billet-doux to me. Light another candle and open the thing if you like. It won't do him a bit of good."

She lay with her eyes closed against the light. Her head ached miserably. She could hear Prue breaking sealing wax and rustling paper.

"Well?" she said.

"Look!"

Fannie turned her head and saw a large enameled locket dangling on a thin gold chain. She sat up with a bounce, all headache gone. She seized the locket from Prue and opened the catch with twitching fingers. And there she saw William, a head-and-shoulders portrait done by some English miniaturist years ago, when he was seventeen or so; the familiar coconut pointed at the chin and the back of the head, the yellow hair, the dimpled chin, the full-lipped avid mouth, the nose hooked at the tip, the pink cheeks, the wide blue eyes. The locket lid held a scrap of paper with four penciled words, laboriously small. "For kindness, a remembrance."

THIRTY-FOUR

M~R. WENTWORTH~ selected a quill, trimmed the point with his penknife, dipped it in the ink, made some preliminary twirls, and began a letter to the Reverend Jeremy Belknap.

> Friar Laurence's Cell,
> Near Halifax,
> May 15, 1791

Dear Sir,

It is a long time since I have rec'd such sincere pleasure as your letter has given me. I was much pleas'd on hearing you were continuing the history of New Hampshire, having rec'd so much satisfaction from the first volume, and being myself more interested in the two next. I herewith send you the papers you desire, as far as I can find them. Most of my papers were destroy'd during the late tumults. Their loss is now particularly regretted as they might have been useful to you.

I now declare to you, in private friendship, that on a review of all my public conduct to this day, I acted with zeal for the King's service and the real good of his subjects, which I always did and do now think were inseparable. Nor did I ever know any intentions to impose arbitrary laws on America, or to establish any system repugnant to British liberty; and I do verily believe that had the true, wise, and open measures been embraced on both sides, that their union would have been many years establish'd and their prosperity wonderfully increas'd.

Their independence having been consented to by the Government which entrusted me with its powers, I most cordially wish the most extensive, great, and permanent blessings to the United States. If there is anything partial to my heart in this case, it is that New Hampshire, my native country, may arise to be among the most brilliant members of the confederation, as it was my zealous wish to have led her while under my administration.

With the most cordial good wishes I am, dear sir,

Your Obed't Serv't,

J. Wentworth

Johnnie laid down the pen and slouched in the chair, brooding. The old letters and documents brought back all the memories. Four-and-twenty years ago he had arrived in Portsmouth as the new Governor, with the applause of the whole province. Sixteen years ago he had fled, a fugitive with scarcely a soul to raise voice or hand in his defense. And now he was just a page or two of history. A relic of the past at fifty-five!

For there was nothing now. Indeed, looking back, he could see nothing in his life from the moment he fled Portsmouth. The dreary emptiness had set in then. The corroding idleness at Boston, Long Island, and then in England. And nearly eight years of this existence in Nova Scotia, with even his private honor gone into the shadows with Fannie's lovers. What was there to show for it all? On one hand the bundle of New Hampshire documents, the last mark of a time when he was a proud and happy man, the most popular and the best of royal Governors in America. On the other hand—he glanced at them with distaste—a stack of bills, dishonored drafts, and dunning letters, the history of his exile, one long record of failure.

In a moment of self-pity it seemed to him that his fortunes had begun to change for the worse when he yielded to temptation in the Portsmouth garden, all those years ago. But pshaw!— that was what Adam said, wasn't it? And what was the truth or even the use of blaming Eve? She couldn't help being what she was, made as she was. You had to get along with her and with the serpent somehow, even in the wilderness. And even the serpent was getting weary now. A little over two years ago Fannie's prince had sailed away to England forever, and within a few more months the gay companion Dyott had marched with his company to a fort on the other side of the province. Dyott still appeared in town on leave at long intervals, and dined in polite cheer at the Wentworth house and at Brinleys', but the rest of his leave was passed in revel with gay dogs of the garrison and the ladies of "the hill."

Fannie herself had changed. She still kept herself the best-dressed woman in Halifax, and, although she did not like the saddle any more, she still drove about in her carriage and drew the company of the younger puppies in scarlet and blue. But there was something a little sad about these gestures. She had a haunted look, as if the secret spring of her youth were failing at last and she could not bring herself to admit it.

Johnnie's eyes came back to the bills and duns. He took a silver dollar from his pocket, chose heads, and spun the coin in air. Heads it was. Very well! He locked the cottage door, taking only the letter and the bundle for the Reverend Jeremy, and went slowly down the steps to his horse, tethered in the trees below. In another minute he was trotting along the road to town. It was a bright spring day. The birches about the cove were just breaking into leaf, and on the farther hillsides the white bloom of Indian pear made patches like snow. Beside the road the dandelions were showing, and in the shade of the trees in low places the white and blue of violets, and in sunny places the bank was spangled with white blossoms of wild strawberry. The trees swallows were back from the south and busy nesting, and there was a music of sparrows and bobolinks, and robins were everywhere.

As the road climbed to the lip of the plateau above Bedford Basin he halted beside the tottering ruin of a blockhouse, built to defend the rear approach to Halifax in a time long gone. There was a broad view of the Basin, blue and sparkling in the green bowl of hills. It was like standing under the big pine on Mount Delight and looking at the beloved lake in the hills of Wolfeborough. God, to be back there again, with all these dreary years nothing but a mince-pie dream!

When he reached home Fannie was lying down in her chamber with the shades drawn. She did this nowadays whenever she returned from an excursion in the company of her cavaliers, like an actress tired by her performance under the eyes of the crowd. Her chamber door was open, and he paused there.

"May I speak to you for a few minutes, my dear? I don't like to disturb you, but it's a confidential matter of some importance."

"Very well. Come in and shut the door."

The sunlight through the crimson shades made a deep rosy light in the room, and Fannie lay in it like an elegant corpse. He sat in a chair and crossed his knees, gazing down at the lifted riding boot and spinning the rowel of the spur with a finger.

"It's the matter of money," he said.

"Oh, that again!"

"Yes, that. My dear, I'm afraid we're at the end of the tether. My creditors have got together, and I can't put them off any more. Some of my notes go back years. They threaten to clap me into jail."

"Fiddlesticks! Those tradespeople always do."

"They mean it now. Apart from anything else, a good deal of my paper is in the hands of certain merchants in the town— the ones whose ladies you despise. I'll get no mercy there."

"Bah! Now you want to blame me for your own incapacity, and I won't have it, Johnnie. What did you do with all that money you got from your loyalist claim?"

"The government reduced my claim to five thousand pounds and paid me that two years ago. Every penny went as payment on the principal and interest of my debts and to support this house—your carriage and ponies alone cost £200 a year, d'you realize that?—and of course the milliners and dressmakers who wouldn't do another stitch for you without pay."

"And what about your own tailors and saddlers and bootmakers, and the rest? More important, what about all the debts you've run up on behalf of Paul Wentworth—the slaves, the cargoes of timber and fish, and heaven knows what else—all the things he's asked you to send to Surinam? You've always refused to dun him. What does he owe you?"

"Four thousand pounds or more."

"Ah! And what are your debts altogether?"

"Close to double that."

"Very well. Draw on Paul and pay your creditors the four thousand. That will satisfy them for another year or two. Why do you bother me when it's all so simple?"

She turned on the bed and presented her back, the familiar attitude.

"For your information, Fan, I drew on Paul for the full amount last year. When the spring mails came I found my draft dishonored. There was no explanation, but a friend in London gave me a bit of gossip. As you know, Paul's been very intimate in Paris for years, and since the American war he's had more luck there with his speculations than in London. In short, his interests are more French than English, though he still travels back and forth."

"Well?"

"May I remind you that the French have been in a state of revolution for the past two years? With their king and queen held practically as prisoners?"

"And serve their damned king and queen right. That's what they get for helping rebels in America."

"Maybe. Paul remembers the American revolution too. He remembers who came out on top. So for the past two years he's been playing his hand with the revolutionary committees in Paris. For his own purposes, naturally. But that makes him suspect in England."

"Why?"

"You should read the newspapers now and then, my dear. The King and the Tory party fear a revolution in England. It's their bogey. They're arresting all sorts of people and putting 'em on trial for treason, on the least excuse."

"What's all this got to do with your debts?"

Johnnie sighed and fingered the spur again. "I must find what's happened to Paul. I must get that four thousand pounds. In the meantime I must get out of Nova Scotia. Otherwise I shall find myself imprisoned for debt. The law of the land applies to me the same as the poorest cobbler in the town. My creditors can throw me into jail and keep me there at their pleasure, so long as they supply me one pound of hard biscuit every day. And what would become of you?"

Fannie was sitting up now and staring, as if behind him she could see all her she-enemies gloating. She put her hands to her face and drew the fingertips slowly down to her chin, as if to erase the picture.

"So we must run away? How I hate to give those cats the satisfaction! But I confess there's nothing else to do. And heaven knows I've nothing else to hold me here. I've always hated the place. It'll be something to see England again and the Fitz-Williams and our other friends—and young Charlie of course. How soon do we go, and how?"

Johnnie said, "You understand of course we'll come back here if I can get the money from Paul. Otherwise I must throw up my post along with everything else. I've thought it all out carefully. We'll take the first ship for England. Prue shall stay and give out word that I've got leave to go to London, that we've gone to see our boy, and we'll be back next year. Our establishment will remain exactly as it is, and I'll leave Prue enough money to keep it going for a year."

"But I can't get along without Prue for a year—even for a month!"

"You'll have to. She's the only person I can trust to keep up appearances here. Otherwise my creditors will seize the place and sell up all we've got. As it is, they'll hold their hands. I've told 'em I have a large sum owing to me over there. And besides, they'll figure I won't throw up a post worth £800 a year here. The present notion is to throw me into jail for a time. Then, when I'm desperate enough, I'll assign the whole of my salary as Surveyor General to the payment of my debts. They know I get a pension of £300 a year besides, and as far as they're concerned we can damned well live on it."

"Like a pair of church mice! How they'd love that!" Fannie

reflected for a few moments. "What if you can't collect from Paul?"

"Then we'll send for Prue and abandon everything here. We'll cast ourselves on our English friends, and then perhaps FitzWilliam will find a post for me in some other colony—there's no hope of one in England."

She sprang off the bed and threw back the curtains, gazing with a sudden animation as if England lay just at the end of the Mall.

"London! London again! Huzza! Set about it as quick as you can, Johnnie! I can hardly wait—I can't wait at all!"

THIRTY-FIVE

So it was London again, after seven years for Fannie, and for Johnnie eight. They put up at a genteel lodginghouse in Clarges Street, and at once Fannie insisted on driving about in a hired carriage, drinking in all the old impressions as if she had never seen the town before. The handsome houses and churches—not a wooden building to be seen—the rich goods in the shops, the fashionable customers stepping in and out of chairs and carriages, the lively hubbub of voices and feet and wheels, all the familiar things. Even the lesser folk delighted her eye: the piemen and the nosegay girls, the chimney sweeps, the milkmaids with tubs and measures balanced on their heads, the knife grinders, the butchers and bakers, the crossing sweepers, the paving gangs, the oysterwomen crying their wares, the soldiers on horseback and afoot, the sailors from Wapping, the beggars blind or crippled; and in side streets here and there a laughing group about a puppet show or a pair of tumblers or a juggler. Hyde Park's trees and fields looked the same as ever, although the riders of the *ton* wore another fashion now, and passing views of Ranelagh and the Pantheon called up all the old exciting memories.

The next day they went to see Charles-Mary. At the Westminster School they were ushered into a musty little sitting room with India curtains and hard chairs and a badly worn sofa, and after a time one of the masters, a lean suave man in a blue coat and scratch wig, brought the boy to them. Fannie was prepared to rush at him with a glad cry, throwing her arms about him and smothering his face with kisses. But at sight of him the notion perished. Charlie was tall for sixteen—taller than Johnnie himself—and slim in brown velvet coat and breeches. His brown hair, gathered in a neat club at the nape, had the soft shine that comes of careful daily brushing. He had his father's large gray eyes but nothing else that was Johnnie's. The face was pale, the mouth soft, even weak, and he walked with a peculiar grace and made little girlish gestures as he talked.

He gave them a limp hand to shake, regarding first Johnnie and then his mother with a well-bred curiosity but no visible affection. He seemed concerned that he was missing an important Greek lesson. He mentioned that he was in the top form at the school and that next year he expected to go on to Oxford. He spoke of his high marks and said that Lord FitzWilliam had invited him to be his secretary when he came down from Oxford. The ivory face lit when he said this, and it was the only emotion he displayed. When they left at the end of half an hour Johnnie said, a little heavily, "He's grown a nice lad. A scholar, every inch of him."

"Yes," Fannie said. Her son was not what she had expected. Charles-Mary seemed not quite so much Charles as Mary. An exquisite creature of course. Such beautiful speech and manners. She could display him for a time when he came down from Oxford, the very model of a well-bred young Englishman. She would be fifty then—no more nonsense with men—and they would make a striking pair, the pretty youth and the handsome mother who could not be much more than forty, with Johnnie gray and distinguished in the background.

Charles-Mary's father had his own thoughts. He retained his old affection for the boy, but he was disappointed. All this time he had pictured Charlie as he had been himself at that age, eager to grapple with the world, and with an eye for a gun or a horse, as well as for books and pens. He tried now to picture Charles-Mary in the American woods, and his imagination failed. He could not even picture Charles-Mary taking a wife and siring boys to carry on his name. In fact Charlie seemed a changeling, not at all the boy of whom he had written so long ago, "he'll do to pull up stumps at Wentworth House."

If the renewed acquaintance with their son had proved a surprise, a visit to Hammersmith, expecting to see Paul, gave them quite another. They found Brandenburg House in the hands of strangers. All they could discover was that Mr. Paul Wentworth had got into trouble as a suspected radical on this side of the Channel and as a suspected English spy on the other, and that he had sold up everything in a hurry last year and gone away "to some wild place in South America."

That could only mean Surinam. So Paul had retired to the plantation that he had preserved and built up all these years. It seemed good sense, as Johnnie observed.

"Paul's sixty-odd. He lived some years in Surinam long ago, and no doubt he's always planned to retire there. No fogs, no winters, nothing but ease and sunshine. It's strange, though, that he didn't write to me about all this."

"Letters get lost," Fannie said hopefully.

As soon as they got back to Clarges Street Johnnie sat down and wrote a long and urgent letter to Surinam. He fretted at the delay. It would take at least six months to get a reply and possibly a year. In the meantime he could only trust that Paul would realize his straits and pay the old account promptly.

At the end of the week they left for Yorkshire, and there at all events found what they had expected. The green sprawl of the park, the stately pile of Wentworth Woodhouse, the settled air of quiet luxury that centuries could not change, and best of all the delighted welcome of the FitzWilliams. It was the happiest of reunions. They were given the same apartment, and within a few days they had slipped into the old pleasant Woodhouse round of country balls and parties and race meetings, and carriage tours of the countryside when there was sunny weather. In this easy fashion the summer passed into autumn, and the autumn fled.

When November came they prepared to return to London for the winter. So far Johnnie had said nothing of his plight, and the noble lord had not mentioned the old dead subject of a post in England. On the evening before they left Johnnie took the plunge. Dinner was over, and the ladies had withdrawn, leaving their men to the port and walnuts. Johnnie told his story simply, ending with, "You understand, my lord, I'm not seeking a loan. Far from it. I have too great a debt of gratitude to you as it is. And as I've said, Mr. Paul Wentworth can relieve me of much anxiety on this matter of money. But my problem in Nova Scotia remains the same, even if my old debts were extinguished. The income from my present post isn't enough to make ends meet. In another two or three years I shall be in trouble again. The only remedy is a more lucrative post—and it doesn't matter where."

His Lordship looked embarrassed. "I fear, my friend, that I can't do any more for you now than I've been able to do since you left for Nova Scotia. The Tories remain in power, and all the government patronage lies in their hands. The Whigs are too divided ever to upset them." He hesitated. "I don't mind telling you that I'm somewhat in your position myself. I can't content myself with a vegetating life on these properties. My uncle always sought public service, and I'm of the same mind. I speak from my seat in the Lords, naturally, but the speeches of Whig lords nowadays are just a whistling down the wind. I feel there should be some use for my abilities in the government of this country. I feel myself out of sympathy with many of the Whigs; they're too full of this French republicanism for my liking, and I have a growing respect for Mr. Pitt, a very capable young man. I have reason to believe he regards me as one Whig of ability and sound principles."

He took a walnut from the bowl and cracked it with great care, as if it were a problem. "This revolution in France—an evil business to have just across the Channel. Paris seems to be in the hands of madmen, and their affairs go rapidly from bad to worse. Unless I mistake the signs we shall see something frightful there in a year or two, and the men in charge will start a war with us merely to distract their own populace. Our government's taking military precautions, as perhaps you know. Now, my dear sir, if war should come, all Englishmen must unite. Mr. Pitt knows that as well as anyone. And in that case I may be offered a post in his cabinet. I have no more than a hint, but we shall see. If that happens I shall be in a position to do something for you. In the meantime I can only wait, and so must you."

When Johnnie repeated this conversation to Fannie on the road to London she gave an impatient "Humph!" And then, "If-if-if! I'm sick of If! There's only one thing to do. I'll go to see Prince William."

"My dear, your friend William has turned Whig, like his brothers, just for the sake of kicking up his heels. He has no more influence on the present government than an Indian in the wilds of Nova Scotia. What's more, the King recovered from his fit of madness long ago. There's no question of a board of regency, with or without your friend."

"I don't care two pins!" Fannie cried. "William got himself made Duke of Clarence, with a grant of £12,000 from this precious government, didn't he? So he has influence, never fear. Lady Charlotte tells me he's still the favorite son of the King and Queen. And that's enough. We have a voice at court if we care to use it, and William owes us a word or two—as well you know."

As soon as they reached Clarges Street, Fannie began inquiries. Prince William, it appeared, was living at Petersham Lodge in Richmond Park, a nine mile drive outside the town. Johnnie had some acid detail.

"Your royal friend didn't waste much time after that last dance at Halifax. He crammed on sail and got to Spithead in three weeks—a mighty smart passage on the eastward run in April weather, even for a frigate with a lot of hands and canvas. Soon after he reached London he was briskly engaged with—um—the larboard watch, in particular a Miss Polly Finch, I believe. And that same fall he bought Petersham Lodge and set up housekeeping with her there."

Fannie's lips tightened. She refused to be discouraged. She had a new daydream of meeting William somewhere, at Ranelagh say, and skipping off with him to a cozy rendezvous in town, as she had with the Horse Guard long ago.

"He must come up to town sometimes," she said.

"Oh, yes indeed, my dear. Miss Finch, it seems, has served her turn and been dismissed. For the past several months he's been wooing a Mrs. Jordan, an actress at Drury Lane."

A few nights later they sat in a box at Drury Lane, in the second tier, and close to the stage. It had cost precious money, but Fannie insisted. Curious to see William's current taste in women she had armed herself with a borrowed opera glass, and she sat impatiently waiting for the curtain to go up. The boxes on both sides of the house were filled with lively members of the *ton*, a new *ton* in which she could not recognize a single face. Johnnie regarded them with a slow contempt. A lot of patent whores, and fops with quizzing glasses, some of the men with their hair unpowdered and cut off at the nape, imitating the new fashion of the French republicans. It was more interesting to watch the squirming commonality down there in the pit.

Before long Fannie noticed a titter and a craning and passing of opera glasses in the adjoining box, where two young officers of the Coldstream Guards sat with a pair of painted creatures wearing a droll travesty of the Quaker dress. She turned her own glass in the direction of their amusement and found the cause at once, a long rent in the stage curtain near the hither end. In the oblique view from these boxes there was an odd little peep show through the gap. Prince William—there was no mistaking that head—stood chatting and joking with an actress composing herself in a chair. Other members of the cast were moving about, getting themselves placed for the opening scene, and Fannie could not get a good look at the woman.

One of the pseudo-Quaker ladies, seeing her interest, leaned over with a confidential wink. "Sailor Billy and Dolly Jordan—he drives her up to town himself, every performance. D'you know her?"

"No."

Another wink. "She has five little tokens of her old affairs, but that don't bother Billy a bit. He's got the whole brood out at Richmond with him—ever since October. And he's had no money so far from his Parliament grant. So the question is—does he keep her, or does she keep him?"

Another gale of laughter from the other box. But now William disappeared from view, and in another minute the curtain rose, and the play began. It was a comedy, but Fannie had no mind for humor or the plot. Throughout the performance she saw nothing but Billy's fancy, a creature of voluptuous flesh, bouncing on and off the stage, now in skirts and now in tights, speaking her lines in an undisguised Irish brogue and sending the audience into roars of laughter. She was anything but pretty, but she had a bubbling sense of fun that passed easily across the footlights to the crowd.

As they came away Johnnie murmured, "Well, what do you think of your successor?"

"She's fat and vulgar."

"I heard someone say she's the best comedy actress since Kitty Clive."

"She must be thirty if she's a day."

"Ah, that sounds familiar. And William's now, what, six-and-twenty? Not a boy any more. D'you still think of going to Richmond for an interview?"

"With that creature there? Impossible!"

At Christmas they journeyed out to the village of Hope, in Hereford, to spend the holidays with Benning and his pretty English wife and children. The erstwhile captain of loyalist volunteers had found an Oxford education of no help in getting suitable employment. He was living very modestly on his half-pay and an allowance from his father-in-law, hoping year after year for a government appointment that never came, like so many others.

He had some small news of the loyalist refugees in England. Most of them had scattered away from the expensive living in London and vanished into the countryside like himself, or gone back to North America. Old Colonel Boyd had returned to New Hampshire, tombstone and all, and was buried under it not long after. Robert Rogers, that hopeless sot, had vanished in the London stews. Young Ben Thompson alone seemed to flourish in foreign air. Soon after Johnnie saw him last Ben had entered the service of Prince Maximilian of Bavaria, and applied his many-sided genius so well that he was now Grand Chamberlain with almost supreme authority over the whole state.

"He always makes a first-rate job of everything he does," said Benning with enthusiasm. "By God, he's marvelous, and all Europe knows it, not to mention Britain. This year he was made a Count of the Holy Roman Empire. And chose his title from his wife's place in New England too. Count Rumford, if you please. How's that for a Yankee boy abroad?"

"Maybe we should all move to Bavaria," said Johnnie with heavy humor. "Here we seem to be just the discounts of the lowly British Empire."

In the dark days toward the end of December he and Fannie returned to their chilly lodging in Clarges Street. A few doors away a pair of servants were helping a crippled female into a coach. She was well dressed, and it was pitiful to see her moving with crutches and dragging her almost helpless feet. Her face in side view appeared to be that of a pretty woman in the mid-thirties, and there was something oddly familiar about it. Johnnie had gone inside, and their landlord stood holding the door.

"Who's that?" Fannie said.

"Eh, ma'am? Oh, her! That's the famous Missus Robinson. She lives there. She had a rheumatic fever some time back that crippled her legs."

"What! Perdita?"

The man chuckled. The coach was just driving away. "Ay, there's some still call her that, though she ain't been on the stage for years. They say she still gets a small allowance from the Prince of Wales—him they called Florizel—though she's lived the past ten years with Colonel Tarleton. She'll need that money now."

"Why?"

"Tarleton's left her." Again the irritating chuckle. "They all come to the one end, them affairs. Another pretty face and off he goes, with not so much as a thankee."

Fannie stalked inside wrathfully. She had fancied herself so often as another Perdita, the darling of gallant soldiers and a prince, that this revelation was like a sharp needle in the heart. Men! What ingrates! What cruel selfish animals, the whole lot of them!

In their chamber she found Johnnie with an open letter in his hand and a face as gray as the winter sky. He glanced up, crushed the sheets into a ball, and flung it across the room.

"From Paul—he can't pay me a penny. Says his money's tied up in the plantation, and no getting anything out of it in these hard times. Assures me my investment's safe, of course, and hints delicately about all the money he let us have in time past."

"He would!"

"So, you see, we can't go back to Nova Scotia. I've simply nothing for my creditors."

"Whatever shall we do?"

Johnnie shrugged and went to the window. Not far away, at the end of Clarges Street, he could hear the rattle of Piccadilly. "There's a letter for you. From Prue, I think. The address looks like her hand."

"Poor Prue! We can't afford her passage here now, let alone her wages. How shall we ever tell her?"

She broke the wax and unfolded the single sheet slowly. Johnnie heard a gasp.

He turned and saw Fannie's pale face lit from within, like one of those transparencies at the dance aboard *Andromeda,* but her voice seemed almost lost. Her lips moved, and he heard a hoarse and rapid whisper.

"Johnnie! Johnnie, he's gone—he died of a stroke five weeks ago!"

"Who?"

She had found her full voice now, and the words rang in the room like a war whoop. "Old Parr—Governor Parr!"

THIRTY-SIX

SNOW was falling in large flakes, without a wind, settling like scraps of swansdown on the wayside roofs and fields, even putting a white skin on the deep mud where the post chaise plunged and wallowed. It might have been a New Year's Day in New England except that the cold was a damp and miserable kind, nothing like the tingling frost of America. The trees stood black and bare, except for the white snow-tippets along the branches. The hedgerows wore the tippets, too, and the tops of the walls about fields and gardens. Sometimes there was a glimpse of the Thames flowing like molten lead between the pure white banks. The houses and villas along the riverside, always so charming in the summer greenery, had a grim besieged look now; the smoke from their chimneys told a tale of urgent fires and busy scuttles and bellows, and nobody seemed to be abroad.

The driver's brown greatcoat had several overlapping shoulder capes. He sat huddled in it like the top of a monstrous pine cone, with a wool scarf bound over the crushed cocks of his hat and tied in a great knot beneath his chin. Inside, Fannie sat bracing herself against the heaving of the chaise. She had a new cloak with a tall calash hood, stiffened by whalebones to protect her headgear. It was of good cloth, but she wished heartily for the fur cloak left behind in Nova Scotia. The nine miles seemed endless, and when the chaise reached Richmond Park the bristle of naked trees in acres of snow might have been a hard-wood forest in the wilds of Canada.

The driver turned into a private carriageway and pulled up at last. To right and left a high stone wall shut off all view except the upper tangle of trees, but through the intricate ironwork of the gate Fannie could see a brick villa half masked and half exposed by barren shrubbery. There was a small gatehouse, and the door opened, and a stout man in blue-and-yellow livery stepped out to the post chaise. Fannie had told her driver what to say. The reply came bluntly.

"The Jook don't see nobody, specially ladies in po'-shays."

She opened the window. In a clear voice, using her well-bred English accent to the full, she commanded, "My good man, have the goodness to open the gate and let me through this minute! I am an old friend of His Highness." But the fellow held that stubborn insolent look. He seemed to be used to lone females approaching in just such a way, and clearly he had orders. Thrusting back the cloak, Fannie unclasped and drew from her neck the Prince's locket, the pride of her life, and held it open for his inspection.

"You recognize your master, I trust? Take this to him—him alone, you understand? And say that Mrs. Wentworth—Mrs. Wentworth from Nova Scotia—begs the favor of a word." He took it, with a comical mixture of awe and suspicion on his round moon face, and trotted away up the carriageway. The gate remained barred. After five minutes he came back at the same trot, trampling his own tracks in the snow.

"You may come in, ma'am, but the shay"—there was a rich contempt in his voice for the shabby hired thing—"must stay outside." He admitted her through a little side gate, and Fannie walked up to the house with what dignity she could summon. She was chilled to the bone and disheveled by the long drive on a road at its winter worst, and when a footman opened the door and showed her into a small sitting room she made straight for the fire and the mirror above the mantel.

Almost at once there was a rustle of skirts. In the glass she saw a woman coming into the room. She turned, and they regarded each other. It was Mrs. Jordan. The actress wore a much-embroidered gray silk gown in the new high-waisted fashion, which made a notable parcel of her bosom; the puffed sleeves stopped well above her elbows, and a pair of long gray mittens covered her lower arms and the palms of her hands. The naked fingers glittered with rings, and from one finger, dangling by the chain, hung Fannie's locket.

Dolly Jordan had neither rouge nor powder. Indeed she needed none off the stage, for she had the soft skin and color of an Irishwoman still on the sunny side of thirty. A white mobcap of many ruffles and a large blue bow covered her hair. Fannie could see no beauty in her face. A snub nose, big green eyes, a mouth as broad as her native Liffey. Yet she had that air of animal good spirits which Fannie had noticed at Drury Lane; there was warmth as well as humor in the mouth, and now as she inspected Fannie's pale set face under the hood of the calash a good deal of the hostility went out of her eyes. Fannie could almost hear her shrewdly counting up her years and coming to a reassuring sum.

Without removing her gaze Mrs. Jordan opened the locket, not for the first time, for the little scrap of penciled paper was gone.

"You seem to have found William when he was just a boy," she said. There was a faint note of derision in the brogue.

"Not so long ago," Fannie answered defensively. She saw the disadvantage of her position. This creature had the real William in her fingers just as she held the locket now.

"What do you want to see him about?"

"We—my husband, Mr. Wentworth, and I—had the honor of the Duke's acquaintance in Nova Scotia. He was good enough to make our house his *pied-à-terre* whenever he was ashore, and he left us the little picture as a memento."

"So I see."

"Please—it's Mrs. Jordan, isn't it?—I've come to ask a favor for my husband, not myself. If I could see His Highness for a few minutes. . . ."

"If it's money," the actress said with a laugh, "he hasn't a ha'penny. I can tell you that. The Parl'mint's passed a grant to him, but they're a bit slow with the dibs."

It came to Fannie suddenly that William was not far, that he was probably lurking in earshot, somewhere beyond that open

453

door. She raised her voice to a note of piteous appeal. "Oh, please, please, don't misunderstand. It's the matter of a post for my husband. He sacrificed his position and fortune for the King, in the time of the war in America, and ever since he's had to earn our living in the woods as a surveyor. Summer and winter. You may imagine the hardship. And my poor man's getting old—he's fifty-six."

Without moving a step Fannie seemed to throw herself at the woman's feet. There were two actresses in the room. And now she read a friendly light in Dolly Jordan's green eyes. She had touched the quick Irish sympathy.

"There's something just come vacant," she went on breathlessly. "The Governor's post in Nova Scotia. It's one that my husband could fill very well—he's been a Governor before in America. But you see we have no friends in Parliament. If His Highness could use his influence . . ."

"Ah! Well, he's got a little of that, to be sure. And why not?" Dolly Jordan closed the locket, gave it a little twirl on the chain, and then held it forth. "You may as well keep this," she chuckled. "He'll never look as innocent as that again, I warrant you."

She whirled about and left the room in the swift dancing way she had, on the stage and off. There was a murmur in the hall. Then William walked into the room with his familiar nautical gait, planting the feet well apart as if the floor might heave on a sea at any moment. His cutaway blue coat had a naval shape and plate buttons, opened below the breast to display a bright scarlet waistcoat. In the Whig fashion affected by his brothers he wore tight buff breeches with the coat—to show the party colors.

He had put on fat in the past two or three years in England. With the buff legs and the round red belly and breast he was like a preposterous robin. His big blue eyes were clear. There was nothing of that bloodshot look in the whites which she remembered, the result of those Halifax drinking bouts, and under English skies his face had lost the sunburn of the West Indian winters, which had given his hearty complexion such a purplish cast. His cheeks now were those of a fresh-ripe Devon apple.

"Your Highness," Fannie murmured, and curtsied. He brought his heels together and gave her one of his stiff little bows. "This is an unexpected pleasure, ma'am. Your husband's with you in London, I take it?"

"Oh yes, Your Highness."

"And there's a Governor's post in the offing, eh?"

"Yes, Your Highness."

He sat in a damask armchair and motioned her to another across the little room. By chance it placed her with the window light at her back, leaving her face shadowed in the hood, and she was thankful. She could match her figure against Dolly Jordan's, but she shrank from any comparison with that exquisite skin. She wondered what was passing in William's mind. The locket was still in plain view in her hand. Surely he must be thinking of those three seasons across the sea? She could remember every kiss, every touch of his hands. However rude and greedy he had been, there was a warm autumn haze of romance about those kisses and caresses now. She kept them pressed between the pages of her mind like petals. The great love of her life. And the last, for she would have no other now. She told herself that William had carried off her heart, when what he had really taken was her looks. As if her beauty had kept its fresh appearance through the years for that one supreme affair, and then gone to pieces, like a September rose at the shake of a wandering child.

"Those fellas in the Government," he was saying ponderously. "I've got no influence there, you know. Before they'd let me have my dukedom and make the money allowance, I had to threaten 'em with a broadside at the water line. Fact, I assure you! I said if they were going to keep me a commoner I'd dam' well be a commoner. I told the newspaper fellas I was going to stand for election to Parliament, so I could tell the people of my grievances. I had a seat picked out, too, down in Devonshire at Totnes. And the people would have listened, you may depend. I haven't had a safe and comfortable life, like my brothers. I've served my country in the wars, and at sea, where nothing's ever safe or comfortable. The people know that. I'm not called the Sailor Prince for nothing. Well, the Government couldn't have that, eh? Nor could my father, eh? Never never do! So suddenly I was made Duke of Clarence and Saint Andrews and Earl of Munster—titles I should have had long ago. But that's not what you've come to talk about, eh? Eh? What's happened to old Parr?"

"He's dead of a stroke, Your Highness. We had word a few days ago."

"I see. But you've got other friends to speak for you, eh? I've often heard you mention Lord FitzWilliam, and so forth. But Whigs—Whigs, the lot of 'em. All the oars on one side of the boat. Deuced awkward rowing, that! But of course there's His Majesty. A Tory if one ever lived. That's what's on your mind, eh? Eh?"

"If His Majesty spoke to Mr. Pitt," Fannie said meekly, "and Mr. Pitt put in a word at the Colonial Office . . ."

"Ah! So he might, so he might! Well, let's see, what should I say to His Majesty? Mr. Wentworth's an American gentleman, the former Governor of what d'you call it?—New Hampshire?—yes, of course. Gave up everything for his King, went into exile, and so forth. Long service in Nova Scotia since, looking after His Majesty's forest. Deuced rough business, that. Zounds, I found it rough enough hunting partridge in the edges. And he's getting on—fifty-six, eh? Time he was rewarded. By gad, yes. A governorship at the very least. Nothing's too good for a man like that. Nothing!"

"During the late war," Fannie pursued, without hesitation and in the same small voice, "Lord Germain told Mr. Wentworth he deserved a baronetcy. But of course that was lost sight of when the war ended, like all the promises."

"Oh?" He pondered that for a moment or two. "Well, we must tackle one thing at a time. First thing's this post in Nova Scotia. The rest can follow in due course. Point is, we'll be at war with those damned Frenchmen in a twelvemonth, as sure as you're sitting there. Sea war, mainly. And the French have a station up by Newfoundland; those islands, Saint Pierre and Miquelon, I've seen 'em, right on the way into Canada. Damned dangerous, you know. And there's Halifax, your Governor's seat, the only British naval station left on the whole continent of America—vital, you know, vital! I may be stupid about a lot of things, but I know my own profession, damme. Used to talk over all these things with my friend Captain Nelson—another man I'll see promoted, mark you, when the war begins. Well, there you are. As soon as the shooting starts it'll be time to pull the halyard for a title. It can be done, I give you my word for it. A little patience, and there you are."

As William rattled off these remarks he seemed to keep an ear cocked toward the door. And now, as if at an unspoken command, he jumped up to end the interview. Fannie rose at once, curtsied respectfully, and moved toward the door, slipping the locket once more about her throat. At that moment, in some distant room, there was an outburst of children's voices and the jolly laughter of Mrs. Jordan. She had felt quite sure of William, then.

For the first time the Prince dropped that stiff and distant attitude, stepping forward and catching Fannie's hands in his. "I must tell you something, my dear—something you'll understand as no other woman would. All my crazy frolics over there in Nova Scotia and the West Indies—I wasn't just a silly colt feeling his oats and kicking up his heels, though I admit that was part. But I was in a temper all that time. I mean to say, my father and the Admiralty packing me off the way they did, like a press gang picking up a young lout in the street. My brothers could enjoy themselves in London, but not William. William hadn't answered Papa's helm, so William must fry in the Caribbees, and freeze in the Canadian winds, and rattle up and down the seas between, for years—years!"

He snorted at the memory. But the bitterness left his voice at once. In a warm tone, and with a surprising sensibility, he went on, "I'm not a drunkard by nature, nor a rake for that matter. I didn't know what I wanted, really. Till I met you. You were much older than me, I always knew that. And there was something about you the young baggages didn't have. You—you satisfied me. You made me feel content. I think I told you that. I'd gone to sea at thirteen. We're a big family, and I'd never had much of my mother. I never had a playmate. And when I grew up and found what women were for I wasn't allowed to take a wife. And there you were, all three somehow. After I got home to England I took up my old antics for a time, but it was no good. Then I met Dorothea. You can guess the rest. I've never been so happy in my life. I never drink more than five glasses of wine at dinner now. And no more capers—none. I even lock the doors myself each night, to make sure the servants don't stay out late and give my house a bad name. Whatever some people may think, I'm perfectly respectable. I'm like a married man—Dolly tells me I'll be a father next autumn, fancy that!"

There was a sound of Mrs. Jordan's voice again, closer now, and the thump and patter of her children's feet. William released Fannie's fingers hastily.

"Give Mr. Wentworth my compliments," he said in the stiff loud voice, "and assure him I'll do everything in my power. And now be off with you, my dear lady. Good-by—Good-by!"

Through the cold and dismal January of '92 they waited in their lodgings, Fannie in high heart, Johnnie in a mixture of dour patience and disbelief. He pictured a dozen English candidates for the post, each with the proper Tory influence. Somewhere in the mysterious clockwork of empire about Whitehall the wheels and cogs were turning in their slow inhuman fashion. Eventually there would be a click, unnoticed in the London bustle, and a little figure would emerge from the clock and set off to rule distant Nova Scotia.

Early in February a messenger came to Clarges Street with a

document that bore the Colonial Office seal. Johnnie passed it to his wife.

"You open it. I haven't the heart."

He threw himself into a chair and sat slumped, feet out, chin on breast, eyes closed, the old attitude of despair that Fannie so despised. She broke the seal quickly, glanced at the letter, and slid it under Johnnie's nose.

"Read it, if you please, Your Excellency!"

He opened his eyes and sat up. And there it was. *It has pleased His Majesty to appoint Mr. John Wentworth, Esquire . . .* and so forth, and so forth. Mr. Wentworth was requested to call at the Colonial Office at the earliest opportunity, to receive his commission and receive instructions. He must expect to sail for Nova Scotia as soon as the March gales were past, and one of His Majesty's ships would be provided for the passage.

It seemed so incredible, after all the years and all the disappointments, that he read it over and over again to assure himself that he was awake and the paper real. After a time he was aware of Fannie's silence. He looked up.

"Well, my dear, why aren't you crying Huzza and dancing?"

"For this?" she said, giving the paper a tap with the back of her hand. "I knew you'd get this. You were always the doubter, not I."

And seeing his puzzled look she went on, "There are other things in view, my Governor. Our luck's turned at last, as I always knew it would. And nothing can stop us now. Next year there'll be war with France—I have it on the best authority—and there you'll be, my trusty Governor, commanding His Majesty's loyal province of Nova Scotia, the only British naval station on the coast of North America. And what's in the offing for a man of such importance? Nothing less than a title! Oh, don't give me that irritating smile. Lord Germain hinted at a baronetcy, years ago, didn't he? This time it shan't fail, I promise you. Think of it—Sir John and Lady Wentworth!"

"That's a little premature," he said.

"Fiddlesticks! You must start your preparations now. You'll

need a coat of arms, and I don't see why you can't use the arms of the Yorkshire Wentworths, with some little addition of your own. The first Wentworth in New Hampshire came from Yorkshire or thereabouts, and there's sure to be a connection of some sort if you trace it back far enough. Write Lord FitzWilliam and ask if he'd have any objection—but he won't quibble, you may be sure of that. Lord Rockingham always received you as one of the family. Go to the Herald of Arms, or whatever the deuce he's called, and get a little advice on your own addition to the Wentworth arms. You must have everything ready when the title's granted."

Johnnie regarded her in astonishment. "When did you get this ambition?"

"I've dreamed of it for years. And that's not all I've dreamed."

"Oh?"

"Someday, Your Excellency, I shall be presented at court—Lady Charlotte will do it gladly when the time comes—and because of my handsome looks and your long distinguished career I'll be made a Lady-in-Waiting to the Queen. What do you think of that for Fannie Wentworth?"

"A nice dream."

"Dreams come true. Mine will, you'll see. A matter of time and patience, and a friend or two in the right places. And do you know why I've dreamed all this—what I want all this for—why I'll have it all before I'm done?"

"No."

Her eyes glowed in the taut ivory face, as if some inner fire, smoldering for years, had burst into flame at last. Johnnie was startled. A woman's eyes should only look like that when one is making love. She was a handsome creature still; she would never lose that figure, slim, erect, and utterly feminine, as imperishable as if carved in marble by some cunning Greek or Roman in a time going back into the shadows. But the lines of forty-six were plain now in her face, and the gray was showing thickly in her hair, impossible to disguise except with the dye pot, for powdered heads were out of fashion now, like wigs for gentlemen. She was past the age for love at last, and what glowed in her eyes made her face look older still. It was hate.

"Those people in Portsmouth," she began. The words came out between her teeth, low in tone but tingling in a way that made his flesh creep. "Those people in Portsmouth, the ones that considered me beneath them because I came from Boston, that gossiped about me—that cast us both out finally—I want to show them Frances Wentworth moving in a better society than they ever knew. But that's not the main thing. That little group of pious prigs, those smug she-cats who've ruled the society at Halifax all this time! I can't wait to get back there now, my Governor! They wouldn't call on me, they wouldn't even speak to me if they could help it. And now they shall bite their fingers and wish they had. Fannie Wentworth's the lady of Government House, and she'll still be there when half of them are dead and gone and damned. She'll entertain as that stingy old Parr never thought of doing. There'll be such a round of dinners and parties and balls as Halifax never saw; and with a war on, and all sorts of great people, army and navy, coming and going. And, my Governor, I'll see that not one of those creatures ever steps inside my door. They'll be shut out of everything that matters. So will those purse-proud husbands of theirs—those tradesmen! I shall write you a list. Not one on that list is to get a penny of government contract money—ever. You'll make sure of that. They made me suffer eight long years. I'll make them suffer twice the pain and twice the time before I've finished with them. Do you see now?"

He nodded dubiously. The old question hovered in his mind. Why make enemies? When you ruled a province you found enemies enough in the course of time—New Hampshire had proved that. And that little group in Halifax included some of the ablest and most useful men. But it was useless to argue with Fannie in this high mood. Perhaps she would grow out of it.

"Well, don't waste time," she said briskly. "We have a thousand things to do. We'll both need a new wardrobe. We'll need new furniture and china and silverware—I never saw what the

Parrs had, but all my officer friends used to laugh at it. And we'll need servants experienced in genteel households—we must engage them here and take them with us."

"What about Prue and Juno?"

"Juno's the best cook in Halifax. She shall be in charge of our kitchen. But we must have a pastry cook who knows the fashion here. And they must have some well-trained helpers—it's one thing to prepare a dinner for half a dozen and quite another for three hundred. As for Prue, dear Prue, she shall be housekeeper —we couldn't get a better in the world. I'll engage a lady's maid here. A lot of those French *émigrés* brought their maids to London with them when they ran away from the Revolution, and can't support them now; and there's nothing like a French maid. As for you, you must get a set of English footmen like those you brought to Portsmouth, all of one height and properly trained, and dress them in a good smart livery. One to act as coachman. And that reminds me, our present horses and ponies in Halifax will do for the time being, but we'll want a new glass coach and phaeton. You must order them now. Go to Benwell of Long Acre, he's the best in London."

Fannie paused for breath, and he said mildly, "Where shall I get the money for all this?"

"Borrow from Drummond the banker. All you have to do is show him your new commission—that letter will do. What a silly question to ask!"

THIRTY-SEVEN

*A*LL THE WAY to Falmouth, rolling through the green length of southern England in an air scented with primroses, Johnnie had the odd sensation of traveling back through time. This was the way he had come, sick at heart, in the spring of '78, seeing from the coach window nothing but America torn and bleeding, and himself forbidden ever to set foot at home again. But the hands of his life's clock were turning much farther back than that. He was leaving England to govern a province on the other side of the ocean—he was living again that homeward journey in '67.

Some things were different. A rider with a bugle went ahead of the imposing little procession to warn the inns of important folk approaching; then came the leading coach in which he sat with Fannie, and behind that four others laden with baggage and servants. When at last they rattled into Falmouth the captain and crew of H.M.S. *Hussar* were duly impressed. Half an hour later the Governor and his lady stepped aboard to the chirrup of boatswains' pipes, with the seamen drawn up at stiff attention and the captain and officers saluting, a pleasant little taste of their new importance.

In consultation with the Colonial Office and the Admiralty Johnnie had chosen his sailing date with care. Although the wild March gales were safely past there was still a prevalence of westerly winds, and the voyage would take a month or more. It was now the seventh day of April, so they would arrive in Nova Scotia well on in May, when the sun's warmth had returned to northern latitudes and the last of the snow had vanished.

Fannie was gratified to find the commander of the *Hussar* no coarse old salt, but a Londoner of good family with a house in

463

Park Lane. Captain Rupert George had given up his own spacious day and night cabins to the distinguished passengers and fitted them with especial care for a lady, even to fresh flowers and potted plants, well secured in a rack by the great stern window. He had laid in a choice supply of provisions and wines for his table, and even provided a stock of books for the long idle days of the voyage. On the second day at sea Fannie discovered among the novels *Vancenza*, poor Perdita's latest effort to support herself, and one that was bound to set London agog.

In the course of the next five weeks she read *Vancenza* several times. It was Mrs. Robinson's apologia in thin disguise, of course; and the theme was in one stately passage to which Fannie returned again and again.

Small is the triumph of chastity that has never been assail'd. The female heart has little right to exult in its resolution till it has resisted the fascinations of pleasure, the voice of insidious flattery, and the fatal allurements of example.

Whenever she read these words she felt increasingly virtuous. They might have been addressed to those censorious females across the sea in Halifax.

But in spite of novels, of whist in the evenings, of all the little diversions and comforts of this pampered shipboard life, she found the voyage very long. Her French maid was seasick most of the way, and she had to make her own toilet. It was impossible to apply her new hair stain properly through so long a time; the gray showed near the roots and sometimes, she was sure, at the back of her head, where a hand mirror combined with the big glass on the bulkhead gave no satisfactory inspection. She felt this whenever she arrayed herself to meet Captain George and his keen-eyed company. But she put a good face on it; her accent and manner as a well-poised Englishwoman of fashion were faultless now, and she wore them like an armor.

At the proper times she could be far more imperious than

dumpy little Queen Charlotte; and again she could be the gentle-woman at ease, whiffing a segar, shuffling and dealing cards, or discussing wine, French cookery, horses, politics, art, and London plays with the facile tongue of one who had known these things always as part of her life. Casually she mentioned famous lords and ladies as close friends of hers, and she talked much of the Duke of Clarence—"dear Prince William, a sailor like your-selves"—who had been such a charming guest of Governor Went-worth and herself for three seasons on the North American station.

Sometimes she threw out a light allusion to Prince William's amusements there, with a roll of her fine eyes, as if to say that she could tell a little more on that point if she wished. But somehow the point was lost. The officers regarded her always with the polite impersonal eyes of young men toward a woman in middle age, as if she could never have been pretty and young and exciting. It nettled her at first, but as the sea weeks went by she became resigned. She had always been happiest in the company of men, and she would prefer them to women till the day she died, but the familiar devil had deserted her flesh at last and taken her youthful looks in the going; she was merely a handsome relic in their eyes now, and she must content herself with memories.

What annoyed her now was an amazing and quite absurd return of youth in Johnnie. He spent every possible moment on deck, walking the holystoned planks with a spring in his step that she had not seen in years. He had the daring eye and at times the very sinew of the young Johnnie Wentworth who chose and felled mast pines in the forest for his father. More than once, when the lookout reported a whale or some such thing in the offing, her Governor climbed the rigging to the foretop, with surprising skill, and made a point of reaching that perilous little platform by the difficult outside way, instead of popping through what the seamen called the lubber's hole. His old lively humor was back; he joked with the officers and often set them in a roar of laughter with some droll tale of the backwoods, told in the country dialect of New Hampshire or Nova Scotia. His whole air was that of a man half his age, which Fannie found ridiculous. What the deuce had got into him?

Johnnie hardly knew himself. His head was fizzing, just as it had on that voyage five-and-twenty years ago when he was on the way home from his first stay in England. His journeys in Nova Scotia had made him familiar with every part of it, and he had long seen the things that ought to be done, as old Governor Parr never could. Plans, wonderful plans!

Roads first, just as in the New Hampshire days. Improve the so-called Great West road, which actually was nothing but a wagon track winding through the woods from Halifax to the Annapolis Valley, and the south shore road, which was a mere bridle path. The eastern half of the province was still a wilderness. Open it, then, with a new road through the forest and over the hills to Pictou, where some pioneers had come by sea. There was good land up that way. Grant himself a large tract there and put some settlers on it to show what could be done, as he had at Wolfeborough long ago.

But roads were not all. In England he had seen what a canal could do. And what couldn't a canal do for the settlers on all those fertile lands about the Bay of Fundy? A waterway across country to Halifax could move the country produce easily to the capital, and merchandise from the Halifax stores could move as easily in return. He had gone over every inch of the ground, and he knew a canal was feasible, using a chain of lakes behind Halifax harbor, and northward the long run of the Shubenacadie River.

Start a flour-milling industry at Halifax, using native grain. Why should the town, the garrison, and fleet depend so much on flour bought abroad? A fat profit to be made there, too, when the war came. His loyalist friend, Hartshorne the merchant, could build the mill and get the government contract. Then the matter of mines. Cape Breton was one big lump of coal, so far unscratched except for a few shallow pits to serve the army posts. Get permission from London and encourage men of money to come and develop real mines, as he had seen the great land-owners doing in Yorkshire. A tremendous prospect in this country of cold winters—more, there was a market on the whole American seaboard, where people still used wood for fuel. And the Nova Scotia coals right beside the sea, a mere matter of tipping the carts into the ships! A dozen other matters of this kind. Put 'em all in motion. Start a new tide of prosperity that would double the population in ten years. Just what he had promised in New Hampshire—and look at New Hampshire now!

As for government, Fannie was right; he must avoid his old mistakes in New Hampshire, especially in view of this new and dangerous French republicanism which seemed to be catching so many minds, even in England. Take no nonsense from the Assembly. Fill the Council with men loyal to himself as well as the King, and leave no opening for another Peter Livius at the board. Deal justly with the "old settlers," but give the loyalist refugees a preference, because they deserved it. Support the Church faithfully, and get a royal charter for the new college at Windsor as a Church institution, as he had failed to do for Dartmouth College in New Hampshire. And of course—since loyalty begins at home—as soon as a decent post is vacant send to England for Fannie's brother Benning. And when Charles-Mary graduates from Oxford bring him out, too, and make him a member of the Council.

Johnnie liked to walk the deck alone at night, thinking of all these matters, because in the darkness they passed before his mind's eye as finished realities, one after another, like the painted slides of a magic lantern. And as the voyage went on he became aware of something else, not a plan, not even a dream like so many of these things. He had not thought of a woman in a romantic way for years. His old faithful love for Fannie she had killed herself, and he had no pangs about that any more. And now, in this strange return through time to the year '67 he felt in his blood a new stirring where all had been quiet for so long.

Sometimes on deck in the darkness, where there was nothing really but the sea, the sails, and the topmasts scraping at the stars, he seemed to hear sometimes the laughter of a girl. That, and the sound of a light wind in trees, as if some sprite of the forest awaited him in the invisible land toward the west. Where, exactly? He amused himself with the idea. The sound of trees suggested Friar Laurence's Cell. Would she come to him there? He could picture that scene well enough but not the girl. Perhaps she was only an unconscious wish, a longing for some lively mischievous creature like the Fannie of the Portsmouth garden, but without Fannie's selfishness and with no ambition except to please him and to give him back his youth for a time. A crazy conceit; yet there it was, something to be fulfilled with all the other things, one spell of Indian summer in his life before the winter came! He felt as sure of the mysterious wild girl as Fannie was sure of her titles and honors in the time to come.

Fannie reminded him of those on the night before the *Hussar* sighted the Nova Scotia coast. "What have you done about a coat of arms?"

Johnnie opened a dispatch case and took out a drawing. She had seen the arms many times at Wentworth Woodhouse, but she had given them no close examination. Now she did. The heraldic symbols of the Yorkshire Wentworths were rather odd. The whiskered heads of two cats glared popeyed from the upper portion of the shield. A third cat glared below, shut off from the others by a chevron. A griffin pranced on the shield top, and at the bottom was the family motto, *En Dieu Est Tout.*

Fannie looked at the three grimalkins and laughed. "How very appropriate! I'm the lone cat inside the bar, you see, and the others are the Halifax tabbies, watching." And then, seriously, "What do you propose to add to these arms for yourself?"

"Two keys."

"Where?"

"One on each side of the lower cat."

"And what will they represent?"

"Fidelity."

The smile left her face. She looked up, startled and furious.

"That's a very bad joke—in fact it's ungrateful and hateful. Where would you be today if it hadn't been for me?"

"Sometimes I wonder, my dear. But as it happens your interpretation is quite wrong. The 'cats'—and they look exactly that, I admit—are supposed to be leopards. And the addition of the keys is to mark my own fidelity to the King, in New Hampshire and in Nova Scotia."

She saw that he was in earnest, and to turn his calm gaze from a very red face she pointed once more to the drawing. "What's that ugly creature on the top?"

"A griffin. Half lion, half eagle. Griffins are supposed to guard the family's gold and all treasures of that sort."

"Humph! It won't have much to guard in our case. What do you intend to do about your debts at Halifax? You've got Drummond to pay now."

Johnnie shrugged. "My creditors can't very well arrest their own Governor for debt. He's got too many favors in his power. I'll offer 'em a system of payments stretching well into the future, and they'll be thankful to settle for that."

"You'll have to make the payments precious small," she said tartly. "Our expenses will be heavier than ever now, remember that. We have a position to maintain. Can't you find some money outside of your two salaries as Governor and Surveyor General?"

"There's a chance, when the war with France breaks out. I'll raise a regular regiment for home defense in Nova Scotia and get myself made colonel. That should give me another thousand a year, if Prince Edward approves."

"Edward? You mean William's soldier brother? He's posted at Gibraltar. They're treating him just the way they treated William. What's he got to do with you?"

"He's commanding the forces in Canada now. He was sent out to Quebec last year."

"Oh? I didn't know that." Fannie considered this news for some moments. "That means he'll be coming to Halifax for garrison inspections!"

"No doubt, when the war begins." And seeing the sudden

469

interest in her eyes he added blandly, "I'm told he's acquired a little French mistress at Quebec, and that he's very much in love with her. She's on the sunny side of five-and-twenty."

"While I'm a hag of seven-and-forty! Why don't you say that too? As if I had any intention . . . but of course you just want to be cruel. Sometimes I think you have no heart at all!"

"I have a head, at any rate, my dear." He put the drawing back into the dispatch case carefully. "We've come a long hard way together, my dear Fan. If I've learned anything it's not to fret over whatever's past and can't be changed. All I see now is the present and future, and they look very pleasant to me. Dignity again, and work to do. Shall we let our sentiments rest on that?"

The *Hussar* raised Cape Sambro on the twelfth of May, having sighted and followed the coast all the previous day. Then Thrum Cap appeared, and Devil's Island, and in the distance the green tip of Citadel Hill. The frigate entered the harbor in perfect weather, a hot spring morning with just enough breeze to fill the sails and bring her to an anchorage off the town. On the harbor slopes the snowy bloom of Indian pear was showing in the woods, and the fields and pastures had their freshest green. In the town itself the well-kept mansions of officials and merchants shone like painted faces in the morning sun, and the tall white bulk of Government House peered over the water-front sheds toward the frigate lying off King's Wharf. There were the familiar red and yellow barracks on the shoulders of Citadel Hill, and the sprawl of houses and shops and warehouses down the slope to the water, all with a clean look at this distance, as if the March winds and April rains had scrubbed them for the occasion.

Johnnie could not have wished a better time of arrival. It was Saturday. All the preparations for their reception could be made today, while they remained on board. And tomorrow they would make their landing, after the churches emptied, when the whole population, dressed in its Sunday best, would pour down to Hollis Street to watch the show. He considered the arrangements carefully and sent notes ashore to old Mr. Bulkeley, President of the Council, who had been administering the government since Parr's death; and to General Ogilvie, Chief Justice Strange, and the other dignitaries, while Fannie herself dispatched a note to sister Mary and a long list of instructions to Prue.

They slept little that night. There was too much to think about, of the past as well as the morrow. They were up at daylight, Fannie calling at once for her maid. For hours Emelie fussed over her mistress, while the sun climbed and the air grew hot, in spite of the open cabin window. Miladi's hair, now a dark and flawless brown, was dressed in the new mode, fairly low, and full at the sides and back. The face lightly powdered, with deft touches of rouge and lip paint to take away the pallor of her face. The chosen gown was in Fannie's favorite blue, with the new high waist and short sleeves, and at the neck a modest V and a rich froth of lace. White gloves to the elbow, a white turban with twin ostrich plumes pinned by a diamond brooch, and on one hand a white feather muff. When the Governor's lady stepped on deck at last she heard a flattering murmur from the assembled crew.

"There, I venture," breathed Captain George to his first lieutenant, "is one of the handsomest women of her age to be seen outside of London!"

It was past noon, and she found Johnnie at the rail gazing eagerly toward the shore, where he could see the trim ranks and musket barrels of the 21st Regiment, and beyond them a gathering multitude. For his own dress he had copied instinctively what he had worn on that triumphant entry into Portsmouth all the years ago; white silk breeches and stockings, a waistcoat in red satin, a coat of red velvet with silver buttons, a cravat of white ruffled silk, a hat with tall military cocks edged in gold lace and bearing the black cockade of Hanover. The gold hilt of a dress sword gleamed in the open sweep of the coat. His hair was white with pomade and powder, the queue neatly clubbed at the nape with a scarlet ribbon. His face, bronzed by five weeks in the winds and sea glare, made a frame for the calm gray eyes and the resolute mouth. From head to foot he looked every inch the man chosen to govern a key post of the empire in the coming war.

The ship's rigging fluttered every scrap of bunting to be found in the flag lockers, and now a larboard gun fired, the first of a fifteen-gun salute, startling the maid Emelie half out of her wits, and seamen swarmed aloft to dress the yards, standing erect and motionless on those lofty perches like rows of trousered sparrows. At the foot of the gangway the captain's barge waited, with oarsmen in green jackets and black caps. The Governor and his lady embarked, the long oars rose and fell in a beautiful flashing rhythm, and the barge swept in to the stone landing steps just as the *Hussar* fired her last gun. It was exactly one o'clock. And now the battery at Grand Parade began the reply.

Sixteen years ago Johnnie had watched Governor Legge departing from these same steps amid the curses of a Halifax mob, but if there was a lesson in that scene he had forgotten it. At the head of the steps His Excellency received the official greetings of General Ogilvie and his staff. The Admiral was missing—the North American squadron was on its way north from the winter station in the West Indies—but the Commissioner was there to do the naval honors. The troops presented arms, with a smart slap of hands and click of heels. And now the procession formed, at the foot of an avenue of scarlet and flashing steel that ran all the way from King's Wharf to the portico of Government House.

Fannie tucked a hand in her Governor's arm. Emelie, a pace behind, held forth a tall white parasol to shield her mistress from the sun. Behind them came the General, the Commissioner, the Chief Justice, and the Secretary of the Council; the senior garrison and dockyard officers; the members of the Council and the Assembly; and finally a concourse of leading merchants and citizens anxious to show their respect for the new power in the land. Among these last, Fannie's sidelong eye noted with a gleam, were the husbands of "that little group of prigs."

They moved off at a slow majestic pace. Hollis Street was a solid human mass, held back by the red files of infantry. Most of the people were townsfolk, but Johnnie's alert gaze noted the farmers up to town for the market, sawmill men from Dartmouth and the Sackville River, sailors from the merchant ships, dockyard hands, fishermen from Eastern Passage, Herring Cove, North West Arm, and Sambro. The crowd extended up George Street and Prince Street, and there was a mass of carriages along Granville Street. People hung from open windows all about the square, and daring boys and young men were clustered on the roofs wherever there was a foothold. There was a patter of polite hands as the Governor and his lady moved across Hollis Street. And then a sunburned fellow in country dress, perched on a lantern pole, shouted cheerfully, "Ah, there he is! Huzza for Governor Johnnie!"—and in a moment the crowd was roaring and waving hats and handkerchiefs.

Johnnie's eyes went wet, and there was a lump in his throat that he could not swallow. It was Portsmouth all over again. The twenty-five years since had never happened. He looked up at the portico, half expecting to see the lean figure of old Theodore Atkinson, where in fact the President of the Council was waiting with a formal address of welcome.

Fannie, smiling at his side, had no such illusion. Her mind was entirely on the future. She walked along, inclining her head and plumes graciously from side to side and thinking of a grand dinner and ball to celebrate the baronetcy. It would be wartime, of course, and the town thronged with the army and the fleet. And it would be evening, with magnificent decorations and a blaze of chandeliers in every chamber of Government House, a feast prepared and waiting in the dining room, and musicians playing on the balcony. Sir John and Lady Wentworth would come down the staircase to the levee room at the exact moment when Prince Edward and his glittering staff arrived at the Hollis Street steps. There would be at least two hundred guests assembled; and in all that favored company, cherishing her invitations like tickets to Heaven, not one—not a single one of those creatures on her black list! She could taste the moment now, like the first sip of a delicious wine that had been years maturing.

The guns at Grand Parade fired the last shot of the fortress salute, and the procession halted. On the grassy terrace of Government House the band of the 21st were lifting their instruments. Johnnie blinked the water from his eyes and turned a steadfast gaze upward to the terrace, to the flagstaff, to the British colors stirring in the light air off the harbor. With an imperceptible movement he slipped off Fannie's proprietory hand and took a single pace forward, sweeping off his hat and standing as he had stood in the Portsmouth square all those years ago, free and alone.

At that moment the tense waiting silence of all those gathered people was broken by one sound, the naive happy laughter of a girl. And then the band crashed forth the notes of "God Save the King."